KILLER'S ISLAND

ANNA JANSSON

First Published in the United States in 2014 by
Stockholm Text, Stockholm, Sweden

FOR INFORMATION CONTACT:
Stockholm Text
Kungsgatan 58
111 22 Stockholm
Sweden

stockholm@stockholmtext.com

Library of Congress Cataloging-in-Publication Data
is available from the Library of Congress.

TRANSLATION BY Paul Norlén
COVER DESIGN BY Ermir Peci

Manufactured in the United States
FIRST EDITION

1 3 5 7 9 8 6 4 2

ISBN 978-91-87173-99-8

Swedish streets and places will appear with their Swedish names
throughout the novel. For English translations, please see the last
page of the book.

Lost

The moon comes, the sun goes,
the dream made you lose yourself.
The dream of lily years
made us ever lose ourselves.
Thistle paths and charred earth
you trudge upon now, with broken shoe…
—The dream of lily years made you lose yourself

Nils Ferlin

By simply tapping the keyboard he was able to watch, via satellite, the day-to-day lives of ordinary people; how they opened their front doors and took their dogs for walks or bumped into friends on street corners, as if things were ruled by chance—for these superstitious, dim-witted beings still believed in chance. His constant observation of them made him feel powerful. He registered their habits, began to predict where they'd be and who they'd meet. It had been child's play hacking into the Russian satellite that monitored the gas pipeline near Gotland. That its reception was so technically advanced came as a surprise. When weather conditions were favorable he could even watch their unsuspecting faces. This, perhaps, gave him more satisfaction than anything else.

Chapter 1

Friday, June 7, was an unusually hot day. Long into evening, the heat still lingered in the narrow alleys of Visby. A pale dusk lay over the creased surface of the sea, lighting up the dark bastions of the city walls and the monastery ruins hailing back to another, more powerful time. The silhouettes of the stepped gable houses that had been warehouses in Hanseatic times stood out eerily in the red-glowing evening light. In the distance someone was playing a wooden flute. A sad, medieval melody.

When Maria Wern started wandering home from Quay 5 at about nine o'clock, she immediately cursed her choice of shoes. Admittedly quite gorgeous, with sharp heels, pointy toes, and ankle-straps, they were nonetheless nearly impossible to walk in. The air was still clement. On the whole, she reflected, it had been a pleasant evening, apart from the last hour when Erika, as the situation warranted, had worked herself in a tizzy about a man. At such times she grew deaf and blind to anyone else. It was at that point that a fruity cocktail equipped with a straw and umbrella had landed on the table in front of Maria.

"Something for the lady, from that gentleman by the

door." There was a scarcely hidden, teasing quality in the waiter's smile.

Someone had weighed up the situation and was now opportunely moving in for the kill while she sat there, left to her own devices. Maria glanced up toward the door. The gentleman in question winked at her and carefully rotated his open palm in the air—like in a comedy movie. *Hey, it's me!* No, she wasn't quite as desperate as that.

"I think I've reached saturation point. Tell him thanks." Maria stood up and tried to make eye contact with Erika, now deep in conversation with her new acquisition. His name was Anders, he was a district medical officer in town and seemed unusually sympathetic. Was he married or a sociopath or a drug user or annoyingly perverse? There was usually something wrong with good-looking men who were apparently still available. When Erika invited him home, Maria couldn't help but feel a little tingle of anxiety. As a police officer, Erika knew one could run into crazies in a bar.

"Careful!" Her text message did not seem to get through. Although, when she thought about it, it occurred to her that *he* might be the one in need of a warning. Erika was usually more than capable of taking care of herself. "Erika, is your cell phone switched on?" Maria whispered as she stood up.

"Mother hen! You know I won't be calling you tonight." Erika laughed affectionately and gave her arm a squeeze. "Everything's totally cool, okay?"

"Exactly." Anders cut in. "Too cool if you ask me. I've got my daughter at home and my old mom babysitting. She'll be wanting a lift home at a respectable hour, so it'll just be a peck on the cheek at the door, I suppose. After that I'll be making my own way back through the dangerous streets of Visby."

They all paid for themselves, then walked out into the lukewarm night. There was a gusting southeasterly wind pushing them away from the edge of the quay. The street-lights reflected in the black water. Music and humming voices could be heard from the boats in the marina, but the main seafront was almost deserted. They separated at Donner's Place and Maria continued homewards down Hästga-tan toward Klinten. Her feet were insanely sore. She tried walking barefoot, shoes in hand. Noticing the glimmer of glass and sharp bottle caps here and there, she was careful about where she put her feet. A taxi stopped and picked up a couple in party clothes. A taxi ride was not an option for Maria, whose finances were stressed. Anyway, she was al-most home. She continued to Wallers Plats and then turned off down Södra Kyrkogatan toward the Cathedral, whose black steeple could already be glimpsed over the house roofs. She avoided the main square and headed for Ryska Gränd so she could take the long, steep Cathedral stairs up to Klinten as a workout—a punishment for being lazy and staying away from the gym all week.

Further down Ryska Gränd, Maria heard a call for help. A pubescent voice, just at the cusp of breaking. At first it seemed unreal: three hooded men standing around some-one on the ground, kicking him. The lane was dark, but she could see some of the kicks hitting his head. The figure on the ground was a boy, no more than perhaps thirteen or fourteen—just a few years older than Maria's own son. Every kick catapulted his gaunt body off the ground. He was screaming.

"Stop that! Stop! Police!" Maria got out her police badge and tried to make her voice as strong and authoritative as possible, although she was trembling inside.

The three men looked up. They seemed to weigh her up, measure her with their eyes. If she could calm things down and make them respect her, she might just be able to resolve this without further violence. Purposefully she walked up to them. One against three. She dialed the emergency number on her cell phone. At best this would make them leave the scene, so she could save the boy. *Answer the phone!* She was placed on hold, an automated voice telling her the waiting time should not exceed three minutes. Three goddamn minutes! The tallest of the three men smiled scornfully at her as he unleashed another kick into the kid's stomach. The boy went completely silent, likely unconscious. One of the other men hit Maria hard, knocking her cell phone out of her hand and then crushing it under his steel-toed shoe. Maria bent down to see how things were with the kid. His face was been beaten to a bleeding pulp, his body was limp, and he was no longer shielding himself with his arms.

"Stop! You'll kill him!" Only then did the fear really hit her.

A tall man in his seventies wearing a cap and a light-colored overcoat appeared in the lane. Maria cried out for help but the man hurried by as if he were deaf and blind. His long overcoat flapped around his legs. He didn't even turn around. She saw the gray hair down his neck, hanging over his collar.

"Hello! Can you call the police! Help us! Call the police!" Her voice was still strong and authoritative.

The man disappeared. He was out of the game. Coward! Next time you'll be the one who needs help! You'll have to live with this for the rest of your life, Maria wanted to shout after him. He *must* help them, he *must* pick up the phone. Couldn't he see that? She filled up with impotent anger. The next few minutes would determine whether they came out of this situation alive.

"Don't come here poking your nose in this, fucking cop cunt!" The tall one aimed another kick at the boy. Maria didn't know where she got her strength but somehow she managed to shove him so that he lost his balance and fell. His kick missed the victim's head. One of them, shorter and fatter than the others, seemed to be drugged. His movements were floppy and his pupils tiny, like fly-specks. "Shit, Roy, maybe we should leave it and get out of here." The others weren't listening to him. The tall one resumed his attack on the defenseless boy on the ground. Maria screamed, called for help, clawed them, tugged at them, fought like a wild animal. They'd kill him if she didn't manage to stop them. That boy was not much bigger than her son, Emil. In her mind, he might as well *be* Emil. Maria gave it all she had. She punched and kicked and roared for help, then managed a direct hit in the tall one's groin, leaving him doubled up. At the same time she was kneed in the small of her back by one of the others. She fell to the ground, a hissing sound in her head. A hard fist slammed into her face. There was a taste of blood in her mouth. The pain had winded her. She crawled up again, took a kick in her back and lost her balance. Fell. Crawled to the boy on the ground and laid on top of him to protect his head, using her body as a shield. A powerful kick thundered into her side. Then another. She felt as if something inside her just exploded into smithereens. The pain was unbearable. She went into deep concentration, focusing on protecting the boy's head and also her own.

"Fucking cop cunt!" The tall one moved in close with a syringe in his hand. Maria saw him in the corner of her eye. The syringe was gleaming, filled with dark red blood.

"Please, I.... Don't. Don't. Ouww, oh God!"

He squatted down on her back. The others held on to her arms and legs. For a moment Maria thought that they were going to rape her, that they were only using the syringe as a threat. But it was far worse than that.

"Welcome to hell." The taunting voice cut into her. The needle pierced her trousers and skin, went in deep and grazed her femur. Maria tried to kick herself free. The needle glided out. Maybe it had snapped inside her flesh? She didn't know. He continued stabbing her with it. She had to try and mark him. She bit, scratched, clawed at his masked face. He spit at her. Right in her face. His eyes were overflowing with hatred. He stood up to kick her one more time.

Someone opened a window and a woman's voice called out.

"If you don't stop that racket I'll call the police!"

"Do it! Call the police!" Maria's voice did not carry. Another kick slammed into her, she convulsed and gasped for air. Her back was smashed. The pain was beyond endurance.

Another window opened.

"What's going on?"

"Help!" Maria's voice made a hollow, croaking sound.

One more kick swished into her. She tried to protect her head with her arm. Another kick. There was a cracking sound. The pain made her black out.

"Call an ambulance! Please...." Her voice was no more than a whisper, maybe just a thought. Everything went silent. The kicking stopped. Dark figures moved indistinctly round them, like a dance of witches. Steel-toed boots. The voices from the windows turned into echoes. A last kick cut clean through her whole body.

When Maria regained consciousness she only saw the staring eyes at first. Black human bodies with long legs and eyes. A quiet murmuring of perturbed and dismayed voices. Echoes, half-perceived words to cling onto in a sea of raging pain. She tried to make out the words but they remained indecipherable. The sound of an approaching ambulance accentuated everything. Someone touched her, tried to move her. The pain was indescribable.

A new face came up close to her. A man with an anxious gaze, though his words were calm. Clear. A kind voice. She wanted to cry.

"How are you? Where does it hurt?" The ambulance man was speaking to her.

"Is the boy alive?" He couldn't hear her. It was painful to breathe.

"Where does it hurt?"

She couldn't make herself understood. Her lips were swollen and she couldn't project her voice: each word felt like internal bleeding or a fractured neck. Her whole identity seemed to be in swaying motion, without any firm grip. The man's voice took command. Passively she let herself be moved. They were placed on stretchers and transferred to the waiting ambulances. She caught a glimpse of the boy's limp body. He simply had to pull through, had to survive, in spite of all the blows and kicks to his head. Where were his parents? Soon they'd find out. Maria felt a fit of weeping in her body, but without tears. Every time the car jolted, an excruciating pain coursed through her. The ambulance man was there, the one with the anxious eyes and calm voice. All the way on the bumpy road to the hospital he was there with her. He told her his name was Tobias. She held onto his name as if it were a mantra.

The fluorescent lights in the white room cut into her eyes. White-dressed figures flitted past like bright butterflies. They were hands and voices in a sea of pain. A doctor introduced himself but Maria couldn't fix his name in her mind. His face was round. He was sweating and his glasses had slipped down his nose; his lower jaw masticated as he spoke. He'd nicked himself on his chin with his razor. A tiny, bleeding cut. He seemed to be saying something about an X-ray. He asked a question, wanted an answer. But the pain engulfed her in darkness. The voices came and went in her wavering consciousness.

"The boy, is the boy all right?" Maria grabbed hold of a white coat. She had to know.

"Is he your son?"

Maria shook her head.

"He's in intensive care. The police want to talk to you later." The woman's voice was soft and calm. Do healthcare staff have to take an oral exam before they're offered a job? The quieter and calmer they sound, the more serious the situation. One can see it in their eyes. Only there does the truth leak out. At times of utter silence one knows death has showed up; death is beginning its struggle with life.

Maria was helped to crawl over into a bed. "They stabbed me with needles!"

"We'll take you for an X-ray in a minute." Two voices talking. No one heard her. The bed started rolling along.

"I could be infected. My blood." Fear cut through her body. "I could be infected!" Still they could not hear. The bed took off. The blinding lights along the girders flashed by overhead. White coats swished past, silent as shadows in a dream. Only the hushing of fans and the scraping and singing of the bed's wheels against the concrete floor could be heard. "I've been stabbed with a goddamn syringe!" Maria tried to make eye contact with the auxiliary just as he was greeting a passing colleague. "I may have been infected with HIV!"

Chapter 2

When Maria woke up, Commissioner Tomas Hartman was sitting at her side looking tired, his shirt creased and his curly gray hair standing on end. It took a moment for Maria to realize where she was. She took shallow little breaths.

"How long have you been sitting there?" Maria looked at her watch. It was quarter past seven in the morning. The white coats were changing shifts—old faces disappearing and new ones coming in. Spick-and-span, middle-aged Lotta had gone home just as Maria had worked out from her tag what her name was; she was replaced by young Daniel with Rasta dreadlocks.

"A few hours. They called in the night."

"The boy! How's the boy doing?" She clenched her fists hard round the mattress and steeled herself. "I have to know."

"He's in intensive care." Hartman paused, to see how Maria was taking it.

"I want to know!"

Hartman gripped her hand, closed his eyes to compose himself and then looked directly at her. "Several of his ribs are broken. Bleeding lungs. He's unconscious. Those kicks

17

to his head… they're not ruling out more internal bleeding. He's been moved to the operating room."

That was the point when she started crying. Hartman caressed her hair with his big, awkward hand, trying to calm and comfort her just as he'd comforted his own children when they were small. No words. Just being there. A secure presence, listening.

"But he'll pull through?" she entreated. "He's got to pull through!"

Hartman slowly shook his head.

"The doctors don't think there's much hope. He's very badly injured. Are you up to telling us what happened?"

Maria sat up in bed with great effort and started talking. As she began to re-live what had happened, she had to confront her fear. She wept. Again and again, Hartman had to ask her to repeat and be more clear.

"Why did they have to hurt him?" Maria looked her chief in the eye but she didn't expect an answer. "Why? There used to be a sort of cowboy's code of honor. You didn't hit someone who was smaller than you, if you had a fight it was one against one. What happened to all that? Do you know what was going on before I turned up, why did they go for him?"

"No. I've spoken to his parents. At around nine o'clock last night he said good-bye to his friend Oliver. He only had a few hundred yards to walk, his mother lives one block away. Another two minutes and he would have been safe."

"So close… and yet they knew nothing about it." said Maria, thinking about her own son. You had to give your children freedom so they grew up—which meant letting go of your need to protect them from every possible danger.

"What else do you remember? What did they look like?"

"They were wearing balaclavas. One of them was taller than the others. He seemed to be the one making the decisions. He was also the one really laying into the boy, kicking him, while I was watching. They didn't sound like they came from Gotland. The tall one had a sort of mixed dialect." Maria fell silent and her eyes grew large and black. "They stuck a blood-filled syringe into me. 'Welcome to hell,' he said. I may be infected."

"What has the doctor said about that?"

"They don't know about it yet. They're concentrating on my injuries; no one listens to me. I can't make them listen, I don't have the strength for it. And they're all in such a hurry."

"So I'll speak to them. Rest now, will you. I'll take care of it."

A new face popped up in the doorway. "The police told me you were stabbed with a used syringe. There's an infection specialist on his way, he'll have a word with you about it." The nurse disappeared with her cart into the next room. Maria sat up on the edge of the bed. Her belly ached, also her back and head. Her chest was full of cutting knives. In fact, everything hurt absolutely everywhere, except her right arm. She stood up and tottered across the floor with a spinning head, then grabbed the door frame and felt close to passing out. She lay down on the bed again. Far off she saw someone moving toward her down the corridor: it was Jonatan Eriksson, the infection specialist who'd taken such good care of them when Emil was ill. How wonderful to see him. The tears came streaming again. Here, in this alienating hospital world, was a familiar face. Someone to trust.

"Maria! How are you?" He sat in the chair Hartman had just vacated, gripping her right hand and, with his other hand, gently patting her left arm. His face came up close. She smiled at him, feeling her swollen lips tightening.

"I look a wreck, don't I? I've been better, I have to say. We have to stop meeting like this, Jonatan."

The joke amused him, his face widening into a big smile.

"We have to stop meeting in hospitals, you mean. I came as soon as I heard what had happened. Do you know who he is, the guy who stabbed you?"

"No. He was tall, he wore a mask. Gray or green eyes. One of his friends seemed under the influence of drugs. His pupils were tiny, as if he was on morphine. He slouched. The one who stabbed me wasn't high, as far as I could see. He stabbed me many times, it was like he was in a fury. There was blood in the syringe. He did it on purpose. There were three of them. I couldn't do anything." Maria felt her fear surging back, more intensely every time she put words to her experience. Flashing images passed through her mind: the needle as it punctured her skin. "Am I going to die now?"

Jonatan shook his head. "The risk of HIV infection is minimal. There's a greater risk of hepatitis B and C. In which case your liver could take a bit of a beating. The first thing we do now is to test you for antibodies, then we check if you already had the disease. Then we'll give you a quick vaccination against hepatitis B, also immunoglobulin. After that you shouldn't have to worry too much."

"But what if I get HIV?"

"We'll give you an HIV test now to make sure you weren't already infected with it, then we'll test you again in three months' time, and then again in six months. We'll test you in the same way for hepatitis. The last test will be in nine months."

"God! Do I really have to wait nine months to know if I've been infected? Is there no quicker way?"

"I can understand it's stressful. But if you're HIV-negative after three months it's extremely unlikely for you to have the infection. The six month check-up is just to be on the safe side."

"Three months.... But there are medicines, aren't there...

inhibitors? People with HIV get inhibitors so they live longer." Jonatan had made an exception before, when Emil was ill and wasn't allowed visitors. Surely he would also help her this time, even if it were against the rules?

"These aren't risk-free medicines, you don't take them unless you have to. If we knew that the guy who stabbed you had HIV or if you test positive, we'll give you an inhibitor, but not until then."

"But we don't know who he is! What if we don't catch him? And surely there's a difference between just being stabbed with a blood-filled syringe and actually being injected with the blood."

"Of course the amount of blood does make a difference. But for the moment I want us to wait and see. For your sake, Maria. If you were my own wife I'd do exactly the same." He looked into her eyes, looked at her earnestly and with warmth until she dared take the mental leap into trusting him.

"Okay…. How is your wife, actually?" Maria had thought of them sometimes, particularly about what Jonatan had told her in confidence, that his wife was having serious problems with alcohol.

"We don't live together any more. She moved in with another man who drinks just the way she does. I can't do anything about it… nothing. She won't live very long if she carries on…. I really don't want sympathy, I just want to be clear about the realities of the situation. I wasn't able to deal with it, I couldn't be there to help her through it. If you want to meet for a coffee some time… and to talk… you know where I am."

"I'd like that." She meant it.

"And how have things been with you?" he asked, his expression indicating that he was expecting confidences, not platitudes.

"There's a man I love…" Maria grew silent. It was not easy explaining her relationship with Per Arvidsson.

"But.... I think I can read between the lines... and there's a 'but'..."

"But... it's not entirely uncomplicated. His name is Per Arvidsson, he's a policeman. Remember that policeman who was shot while he was on duty? Physically Per's back to normal. But he gets depressed sometimes. He's gone back to work, part-time. He just separated from his wife; the children spend every other weekend with him. We see each other sometimes but he's not up to a relationship, and he can't cope with my children, they're too demanding for him. Everything is too much on their terms. So we see each other on the weekends when we don't have our children staying and we try to think of things to do together. He doesn't even know for sure if he loves me.... Everything just feels empty, he says."

"Is that enough for you?" Jonatan looked at her very attentively. "Sometimes I think people try to be satisfied with the crumbs from the table because that's all they feel they're worth.... That's how it was for me. I always wanted something wholehearted, not just a bit of affection now and then when she needed consolation. Now that she's moved out I wonder how things could have ended up like they did."

"What Per gives me is good enough... if that's all he's got for now. He's getting better. I'm hoping it'll work itself out if he can have the time he needs."

"Take care of yourself, Maria. And call me." He kept his eyes fixed on her for a long time, until she felt a tingling sensation in her body. There was a kind of tension between them. It had been there from the first moment a few years ago when she blew up at him over the telephone—as a result of a confusion. That seemed an eternity ago. To her own chagrin, she felt herself blushing.

He noticed, and let go of her hand. "I appreciate your friendship," he said as if he'd read her thoughts and didn't want to cause her any more embarrassment. After all, he'd just made it clear he was free and this might be misconstrued as an unsubtle come-on.

A nurse stuck her head in between the curtains separating the beds.

"Jonatan. They're looking for you at the ward. Did you turn off your pager?"

He rummaged in his breast pocket. "Must have left it in the staff room. See you again, Maria. Promise. Call me when you want to."

"How long do I have to stay here?" she called out down the corridor as he was walking away.

"If it was up to me you could go home after we've finished the tests. But you have a couple of broken ribs and the surgeon may want to keep you here for a while to make sure there's no bleeding or perforations to the lungs." Maria saw a final glimpse of his white coat as he swung round the corner.

As soon as she was by herself, her thoughts started churning. Again and again she ran through her harrowing ordeal, trying to remember more details. The tall guy had worn steel toe-toed boots, Dr. Martens. Kilroy jeans. A guy with money? Or loaded, big-spending parents? His age was difficult to tell. The other two had spoken in a dialect that was probably from somewhere around Västerås. Thick sounds.

Shit, Roy, maybe we should leave it now, get out of here. So the tall guy went by the name of Roy. Hartman was cross-checking against well-known local criminals and gangs. He would also be calling for witnesses on the radio and the local television news—asking them to come forward. What a waste of time to lie here waiting! She wanted to help, but she knew she wouldn't be allowed to take part in the investigation. Not now that she was directly involved.

"The boy's parents want to talk to you. They're in the intensive care unit, if you feel you're up to it." The nurse with the cart of needles again. "I just have to take a bit more blood and then you can get out of bed." She clamped Maria's right arm with a blue cuff and looked for a suitable vein. Her skin turned blotchy and a vein swelled in the crook of her arm. Maria looked away and tried to breathe slowly and deeply. She'd never been afraid of needles before. Now the mere sight of one made her tremble uncontrollably. She burst into tears. Then cursed her own sensitivity and had a go at the nurse, who was trying to comfort her.

The intensive care unit was bathed in blinding, white light. Maria passed a group all in green and clipboards in their hands, like a detachment of Roman soldiers with shields. At the far end of the corridor stood a muscular man in his forties. His eyes had something hunted in them, his eyelids were swollen and his sparse hair bathed in sweat. He came to meet her.

"Linus's dad." He offered his hand and fought back the tears. "I could kill the pigs who did this to my son. Do you understand? I could kill them! No punishment could ever be enough. Fucking bloody lunatics!"

"I can understand the way you feel." Maria backed away from his terrible wrath. No doubt about it, if he ran into them now he would be capable of killing them.

"I'm going to find out who they are and I'm going to kill them!"

"Calm yourself down, Ulf, think about what you're saying." A buxom woman in a pastel-hued dress tried to put her arm round him. "Taking revenge won't bring Linus back. I wouldn't want you to go to prison. You have to calm down. You're scaring me, Uffe."

The woman started to cry. His words had lashed like a whip.

"It's your goddamn fault! If he'd been with me there'd have been different ground rules. You think you're nice when you let him stay out as late as he likes, it's goddamn sloppy. If he'd lived with me this would never have happened."

"Ulf." Her voice was pleading. "Please stop."

He blocked her attempt to put her arms round him, holding out his hand and stepping back.

"This is all your goddamn fault, Katarina!"

Maria went between them. It was unbearable hearing them arguing.

"How is Linus?"

"Don't you know!" Ulf stared at her with deranged eyes. "He's dead! Dead! I'm going to get hold of the fuckers who did this if it's the last thing I do. I don't give a damn if I end up in prison. I asked for you because I want to know exactly what happened. Do you know who they are?"

"No. I didn't know... he was dead." The information came as a shock, even though she should have been prepared for it. "I'm so sorry. The last I heard before I came here was that he was on his way into an operation. Can we sit down somewhere and have a quiet talk?" Maria's legs were scarcely capable of holding her up; the pain in her chest was almost unbearable. She mustn't pass out. Not now. Not make a nuisance of herself.

"He died almost three hours ago. They didn't even have time to prepare him for the operation. A rib punctured his pericardial sack." The woman's voice broke up in a new fit of weeping. "And even if they had managed to save his life he would have stayed on life support. He wouldn't ever have woken up again, the doctor said. The damage to his head... led to inner bleeding. He'd never talk again, or eat or move...."

"Stop it, stop for God's sake, Katarina! I can't listen to this any more." Ulf turned away and walked off with long quick strides, as if it were possible to run away from the words.

They sat down at a table in the room set aside for next of kin. Ulf immediately bounced up and started pacing to and fro before them.

"Damn it!" He crunched his fist into the doorframe. "Damn!"

"I'm so sad for you. It's so hideous, I don't know what to say." Maria put her arm round Linus's mother, who looked back at her with deep gratitude. "Is there any chance that Linus knew these men? Any kind of situation where he might have run into them?"

"Not a goddamn chance." Ulf started criss-crossing the floor again. "Linus didn't have a lot of friends at all. Mostly he just sat at home." Katarina glanced at Ulf, checking to see whether it was advisable to add anything to his statement. "He had serious asthma and couldn't hang around with the other boys in the class or play football or things like that. Any kind of physical exertion made it worse. I was so happy he had Oliver to play computer games with, so he wasn't completely on his own. I tried to think of things we could do together, but it's not ideal. A boy of his age should be with his friends, not his mom. I did all I could to encourage him to meet people of his own age." She gave her husband a long-drawn gaze, which seemed to say: thanks for letting me finish without interrupting, and explain myself.

"He wasn't exactly bullied at school, but at the same time he wasn't really one of the group," Ulf offered. It was as if the air was slowly deflating now, and he could no longer find a reason to scream at Katarina. He sank into an arm-chair by the door. The worst of his fury seemed to have spent itself. "Tell us what happened."

As mercifully as possible Maria described the assault without going into any details about the assailants. Apprehending them was a matter for the police.

"We're going to put all our resources into finding these people. I won't be able to work on the investigation, but I will be a witness. I feel just like you, Ulf, I'd like to beat the life out of them. But if you feel like that you can't do a good job as a police officer. My chief, Tomas Hartman, is a highly competent police officer. He'll do his utmost." Maria realized her words were not sounding very convincing. There was an unpleasant determination in Ulf's voice. She really hoped he would calm down and trust the police to do their work.

"Thanks for having the courage to... for trying to save Linus." Katarina gave Maria a heartfelt embrace and looked at Ulf. But he could not show any gratitude; he was too blinded by his hate.

"There was a witness, you said, a man who passed by without helping you. Can you describe him better?"

Chapter 3

When Linn Bogren knocked off her shift at the hospital it was almost eleven o'clock. Just before the end of the night shift, a case came in from the intensive care unit. They were in the middle of the run-through. If the decision had been made an hour earlier it would have been much smoother. The medical department would have taken charge of a man with multi-symptom illness—inserting a catheter, putting him on a drip, and measuring his urine. He was given blood electrolytes, proteins, and fat; also oxygen, a respirator, and a pain pump they'd never seen before. There wasn't even a set of instructions for it. It took a while to get him installed and inform his next of kin that he'd been moved out of intensive care because of a lack of space. The ICU had taken custody of a badly injured boy that night, who was more in need of the bed. Of course it wouldn't quite be put in this way to the old man's family. It was better if they interpreted the whole thing as good news. The situation has stabilized: "Our view is that he can now be moved to a normal ward." In the old days when finances had been better, there'd been extra personnel available. The old man could do with constant monitoring, given the confusion he was in. In the short term he'd been in the ICU he'd already had time to pull out the needle twice, so that blood and drip solution leaked into the bed and they had to change the sheets. Of course the man needed a room of his own, so they had to rearrange half the section. One lady was moved into the corridor. She was a bewildered old thing, who also needed individual attention.

Linn walked homeward at a brisk pace under the streetlights along the beach promenade by the city wall. Far away on the ice-blue horizon she could see the Gotland ferry like a white sugar cube on its way into the harbor. She tried to disconnect from her thoughts about work, tried to breathe calmly and relax, but it was impossible. She thought about the badly injured boy. A colleague in ICU had told her he'd been assaulted and that his injuries were life-threatening. She'd seen his parents on the stairs. Their evident despair had shaken her deeply.

But she must stop agonizing about work, had to calm down before she got home, so she could sleep. Tomorrow she was back on duty at seven o'clock. At best she'd get about five hours of sleep. Once you started checking your watch it was already too late: five more hours to get some sleep, four hours, three, two, one, zero. Just before the alarm went off she usually fell asleep like a dead person. Her old job at the health center had been better. Just a straight week, 8–5. But she'd committed to the hospital over the summer. They needed people. She'd been very hesitant about going back for a number of reasons. But in the end she'd given in. She was in dire need of money; this year she'd have to make do with a week's holiday in November.

She lingered a little by Kärleksporten in the city wall. Twelve years ago she'd gotten engaged in this very spot, on a sunny but cold spring morning as the waves lashed against the rocks on the beach. She'd been so happy... or was that true, in fact? At that time she was a young girl, perhaps more in love with love than the actual man she was getting engaged to. He'd wanted this and his willpower was so strong. He was older, he knew best, he was so much surer about everything. They suited each other, he'd said. She'd been hesitant about it even then. But so many things in life were like this. She hardly ever knew what she wanted, and in the end you had to decide on something, right? If you didn't choose someone to live with, you ended up alone and nothing could be more frightening than that.

She passed through Kärleksporten and turned into Studentallén. There were a lot of people out and about, mostly young people celebrating the end of term. The time had not quite come yet for the big tourist influx, and Medieval Week was much later in August, but the mild weather had brought people out of their hollows to socialize. A bride in white was standing outside the Wisby Hotel with all her entourage. They were all laughing and talking, hugging and being silly. It looked like the reception had been a success. The bride was very beautiful. Linn felt a pinprick in her heart and thought about Sara. The bride looked so similar to her beautiful, irresistibly courageous Sara, with that light red, wavy hair and those lively gray eyes.

Sara had first come to the hospital diagnosed with cystic fibrosis. Incurable. Unfair. With every passing phase her breathing deteriorated. Her days had been filled with physical therapy and massive courses of antibiotics. She'd had a great need to communicate. Linn had often stayed on far beyond her normal working hours because she wanted to, wanted to stay more than anything. And not just for Sara's sake either... it wasn't a sacrifice on her part. They became close friends. They went to the theater and movies together, listened to music long into the night, shared experiences and discussed them. One shouldn't socialize with one's patients. It's no good. One has to keep a watertight seal between work and leisure. Anything else spells disaster, every professional nurse knows this. But her feelings ran away with her. Each time there had been a further deterioration when Sara came into the hospital, it felt like a personal loss, a punch to the stomach. Sara often called ahead before she came in—"I can't stay at home any more, I have a temperature again." The intake of oxygen was increased every time. Her infections hit harder and harder. Her lung capacity dwindled and death put its mark on her cheeks. She was so young, not even thirty. The only possibility left to her was a lung transplant: new lungs would give her new life. She was placed on a waiting list. There was a slim chance, the waiting list was long. The lungs had to be compatible. The organ donors were few, and the wait was macabre in its way—the very idea of hoping for someone else's death in order to live oneself! Linn had not wanted Sara to think so negatively, so crassly, about it. Something good can come of another person's meaningless death, a part of the body can live on, can give life. The weeks passed and Sara did her best to stay in shape. She maintained a good diet, worked out, stayed positive, slept as much as she could, rested and worked out again. It was going to be all right. It had to be all right.

Then the day came. A new pair of lungs were available. She was due to be flown to the Karolinska Hospital. A life-or-death journey. Linn stayed with her at the hospital that night. Neither of them could have slept anyway. There was a full moon and the lights were all out in the ward. In the silvery glow she'd seen Sara's white face, the gleam in her black eyes. Her skin was worryingly shiny. At around midnight the fever broke out, and Sara had a shivering fit. Her face grew red, her eyes glittered, her forehead dripped with sweat. That night another person on the waiting list was given a chance to live. If you're sick you can't have an operation. Sara deteriorated even more. Lost weight. In the end she was taking fifteen liters of oxygen through a mask and still she breathed as if she'd just run a marathon. She wavered between life and death in a sweat-soaked struggle with the infection that would not give in.

You have to go home, said Linn's colleagues. You really must sleep if you're going to be able to do your job. The clinic manager, Sam Wettergren, had a long talk with her. He had realized how things stood and now offered his own interpretation. It made everything sound so ugly, the way it came out of his mouth—everything that had been care and commitment. He said straight away that she should resign. If she refused, he'd transfer her. A nurse cannot have a personal relationship with a patient. There was no way this would be allowed in his clinic.

Rather than playing the coward and denying her feelings for Sara, she abstained from commenting on what he'd said. She was not going to make a victim of herself. If he put any ultimatums on her, she'd counter with certain things that were less pleasant for him. He, who was supposed to be a good example to all. It would be enough to allude to one particular fateful error he'd made, which could be enough to ruin his career for ever.

"What are you going to do about it?" Sam Wettergren had said, and she'd seen the fear sweeping over his haughty face.

"Nothing—if I'm just left in peace," she'd replied. The first round ended in a draw, then. As long as he kept in line she wouldn't share what she knew with others.

"Does Sara know anything about the medical research? Have you said anything to her?"

"No, you're her doctor and she trusts you. I don't want to undermine the confidence she has in you. I won't say anything to Sara if you take care of your business and leave me to mine."

After a week, there was a turnaround. Sara improved once again; it was miraculous. Her temperature returned to normal and the oxygen levels were reduced, although she remained at the hospital. With incredible determination, Sara continued exercising. Cycling with oxygen, mile after mile, while waiting for the last chance. Rest—exercise, rest, exercise, and a total avoidance of contact with people who might have a cold or any other contagion. Linn had waded in and read the riot act to a consultant senior physician who'd been about to go into the ward even though his nose was running.

And the chance came again… one rainy November evening when Linn was on duty. She would never forget that evening. Not for as long as she lived. The telephone call came through from the coordinator. There was going to be an operation. New lungs had come in. Linn got her instructions about oxygen tanks for the helicopter journey, orders for preparation of the patient, forms to fill in. She called in the doctor on duty. Her whole body trembling, she'd woken Sara to give her the marvelous news. They'd laughed and cried. The fear and joy washed over them like breaking waves. Now everything had to work to perfection. Linn calculated oxygen volumes and asked her colleague to double-check. She was on pins and needles. The ambulance crew was there in no time at all. "See you very soon!" Linn had said. See you! She'd hugged Sara. This might be their last embrace, Linn's last glimpse of her still alive.

"I love you, Linn. For real," Sara had whispered into her hair.

"I love you, too. More than anything else in my life." And thus it was out in the open. The forbidden thing had been spoken; a bridge constructed over the void. A tremulous joy, a vertiginous fear. May it give Sara the courage and strength to live.

For the rest of that shift Linn had neglected the other patients. She had Sara in her thoughts the whole time. It was a wonder that nothing more serious went wrong than a significant delay in the administering of evening medicines, and the fact that many patients fell asleep without their sleeping pills.

When Linn came home that night she'd been unable to sleep. She'd sat by the window, staring into the rain and praying to that God she didn't even believe in—asking for Sara to live, for the operation to be a success, for Sara to cope with the medicine that calmed her immune system so that the lungs were not rejected. I love you, Sara. Only now had she spoken those words to herself. What she'd known all along deep inside without even daring admit it to herself. Against all common sense. A patient. A woman. Where would this lead? No, there had been no sleep that night. Not a wink.

Marvels can be accomplished while you wait, miracles take a little longer, as magicians like to say. At first they didn't recognize her: a fresh young woman in a summery skirt and hair hanging loose in red waves, who wandered calmly into the ward. Her eyes were radiant and her smile like the sun.

"Sara! Darling Sara, let me look at you! It's fantastic! No oxygen." Linn hadn't been able to hide her joy from anyone. And Sam left them in peace that day.

Chapter 4

Linn hurried her steps toward home. Her whole body ached with tiredness. Those last few days she had not had much in the way of sleep either. Claes was at sea and before he came home she had to make the decision about whether to leave him. He'd been gone for almost a month and he'd be home for a whole month. Every spare moment he'd be there, and she'd miss being at work so she wouldn't have to feel his hands on her body, and all the expectations of what she did not want to give him. It would be best to pack her bags and move out before he came home. And only bring what was most important. He could keep most of it. In actual fact there isn't much one really needs: clothes, a few keepsakes, books. The thought of packing while he watched, while he tried to persuade her to stay, turned her stomach. He wouldn't become violent or angry. He'd just give her sheepish looks—silent, cut to the quick, watching what she was doing. His implied accusations would be worse than any hard words. Maybe he'd remind her of all the things they'd experienced together, their friends, the house downtown that neither of them would now have the means to keep. The house into which they'd plunged all their money and creativity. Mostly his money, but certainly her creativity and time. As a nurse she only made half his salary. A separation would put her in an entirely different situation, she realized.

What would her friends say? Her colleagues at work? His parents? In the thirteen years they'd spent together she'd grown so close to his family. She loved her mother-in-law, who'd become the mother she'd never had. And his siblings: they always saw each other during their holidays. At Christmas, New Year, Easter, and Midsummer they had lovely parties and every autumn she went on vacation with his sister Lotta. This year they'd been talking about going to Tenerife. All this on one side of the scales, and Sara on the other. Linn tottered along over the cobblestones. Everything was silent and still. Her thoughts whirled round and sought a hub to fix onto, a decision to stick to. She had to make her mind up very soon. Wonderful, entertaining Sara. When they were together there was not a shadow of doubt, but in her lonely moments the choice was not as simple.

And if she did leave him? Then she'd move in with Sara. Sara would never want to leave her house in her blooming rose garden in Lummelunda. How does it feel to move in with someone and not have anything of one's own? To be a guest in Sara's home? To pay half and own nothing? And what would happen if Sara got ill again? Properly ill. What if she died just when Linn had left security behind and jumped over the precipice? Later there would be no way of repairing the deceit and turning back. And then the loneliness would become unbearable, with neither Sara nor Claes there. The way things were now, she had them both. No, she couldn't be so calculating about it. Linn tried to shake herself, rid herself of such low principles. What would Sara's family say? They didn't know anything. They thought the reason she never met any men was because she was ill and didn't want to involve anyone. Or maybe that the illness took so much time that she had no opportunity to meet anyone else. They had stopped asking long ago.

There was just another week now until Claes came home. If she decided to leave she'd have time to pack this weekend. On Monday next week Claes would sign off the ship. She could still choose to stay in her dull security and pretend everything was just the same as always. Nothing had happened. Which would be deceitful to Sara and also to her own deepest feelings. Of course she also felt guilt, but it was not only her own fault the way things had gone. She needed something else, something Claes could not give her. Maybe it was time to reassign whose fault it was, rather than just piling it all on her own head? Something in their ability to feel intimacy had been lost. He needed sex to help him drum up the courage he needed for closeness, whereas she needed closeness to even want to have sex—things could be summarized more or less like that. And then things had also grown so unbearably dull....

Linn looked at her watch. She should call Sara and say good night, but something held her back. They had already started planning their life together, but Linn had not been quite sincere about her hesitations. She didn't want to make Sara upset or insecure. Surely it was quite enough for her to be obsessing over this. You decide. It's your life and your decision, Sara had said. And that was right. Linn would not be able to avoid it.

Linn crossed the parking area by Ordnance Tower to pick up a bag of clothes in the car. She'd been buying new clothes for her new life. She met no one, yet had a feeling of being watched. Maybe it was her bad conscience putting ideas in her head? She grew more watchful, avoided walking too close to parked cars. A door could suddenly open, and someone grab her and pull her inside. She threw hurried glances on either side of her and hurried along. In through the gate in the wall and up onto Fiskarplan. Almost home. Specksgränd lay in darkness. What had happened to the streetlights? Were they all broken? A beer can rolled across the road. It was unexpected. The rattling sound was deafening in the silence. She tried to look into the doorway from where the can had come rolling, but she couldn't see anyone. Her knees felt like rubber. One foot in front of the other. She had to get out of here. Didn't even dare look round. But there was someone there, just behind her. Rapid steps behind her back. From the next doorway up ahead, a shadow emerged. A tall hooded figure with a chain around his wrist. The steps behind her were clearer now. They slowed down. A glance over her shoulder and she looked into a pair of glimmering eyes. From a side street came a third man. She wanted to scream, but her voice wouldn't do as it was told.

"You got a smoke?" The tall one was standing less than three feet from her. His breath stank of alcohol. His gaze was bloodshot and wild.

"Sorry. I don't smoke" she minced.

"I couldn't hear, what did you say?" His face came right up close and she backed away automatically.

"Shit, you're pushing?" The voice belonged to the guy behind her. He was shorter and had slightly protruding front teeth. His muscles tensed under the rolled up sleeves of his hooded jacket.

"So you don't have a cigarette?" The tall one rattled his chain.

She shook her head. Her voice could no longer be relied on.

She saw his green-gray eyes flick from side to side. As long as he didn't touch her, as long as he limited himself to

38

words, everything would be all right, she told herself. She had to keep it on that level. If she remained polite and co-operative, they would let her pass.

"You have to offer us something else, then." He grabbed hold of her between her legs, tightening and maintaining his grip. She tried to push his hand away but he was so much stronger. It hurt. At first she was more frightened than disgusted. The disgust came later… and would not go away. He jeered at her. She felt a hand on her shoulder. The third guy was standing right by her. His pulled-down base-ball cap covered the upper part of his face. He was slimmer than the others. Just a gray shadow. Three against one. The lane was deserted.

"Leave me alone! Please, let me go."

"Depends if you're a good girl and do what we say.…"He released his grip and started opening his fly.

The other laughed. She got a shove in the back. Her arm was wrenched and someone pressed down her head.

"I don't want to. Leave me alone."

"If you scream we'll cut your throat, you got that?" His grip hardened. "Do you get it?" He pulled down his un-derpants. His purple-blue skin down there glowed under a straggly covering of hair.

"Yes." She was forced down on her knees. Caught the smell of genitals; the nausea came over her in a torrent. She sobbed and cried. He slapped her face and cursed. At that moment a door opened in the apartment opposite, and the neighbor emerged with his dogs. The gang dissolved and were gone as suddenly as they had first appeared.

"Can I help you with anything? Are you okay?" Harry, her friendly neighbor, was standing next to her, ready to help her up on her feet. Her knees shook and she was having difficulty regaining her balance. "It's easily done, having a few more than you can take when you're enjoying yourself with friends. Can you manage on your own?" He clucked with laughter and turned his friendly eyes on her.

"Yes, yes, I can." She tottered along like an old woman. "It's not like you think," she tried to say. But he winked at her, clearly unwilling to listen to any excuses.

"Well, we've all been there. But I think I was a bit younger than you when I tested the limits. Oh the parties!" He tugged at the lead. "Mirabel, Gordon! All right, I know you're in a hurry. We'll have to walk on. They're impatient."

She would have liked to tell him. Explain the situation, what had happened. But his joviality was so dense that she didn't have the strength to force her way through it.

Linn stumbled through the gate. She locked her front door behind her with fumbling hands, wedged a chair under the door handle and got out the biggest kitchen knife she could find. Her pulse thundered rapidly in her body and she was too frightened to relax, sitting there with the lights off, almost bursting with tension and staring into the darkness. Had they noted where she lived? As she stumbled toward the door she hadn't given a thought to that. All she'd wanted was to save herself and shut the door behind her. Now she cursed her stupidity. She should have told Harry what had happened. She could have asked him to come inside, into the safety of his house. But something in her had resisted. It was partly his whole interpretation of the situation, partly the shame, the shame that was not hers—yet nonetheless it was there, in all its stickiness. "Things like this don't happen to good girls. It was your own fault!" Who would believe her if even Harry—and he was kindness itself—didn't? Why would the police see things any different? She'd have to go through the whole repulsive thing again. Then, maybe, in the end, they wouldn't even believe her. Anyway, nothing had happened. Or had it? Certainly it hadn't been rape. Sexual molestation, what was the punishment for that? No, she didn't want to put herself through all that. She didn't want to explain the nauseating thing that had happened in interviews, to strangers, who might nonetheless conclude that was she partly to blame. Why didn't you resist? Yes, why not? Because I tried to get out of the situation without violence; they were stronger than me and I was outnumbered. But there was also something else. My body would not obey me, it turned to rubber and couldn't be relied on. She'd been unable to run, only totter along, half-paralyzed. So unsure on her feet that Harry had thought she was drunk.

Linn lay down on the bed. She was determined to sleep with her clothes on, and her sneakers. The knife was on her bedside table, and a baseball bat. The cell phone lay next to her in the bed. It was past midnight, she had a few hours to sleep before she had to get back to work, fully focused on her patients and solicitously avoiding mistakes. She had to call Sara before she fell asleep. If Sara were to get worried, she'd take the car and come to her. Nothing could stop her. But there were a thousand eyes in her street! Someone would see Sara coming in the middle of the night and then tell Claes. It mustn't happen, not now! Not before she'd thought it all through clearly and decided what to do. Linn felt her tiredness like an iron band round her head. There was a creeping sensation in her body. There would be no sleep. She had to call Sara.

Two souls and one thought. When the cell phone rang, Linn jumped bolt upright in the bed.

"I wanted to hear if you were still alive. You haven't forgotten me, have you? My name is Sara and I'm your love."

41

"There was a lot on at work. I only just got home."

"I miss you. It's lonely here."

"I miss you, too, more than you think."

"Has anything happened?"

"No, things just messed up. We had a patient brought out of intensive care right at the end. They didn't have space for him, a boy came in who'd been assaulted. Has there been anything about it on the radio yet?"

"I didn't hear anything. How are you?"

"I'm so insanely tired."

"So I'm going to let you sleep. We'll talk tomorrow. Did you decide yet if you're going to tell Claes about us? You have to decide, Linn. You know that, don't you? You can't play it both ways. I can't take it."

"I'm going to talk to him. As soon as he comes home. I promise. Love you. So enormously." The words were the right ones, but she couldn't quite manage to make her voice sound convincing.

"I love you. And soon we have to be very brave." Sara inhaled.

"When we're together we're really brave. Good night." Linn didn't have the strength to carry on talking.

There wasn't a chance of Linn being able to sleep. The feeling of vulnerability made her too frightened to stay in bed. She lived on the ground floor and someone could easily break a porch window. She listened for sounds in the street. Wandered from room to room. Looked at the things she and Claes had bought together. The big wedding photo, printed on canvas like a painting. She was in a creamy white plunge-back dress with a prudishly high collar; he, in a black dinner jacket and a pink bow tie and short-trimmed hair. How very young they'd been. They knew so little about each other, about love. They had never stormed the gates of heaven. It was more of a friendship, a warm and comfortable embrace. She had called it love. Before she met Sara, she'd believed that's what it was. Linn touched the necklace she wore. Since the wedding she'd worn it every day. It had been a gift from Claes's mother, a precious heirloom passed down for generations. It had become a part of her. Rather than the wedding band, which she could not wear at work anyway, the necklace had become symbolic of the fact that she was Mrs. Bogren.

Most of the furniture had been bought second-hand on the Internet. For less than twenty-five thousand kronor they'd put together all their household goods. Expensive quality furnishings costing trifling amounts. She didn't want to keep any of it. Those things would always be associated with the life she'd lived with Claes, and they would not fit with Sara's light interiors and Bohemian style.

A sound from the street catapulted Linn back into the fear she'd managed to push away for a moment. The gate screeched slightly. Steps on the gravel path. She tensed her ears to the utmost, then ducked under the window as she quickly returned to the bedroom, where she pocketed the cell phone and picked up the knife. Then she crawled behind the sofa. There was a careful knock at the door. From her hiding place, in the faint light, she could see the door handle being pressed down. Her heart was racing in her chest. She held her breath until she thought she'd suffocate. There was another knock. Then, after what seemed an eternity, she heard the steps on the gravel again. The porch door handle was also pressed down. What would she do if the window were broken?

Everything went back to silence. Nothing happened. The trees out there swayed lazily in the wind, scratching against the walls. She tried to tell herself it was only a branch scraping the façade. There… a face in the window. She couldn't see who it was. His hands were cupped and his nose pressed to the windowpane.

Linn wanted to scream, but the sound lodged in her throat. She dialed the first two digits of the number to the emergency services and waited. If she reported these guys they'd find out who she was, and then she might never have a moment's peace again.

Chapter 5

The waiting room at the health center was filled to bursting. Linn was trying to concentrate, reading a report on insomnia in a magazine, when the doctor emerged and shook her hand.

"Please!" Anders Ahlström pointed at the empty chair on the other side of his desk. "You work here sometimes, don't you?" He had a vague memory of having spoken to her not too long ago in the coffee room.

"I got a job here recently but I'm working at the hospital over the summer." She twisted. "I need the money. I'm taking my vacation in the autumn this year."

He nodded by way of an answer. The computer was on, the printer fan whined. "What can I do for you?"

"I can't go on like this!" Linn Bogren's eyes filled up. "I'm too exhausted for work." She covered her eyes with her hand, could not quite face meeting the doctor's sympathetic gaze.

Anders Ahlström handed over a few tissues and waited for her to go on. When she remained silent, he asked: "Why are you too exhausted to work?"

When Linn still couldn't regain control over her voice, he

continued: "Has anything happened at work that makes it difficult for you to go? And this stays between us."

"No, no, it's not like that." Linn wiped her runny nose and rubbed her eyes with the back of her hand." I like my work, both here and at the hospital. It feels meaningful and I like my colleagues. But I need to go on sick leave because I can't sleep. I think I'll go mad if I don't get a full night's sleep."

"I understand." Anders had seen many patients in the same situation. "What exactly is your sleeping problem, can you describe it?"

She sighed heavily. "Every scrap of advice I've been given, I've tried to put into practice. I listen to relaxation tapes. I don't work out before sleeping, don't eat too much, don't drink coffee, no alcohol. I wait until I'm tired before I go to bed, the bedroom is dark and cool. And still I don't sleep… the clock ticks away and midnight starts closing in and I get stressed out because I know I have to get up and be on time for morning report. The night shift has to go home in the morning. They hate it if you're late. I've always been a morning person, so it's never been a problem getting up early, not at all."

"So you're working shifts right now? C shift until 11 p.m. and then A shift? You start at 7 a.m.?"

"Well, the worst is when I've done the evening shift and have to be up early in the morning. It's been like this all year, that's why I applied for the position at the healthcare center. I thought it would make a difference working normal hours. I know what you're going to say, that I should drop my summer job at the hospital. But I can't afford to."

"Are you taking any medicine?" The doctor glanced at the note made by the receptionist when Linn called to book a time.

"I've tried sleeping pills. They help me sleep for a short

while, then I often wake up frightened. In a panic. It feels like someone's watching me through the window, so I let all the blinds down. I've even taped up all the cracks so no one outside can spy on me. But I feel like I can hear steps on the stairs outside. And even though I'm so terribly frightened I make myself open the door to have a look. There's never anyone there. I fall into a doze and dream and suddenly there's someone in my bedroom. He has a knife and he slashes at me. I try to roll out of the way and he misses a few times and stabs the mattress, then gets me in the stomach. Here...." She showed him an area at the top of her ribs where the anxiety tended to manifest itself.

"Have you ever been robbed or been subjected to anything else that's frightened you?" Carefully he studies the reaction in her face as she thinks about it. She shakes her head, blushing and then nodding.

"I thought I saw a face in the window last Friday. Someone who was in my garden, staring at me. But it never happened again. Maybe it was just my imagination. This isn't the reason why I'm asking for help. I need stronger sleeping pills to cope with my job this summer. The nightmares started before I saw the face in the window, but they've grown worse since then. That same night I ran into a gang of boys and they frightened me. They were making trouble, I couldn't do anything about it.... If my neighbor hadn't come by at that precise moment anything could have happened." Linn smoothed back a dark lock of hair from her face.

Anders Ahlström fingered his prescription pad. How easy it would have been to write out the prescription she wanted, then bring in the next patient. He was already behind schedule because he allowed his patients to say what they had to say, then followed up with questions and listened to their replies. In the long term it was actually a time-saving device. Confident patients did not call back as often. If they received proper help the first time round they didn't have to come back. But in the short term it led to annoyance, less from the patients who had to wait than from his colleagues, who often did not get home on time.

"Is there anything else weighing on you?" He scrutinized her intensely, with a feeling she was not telling him the whole truth. "There's no rush. I have time to listen until you've told me everything."

"No, not exactly." She fixed her eyes on the prescription pad. All he had to do was to scribble something on it and she wouldn't bother him any more.

"That face you saw last Friday night… was it real? Were you dreaming?" He rolled back his office chair slightly, to give her space.

"I'm pretty sure it was real." Linn sighed audibly. He had to believe her. She didn't have the energy to be called into question.

"So there was a stranger in your garden in the middle of the night and he pressed his face to your window. That's a disturbance of the peace. Did you report it to the police?"

"No, nothing happened. Sleeping pills, that's what I need. Just do me a favor, will you. I know they're addictive, I won't take them unless I have to. Please…." She shifted in her chair. He could hear she was on the verge of tears.

"If I thought sleeping pills were the solution to your problem I'd write you a prescription right away. But quite honestly I don't think I'd be doing you much of a favor. With pills you don't sleep as well. Just like with alcohol. It's easier to go to sleep, but you sleep much worse. I can arrange an appointment with a colleague who works with insomniacs." It wasn't easy saying no to Linn Bogren—after all, they were colleagues. But how many suicides were assisted by prescription drugs issued by doctors? Too many. Something about Linn's attitude worried him. There was a disturbing level of anguish under the surface, he grew more and more sure of this as their conversation unfolded. What worried him most of all was her absolute determination to get hold of the pills. It would be difficult for her to amass enough pills at work because they monitored everything. But surely she'd also be able to get hold of a few more pills there if she really wanted to. Patients fell asleep before they'd taken their evening medicines. Drugs were discarded once they passed their expiration dates or when patients left the hospital. Any pills he gave her now and a few more she could procure for herself would be enough for a one-way ticket to eternity. He wasn't usually so suspicious, but he had a gut feeling this time.

"An appointment! Thanks a lot. You know as well as I do it'll take months before I get to see your colleague. I need to sleep *now*. If I don't get some help soon I'll kill myself." She burst into floods of tears and he looked on helplessly. He knew she was right in what she was saying, it probably would take months.

"If you'd rather talk to a psychologist that might be a little quicker. I get a feeling you're not telling me the whole truth, Linn. Maybe you don't think it has anything to do with me. In order to be able to help you, I have to know why I am giving you the medicine."

"I'm leaving my husband. Are you satisfied now? I'm in crisis. I need to sleep so I can think clearly and make the right decision."

"Okay." Her explanation gave him the alibi he needed. "I'll write out a prescription now for ten pills, and I'll set up a new appointment for you in a week's time." He saw the disappointment in her face and steeled himself against making any further concessions. She snatched the prescription out of his hand as soon as he'd lifted his pen from the paper.

"Next time we see each other I won't be your patient. I'll

be your colleague." She wiped her eyes with her sleeve. Her bearing was straight and proud and she was out of the door before he'd had time to rise out of his chair.

Anders Ahlström grabbed his tape recorder and dictated his journal entry. The next patient was waiting and had already been waiting forty-five minutes. Lunch was out of the question. He was all right with that. The worst thing was his craving for a cigarette. He'd promised himself and also Erika, whom he'd met in a bar, to stop smoking. She hated the smell of smoke. Kissing a smoker is like licking an ashtray, she'd said with fierce emphasis. He wanted to make a good impression. As a doctor he knew all about the damaging effects of smoking, but logic does not help very much once the pleasure center is stimulated. He smoked on the sly, so his daughter Julia wouldn't worry. "I don't want you to die like Mommy, then I won't have anyone left," she used to say. One time Julia had almost caught him when the steering wheel smelled of smoke from his hands. He had to stop, but right now he felt he wouldn't be able to concentrate at all unless he had a few drags. He'd finished his last pack the day before and intentionally not bought another one. He searched his jacket pockets and the brief-case. Nothing. Maybe he could borrow a cigarette from someone? Lisa, the receptionist, smoked, but she'd left and Siv was on vacation. Damn it! His hands were shaking and he couldn't think of anything else. Outside the window he saw a homeless man hanging round by the waste paper basket with a cigarette butt in his mouth. Without hesitation, Anders headed for the exit. This was an emergency. The man looked up, startled, as the doctor came steaming toward him in his white coat. With his foot he pushed the plastic bag from the liquor store into the nearest bush and prepared himself for a lecture on the dangers of smoking so close to the entrance.

"You wouldn't have a cigarette I could buy off you, would you?"

"What?" The man smiled broadly, exposing a row of worm-eaten teeth. Then thoughtfully rubbed his nose. "What!"

"Have you got a smoke?"

"I've run out, but you can have the butt." He took a deep drag. The cigarette was filterless and glowed two centimeters from his grubby thumb before he passed it over. "It's on me."

"Thanks, very decent of you." Anders Ahlström took the last drag on it and waited for the rewarding stimulation in his brain. "That was good, damn good."

"It was you who told my buddy to stop smoking? Poor schmuck had a heart attack and dropped dead last week."

"Probably was, yeah." In your moment of humiliation it's best to just come clean. "I should stop as well, but it's not so easy."

The old man agreed. "You're right there. Goddamn nightmare."

"A real goddamn nightmare." Anders felt strangely comforted by their understanding.

Chapter 6

He wasn't really so afraid of death. He just didn't want to die unless he had to. That was the reason why Harry Molin was sitting there—and suffering—in the health center waiting room. Through the window he could see his good-for-nothing doctor having a smoke with one of the down-and-outs, in spite of the fact that smoking was prohibited outside the entrance. At the turn of the last century pharmacies had sold ready-stuffed pipes as a remedy for asthma and hysteria, but surely science had moved on since then?

Anxiety about one's health must be like wanting a smoke, Harry reflected to himself. The kick when the nicotine hits your brain is like the euphoric relief you feel when you get confirmation that you're not suffering from a deadly disease. A short moment of bliss. But no long-term happiness. The need is still there, looking for new kicks. It's a beast that always wants more.

The last time he came he was sure he'd contracted MS. He had all the symptoms. First the twitching in one of his eyelids, the giddiness and the shaking hands. He'd held them in front of him for a long time, and then they'd started shaking uncontrollably. Later there was the numbness and the pricking sensations, and he may possibly have had a slightly worse sense of feel in his right leg than his left. It was a close call, but after squeezing them for a long while that's how it seemed to him. He also needed to pee a lot. The doctor thought this was caused by nervousness. But you couldn't be sure about it, could you? Nor could his insupportable tiredness be explained away by the fact that he'd lain awake worrying about his symptoms. It was difficult trusting this young doctor. He didn't run all the necessary tests. You could read on the Internet exactly how the tests should be done. And in Poland there was a doctor who ran extra tests, just to be on the safe side.

The doctor had been just as nonchalant that time Harry came to see him because of his suspicion that he'd caught HIV. His Alsatian had snapped at him, so there was a little cut; afterward, he'd accidentally touched a coin. There could have been infected blood on that coin. After that he felt his immune system weakening. He ran a fever, had swollen lymph glands and a sore throat and that's how it all starts when you catch HIV. One long-drawn cold after another had followed as winter turned to spring, and he'd been hard-hit by the flu. Could things be any clearer than that? His immune system had started running amok. Already at that point he'd started thinking about changing his doctor. Doctor Ahlström saw no need for an HIV test. For an hour and a half, Ahlström had gone through all the symptoms and explained them away. And the agreed conclusion was that if it weren't HIV it had to be something else, and it was this that had occupied Harry ever since. It had to be something. He just didn't feel healthy.

Things had been better while Doctor Wallman was there, before Ahlström arrived. Wallman had actually been a surgeon; he was a man of action. If you came to ask about a mole he had no problem removing it. True, he never had time to wait for the local anaesthetic to take effect before he picked up the knife, but you felt better afterwards. Sixteen moles had been removed by the time Wallman retired, and since then there had been a total stop. Ahlström never thought any of Harry's moles looked dangerous. As if he could tell. Somewhere a few cells start changing and it takes time before the human eye can tell. Surely it's better getting rid of the mole before the cancer has time to spread. It was the same with antibiotics. Wallman had never been stingy about prescribing them. The same went for painkillers. If you're in pain you're in pain. It's a subjective experience. Of course it would be best just to stay on antibiotics the whole time. In that way you'd avoid infections. Antibiotics should be a supplement, a way of enriching one's diet, quite simply. Every kind of antibiotic in a cocktail.

"That would avoid a lot of sick days," he'd commented to Doctor Ahlström.

"And we'd have lethal illnesses springing up which we couldn't treat because of the bacteria growing resistant to antibiotics," Ahlström had countered. Sometimes he was a bit drastic, that doctor. The real problem with antibiotics was that they gave you diarrhea. You didn't know if your bowels were loose because of the antibiotics or if you had some other illness. It could be salmonella or some inflammatory illness of the intestine or cholera or campylobacter from improperly handled mince meat. How do you know what's a side effect and what's a new disease? It's absolute hell sorting it all out.

"Harry Molin, please come in." Harry stood up and reluctantly shook the doctor's hand. Once he'd asked if the doctor really disinfected his hands after every consultation. Ahlström laughed and said that if the King and Silvia survived shaking hands with hundreds of people at bridge inaugurations and the official openings of new concert halls without dropping dead, then maybe one needn't agonize so much about it. The immune system had to be kept sharp. It was an answer that had annoyed Harry. Now he didn't dare ask; nor could he been seen to be avoiding handshakes and thus making himself look ridiculous.

Anders Ahlström sat down at the desk where Harry's medical file, all four thick files of it, had landed in a pile. There was really little point in running to and from the records storage with them all the time. They might as well just stay in the bookshelf.

"What can I do for you, Harry?"

"This time it's really serious, doctor. Really bad." Harry paused and thought about how to begin. He had to make himself understood this time, had to be taken seriously. The nurses had tittered behind his back when the receptionist said: "So it's you again, Harry. Have you missed us?" So humiliating. If he'd been in a position to choose the company he kept, it would hardly be that moronic receptionist person and the other nurses. Right now she was at the top of the list of people he'd bite if he caught rabies. That's exactly what he told her, too. If he'd been healthy, he'd go to work with an easy mind and socialize with friends in his spare time. Instead he had to humiliate himself time and time again because he was ill, and pay a lot of money, too, out of his hard-stretched reserves. There were certainly better ways of enjoying one's money.

"Tell me. What's the matter?" The doctor wasn't sounding sarcastic. Harry felt a vague spark of hope that maybe, in spite of all, the doctor was interested.

"It's my stomach acting up. *Yesterday I read about colon cancer in a newspaper… and everything fits.*"

Anders Ahlström couldn't stop himself groaning out aloud. He'd also read that blazing article and reflected on the costs to the taxpayers and the growing lines for those who actually needed treatment. Just a lot of scaremongering: "You could have cancer of the intestine. We know the symptoms. Read the full list!"

"You don't believe me!" Harry felt a lump in his throat. He was close to tears. He was so anxious that he couldn't sit still. He had to be properly checked out, even if it turned out to be really unpleasant. Rectoscopy, coloscopy, gastroscopy: he'd read about the procedures and they were not the sort of thing you exposed yourself to without good reason.

"Sorry." Anders quickly noted down the patient's concerns. "I'm groaning about the evening papers. Nothing else. I believe what you're telling me and I'm listening."

Harry drummed up some courage. What he was about to say sounded really stupid, but he had to say it.

"I'm passing feces as thin as pencils. If you have changing intestinal functions this could be a red flag that you need to seek treatment. I read about it in a medical journal on the Internet. Of course I felt very nervous about it, so I read everything I could find on the net. It described in detail what sort of surgical procedures are done. Sometimes they use radiation, sometimes both surgery and radiation. I couldn't sleep. I went to the toilet many times."

"Did you see if there was any blood in your feces?" Doctor Ahlström made notes in his pad to help him remember. His thoughts had a tendency to drift. Right now he was thinking about how to get hold of cigarettes before Erika met him after work. He was dying for a smoke; it was almost more than he could stand.

"It could be such a small amount of blood that it's not visible to the naked eye. That thing about feces thin as pencils isn't normal, is it? I had to know if it was dangerous. But everything was closed on Friday night except the emergency room. So I thought I'd go over to my neighbor, Linn, she's a nurse. It was almost midnight but she comes home late and

I was hoping she hadn't already gone to bed. I didn't want to call and disturb her, in case she was already sleeping, so I went over to see if there were any lights on. I knocked on the door, but no one opened, so I tried peeking in through the window to see if she was in the living room."

"What did you say? You did what?" Anders had to ask to make sure he'd heard him right. Of course it could be a coincidence, but nurse Linn Bogren and Harry Molin lived on the same street.

"I went over to my neighbor to see if her lights were on. What's so special about that? We're talking about colon cancer here. That's what's important." Harry shook his head. This doctor was really slow on the uptake sometimes.

"Did you put your face to the window? Is your neighbor called Linn Bogren?"

"Yes, but what's that got to do with anything?"

"Nothing. Carry on. Did she open the door? What did she say?" Anders Ahlström remembered Linn's story clearly. So the frightening experience had a natural explanation.

"I thought she'd be awake. She came home late and seemed groggy or slightly drunk. Apparently she ran into three men in the street. Seemed upset about something. When I got to her place every window was dark and I let her sleep and went home. But I didn't get a wink of sleep."

"Okay, this is how we're going to do this. I'll give you three small envelopes to take home, and I want you to leave three stool tests, on consecutive days if possible. If there's no blood in the excrement there's no danger. We'll test it when you come back here, we can get the result right away."

"If you've been constipated you can have a bit of blood, anyway. I don't want an operation if there's no reason for it." Harry felt at a loss and more and more worked up. In one sense it was better to be opened up so they could check what was wrong, but some surgeons weren't as skilled as others.

"Of course not. Obviously we'll carry on investigating if there's blood. But right now it's enough to know if there is or isn't."

"Before I go I have a tip for you, doctor. A new promising drug has come out for people who want to stop smoking. It's called Fumarret."

Harry blinked and stood up to say his goodbyes. His ingrown toenail hurt like hell. But he didn't want to bother the doctor with it. It wasn't life-threatening, he knew that, and if you wanted to be credible and have people listen to you, you couldn't bring up too many illnesses at the same time. A little ailment can divert attention from something you really need to deal with. In that respect doctors were often bad at prioritizing, he thought. A small but visible problem often had far too much time devoted to it while the important stuff was forgotten because it seemed too far-fetched. Time ran out and you were pushed out. You have maximum one minute to capture the doctor's attention, three minutes to explain complicated factors, and then your time's up. Every time Harry went to the doctor he practiced carefully beforehand, both what he was going to say and how he was going to say it. Today had been a really successful appointment. You could say what you liked about Ahlström, but he wasn't stingy about the amount of time he gave you.

On his way out of the health center, Harry passed the magazine rack. At the top was a small brochure about tick bites. He took a copy and dropped it into his pocket, to study it once he got home. True, he was vaccinated against TBE, but you couldn't vaccinate yourself against borrelia. You had to keep your eyes open. He must have pulled ticks out of his skin at least ten times. The dogs brought them in. When he got home he'd check the symptoms of borrelia.

Was there a more venal sin that failing your nearest and dearest or denying your own kith and kin? If murdering a stranger could result in a life prison sentence, faithlessness to your nearest and dearest should be punished even more severely. Capital punishment. And how could we be so sure that death was a punishment? Maybe it was just a way of slipping out the back way and avoiding punishment. Wasn't this in fact how we dealt with animals—putting them down as a way of showing how merciful we were? Because they were only animals and therefore not answerable for their own desires. Our human consciousness demanded a greater level of responsibility in us. The punishment had to calibrated. If you failed those who were nearest to you the punishment should not be death, but suffering. Not the suffering of the body, that was not the worst. But the soul. The slow breaking down of dignity and then the shame and realization that one had directly been the cause of all the evil that had taken place. And that one could have prevented it.

Chapter 7

The scent of Harry's cheap aftershave hung heavily over the room. Anders Ahlström banged his head against the table before he went to open the window. A passing nurse popped in with a paper to be signed. As if she were a persistent fly, he waved his hand to get rid of her. He had to have a minute to himself. He stayed by the window, breathing in the air. He felt exhausted and inadequate. If the waiting room had not been so full of people he would have dealt with Harry and his hypochondria in a better way. "Hypochondria" is not a good word. The anxiety was real. Harry really believed he was dying. And eventually, if he carried on subjecting himself to excessive medical attention, he might actually catch something. Hypochondria is a serious illness, in which the patient risks operations or inappropriate medication—or ultimately, being passed over and ignored when the appointments grow too frequent. Living with constant anxiety is corrosive to body and soul, and not being taken seriously is damaging to the self-confidence. Anders knew this better than most, maybe it had even been what made him become a doctor. An infinite number of times he had asked older medical colleagues for advice, letting on that it concerned a patient rather than himself. Not just in the early days but now as well, when he had started considering the risks of getting lung cancer. Maybe doctors are the worst hypochondriacs of all. The more knowledge there is, the greater the burden. Which did not stop him from keeping up his nicotine abuse. He had long since lost count of how many times he'd tried to give it up. Once he stopped for almost a whole year, then lost it when he had a single cigarette at a party, but mostly he couldn't even keep it up for a single day. One early spring when he had his first bout of pneumonia he thought his life was coming to an end. It made him so nervous that he smoked twice as much as usual. This just wasn't good enough. The new medication Harry had tipped him off about was a type of Antabus for smokers, causing nausea, heart palpitations, and giddiness—not much of a pleasure kick there. At the same time it contained dopamine, which reduced the hankering for nicotine. It was a constant reward, in other words, and a punishment if one lapsed and had a drag or two. Might be worth a try. Anders Ahlström got out his prescription pad and scribbled down the name of the acrid medicine for himself. Erika wanted him to stop smoking. In the honeymoon phase you're still malleable. Now was the time if ever.

The afternoon moved along at a snail's pace. He avoided coffee to minimize his cigarette cravings. The caffeine shortage gave him a headache and when Erika met him at the end of the day he was not at his best.

Erika noticed that Anders was less than peppy at once and quickly said, "I missed you," while slipping her arm under his and looking at him intently. Maybe he didn't want his colleagues to see them? It was all so new. There was no guarantee. He had probably not even told them he'd met someone. "They didn't want to let me in because I hadn't booked a time, so I said I was your lifestyle coach. The goal is a new and better life."

He shrugged his shoulders, feigning indifference.

"Not my fault I'm so immeasurably popular. Sorry to keep you waiting."

"What do you want to do?" Erika smiled at him. She'd been looking forward to the evening. Rushing home like a lunatic from work to have time to shower, get changed and fix her hair. He was worth it, although he looked as if he'd been sleeping in his clothes. His shirt under the doctor's coat was wrinkly and she felt that his hair was all sweaty at the neck when they kissed outside the foyer. He tasted of smoke. A letdown.

"Hm… I can't think of anything much." When he saw Erika's face he laughed uproariously. "I'll do anything as long as I can do it with you."

"Where's Julia, then?" Erika found herself wishing that his daughter could spend the night somewhere else.

"At the stables. I'm picking her up at ten o'clock. So we have four whole hours to spend together." He looked so full of anticipation that Erika couldn't stop herself from laughing at him, even though deep down she was disappointed. So nothing would happen tonight, either. And she'd made up the bed with clean linen, bought fresh-squeezed juice and freshly baked bread for breakfast.

"Tell me about your daughter." Erika thought she might as well find out about her number one competitor for Anders's favor.

"She's like most eleven-year-olds. A child but sometimes far too grown up. She likes horses and soccer. Finds it a bit difficult making friends at school. But there's a teaching assistant who means a lot to her and who's trying to help her find her feet. He's not officially there for her, but he's taken her on. Otherwise it's just always been us. So it might be a little difficult for her, you turning up. We have to take it a bit easy."

"What about her mother?" Erika was relieved to be able to ask the question. He had never mentioned another woman or whether he was married. It worried her slightly. Discretion in front of the daughter and not a word about the mother, it gave her bad vibes.

"You want to see a photo of Julia, so you recognize her if you bump into her in town?" He opened his wallet. There were two photos of Julia. A chubby baby in a cap and diapers; then a very pretty young lady on the back of a horse.

Erika commented on the photos and repeated her question. How typical if he were taken. Of course that was it, that was exactly it! He was too good to be true. The least he could do was come clean about it so she could decide whether to stay with it or walk away. Several times that day while sitting by the computer at the police station she'd come close to opening the registers to check him out. It had been very tempting, but the prospect of punishment if she were caught dissuaded her.

"Julia's mother is called Isabel. She's not alive any more."

"I'm really sorry. What happened?" Erika immediately noticed the change in his face. Maybe she'd gone too fast here. This was not something he wanted her to start digging in.

"Let's talk about it another time. Have you any plans? What shall we do? Oh, did I say... you're looking lovely. And you smell good, too."

She would have liked to suggest wild and passionate sex in the cottage she was renting in Lummelunda. An artist's studio with big windows and a generous view of the sea since they cleared the vegetation on the ridge. But she didn't dare say it, not yet.

"Maybe we can find some cozy café with outside tables."

They climbed Hästbacken until Adelsgatan, then strolled down the pedestrianized street. Anders stopped by the bookshop window. He pointed at a book in the window. *Myths and Legends of Gotland.*

"I have to buy that. It won't take a minute."

He came back with two copies.

"One for you and one for me. Read it and then I'll tell you something afterward."

"Anything special I should read?"

"The mermaid," he said, observing her with a slight tension. This was clearly something important for him, but she chose not to ask any more questions for now.

They decided on the Crêperi on Wallers Plats and ordered a beer each and a pancake baked with spelt wheat, blueberry jam, and cream. The evening sun was pleasantly warming, and their view over the town quite spectacular. They talked about travel, cooking, and work. As soon as Erika tried to move one step closer, talking about family and friends, Anders grew silent and distracted.

"Sorry, I'm not quite myself—and it's all your fault."

"Is that supposed to be a compliment?" Erika really wasn't sure.

"I'm trying to stop smoking. As soon as anyone lights up and I catch the smell I'm toast. But I'm going to make an honest attempt for your sake."

"I want you to do it for your own sake, the decision has to be your own." Erika didn't want to be some kind of moral guardian.

"If you're going to get out of drug dependence you have to have an antidote. The best antidote is falling in love." His eyes latched onto hers.

"And are you? In love?" she asked, laughing away the seriousness.

"Yes, I've never met anyone like you. I think about you

all the time, Erika. The first thing I think about when I wake up and the last thought in my head before I fall asleep is you."

Amazing that such jaded phrases could sound so fresh. She wanted to believe him and, against her will, she took in every word.

"I feel the same." She took his outstretched hand in hers. He still wore his wedding ring on his finger. It made her wonder, but she did not want to ruin the magic moment by asking.

Right at that moment, Anders's cell phone gave off a jazzy melody.

"What? Pick you up now? But we said ten o'clock... all right, then... all right! No, you don't have to go back by yourself."

Erika gave him a quizzical look.

"That was Julia. She had an argument with the girls at the stable and wants to be picked up earlier than we said. I'm sorry, Erika, this is how my life looks at the moment. It's all very intense at that age. The girls are best friends and love each other more than anything else in the world, and then suddenly it's all over and they hate each other. I suppose they're training for the adult world. Julia seems to have particular problems finding someone to be close to. I don't want her to walk home on her own. You're a police officer, so you probably understand you can't let a girl on her own go through town when there are gang fights and whatnot happening."

"No, of course, you have to pick her up. You're not taking the car, are you?"

"You're right, I'll have to ask her to take a cab and then meet her at home. She probably wants to talk for a while... or not. Sometimes she just locks herself in her room and won't come out until the next day. It's not entirely easy being a father." He grew silent. "Did you catch the people who assaulted that young boy and Maria Wern? I read in the paper that he died and she was stabbed with a bloody syringe. His poor parents and poor her. How is she coping?"

"It's hard. Maria is my best friend. I'm going through it with her. The case is top priority. We have to find out if the syringe was infected. The worst thing is, we don't seem to have any witnesses. People don't want to get involved, they're scared or don't want any trouble."

"Terrible." Anders paid the bill and they started walking toward Österport. "Next time it could be them in trouble. Do you have any leads on who did it?"

"Sorry, but I can't say anything about that. Just like you, I'm sworn to silence." She put her finger to her mouth and kissed it, before touching his mouth. I want you for real, she thought. But she still did not have the courage to say it out loud.

Chapter 8

Erika Lund sat in the hammock watching the sun slowly sinking over the edge of the ridge, and the sky turning blood-red. The sea lay still and reflective. But under the calm surface there were dangerous currents, a downward suction of water where the sea grew deeper—it could pull even the most experienced of swimmers under. There were many frightening stories and myths about that. One of these was the story of the mermaid, which Anders had encouraged her to read. Erika closed the book and reflected.... Was that how she had died, his wife, Isabel?

The fable told of a young, happy couple on their wedding night, taking a refreshing dip after all the dancing. They swam right out into the moonlit water when suddenly the bride was pulled down by the undertow. The man could not save her, despite his frantic efforts. She'd gone and did not come back. But in his dream they met again that night and she told him that if he ever remarried she'd come and take him out into the abyss. They had promised each other eternal fidelity and he must keep his promise or die. Time passed and he forgot the dream and then one day he met a woman he wanted to live with. Just as the priest was about to wed them, a blindingly beautiful woman entered the church and everyone was as if turned to stone. Neither the bride nor the priest could do anything to help the man. Passively the man was led by the mermaid's hand into the sea. Later he was found drowned.

Erika had heard variations of the story in different parts of Gotland's west coast. An old man in the fishing village in Gnisvärd had recounted the following version of it: Four men were sitting one night in Captain Pettson's cottage waiting for dawn, when they were going out to take up their nets. One of the fishermen was a young man, the others were old hands. They drank coffee laced with schnapps and swapped stories about women and the supernatural. Maybe somehow with all their tales they managed to call up a spirit from the past—one of the unfortunate individuals who'd been drowned in the waves. When the young man went around the corner to relieve himself he saw a line of gossamer-fine mist gliding over the grass. He followed it to see what it was and was gripped by an eerie, compulsive feeling. The mist became a shadow, then a figure. He had to follow the creature. When the white mermaid turned around and smiled at him, he saw that she was the most beautiful woman in the world. She was so wonderful that nothing else mattered to him at all, and she enticed him down toward the beach. He could not lose sight of her, because if she disappeared she'd take the whole meaning of life with her. He'd known this from the first moment he looked into her sea-green eyes.

The old men realized something was wrong when the boy didn't come back. Had he got himself into a fight or maybe he'd fallen asleep out there? Perhaps he couldn't hold his drink so well? They went out to look for him. When they found him he was in the water up to his armpits and his black hair had turned white as chalk. He was never himself again. Gone was the lively, fun-loving young man, in his place a taciturn old man staring into the far distance, beyond what any ordinary mortal could see. Not mad, not wise either. Just strange.

What was Anders trying to tell her? That he'd lost his wife in a drowning accident and had been unable to save her? Surely he couldn't be so superstitious that he believed a story like this—or would avoid starting a new relationship for such a reason? Most likely it was about guilt. The guilt of carrying on living after the death of a person one loved deeply. And all the what-ifs... if one had done this it wouldn't have happened and if one had done that she might have been saved. Why couldn't he just tell her straight? Why did he have to take this detour of a book of folk tales?

Erika decided to call him and say good night. Maybe if she did, he'd tell her what had happened. She went inside and fetched the cell phone from her jacket pocket, then sat on the bench against the house wall. Her neighbor, Sara Wenzel, gave her a wave from a window. Her presence felt intrusive when Erika was about to talk to Anders about this sensitive subject, which he might feel brave enough to share with her. Erika stood up and wandered off to the edge of the rocks for a bit of seclusion. It was difficult not to pine for him, and every time they met the prospect of losing him would become more painful. Erika dialed the number and took a deep breath. Everything was still so new and exciting. It was difficult to know whether he actually wanted her to call him.

"Julia Ahlström." The daughter had picked up right after the first ring.

"Hello, my name's Erika Lund and I was wondering if your father's there?"

"I doubt it." The voice sounded snooty and Erika felt like a schoolgirl caught making a nuisance call.

"Do you know when he's coming home?"

"Nope." She was chewing loudly on something, munching. An apple perhaps, which she was demonstratively chomping.

"Can you ask him to give me a call when he gets in?"

"I don't think so," said Julia with a dragging voice. "He doesn't have the energy for any more crazies today. He's tired after work, can't you see that?"

"Why don't we let him decide for himself? He's a grown-up."

Erika heard Anders's voice in the background.

"Who is it?"

"Some nut-job called Erika. We're watching a movie. You promised not to talk to people when we're watching a movie!"

"How are things with Julia?" asked Erika when Anders came on the line, although she wasn't so concerned about his answer. But she did understand it was important to him that Julia should feel happy again after her argument with her friends at the stable.

"She's a bit out of sorts. I promised her a cozy evening. Can I call you later?"

Silly the way one could go around waiting for a telephone call and not get anything done in case he called. Erika had promised herself to never, ever get caught in that trap and now she was pacing the floorboards. Julia was used to having her father to herself and Erika had no experience with that sort of thing. Her own children had been small when she was forced to leave them. How would she cope if his child hated her from the start and wanted to sabotage her? By the time Anders called it was close to midnight and Erika had almost given up hope.

"Sorry. I couldn't get away earlier."

"That's okay." It was a relief hearing his voice. "I read that book you gave me. Can we talk about it?" She heard him close the door.

"If we can make it brief. Julia isn't asleep yet, and she'll want me to put her to bed."

She's eleven, isn't that a bit too old to be put to bed? thought Erika. But she didn't comment. "Was that how it happened? Like in the book?" she asked, to get him on the right track.

"Yes." She could hear the resistance, and when he continued his voice was tense and creaky. It wasn't easy for him to talk about it.

"When did it happen?" In view of the fact that he was still wearing his wedding ring, Erika thought it must be fairly recent.

"Julia was six months old. She was christened at the same time as we were married in Gnisvärd Church. We had the reception at the Fridhem Pension, just by Högklint. Isabel wanted a midnight swim. I had some drinks with the guys and then stayed with Julia in the bridal suite and fell asleep. I wasn't at all sober. After just a few hours I woke up. It was dawn. She hadn't come back. I got worried, woke up my mother and asked her to keep an eye on the baby while I went down to the beach. Isabel's clothes were in a pile. The undertow...."

"It must have been terrible."

"If you knew how many times I've regretted not going with her. She wasn't sober, either. I wasn't thinking straight. I could have left Julia with my mother who was sleeping in the room next door. But I didn't. Instead I had another drink with the guys before they went back into town and then I passed out."

"So what does the actual myth mean to you, then?" Erika had a gut feeling that her question was warranted. Normally, legends and myths are created so that people remember to watch out for a particular danger. The Dryad haunted the rapids so that children took extra care when they went there and so that women were not seduced by violin-playing foreigners and enticed into extra-marital escapades. The Siren of the Woods was invented so that children were careful about not getting lost in the forest and men guarded over their virtue. The Mermaid was all about watching out for the undertow. And that was why the stories were passed on from generation to generation, so that the living did not make the same mistakes as their forebears. But what did it mean to Anders?

He delayed answering, and when his answer finally did come it was apologetic and full of hesitation. "I know that dreams and fairytales are sometimes as real to me as reality itself, even though I'm a doctor and have been brought up to be scientific. It's obviously about guilt and it's possible that I'm still punishing myself because I wasn't there for her that night, on our actual wedding night. Obviously it does affect my relationship with Julia. I can't deny her anything. I obey her slightest whim to compensate for the loss I can never repay. She never had her mother. I've tried to meet other women since then, but nothing ever developed because I didn't dare. Julia takes all my attention. It's not easy. And now you know."

"So what do you think about us, then?" Erika felt as if she'd had a cold shower. Wasn't he serious, then? Didn't he even want to try? Her disappointment turned into an ache in her stomach. She hoped he wouldn't begrudge himself some life just because one time he'd made a mistake. This wasn't good for him, and not for Julia, either.

"I want to try. But you're going to have to be patient with me and Julia. I'm crazy about you. I want to be with you. Who knows, you might be the good genie who releases me from the curse."

So send the kid to a finishing school, stop talking non-sense about genies, and come over and make love to me, Erika wanted to say. But she held her tongue, of course. It would have to take its time. She would be patient. Something told her he was worth it.

Chapter 9

Maria Wern had gritted her teeth at the pain and taken extra shifts over the weekend. Her colleagues thought she should go on sick leave, but Maria had refused—anything not to have to think about the assault. It was more than enough to be constantly dreaming about the dead boy and waking up with grinding jaws and stomach aches. Then all the brooding about the possibility of infection—what if she were infected and got so ill that she couldn't take care of her children? And what if she died and disappeared from them? She made herself push the thought away. There was still all the paperwork to get through. She worked out at the gym as much as she could despite the broken ribs and swellings. If she worked until she was worn out in body and spirit she might be able to sleep. The others had long since gone home. The fans whirred in the office at the police station, where she sat typing with her right hand—the left was still too swollen. An interview with a car thief. The work pushed away her brooding about the test results she was waiting for: HIV, hepatitis, or a clean bill of health?

The car thief she'd questioned had been found asleep in a stolen car at an industrial park. The trunk was completely stuffed with cans of diesel fuel, which he'd most likely siphoned from other vehicles and machines. When the staff arrived at their workplace in the morning, they'd knocked on his window to wake him up. He'd locked himself in his car before falling asleep, heavily hung over. When they managed to rouse him he tried to start the car to get out of there, which was impossible, because he'd filled the gas tank with diesel. In his dazed state he'd admitted to a crime. This was not the first time, not even the first time this week, he'd been caught. Twice before he'd tried the same thing and blown it. Every time a new interview report had to be carefully drafted, which the crook thereafter had to approve word by word. At this point he grew stickier than chewing gum. When the first theft was brought before the court he denied the accuracy of the report and said he'd been pressed too hard by the police. Maria couldn't stop herself from laughing. The guy was like a mountain and the woman police officer who'd interviewed him measured no more than 5'3" without her shoes. The best option would obviously have been to bring him down to the police station, write down the sequence of events, and let him sign it directly, page by page. If a police officer does not report a crime, he can have his salary docked, but if he does report it, an avalanche of paperwork follows. Is it reasonable to report a graffiti offender for the sixteenth time when the maximum sentence gets handed out after five offenses? Is it reasonable to write reports for half of one's working hours? To Maria, it all felt more and more frustrating. Then there was another car that had been stolen outside the Department of Technology, for just a few hours, only to be found a block away. A report that was very unlikely ever to lead anywhere.

Hartman had told her about a time when there used to be a whole room of typists at the police station. Civilian employees who were laid off in the general enthusiasm for budget-slashing. What sort of budgeting could ever work as long as police officers had to type out their own reports with two fingers? Not even tape-recorded interviews were particularly easy to document, because every *ah* and *hm* had to be transcribed and every silence pointed out.

But right now it was work she needed. Work, to dull her thoughts. Hartman was running the investigation into the lethal assault and she knew he was doing it competently. Nonetheless it was frustrating not being able to take part in the process. It was as if the three men had been swallowed up by the ground. Very likely they had committed crimes before. Someone had probably run into them before. If people had the guts to report these things, there'd be more clues and a significantly improved possibility of catching them

Maria quickly checked the news on the Internet. New excavations had started on Galgberget. Judging by the findings, the place had already been in use in medieval times. Some thirty bodies had been found, including one interesting discovery of two wooden coffins. One of them contained two bodies. It was not known why they had been interred in a single coffin. There were no votive offerings that might indicate their gender. But surely this could be determined by the pelvis, thought Maria.

Maria had been on Galgberget quite recently. The old place of execution was barren, a scene of natural beauty. Situated on the ridge above Visby, with a view of the sea and the red brick buildings of the hospital, there were three stone pillars that had once born up the beams from which the prisoners were hanged. Through the ages people had sat there watching the executions as entertainment—dismemberment and whippings of the unfortunates, or bodies broken on the wheel. Most, however, were hanged and then mutilated and buried on the spot.

The online publication also reported on a landlord who'd

been in touch about a bucket of bones discovered under the stairs. He thought they might be human remains and that a murder had been committed. But when the police arrived on the scene it was found that one of the participants in the excavations had taken the bones home, intending to pass them on. Because, for the moment, there was no other safe place to keep them.

The next headline on the site was about Gotlanders, and how the incidence of drinking and driving was lower there than anywhere else in Sweden. Maria wondered how the study had been conducted? Last summer, when four-fifths of the islanders were from the mainland, or even during Stockholm Week when the entire population of the exclusive bars around Stureplan were blowing their minds with drugs. There were 448 crimes that week alone. Rape, robbery, vandalism, drug offenses. Half of the reports went straight into the archives without any investigation, because of a lack of leads. If there's nothing to go on, no witnesses, there's nothing to investigate. If anything else happens the investigation can be reopened, but unfortunately many of the crimes are never cleared up.

Maria packed up her things and left the police station. Dusk had fallen. It felt unpleasant walking home alone, even though it was such a short distance. There were plenty of people around, but she could not be sure anyone would intervene if she were attacked. A couple of youths in a group were hanging round and pushing each other a bit outside McDonalds. Maria felt her discomfort intensifying under her skin. She stood there observing them for a while, her heart in her throat. One of them was somehow similar to the leader of the gang who'd assaulted her and the boy. Something in his bearing, the long, lanky body. She felt herself breaking into a cold sweat. But when he turned around she saw that his eyes were not at all right. Nauseous and weak, she carried on. When she thought about it she'd only eaten a salad that day, and it was almost nine o'clock. Probably she had another sleepless night ahead of her. She'd called Per Arvidsson, but he didn't have the energy to see her, and considering how rude he'd been the last time she saw him it didn't bother her so very much. He was the one who needed help. She would have liked to be there for him, if he let her. The relationship was entirely on his terms.

Maria continued down Östra Tullgränd along the city wall and turned off into Klinttorget towards Norra Murgatan 14. There were a lot of people on the move. She covered her bruised, swollen face as well as she could, not enjoying all the staring eyes. She had never before realized how unpleasant it was to get so much unwanted attention. She was ashamed of her appearance, even though it was not her fault.

Once she got home, Maria sank into the sofa in front of the television. She did not feel like turning it on. A sharp telephone ring cut through the silence and almost made her scream. It took a while to extract the cell phone from her pocket.

"Maria Wern," she answered, out of breath. No one answered but she could hear someone breathing. "Who is this?"

"Uffe, Linus's dad. It wasn't easy finding your number, but I managed." His voice was slightly out of control. Maria suspected he wasn't sober.

"What can I do for you?" His enormous loss made her feel inadequate.

"What's going on at the police? Why don't you bring the bastards in? I called your boss, you know. He had nothing to say for himself. Nothing at all. I can't wait any longer. I don't give a shit what happens to me, as long as I get hold of the people who killed my boy."

"I can understand how you feel. But it's better if you work with the police. Hartman is a good investigating officer, the best."

"Like hell I will, when they don't work with me. They haven't even interviewed Linus's friend Oliver. The police are just digging about in the media spotlight. Now that it's not first-page news any more, you're dropping the whole thing. I can see it." He hung up. Maria called him back, but he'd turned off the telephone.

Chapter 10

Erika Lund put on a CD of Regina Spektor. The lone-liness of her little house in Lummelunda felt more oppressive than ever. Everything had been prepared for an evening of togetherness. Wine in the cooler. The food ready to be put in the oven. She'd never ever do this again for the sake of a man. Next time, Anders would just have to take things as they were. What was she supposed to do now? Stare at the box? Tidy up her wardrobe? So hopelessly boring. Going out and meeting people would have been more appealing, but not by herself. Admittedly she could call Maria and suggest going out, but most likely Wern would not be in the mood for bars, not until the ugly bruises on her face had disappeared.

They had spoken just a few hours ago before Erika went off to meet Anders. But unfortunately there had been nothing new for Erika to report. They'd found some fragments of skin under Maria's nails, and she was sure she'd scratched the tallest of them—the one known as Roy, apparently their leader—on the left side of his torso between the hem of his pants and his t-shirt. Even if it had been difficult for Maria to give a description, the DNA would speak very clearly if they could only get their hands on him. Commissioner Hartman hadn't skimped on his energy in trying to apprehend the hooligan. But none of the trustworthy informers had come up with any leads, not even when they were offered reduced charges and other incentives.

Maria had really pushed herself to try and remember.

"I'm not even sure I'd recognize him if we ran into each other in town. All I can remember is... the syringe and the blood and the label on his jeans. Kilroy. His expensive boots. I checked them, they were Dr. Martens. Leather jacket and a gold chain round his neck. A guy with money? That's what I thought even at the time. Rich parents or the proceeds of profitable criminal activity?"

Hartman had checked passenger lists on planes and ferries. "Roy" as a forename or surname. Ronald, Roland, Robert, Ronny, and probably many other possibilities. The most likely thing was that he'd left the island. If not earlier, then certainly when the newspapers reported that the boy had died of his injuries.

Erika had personally checked the spot where the assault took place. For the sake of the parents they had to catch the assailant. The wait was also unbearable for Maria. She had carried on working as usual, but she was not her normal self. Quieter, more brooding. Erika decided to call her after all. She hadn't already gone to bed, surely?

"Just calling to see how things are. Have you got time to talk?"

"All the time in the world. The kids are with my parents and Per can't cope with seeing me. You know, Erika, sometimes I have my doubts that anything will ever change. He's just lying in bed staring at the ceiling. He needs to see a doctor and start taking medication, but he hasn't got the energy to care. I've offered to go with him, but he pushes it away and says there's nothing wrong with him. His ex-wife is a doctor, she could help him with medicine. But he refuses to see her at all. I shouldn't have told him about the assault and my fears of being infected. It was too much for him. Maybe it was selfish of me. I needed a pair of strong arms, somewhere to find consolation. But he didn't have the energy to listen at all. I don't know what to do."

"Force him to take the medication for his own sake. You can't carry on like this, Maria. And you know it's not your fault. Even if you hadn't told him about the assault he would still have found out at work or read about it in the newspaper. Of course he had to hear it from you."

"I could be infected, I have to be celibate for six months. In three months I'll find out if I'm *probably* not infected, but *probably* is not good enough. Anyway, he doesn't want it. He doesn't want me any more." Maria burst into tears. "What am I going to do?"

"Come over, Maria. I've got wine and loads of beef Wellington. Come over and we'll talk."

"Thanks. Sounds like a dream. Roast beef on a weekday."

Maria Wern leaned back in the armchair and watched Erika, who was clearing the table and pouring a little more wine. "I'm worried about what Linus's father's going to do. Linus was their only child. Ulf says he doesn't have anything more to lose. Not a thing. That's why he's so dangerous. He doesn't give a damn if he ends up in prison or even dies himself. I think he's capable of killing someone if he thinks he's found the guilty man."

"There's a risk he'll go for the wrong person. If he just hears a rumor it might be enough. He's a ticking bomb." Erika sat down in the sofa and sipped her wine thoughtfully. A decent Shiraz.

"What do we have to offer him, then? What sort of punishment would satisfy him? Do we have anything to bring to the table?" Maria had a strong feeling that Linus's father would not consider a prison sentence sufficient punishment. He wanted them to suffer like his kid had suffered—to die while pleading for mercy.

"Not much so far. We've checked the shops selling Dr. Martens boots, but no one remembers any particular purchaser. Those jeans you described, Kilroy, sell in the thousands in Sweden. A scratch to the upper body is a distinguishing feature, but easy to hide. We can only move on once we have a suspect. You scratched him and we got his DNA. If we bring in the right person we've got him. Sometimes I think it's a real pity we're not allowed to use hospital blood samples from newborns' PKU tests to run DNA analysis. I mean, DNA is there in the government biobanks, but we can't get to it."

Maria looked thoughtful. "It's both good and bad. Once the police are allowed to use it, insurance companies may start thinking they also have the right to the information... so they can exclude insurance applicants if they have a higher risk of catching some hereditary illness."

"Yes, and many fathers would be surprised to learn they're not the fathers of their children. But we should be able to get around personal privacy when it's about heavy crime."

"Right now I agree with you," said Maria. "I can't stop myself puzzling over why he went for Linus. I'll go crazy if I don't get a plausible explanation. The meaninglessness is the worst thing of all. If the victim was random then no one is safe. I mean, if the attacker has an overwhelming need to cause harm and that's the whole thing. Someone gets in the way and so he gets sacrificed. But the need must have come from somewhere.... How do you get like that?"

"According to the latest research there are bullies who feel actual lust when they're intimidating other people. They've checked the brain, and the pleasure receptors are actually affected. Before, we used to think it was about lack of empathy... we said they didn't know any better. If they could just reach some sort of insight they'd empathize and become good. It felt better thinking that way. But it's not the truth."

"An individual somewhere is sick in the head, fair enough. But how does he get other people to join in with the violence?" Maria felt her muscles tensing to defend herself when she thought of the kicks and blows.

"One of them tried to stop Roy. He didn't want to join in, but he didn't help us, either. It's cowardly but human. But how do you become totally emotionally cold like Roy? Is it just biology or has he been subjected to terrible abuse and deceit as a small child?"

"It could be both. I don't know how much you've read of John Bowlby's Attachment Theory? We used to believe that the first moment of attachment between mother and child was crucial, but later we've found out that adopted children can also attach strongly, and other adults around the child can play an important role. I hope it's true." Suddenly Erika looked very fragile.

Maria noticed the change in Erika. She never spoke about her two children, but Maria had nonetheless picked up on the fact that they were with her ex-husband in Motala and that she had no contact with them. "What do you think, then?"

"I think it's dangerous for a child to be left in the care of a psychotic or drug-using mother. It can cause irreparable damage if there's no other adult the child can measure reality against and find security with." Erika choose not to get more personal than this, but Maria sensed that the words covered a huge well of first-hand sorrow. There was a long silence and then Erika said: "Do you think his name is Roy or do they just call him Roy?"

"The name 'Roy' makes me think of Kilroy. 'Kilroy was here,' you know. Maybe that's why he chose that brand of jeans?"

"KillRoy! A murderer appearing out of the blue." Erika pulled herself together and became her usual self. For an instant, Maria had been able to look into her vulnerability, but now it was over.

"Regardless of how sorry we feel for this guy, we have to take him in and stop him from hurting others. Sometimes violence is just a long chain of unhappy circumstances leading to more violence. Our task is not to punish but prevent. That's how I see it."A dark shadow passed across Erika's face before she stooped over her glass of wine, then her expression went flat.

Chapter 11

When Linn Bogren opened an old newspaper at work and read about the assault on the thirteen-year-old boy and the woman police officer in Ryska Gränd she could hardly breathe. There had been some talk about it at work but she had not picked up any details. The violation seemed to hit her all over again. The same fear came over her and made her want to flee, close her eyes, hide. She should move far away and never come back again. They knew where she lived. The face she'd seen in the window.... She should call the police. When Claes came back she'd do it, but not now. Not now when she was alone. You can't fight on all fronts at the same time. First and foremost she had to decide whether she'd have the guts to come out, as she'd promised Sara, or if she'd stay in her marriage. Sara had not given her a third alternative. She couldn't take sneaking around any more. There'd be a hell of an uproar, of course. Goody-two-shoes nurse Linn Bogren had fallen in love with a patient. What would her parents say? And Claes? Claes must be the first to know. He shouldn't have to find out from the neighbor or the papers. The best thing would be if she just told her colleagues at work—very direct, very straight. Then her manager would no longer have an angle on her, either. The head of the clinic would be the only outsider suspecting anything, but at least Sam Wettergren would keep his mouth shut. For his own sake. She was sure of that. They had worked together for so long, developing an understanding of their respective good and bad aspects. If on the other hand she decided to come out, he must be told so he could prepare himself against the ensuing hullabaloo. She owed him that.

Linn felt the anxiety crawling in her body. If she let Sara down and chose to stay in her marriage, Sara might start talking to people about it. If Sara were let down so badly, how could she be trusted to keep her mouth shut? In theory she could even report Linn. In the nurse-patient relationship one person holds the power and the patient is in a position of dependence. What the consequences would be, Linn was not quite sure of, but at worst she could have her nursing license revoked and no longer be able to work in the healthcare system. That was no small sacrifice to offer for love. Whatever she did there would be trouble. In real terms there was no possibility of going back. She knew what she had to do. Life is too short to be sacrificed on lovelessness. Claes had to know. Also Sam; she owed them that. She could speak to Sam now. Claes would find out one-on-one.

She plucked up courage, picked up the telephone, and called her boss. Sam Wettergren was full of consternation, of course. She hadn't expected anything else.

"But won't it just pass?" he asked carefully. "Can't you just keep it to yourselves?" His timidity strengthened Linn's conviction. After she'd finished the call she started packing. Once it had grown dark, she carried her clothes, toiletries, and reference books to the car, parked by the Ordnance Tower. In the night it was less likely that one of the neighbors would see her.

She called Sara to say good night. Told her she'd called her manager and what he'd said.

"It's us now, Sara. You and me."

The process she was setting in motion now would have consequences. Possibly they'd be worse than she could predict. She must be careful. Linn looked for her purse in the hall, and checked whether her USB memory stick was where it should be in the inside pocket. The portable computer she'd been using to write her study on plant steroids was still at work. But the material was copied on the stick. Was that enough? Should she for the sake of safety also e-mail it to herself, so she could pick it up remotely from another computer? Claes's computer had been on the blink a week ago, and it was in for repair. The only solution she could think of right now was to ask the police officer who lived across the road if she could borrow his computer. Per Arvidsson. She hadn't seen much of him lately, not since the mulled wine party on the corner, Louise's party, which they'd all gone to. Per looked nice; Harry had told her he was a policeman. The worst thing that could happen was that he'd ask a lot of questions she wasn't prepared to answer yet. It was purely a precaution... a premonition, in case of a worst-case scenario.... If only all this could all be over and done with, so she could sleep.

Linn saw the light on in Per Arvidsson's kitchen window. He was awake, anyway. She rang the doorbell. He was playing jazz at high volume. She really hoped he could hear her. To make sure, she knocked on the kitchen window, too. She caught of whiff of whisky on his breath when he opened the door. But he didn't seem particularly drunk. She related her errand, standing there on his doorstep. He gave no sign of wanting to show her in.

"Do you have a computer I can borrow?" she repeated. When she saw his dismissive body language she hurriedly added: "Just very quickly."

"I'm in a bit of a tight spot right now. Is it okay if you borrow it tomorrow?"

"Please! I need it now."

He was extremely reluctant. Said he needed to be left in peace, but she stood her ground, falling back on an emergency lie and telling him she'd sold her computer on eBay and hadn't had time to buy another. She had to pay for a trip by midnight or the booking would become invalid. Reluctantly he agreed. Afterwards, she regretted fabricating such a complex lie. She should have just said it like it was, that Claes's computer was being repaired. Nerves made everything so silly.

Maybe the body can feel when its allotted time in life is finally drawing to a close? For Linn, the anxiety this night was worse than ever before. She could not stay in bed. She checked all the windows. They were closed. The front door was locked. She lay down on the bed again and closed her eyes. She must sleep; sleep and conserve all her strength for everything that must be done the next day when Claes came home. Anxiety pullulated in her body. The pillow was lumpy. The comforter too warm. She took it out of the comforter cover and threw it on the floor. The sheet tangled round her legs. She rummaged in the drawer of her bedside table for the sleeping pills, and found the carton. "One tablet per night" it said on the package. But tonight her need was greater than ever. She tapped two pills into her hand and stood up with the carton in her hand to fetch water. She let the water run until it was really cold, and put her head under the tap when she drank. Washing her flushed face. Her whole body was boiling with anxiety. All the curtains and blinds were drawn. The mere thought of the face in the window turning up again made her skittish, and she reached for the baseball bat. It was within reach. The kitchen knife was on the bedside table. The cell phone was fully charged. She lay down again and tried to relax. Calm, deep breaths. Tighten and relax one part of your body at a time. It would have been lovely to have some music, but she didn't dare—it would keep her from hearing anyone walking in the garden. She needed to hear, no other sounds could get in the way. She heard voices outside, from the street. When she pressed her ear to the window she could almost hear what they said. Men's voices. Were they here now? The masked ones? She was gripped by a new rush of fear. While her ear was against the glass, someone could smash the window and pulverize her face at the same time. An experienced burglar could use a glass-cutter and suckers to remove the glass from the frame. It would almost be soundless. Would anyone hear her scream? Per Arvidsson certainly wouldn't while his music was at such a high volume. Maybe Harry, if he was out with the dogs?

No, stop! She had to calm down. Find some calming images to reflect on. She pushed herself to think about warm beaches and soft water, but there was no way. The water rose over her head, she drowned and was buried in the sand. Linn turned on her bedside lamp and tried to read for a while, but the words passed over her head. She tried a magazine instead. Makeup advertising. *Tips for better sex during your vacation! Slimming food and summer cakes with strawberries in jelly. Please him with your bikini!* The last four pages were about telling your future with Tarot cards. The fortune-telling ladies guaranteed that they were all experienced at their craft. Only 19.90 kronor per minute to hear a human voice. Linn felt it might be worth it, now that loneliness was eating into the early hours. She dialed a fortune-teller's number—her ad carried the logo of an angel on a bookmark. *Hear the whispers from the other side. Marjatta gives advice and help with relationships.* Marjatta didn't pick up. Most likely both she and her guardian angel were sleeping. She tried the next one. *I see your future. Media advice.* A telephone answering machine asked her to try back the following day. Linn wondered if this also cost 19.90 per minute? On her third attempt a drowsy man answered and seemed to have no desire to answer any questions whatsoever. In the end Linn called the hospital switchboard and asked about the pharmacy's opening hours. A normal, neutral voice—someone she could ask for help if the face in the window turned up. Or if anyone tried to break in.... After that, everything felt a bit calmer. The convoluted thoughts slowly died down. Her body felt heavier. And just as the waves of sleep were towing her out into open water, her cell phone rang. Linn jumped out of the bed to find it and decline the call, before she realized she'd left it on the bedside table. The knife clattered to the floor, grazing her bare foot.

"Linn Bogren." She was drunk and drugged with the sleeping pills. Her mouth didn't quite want to obey her, and her words slurred, as sticky and furry as her thoughts.

"I just wanted to say that I love you and miss you." Claes's voice. A mild, caressing whisper.

"Hi," was all she managed.

"Do you love me?" he asked quietly. The question made her wake up properly. Did he know something? Why else would he be calling in the middle of the night?

"Where are you?" He wasn't supposed to be coming home until tomorrow afternoon.

"We just docked in Gothenburg. Did I wake you, my little darling?"

"Yes." She tried to sound sleepy, although she was wide awake by now. "What do you want?" She looked at her watch. It was a quarter to twelve. If she didn't go to sleep right away now she'd be twisting and turning all night. It was raining. The drops bounced lightly against the windowsill.

"I miss you and I wanted to hear that you miss me, too. Do you? Do you love me?"

"Stop it! It's the middle of the night. I have to sleep. I'm working tomorrow."

"I just want to hear you say it. Then I'll let you sleep and tomorrow I'll kiss you as much as you like. Do you love me?"

"Yes." She wouldn't get away with anything less, even if she felt a resistance. This was not the moment for confessions. She wanted to do it to his face.

"Is it raining in Gothenburg?"

"Yeah, pouring down. It's raining on Gotland, too, I can hear it. Good, so we won't have to water the garden. Kiss, good night."

"Why are you whispering when you're talking, why can't you talk normally? It's echoing like in a bathroom." He didn't hear her. He'd already hung up.

It turned out as she'd feared. After the call it was impossible to fall asleep again. The pills had stopped working. She took another two pills and drank a half-bottle of wine. There was no other way of relaxing. When an hour had passed and she still wasn't asleep, she drank what was left in the bottle. The rain was pouring down outside the window. Claps of thunder bounced between the house walls like dynamite and flashes of lightning passed like hissing snakes across the sky. Darkness pressed against the window panes. She listened, and her thoughts were slowly dulled. She was at home, in the bed she'd known as a child. Great-grandmother was sitting at the kitchen table drinking coffee, and all was calm. The fire crackled in the grate. The cat rubbed itself against her bare arm.

Maybe in spite of being drunk she would have heard the steps on the grass if it hadn't been for the rain. But not even when the window was smashed and fell in pieces over the living room floor did she react. Even less when a hand pressed down on the door handle and opened the porch door. If she'd woken up she would have seen a man whose head was hidden under a dark cape, slowly crossing the floor. He picked up the kitchen knife she'd left on the bedside table and made a deep incision in her white throat; emptying her of blood, as he'd done so many times in his games in the simulator. With heavy steps he went outside into the shed in the yard and fetched the chainsaw in the window.

He'd followed her on the computer screen, from the health center to the pharmacy and home. He knew her working hours and habits. By hacking into and running her registers he knew everything that was required. He had read her medical files from every doctor she'd seen from the time the information was digitized. She used a type of birth control pill known as Beulett and often came in to ask about genital thrush. From time to time she took sleeping pills and sometimes Ipren for menstruation pain. All the information from the region's Social Insurance Office and the Inland Revenue was in her file. Her bank account was 13,436 kronor in the black. Every month, the insurance company charged 166 kronor for a life insurance policy of one million kronor. Claes Bogren was the beneficiary. The list of books she'd borrowed at the library was extensive. He had made a note of every title since 1997. She had a clear preference for triviality: romantic novels and biographies of strong women. He knew when she was having repairs done to her house. He had fetched her garbage can himself and analyzed its contents. Torn tights, convenience food packages, shopping lists. The ease of access did to a certain degree take away some of his pleasure. A little more resistance would have been stimulating, although it did turn him on a bit that her fear had caused her to leave the knife there for him.

Chapter 12

Monday morning was clean and fresh with dew. Maybe slightly on the cool side, at least in the opinion of the visitors who had assembled in the Botanical Gardens to listen to the flute-playing gardener. It was a gentle way to start the day: beautiful flute music, early summer in the offing, accompanied by the sea and muted slightly by the city walls. Long white garlands of material were flapping from the wooden vaults of the pavilion. A discussion started up about the installations which a number of artists had exhibited in and around Visby in the lead-up to the tourist season this year and in years before. Could telephone booths submerged in water really be considered as art? Or giant fried eggs in the town square? Are barcodes tattooed on someone's bottom really an expression of art? It was all up to the observer, not the experts—that was the general consensus. How provocative the installation in the Botanical Gardens would prove to be the group did not know as they wandered up towards Tempelkullen to have a closer look at the arrangements.

None of those who witnessed it would ever forget the horrendous sight that awaited them in the pavilion. The soft vegetation and early summer blooms had lulled them into a false sense of security. Someone had really taken great pains with the contrasting effects. The sweet and the grotesque were shown in a sort of interplay of Life and Death. So repellent was the sight that one of the observers passed out and had to be taken to hospital. The screams could be heard all the way to the Ordnance Tower. Strips of material flapped over their heads like giant serpentines, fixed by thumbtacks to the vaulted pillars. It took less than ten minutes for the police to reach the scene once the call was put through to the emergency number.

Tempelkullen between the herb garden and the rose garden was cordoned off. Chief Inspector Jesper Ek had asked the forensic technician Erika Lund to go with the patrol directly to the murder scene. They wandered up to Tempelkullen, Erika ahead and Ek just behind. Sunlight played in the leafage billowing in the sea breeze.

"It looks like a ritual murder, doesn't it? Nothing hurried about it, no fear of surprise. There was time to decorate." Jesper Ek turned his face away. This was worse than he could have imagined. The vomit lurked somewhere in the region of his throat. He wasn't sure which exit route it would take.

"Do we know who she was?" asked Erika. "She looks like a bride, someone wanted to make her look like a bride." She squatted next to the body and studied the incision. The head had been severed from the body and lay in the bride's lap. There was surprisingly little blood. The woman's face was as white as the lace nightgown she wore and, in her hand, she held a bunch of lilies of the valley. "This is not the murder scene. The body's been moved. The cutting up must have been done somewhere else."

Ek sucked in air. He couldn't bear to look at the remains of this macabre slaughter any longer. How disgusting, how unbearably disgusting. The gaping mouth with the bloody lips. The blood which had coagulated in her face, and the wilted bouquet in her hand. In the midst of all this horror he realized that just a few hours ago she had been very much alive and a beautiful woman. Scarily similar to Erika Lund with her voluminous dark hair, facial features, and sturdy physique. No, he couldn't point that out to her. It was too monstrous. Jesper decided to keep the thought to himself.

Erika pulled on her gloves and inspected the footprints in the ground. Thanks to the rain they were easy to spot.

"Did they all walk up to her to see if she was really dead, or what? Twelve people. It's not so easy getting anything from this mud now." She got out a plastic bag from her briefcase and put in a bottle cap. Then sealed the bag and took out another plastic bag, into which she inserted a small, black piece of plastic, possibly from a trash bag. A cigarette butt. A toffee wrapper. A popsicle stick. The problem was not finding evidence, rather that there was too much of it. Like finding a single hair for DNA analysis at a hairdresser's. Erika held her back; the pain cut into her as she sensed it would when she stood up. What did the flowers mean? Why lilies of the valley? Did the symbolism lie in their whiteness and innocence, or in the fact that the plant was poisonous?

"They must have used a couple of sheets for this." Ek stood on his tiptoes to see if he could reach the thumbtacks securing the strips of material. The one at the top. "It must be someone as tall as me or taller." He picked up the camera and took the photographs Erika wanted.

"The question is why. The immediate impression one gets of these things flapping away on the hill is like a celebration. Big serpentines. Or a huge bridal veil. Did you call Hartman?"

"Yes, Maria Wern will be handling this. I hope she's up to it. You think she is?"

"She is," said Erika. "I'm pretty sure she'll want to come up here before we move the body." Erika went down the hill, and stopped. At the edge of the rose garden, in the shade under a mulberry tree, there were lilies of the valley growing. She bent down. One didn't need a sharp pair of eyes to see that someone had picked some of them from a corner of the flowerbed, someone had scrabbled together a bouquet in an angry hurry. Unfortunately the path was graveled and there were no footprints.

Maria Wern went up the hill with Erika. It was certainly a macabre spectacle. In the gathering heat there were more and more flies. The foul sight presented an almost abstract horror in the full light of day. What sort of person could do something like this?

"I'll be done in a minute, and then we can move the body." Erika stepped back and took another few photographs. It was a source of wonder to Maria that she could be so unmoved. Training, most likely; an ability to disengage her feelings and focus on the detailed work. Not a dead human being, but a body. Preferably Latin names for body parts and phenomena to make it more clinical.

"Do we know who she was or do we have to wait for someone to report a missing person? She looks about thirty. She might have children... a family."

"She wasn't carrying any papers. But she was married. She has an engagement ring, it says 'Claes 4/15/1998' and a wedding ring with 'Linn Claes 8/4/2001' engraved inside."

"It's a start. We'll have to ask the newspaper for help, they can look through their engagement notices and wedding photos. She was barefoot and wearing a nightgown, a white silk lace nightie. Was she asleep when she was attacked by the murderer? Was she at home, in a hotel or maybe with the murderer himself? Or did the murderer dress her in the white nightie? The ritual nature of the crime is clear. She hasn't been buried or hidden in a cellar… the murderer wanted to display her in his own way."

"To scare someone, make them do what he wanted, or just plain madness?" Erika gestured to Ek, who called the ambulance to come and take the body away from the scene. Other officers were trying to disperse the crowd so that the vehicle could get through.

"If it was to frighten someone, why bother with the lilies of the valley? This is probably not about silencing a witness. This is something else, something much more strange. We may be dealing with a psychopath." Maria Wern shivered suddenly, standing there in the shadow of the pavilion. Eventually one of her next of kin would get in touch. The anxiety would already be there as a premonition, and then all that sorrow would lie ahead of them. The investigation, the funeral, the welter of documentation and then the mourning process itself, when there was time for it. First they had to understand what had happened, the how and why of it. They had to take in the whole despicable thing and accept that it had happened. What if she had children? How do you explain to children that their mother has been murdered?

"You want to come with me down to the station?" she asked Erika once the body had been removed in a body bag and the crowd was dispersing.

"Yes. Ek will stay on here a while taking witness names," she said.

"I've asked them to start knocking on doors as soon as possible. Someone could have been awake last night and seen something unusual. There are no tire marks in the gravel to suggest a car was driven up here, so the murderer must have carried her through the garden and up the hill." Maria considered other possibilities for a short while—a wheelbarrow or bicycle? But no wheel marks had been found to indicate anything like that. "Only a person in good shape would manage it. She was either taken close to here by car or someone walked through the lanes with a big sack over their shoulder."

"Or along the outside of the wall... down the seafront." Erika couldn't judge where one ran the greatest risk of running into people in the middle of the night. "I assume the murderer parked by the Ordnance Tower and then walked along the seafront and through Kärleksporten. The hospital parking area is much further off. People are on the move there all the time. Logically speaking the hospital parking area shouldn't be an option."

"If he's a lunatic he's not behaving logically. Anyway, Hartman said he'd handle the media. We need members of the general public coming forward. Better that we put out an early announcement than some witness giving first-hand information to the media."

"Very true. I found a small piece of black trash bag. Maybe he carried the body in the bag and a piece snagged on a branch and tore off. Either that or the plastic comes from some other place. We'll check it for fingerprints." Erika sat in the car, rubbing her sore back. "I had a date tonight but I think I can forget that. Pity. I could have done with some healing hands here and there."

Hartman met Maria on the stairs.

"We have a witness who saw a man with a sack near the Botanical Gardens last night. Or I don't know if I can say 'a man,' she couldn't say for sure. A creature, anyway, wearing some sort of cape. Sort of like a monk in Medieval Week. The witness's name is Jill Andersson. She was walking on Tranhusgatan above Paviljongsplan when she met a man with a sack on his shoulder."

"Is she here, I'd like to talk to her?" Maria felt the blood rushing to her face. Here was a chance of a lead on the person who'd committed this bestial crime, the person it was now her responsibility to track down. Another thing that bothered her was the close resemblance of the woman they found on Tempelkullen to Erika. A sickening thought.

"Jill Andersson had an appointment at the social security office, which she couldn't miss. But she's coming to the station afterwards. She doesn't have a cell phone."

Hartman took a few steps toward his room, then turned round.

"We have another problem. Linus's father, Ulf. He's calling me the whole time. I understand his fury, but at the same time it worries me."

It was inexplicable that he had been capable of such a mistake, but they looked so similar. Two women walk out of a house. One to live, one to die. He had made one tiny error on the way, a miserable little second of carelessness and all the preparations had been in vain. He realized his mistake when he saw her curly head of hair turning up once again in the window of the health center, which he could see from the parking area. She was holding Anders Ahlström, kissing him; then left the building. He followed the wandering dot on his monitor. Was she on her way back to her home address? If he only had her name, address, and social security number: then he could examine her life on the computer screen.

Chapter 13

Detective Inspector Per Arvidsson turned off the alarm clock. His body ached for more sleep, although he'd already slept almost ten hours. The mornings were the worst, when he had to confront the new day with its fresh demands. Just taking care of his bodily hygiene seemed a major venture in itself. He couldn't explain it. Had it been possible, he would have pulled himself together. That was what was expected of him. Occasionally he managed it, then came the setbacks. Certainly day-to-day life had slowly improved but things were still not good; it was as if his energy wouldn't suffice. He could start a project, feeling himself inspired and full of energy, then suddenly run into a wall and, exhausted, give the whole thing up. He'd been on medication for a while and felt better, but did not want to keep taking the medicine if he didn't have to. It calmed his anxieties while at the same time making him impotent. It was a no-win situation: bubonic plague or cholera, take your pick! There was a constantly churning anxiety that life was running away from him, possibilities disappearing without him catching hold of them. Right now he was worrying mostly about Maria—the result of the HIV test. She needed his support so much. Time and time again she had wanted to tell him about all the terrible things she'd experienced; in the end he screamed at her, told her to stop, because he couldn't hear it. He hated himself for it. Maria hadn't accused him. She understood, she said. Darling Maria, she would never fully understand the self-loathing, the feeling of being a burden and a disappointment. She said she loved him. But it wasn't true. She loved the image of the man he had been before he was shot. There were many precious memories, many passionate moments. At this time she was devoted to him, and while this remained so he refused to let her in close. He couldn't cope with being loved when he couldn't love himself. Could she really put her hand on her heart and insist she loved a useless man like him? That was the reason for his hardness, his unpleasant exterior—he admitted that to himself. He kept her at an arm's length by being thoroughly unpleasant, even though there was nothing he wanted more than to take full possession of himself again and hold her in his arms. She had brought the children along a few times when they met. Although they were well-behaved and sweet, it was too much for him. Too much noise, too many demands he could not cope with. Can you play some football with them? Listen to Emil playing the piano! He had asked them to go home. He was such a failure, such a goddamn failure and he wanted nothing more than to be alone with his shame.

Maria had said he must seek medical advice. The days and months went by and life ran through his fingers like sand—without a sense of being alive. Time and time again the thought of finishing it all had come to him. But he had resisted that, for the sake of his own children, he told himself. In fact it was pure cowardice. Not because of the pain, not because of the shame, but because he did not know what was waiting for him on the other side. He had spoken to

Maria about it as they sat on the grassy slope by the promenade overlooking the sea, drinking beer and eating grilled chicken. It was a late evening, everything fine and the wind warm. She was not afraid of death, not afraid of actually being dead. If one isn't conscious then there's nothing to torment one. But the actual process of dying did worry her; growing helpless and dependent on others. Losing body function, being unable to communicate what one wanted to say while at the same time feeling pain or not being able to breathe. "It frightens me and I don't want to think about it," she had told him. "It's lucky we can't see into the future. It's better that way."

Arvidsson was a seeker and a brooder. What if consciousness was not located in the brain? What if there were actually a soul that had to live on? However broken and tormented? He swung between investing his hopes in the great Nothingness and a belief in the immortality of the soul. Worst of all was the thought of being able to see and experience what people around one were thinking and doing after one's death. In his imagination he could hear Maria confiding in Erika. Hartman's complaints. Rebecka's relief when she was awarded sole custody of the children and no longer needed to drop them off every other weekend.

His thoughts of death left him no peace. He did not have the strength to live, but was too afraid to die. There was a sturdy hook in the roof-beam in the living room, where the chandelier was hanging. He'd had it changed, so it would be strong enough. It was there if he needed to walk out of life by the emergency exit. It was a relief to him, knowing that he could decide for himself when it was time. He had got himself a rope, hanging on the coat hooks in the hall, behind his winter coat. He found out on the Internet how to make a slipknot that glides easily and tightens. A suitable stool to kick over was also available. But just imagine if in that moment when the stool is knocked over, one changes one's mind....

He remained sitting at the kitchen table, staring at his hands. Imagined them lifeless. Pale yellow, cold and stiff. His upper arms and the muscles he could tighten now would be released forever, and then rot. His teeth would remain. An ugly grin. He gave in to a sudden fit of trembling. This could not be sustained any longer. He felt he was going to vomit, his stomach ached. Then finally he wept and it was a relief, one which he had not managed up until now. Once he started crying he felt he would never be able to stop. The deep sobs wrenched out of him like an evil spirit he'd borne for a long time—a spirit that had controlled his life. He wanted to live, he wanted so goddamn much to live a normal, straight-forward human life with a wife and kids and a job, just like anyone else. Why the hell couldn't he allow himself this?

In his wallet was a note Erika had written for him. A telephone number to that doctor she was having a fling with. Anders Ahlström.

"He's very patient-focused and thoughtful," she'd said. "I've told him about you. He's waiting for your call."

At first he'd been furious, of course. She had no right to interfere with his private life and discuss him with others. But Erika had taken his face in her strong hands and looked directly into his eyes so he couldn't look away.

"If you don't go and see him I'll club you and drag you there by your hair. You need help, Per!"

Anders Ahlström was thinking about his mother. Late last night she had called because she was feeling so dizzy, and he took Julia with him in the car and drove all the way to Öja, where she lived in a little cottage. She had passed out at the end of her sewing circle meeting, just when it was time for the other ladies to go home. He took her pulse, her blood pressure, and listened to her heart without finding any anomalies. To be on the safe side, they had stayed overnight. The whole thing worried him.

The telephone rang and cut short his train of thought. Anders Ahlström checked his watch. He was actually supposed to go and have his lunch. He had decided to start a new and better life, with regular meal times, exercise, and no smoking. For Erika's sake. When Per Arvidsson called on his direct line to book an appointment, Anders had to skip lunch again. Only with a massive effort of will power did he stop himself from bumming a cigarette from Siv, who had just come back from her vacation.

Per Arvidsson shook hands and spoke his name in an empty, flat voice.

"How are you?" Anders asked the red-haired man who'd sunk down before him at the desk. He smelled of rank sweat and his hair, slicked back along his scalp, looked as if it hadn't been washed for a long time. Proper psychological stress can make a person look like this, even an hour after stepping out of the shower. His eyes were apathetic and filled with sorrow.

"What can I do for you?" he said when his question remained unanswered.

Per Arvidsson burst into tears. He pinched his cheek hard, so that the pain would make him get a grip on himself. "I have this feeling of despair, I can't take it any more." Per fell silent, scraping his nails across the fabric of his pants, making a rasping sound. He couldn't sit still in his chair.

"Tell me." Anders tried to be relaxed in his body language to clarify the fact that he was prepared to listen for a long time.

Per stuttered out his story about the shoot-out when he was wounded, the twenty-four hours when he hovered between life and death. Yet when he could finally go back home, he no longer knew if he wanted to live. He should have been happy that he made it through so convincingly. He was physically completely restored but mentally a wreck.

"What help have you had before?" Anders had listened without taking notes, without taking his eyes off him and thus avoiding any disruption to his story and loss of contact.

"I went to a therapist, who was good. But he stopped and moved abroad. Then I was offered another contact. That one was a real joke, a goddamn moron who thought I should try colonic irrigation."

"Have you tried medication?" Anders rubbed his temples. His headache was now undeniable. He needed a cigarette to think clearly.

"It was rat poison. I was more or less chemically castrated by it. Couldn't get it up. Although I don't much want to have sex now, either, so it doesn't really matter. I suppose shitty genes like mine aren't supposed to be passed on."

"Are you having suicidal thoughts?"

"I was before, yes." The important thing was to tell him just enough to get some medication and stay on part-time sick leave, because that was what he needed. But if he told the truth, the whole truth, he ran the risk of being put under lock and key and suicide watch.

"So what were you thinking?"

"I was going to hang myself. I had a new hook put up in the living room. But it's not a concern any more. I want to try to live."

"A good decision. Would you be interested in some more therapy sessions? I know someone...."

"No, for Christ's sake. It's quite enough for me just to come in and let you know whether the medicine's working.

I don't have the energy for appointments and having to talk to someone who doesn't know which end is up. Or sitting in a group and competing with the others to see who's feeling the shittiest. I don't have energy for any responsibility of any kind. Every bastard out there wants to get you going again, even when you're almost going under with exhaustion."

"You want to start medication again? We can try another sort, with a different chemical composition. There's a good possibility we can find something that works better for you than what you were taking before."

Per drew a deep sigh of relief. "Sounds good."

"How's your day-to-day life, are you living with anyone?"

"No, that would be too much for me. It's terrible but I can't even cope with my own children for very long. They're mainly with their mother, though I try to have them every other weekend. She often has to come and pick them up earlier than we said."

Anders Ahlström got out his pad, wrote out a prescription, and gave it to Arvidsson. "You have my telephone number. Call me if something comes up, promise?"

Afterwards, when Per Arvidsson had left the room, Anders Ahlström was not sure if he'd done the right thing. There was always a risk that people with suicidal tendencies, people who'd been apathetic in their depression, suddenly experienced a new surge of life after the new medication began to kick in—and that was when they finally got the energy to kill themselves. The first month on medication is delicate. Per Arvidsson should not be left alone. On the other hand, he had taken medication before. Anders Ahlström went to the sink and washed his hands, as if to exonerate himself. He grimaced at himself in the mirror. All doctors made mistakes. Sooner or later it happened. There was no way one could watch every patient twenty-four hours a day to make sure no one came to any harm. Some ten to twenty percent of patients who were dealt with in a hurry ran the risk of incorrect treatment. In real terms they would have been better off staying at home.

The telephone rang, interrupting his thoughts again. With a deep sigh he picked up. He really didn't have time for any calls now.

"Dad. I'm going home. I don't want to be in school. The girls are so nasty; they say I smell bad because I don't want to shower after P.E. I don't have time to shower because then I don't have time to go with the others to the cafeteria and then I have to sit by myself. Because they don't give me a space at the table. And anyway I've got a stomach ache."

"But darling, have you told your teacher?"

"She doesn't get it." Julia was almost in tears.

"What about that teaching assistant, can't you talk to him?"

"Only by email. He's not here today. I'm going home now."

"What about the school nurse or some other grown-up?"

"The nurse only comes in when we're having vaccinations, stupid. I don't want to be here. I hate school!"

Anders Ahlström walked into the overflowing waiting room and called in the next patient.

Chapter 14

Harry Molin had been thinking long into the early hours about the dangers of borrelia and at dawn he called to book an emergency appointment. The woman at the call center had been on summer assignment, and thus considerably more helpful than the usual hags. One look at his bulky file had been enough to convince her he was a very sick man. He'd been given an early appointment at ten in the morning.

There was time to take out his dogs. They had been very restless that night. He did not know for sure whether he'd been bitten by ticks, but he'd read an article from Vallhagar in Fröjel about a family that had been assailed by hundreds of them. Their feet were speckled with their black nymphs. It was an image of such horror that it quite destabilized him. Suppose one in five ticks were contagious? This could be a question of TBE or borrelia or streptococcus or staphylococcus or some other terrible thing he did not even know the name of, and therefore even more frightening than anything already known to him. He had gone to Vallhagar to see the old barrows about ten years ago and ever since the symptoms had come and gone, mutating and changing all the time. Tiredness. Flu symptoms. Slight pain in the neck and back. Typical borrelia. But no red marks, as far as he could remember. Because of this he had rejected the possibility; until he read the report that night. Science moves on, new knowledge is always emerging. In the old days they used to say borrelia sufferers were just hypochondriacs. Had anyone received an apology about that? Now we knew better. For instance, we knew that one in four people did not end up with a distinctive ring around the bite. He had read that both on the Internet and in the brochure. So how was one to know if one had been infected?

"And if the tick bites your scalp or your back, how are you supposed to know if you've been bitten at all? What do you think?" he said to the Labrador Mirabel, as she curiously sniffed her way along. Borrelia would explain why he had not been feeling well. The doctor could at least give him a blood test.

"It doesn't exactly fill you with respect for the medical profession when all the time you have to think for them, find things out and make suggestions, without bringing them down a peg," he explained to the dog.

Mirabel wagged her tail, glad of the attention.

"How difficult can it be, figuring all this out?" he said and tugged on Gordon's lead. The Alsatian had clearly picked up some trail, and was pulling with all his might. "Doctors don't figure anything out by themselves, you see Mirabel." The Labrador pricked up its ears and barked. "That's what I like to hear." Of course there were exceptions. He almost worked himself into a fury when he thought about that young whippersnapper of a doctor who'd been interning last summer when Harry consulted him about a problem he'd been having with his urination. There had not been a proper consultation room available, and Harry had been ushered into a corner by a window and exhorted to drop his pants. The young doctor had muttered something inaudible, then shoved his finger up Harry's anus. Just like that. It was nothing less than goddamn molestation and if the nurse had not been there to step between them he would have punched him in some place where it hurt. When it came to humiliation, they certainly didn't hold back.

Harry stopped his dogs. They were pulling frantically. "Sit, sit, I said!" They were absolutely determined to get into Linn Bogren's garden. The garden gate was open, and there were long strips of material flapping from the trees in there. What manner of spectacle was this? It looked utterly bonkers. Maybe it was her birthday? He remembered his own thirtieth birthday. His friends had organized a yard sale with all the useless junk they had at home, and he was supposed to sell it and the money he made was his to keep. He made almost two thousand kronor—a really good present, as he'd also been allowed first choice from the bric-a-brac. Yes, the nurse was probably having a birthday party, that was it. He could bring a bunch of flowers from his garden, congratulate her and at the same time ask whether she knew anything about borrelia. If the gate was open she was probably at home. Gordon gave a low, guttural growl. It was difficult getting his unruly dogs home again; their walk was over before it had scarcely begun.

Harry picked a lovely bouquet of lilies of the valley and forget-me-nots and then added three sprigs of budding bleeding hearts. It looked sweet. He wrapped the whole thing in butcher paper the way his grandmother had taught him. It always made it look more elegant, like bought flowers.

The gate was still open, also the kitchen door, which surprised him as he walked into the nice inner courtyard. It looked pretty amusing, those strips of cloth flapping about all over the place. He tied the dogs to the banister by the front steps. Gordon gave him a reproachful look, but

Harry looked away. Mirabel whined and barked. "Be quiet!" He walked round the white coffee table of cast iron, and knocked on the door. No answer.

"Hello!" Surely the nurse had to be at home? Her door was open. "Hello? Anyone home?" He didn't want to startle her or surprise her in the midst of some embarrassing situation; he made as much noise as possible so she'd hear him. Maybe she wasn't dressed yet, it was only eight in the morning. It might turn out to be embarrassing, he realized. There was no one in the kitchen. On the table was an abandoned mug with a tea bag next to it. There were some crumbs where a sandwich had been. The floor had probably not been mopped all week. Harry washed his floor every night. One had to keep things clean.

He started feeling a little ill at ease about not finding her. "Hello!" He listened as hard as he could, but he couldn't hear a sound. If she were in the shower he should have been able to hear the water running. He went back to the front door. The morning sun was shining directly into the living room. The furniture wasn't arranged symmetrically. It looked as if someone had started rearranging things and then changed their mind. There were moving boxes on the floor. Were they moving? Claes had not mentioned it. They were filled with books, mostly. Harry sat himself down in the sofa and tried to think. Maybe they were taking the books into the attic? He also found it difficult throwing things away, particularly books. Once you'd read them you were a part of their story—you sort of fuse with a book when you read it, adding your own thoughts and reflections and afterwards it is difficult getting rid of it. He noticed something glittering on the floor. What was it? Had the rain come in or had someone been careless while watering the plants in the window? One shouldn't be so careless, it could leave ugly marks in the floor. He stood up to get a better look. In fact they were shards of glass. The window of the door to the terrace had been shattered. How odd…. Now he was starting to feel properly uneasy.

The dogs were whining out there. What was the matter with them? They didn't usually carry on like this. It had been the same all night.

"Be quiet, I said! Quiet!" Had the nurse been home she'd have heard him shouting at them. Surely nothing could have happened to her? This was starting to feel eerie. Harry stood up and was just about to leave the house when he saw the stain by the bedroom door. A red splash just by the threshold. How very careless and filthy not to wipe the floor when you spilled something. It could be wine or cranberry juice… then as he drew closer he smelled a sweet, nauseating odor pressing out of the dark bedroom. He poked his finger into the gooey mess and smelled it. His flowers fell unnoticed to the floor. He fumbled with his sticky hand for the light switch by the door and suddenly the room was bathing in white, merciless light. He thought he'd pass out. He mustn't pass out. He must get out of here. Quick. Away. Out. The white comforter covers were covered in big blood stains and the creamy white wall behind the headboard was spattered with an intense, brown-red color. The bride and groom in the picture above the bed were plastered in blood. In the bed lay an electric chainsaw. The blade was bloody. Harry's legs lost all their remaining strength and he stumbled out. His fingers would not obey him when he tried to untie his dogs. The harder he tugged at the knot, the more it tightened. There was a hissing sound in his head. Maybe the slaughterer who had done this perverse deed was still there, waiting for his next victim. For a split second he thought about leaving his dogs and ensuring his own safety. But he changed his mind. If the perpetrator were still nearby it would be safer to keep the dogs with him. He felt he was going to vomit. He must vomit. But first get himself safe. Lock the door. Cold sweat ran down his body. Into his house, he had to get inside and lock the door. Shut out the evil. There was blood on his hands… what if the police thought he'd done it? How could he prove he'd just been walking past with the dogs? And where was Linn? What had the murderer done with the body? No one could survive such an enormous loss of blood. She must be dead.

Once back home, he washed and disinfected his hands and put the dog leashes and his clothes directly into the washing machine. His nausea churned in his throat. Taking Gordon with him, he searched his house before he was brave enough to lock the front door. The kitchen entrance would serve as an escape route if the murderer came. He sat on a kitchen chair, keeping his skittish dogs close. He held them hard and tried to think, but his common sense was abandoning him and he curled up in his suffocating fear, which gradually turned into palpitations and breathing difficulties. What would he do if they started thinking he was the one who had done it? If they interrogated him to find out where the body was? How could he have been so stupid that he washed his clothes? They'd never believe him now. The best thing would be if someone else found the blood, if he didn't have to meet them and tell them about it. But of course they'd come knocking on everyone's doors, they'd speak to all the neighbors. Someone might even have seen him walking out of her home with the dogs. The police would press him until he confessed.

He'd seen that in a film. It's possible to inflict terrible pain on someone without leaving any marks. There are rotten eggs in the police force, there are some police officers who show a blind eye to such things. No one would believe him, he was convinced of it now. He had demonstrably been on the crime scene. They needed a guilty party. The public would demand someone's head for this.

Good Lord! He'd left his fingerprints all over Linn's home. On doorframes and handles, and those flowers were from his garden. If they got some lead on him they'd easily be able to see that he'd been there and then it would all be over. It would be prison for him and he'd no longer be able to choose his own doctor. From there on he'd get a prison physician. Where could he escape to, where could he go? He had a sister in Arboga, but they had only had sporadic telephone contact these past few years. She would smell trouble if he wanted to come and stay with her for a while.

No, he must calm down. And think logically. If he could just carry on living like normal, he wouldn't give any cause for suspicion. Like normal? How would that be possible? He must summon all the strength he had in his body, steel himself. When they interviewed him he had to answer and come across as natural. He had to think of an alibi. Do his homework, watch the news carefully so he could say he'd seen it on television. But the fingerprints! He had to go back and tidy up. The chainsaw belonged in the shed. It was usually sitting in the window. He had to wipe down all the surfaces he'd touched. He was good at disinfecting things. Remove the flowers. Tidy up. And be quick, before someone else came along and saw the blood. He had to save himself, even if it meant sabotaging the police. One could never trust people in positions of authority. Linn was anyway beyond all hope. She was dead. He understood that; there was nothing he could do about it now.

Chapter 15

The cold fluorescent light at the pathologist's made the badly mutilated body look even more grotesque than in the Pavilion on Tempelkullen. Even though the head had been reattached to the body by means of small, neat stitches, the sight was unbearable. When the green cloth was removed they all involuntarily stepped back. Detective Inspector Maria Wern saw the color drain from Claes Bogren's face. His ash-blond hair lay in damp strips across his brow.

"There she is. There's Linn." His voice was scarcely audible. He swayed on his feet and supported himself with his hand against the wall.

"Come on, let's go and sit down in the room next door." Maria gripped his arm gently and ushered him out of the morgue. His muscular body gave way to her. With a great deal of effort he stumbled outside unsteadily and sank into the chair pushed forward for him.

"It's not true. I spoke to her last night. It just can't be true. She mustn't be dead! She can't be dead!" He rested his head between his knees. Maria looked round for something into which he could vomit, and picked up a kidney-shaped dish from the sink. She held it at the ready. In spite of the low temperature in the room, the smell had been taxing.

"How do you feel? You want some water?"

He shook his head. Maria parted the curtains and threw the window wide open. Outside, the happy laughter of children could be heard, as if from an entirely different world.

"Can I do something for you?" Maria put her hand on his back. His body was shaking. His breathing was deep and tremulous. She kept her hand there, and slowly he regained his self-control.

"I'm okay." He sat up and mopped the cold sweat from his forehead with the back of his hand. "Ask whatever you need to know." His body made an involuntary jerk.

"You were a great help to us when you identified her. We'll take one question at a time, at a pace you can manage." Maria sat down on the other side of the small table, straightening the crooked tablecloth. She waited for a moment, then took out a pen and notepad from her briefcase.

Claes Bogren was a neat and proper man, in a white T-shirt and Armani jeans; a good-looking man, someone who might attract glances in town. Decent haircut, tanned, although a nuance of something pallid seemed to be shining through. Two hours ago he had come back to his wife after a month at sea, he said. He could easily be the guilty one. But Maria hoped he wasn't. She felt she should be able to sense if he were capable of such a heinous deed. The murderer really had to be a lunatic.

"It was so goddamn terrifying coming home. The blood! Blood everywhere in the bedroom. First I thought maybe she was pregnant and had a miscarriage. So I called the emergency room, but they hadn't taken in anyone called Linn Bogren. I searched the house, the street, I asked the neighbors. But she wasn't anywhere. I didn't know what to do."

"They contacted us from the hospital. They heard on

the news about what had been found in the Botanical Gardens, and they assumed you might be her husband. Your first names were engraved in her rings. Until then we didn't know who she was or who her next of kin were," said Maria, as a little prod to make him continue his story.

"I called from Gothenburg. Last night. I spoke to her late last night. She answered in such a strange way, so held-back. I mean, I did wake her…. I felt worried. She wasn't like she usually is…. There was something …something not right. She was very short…."

"What time?"

"It was quarter to twelve."

"What did you talk about?"

"I asked her if she loved me…." His voice broke and tears welled up. He rubbed his eyes frenetically, rubbed and pressed to stop the tears. He didn't want his feelings to get in the way. He wanted to explain and get it out of the way. "She said yes, she did. And then we spoke about the rain. She said it was good that it was raining."

"Were there any other sounds in the background?"

"I didn't notice anything. If I'd caught a plane back she might be alive now. Either that or we'd both be dead…." Wild-eyed, he stared at Maria. "Do you understand what I mean? If I'd taken the plane…."

"Were you going to?"

"No. I wanted to get home as quick as possible, but that's not the way we do it."

"So how do you usually do it?"

"We pulled into Gothenburg Harbor at about 23:00 hours. When we're at sea we're not allowed any alcohol unless we're under Russian command, then we're expected to drink like men. So we usually celebrate once we're ashore. I caught the train to Nynäshamn at about six this morning."

"What time did the ferry leave?" Probably he'd had time

to be on the 12:50 sailing, Maria guessed, but she wanted to hear him say it himself.

"12:50. It was delayed. We should have landed at 16:05 but there was a hard wind and we weren't ashore until almost five."

"Did you meet anyone you knew on the ferry?"

"No, I took a cab. I needed a shower and some sleep."

"Do you still have your tickets?" She saw the consternation in his eyes. "I have no reason not to believe you, it's just routine procedure to back up all information with receipts or tickets. For your own sake. I can understand it feels invasive, but it helps our investigation if we can have them."

"Sure. I'll try to dig them out."

"How did you get back to the house?" Maria made a note in her pad.

"I walked back from the terminal. I hurried up so she wouldn't start wondering where I was. I tried to call a few times, but there was bad reception on the ferry and when the signals went through she didn't answer."

"What did you think about that?"

"I thought it was strange. Because she would have been expecting me to call. I usually call when the ferry's getting close to shore, so she knows it's time to put the spuds on to boil and open a bottle of wine. We usually have a nice dinner and celebrate a bit when I come home." He stood up, closed the window, and then sat down again with his arms wrapped hard round his body.

"Did you run into anyone on your way home from the ferry?"

"I wasn't thinking about it. I just hurried up. My sailor's sack was heavy. I had to put it down for a moment by the Ordnance Tower. No, no one I can remember. There were probably people about but I don't recall anyone in particular."

"And when you got home... ?"

"The gate was closed but not locked. There were strips of material hanging from the tree. I thought: What the hell! What's this? I called out her name. It was a funny way of welcoming your husband home, but she sometimes got funny ideas like that. She wanted to surprise me sometimes." He stopped and bit his knuckle hard, to hold the excruciating pain inside in check. "That's how she was. So sweet, and considerate. She wanted me to be happy." The tears came. The flowing tears he'd fought to keep inside, the tears he so badly needed to release.

"We have lots of time." Maria stood up to hand him a couple of tissues and he gripped her hand and pulled her close so she'd hug him. And wouldn't let her go. He cried and whimpered and made the table jump when he struck it with his fist.

"She can't be dead. I loved her. Loved her so, so much."

Love has its price and that price is sorrow, Maria thought to herself. If one does not have the courage to love, then everything is lost from the very beginning. But she did not say this out aloud. No one ever grew wise from listening to the experiences of others.

"Sorry." He brushed the arm of her sweater, which was drenched in tears, then blew his nose in the tissue. "Sorry. I'm not myself."

"Are you all right to carry on? We can take a break if you want to. I can get you a hot drink. Tea or coffee? What do you say?"

"We'll keep going." He blew his nose again. "I want to do everything I can so you catch the fucker who did this."

Maria sat down at the table again and scrutinized him.

"You came home... there were strips of material hanging from the trees...."

"It was so weird. I called out, but she didn't answer. So I went inside.... The door wasn't locked so I assumed she was at home and planning some surprise. She wasn't in the kitchen. I went into the living room to see if she'd laid the table in there. There were moving boxes on the floor. She'd packed the encyclopedia and her favorite books. I went cold as ice. I don't understand why she packed them. The furniture was rearranged in a funny way. She often wanted to move things round…. How can I ask her now what she had on her mind? Just think if I never find out what she was going to do?"

"Was there anything else she'd packed? Clothes? Toiletries?"

"I don't know. I have no idea. As I was standing there I heard a car stopping outside in the street, and I hurried out. I thought it was her, I thought this was the surprise and that we were going out to eat in some fancy restaurant or something. But it wasn't her. I came in again and then I noticed the door to the terrace was broken. Only then did I start feeling scared. I went into the bedroom, the only place I hadn't been in yet, and in there… that's where all the blood was. Shiiiit!" He was overwhelmed again, his tears came in painful bursts, utterly taking him over. Maria waited. She was ready to postpone the session if necessary. Then suddenly he got himself under control and he gave her an insistent look.

"Why? Why her? So much blood. I called the emergency room and you know the rest. I don't understand who could have done it. A madman…. Everyone liked Linn. I don't know anyone who could have wanted to do her any harm. Do you know? Have you got any ideas? Was she… raped?"

"We can't say anything about that until the medical examiner is done. I'm sorry."

"You said they found her in the Botanical Gardens, in the Pavilion? Why? So she was murdered at home and then moved? Is there any kind of understandable reason for that?"

Maria indicated with a shake of the head that it was also

beyond her comprehension. Linn had been dressed as a bride. That was the feeling Maria got when she looked at her. She had been wearing a white, lacy nightie and there was a bouquet of flowers in her hand. Had she dressed herself up like that, or had someone else done it?

"The white nightgown she was wearing, was that her own? Did you recognize it?"

"She used to wear it when I came home. I gave it to her on her twenty-fifth birthday. Silk. She loved it...."

"Did you have time to notice anything that was missing in your home, something someone had removed?"

"I don't know. Yes, maybe the computer. The computer wasn't there when I was looking for the phone number of the hospital. I just had a total brain breakdown and was going to check it online. No, actually it's being repaired, I remember she told me." Slowly he breathed out through half-closed lips, a moaning sound. Suddenly he looked incredibly old. Maria tried to make her questions more focused.

"I'd like the names of her closest friends. The ones she really trusted. Colleagues? Close relatives? Was there some girlfriend of hers, or some friend she was particularly close to, someone she might tell things she hadn't even told you about yet?"

"Sara Wentzel." His answer came without hesitation.

Chapter 16

Erika Lund opened the bedroom door without backing away from the smell of blood, which had intensified in the heat. Somewhere, instinctive and deep-rooted, the feeling was there: for the smell of blood triggers fear just as much as the color red. Fight or flee. Many years of training had taught her to turn off her sense of smell and feeling of repulsion. She couldn't explain how she managed it, only that it always worked when she got on with her task and focused on the details.

There wasn't enough light for the photographs she needed to take. She pulled up the roller blind and angled up the Venetian blind. Outside, two colleagues were securing shoeprints. The ground was still soft after the rain on the night of the murder, and there were good prospects of finding something of interest. It was something, at least. Rarely in all her years in the technical division had Erika seen such a carefully tidied crime scene. All the door handles, doorframes and surfaces one usually touches were carefully wiped down, almost disinfected. Everything had been tidied away except for the blood, which was on show in an almost demonstrative manner. A remarkable combination of lunacy and perfection. When she saw the mark on the wallpaper, she thought at first it was a coincidence, a lighter band in the blood on the wall that had ended up there after the deed. But then she saw. Someone had daubed a barely visible "K" in the blood.

In the shed they found a chainsaw, with enough dried blood on the blade to rehydrate and analyze. But no damned fingerprints. Everything pointed to this being a scrupulously planned murder. Someone with enough presence of mind to cover every trace of himself afterwards. The perpetrator must have come through the veranda door after smashing the window, then left the house via the kitchen door which stood open. Did the murderer know that Linn Bogren was at home by herself? Did they know each other?

There was still not enough natural light, so Erika rigged up a couple of spotlights from the curtain rail. Only now did she notice the kitchen knife on the floor. The implement was partially under the bed, hidden under the sheet which had slipped down. Carefully she held up the knife against the light. The gleaming blade had clear fingerprints on it. Carefully she inserted it into a plastic bag and sealed it without any exaggerated hopes of the fingerprints being those of the murderer, who in every other respect had been so careful in his desire to cover every trace of himself. She went back to her photography. The mattress had soaked up blood. Blood had also spattered over the wall, over the headboard and the wedding photo. A beautifully smiling couple under a triumphal arch of red roses and oak foliage. He wore a tailcoat and she a wonderful cream-white dress of silk, with a plunge-cut back. Erika's gaze was fixed on the bride's face, which was eerily similar to her own as she used to be many years ago. The hair and eyes. The bridal bouquet consisting of red roses and white freesia. The flowers placed in the dead woman's hand had been lilies of the valley. Did this have some significance? What reason could there be for dragging a body to the Tempelkullen? The blood and the placing of the body seemed to point to some nightmarish ritual, the significance of which was difficult to interpret for any outsider. Erika tried to form a picture of the murderer. A madman working alone, with the ability to think and predict the consequences of his actions? Or a group of people using murder as a performance to frighten others into obedience?

It felt strange, coming into such close proximity to the private habits of others. Silently she asked the dead woman's forgiveness before opening her bedside table. For your own sake, so that whoever did this to you gets their punishment, she thought to herself. At the same time she realized that their detailed investigation into her private life was actually another violation. Erika thought with horror of all the things the police would find in her drawers, if compelled to search them. Things would be held up and dissected in the clear light of day. Certain off-the-cuff comments would certainly pass between the police, while exchanging smiles and glances. Not least for Claes Bogren this was a deep incursion into the sanctity of their private lives. It had been even more unfathomable to him that he could not touch anything in his own home, not even his own computer which they picked up from the repair place.

She found the victim's purse on the floor in the hall. It was unzipped. There was a wallet inside containing about eight hundred kronor, credit cards, keys, and a comb and mirror. If the murderer had been after money, he would have noticed the purse—but nothing seemed to have been touched.

There were two wardrobes in the bedroom. One contained men's clothes while the other one, oddly enough, was almost empty. A red bathrobe hung from a hook; on the shelf above was a sweatshirt covered in paint. Was it in fact as Claes had feared—that she had been on the point of leaving him? In which case, where were the clothes? In one corner stood a dusty computer table with a computer screen and keyboard, two used mugs, a plate, and a lot of other detritus: a hairbrush, CDs, an abstract ceramic sculpture, two pairs of glasses, and a mass of desk paraphernalia. Maria Wern had immediately ordered telephone lists of outgoing and incoming calls both on the landline and Linn's cell phone, still on the bedside table beside the wine glass.

When Erika had finished in the bedroom she continued in the kitchen. There was a lone teacup on the table, a used tea bag beside it and some crumbs from a piece of wholegrain bread. Had Linn been too tired to put these away and wipe down the table, or did she usually leave chores like this at night? Erika opened the fridge. Claes Bogren had been expecting a nice dinner when he came home from his month at sea. But in the fridge there was only milk and yogurt, ketchup, sandwich toppings, a number of jars of gherkins, jam, and taco sauce, and an almost squeezed-out tube of dill caviar. Cooking up a feast with the ingredients in this fridge would be a real challenge. There were two empty bottles of wine in the trash and a corkscrew on the kitchen bench.

Jesper Ek popped up in the doorway.

"We've found Linn Bogren's car parked outside the Ordnance Tower. A Nissan Micra. The back seat is full of stuff. At least two leather bags and a loads of plastic bags."

"So she was probably clearing out. I'll go through the bags later. We'll take the whole car down to the station."

"Maybe the clothes were being taken to the Red Cross collection in Kupan or something," Ek suggested optimistically.

"No, the wardrobe is empty. I think she was leaving him."

"We were just wondering, will you be there for the three

o'clock run-through… if anything new comes up?" Jesper looked at the pile of sealed plastic bags with various objects inside. "Hartman's going to make sure you get some reinforcements, he said."

"I could certainly do with some. I want to carry on here until I'm done. If I find anything I'll call."

"Okay." Jesper's cropped head disappeared round the corner and she heard him whistling. An irritating vice of his; she was glad he took the sound away with him when he left.

The living room did not offer up any surprises. Jesper Ek had taken away the shattered glass from the broken window of the veranda door to check the shards for signs of blood. It would have been a stroke of luck if the murderer had smashed through the pane with his bare fist, thus cutting himself. The furnishings were old-fashioned rococo pieces in wine-red velvet, the covers replicated in the curtains. Inherited stuff or things they'd picked up together at auction? Four modern bookshelves in oak lined one of the long walls, beneath them two small boxes filled with books. Erika tried them for their weight. Most likely Linn would not have managed to pick them up herself. Was she waiting for someone to help her with the move? Where was she going to, and why?

In the shelf furthest toward the window were a couple of photo albums. Erika leafed through them. An entire life. A little dark-haired girl in grandmother's lap. Class photos from first grade. A toothless, blithe girl with pigtails sitting on a swing, tightly clutching a doll. The next album was red with pink hearts. This one featured a lanky teenage girl, slightly knock-kneed, her long hair reaching down to the hem of her mini-skirt. Mountain trekking, two heads jutting out of a tent, a smoking camping stove in the foreground. Then the wedding photo and, on the same page, a photo of the two of them sitting on the front step of their house inside Visby's city walls. End. No photos after that. Maybe afterwards they bought a digital camera or grew tired of taking photographs?

Erika felt uncomfortable rifling through the trash in the bathroom. This was nothing less than snooping in a person's most intimate sphere. What would she find? Something with fingerprints on it? A condom with DNA of interest to them? All the secrets would be brought into the full light of day. When the medical examiner was done with his investigation they would know if Linn had been raped. All the disgusting stuff in the trash could be of immense value. Erika pulled out yet another bag, securing and sealing the contents of the trash. There were expensive perfumes in the bathroom cabinet, possibly presents from the husband who may have bought them on his trips abroad. At the back was a carton with a card of sleeping pills, four gaping holes and six pills still there. The pills had been prescribed as recently as two days ago by Anders Ahlström. It was unexpected seeing his name turning up in this context.

There were any number of nooks and crannies to go through in the house. Thousands of things without any significance had to be checked to find the needle in the haystack that would tip the scales in the courtroom and convict the murderer. It was rarely down to the guns and bullets, Erika thought to herself—if she could put it like that. Extracting the right evidence was all about patience, scrupulousness, and yet more patience. Then and only then could the right person be put behind bars. The broom closet was her next challenge. She stood slightly to one side so she wouldn't block the light. A bucket with a mop. She unscrewed the mop from the handle. Checked the handle for fingerprints. She did the same with the broom, studying the bristle and noticing some short, red-brown hairs stuck in the dust. Dog hairs? The Bogrens did not have a dog as far as she knew. Would the murderer, or murderers if there were more than one, have brought along a dog? Not very likely, and yet if that were the case there was material here for backing it up. The most likely thing was, of course, that some friends had visited—friends with a dog. Another question for Claes Bogren. There were also plant remains in the broom. Small, half-dried leaves and a little white flower petal, possibly from a lily of the valley. Erika held it up against the light. Yes, that was certainly from a lily of the valley.

Chapter 17

Later that evening when Erika was at the movie theater with Anders, she had problems concentrating on the movie. "Archive X" seemed fairly eventless and pale in comparison to the reality she found herself in at this time. But she didn't care. It might as well have been some mid-50s movie about housewives, as long as he held her hand and kissed her in the dark. This was the only thing that made any difference to her. In a way they were a couple and in a way not. It felt slightly uncertain, exciting, nerve-racking, and disorienting. It was Anders who'd called to ask if they could meet. She would have liked to ask him if he wanted to be with her. She still felt a bit bruised after the conversation with his daughter. He'd consoled her, telling her it was nothing personal. "Julia is guarding over my virtue," he said, "it's quite a responsibility." Hearty laugh. "She won't let anyone across the bridge right now, but if we give her a bit of time to get used to it, everything will work out just fine." Erika wondered if he really believed that himself. He hadn't suggested they should see each other at his home, so how was Julia supposed to get used to it? If he really wanted them to be together he had to do better than that. Erika was long since fed up with half-hearted relationships ending up nowhere because of each party keeping up their guard and watching over their own interests without having the guts to go for it. Little input, bad odds, nothing gained. She couldn't help but admire Maria in this sense, because she went in with everything she had, wholeheartedly and without any reservations. Right now she was unhappy, but that was the price of passion. Life is short. Moments of total happiness are priceless—those moments when one knows oneself to be unconditionally loved while at the same time giving back the same love. Am I so different? she self-interrogated. There were things from her past she had not dared tell him; things that grew increasingly difficult the more she fell for him. Would he walk away if he knew?

When the movie was over they wandered slowly through town. There was a light rain and the air was rather cool. Erika buttoned her jacket. Anders noticed and put his arm round her.

"You're very quiet." He applied a little extra pressure with his arm over her shoulder. "Want to tell me what it is?"

She heard the anxiety in his voice. Maybe it was good if he didn't feel too sure of her. "I'm thinking about work, it's always like that when you're in the middle of an investigation."

"I suppose you're thinking about Linn Bogren. Terrible, isn't it. Did you know she was a patient of mine? I have to respect the privacy of my patients, but this is such a serious crime. Linn consulted me about her insomnia."

"Do you feel you can tell me something about it?" It was a relief that he brought it up himself. Really it was Maria he should be talking to, and she'd have to take things over formally.

"It was difficult getting a handle on Linn. It was like she didn't want to talk about the real cause of her problems. I guess she thought it was none of my business. She wanted the medicine, and then she wanted to be left in peace."

"So what did she say to you?" Erika had to bite her tongue not to mention the signs of her preparing to clear out, once she started looking among Linn's things—including the clothes in the car. It would have been a relief to be able to discuss it openly.

"I asked if it was her work. Women working in heath care are an over-represented group when it comes to sleep dysfunction. Stress, shift work, too much coffee and irregular mealtimes all take their toll. But Linn liked her work, she said. It felt meaningful to her; she felt secure with it and up to speed. When I wouldn't let her off the hook without an explanation, she told me she'd decided to leave her husband. But that wasn't all… she also said she felt someone was following her, she felt under threat."

"In what way?" What Anders had said so far fit well with the image Erika had formed of Linn Bogren.

"Some gang. When I think about it now I blame myself for not listening more and asking about it. I was short of time, the waiting room was stuffed. I convinced myself that that she was in a life crisis, going through some major changes."

"Can you remember anything else?" Erika tried to hide her eagerness. Anders stopped, and thought about it. She could follow his entire thought process in his open face.

"She ran into some gang while she was on her way home. Some unruly guys. Nothing in particular happened. Later that night she thought she saw a face in her window, and I had a fairly bizarre explanation for that: the neighbor, Harry Molin, is a hypochondriac. He knew she was a nurse and he wanted to ask for some advice in the middle of the night. I know it sounds a bit crazy, but he's a bit unusual." Anders couldn't stop himself from smiling. "Harry pressed his face to the window to see if she was in. It would have scared the living daylights out of anyone."

Slowly they wandered down Almedalen. Erika had parked outside the library and felt no particular hurry to get there. They hadn't decided whether to go anywhere else after the movie. "But you got a feeling there was something more to it, right? Linn was holding back about something, something she didn't think you had any business knowing?"

"Yes, either that or I've just imagined it, built it all up afterwards... once I heard what happened to her. I didn't ask her anything else about it. I felt that leaving your husband was a good enough reason for insomnia, it seemed a pretty adequate reason for prescribing a few sleeping pills. I don't know if anything else happened when she bumped into that gang. Maybe they assaulted her indecently in some way? The neighbor might know something more about it, I mean Harry Molin. He lays claim to a lot of my time with the discoveries he makes on the Internet; he keeps me updated about all that. That's how the role of the doctor is changing. In the old days we were dictators and the patients were grateful and submissive. Now we've been reduced to consultants and general peons. He even advised me to try a drug for my smoking cravings. And I went for it."

"Maybe it's not all wrong." Erika glanced at him, laughing. They'd reached the parking area and nothing was decided yet. "So... what are you doing now?"

"This...." He leaned forward and kissed her until she was gasping for breath. "And this...." His hand glided down over her bottom. He pressed himself against her as he kissed her again.

"What does that mean? Good night?"

"Not necessarily. When I can't smoke I have to try other stimuli. I mean heavy stuff...." He lifted the hem of her blouse and peered down her cleavage.

"How do you mean? Do you have a plan?" Erika made no move to stop him. Things were looking up.

"We could get into the car and drive to some godforsak-en place and discuss the political climate, the greenhouse effect, celebrity gossip—or not. We'll think of something."

She laughed and gestured for him to get in. So that's what he wanted. A bit of heavy petting in the car. Not home to you and not home to me. Was he serious or did he just want to play a little? Nothing wrong with that—on the other hand, definitely better than nothing. Yet not quite what she wanted, either.

"I want this to be for real." She felt herself blushing hard. It wasn't an easy thing to say. "I want us to be for real."

"We are. For real." He laughed at her embarrassment. "I want to get to know you; to know everything about you. But I think it's good if we take things a bit easy to begin with. I hardly know anything about you. Do you have chil-dren, for example?"

Erika felt the old familiar vertigo coming back. Even though it was a question she'd been expecting, she felt un-prepared for it.

"Two, they're almost grown up. They live with their fa-ther in Motala.... Well, I was very young."

He looked at her, as if expecting her to continue. She had to tell the truth. He'd either disappear if she confessed or they'd get closer. They were at a crossroads. Erika was not going to lie to him.

"I got postpartum depression after giving birth. We sep-arated and he was deemed the more suitable of us. He got custody of the children, sole custody, so I put my energy into my career." Erika sighed heavily. "He's not been very encouraging about me seeing them on my own. Not a day goes by without my thinking about them, how they are.... It's the main sadness of my life."

"I'm sorry, sorry for barging in."

"I haven't told so many people about it. But if we're going to be for real, you have to know."

"And now? Do you have any contact with them?"

"They're strangers to me. I missed out on so much of the time of their growing up; I wasn't feeling so great. I never managed to repair it. I've tried to reach out to them, talk to them, but it gets forced and difficult and I've noticed it makes them suffer. They don't want to see me. I send money at Christmas and for their birthdays, because I don't even know what they want. My ex-husband has to do the shopping with them. He's hardly made things as easy for me as he might have, but I think he's a good father to them."

Erika's sincerity made Anders open up. "I never stop brooding about my wife Isabel who drowned. After we had Julia she turned into someone quite different. She couldn't stand seeing me, everything I did was wrong. And she saw danger everywhere, wouldn't allow any scissors or knives around, and no heights. Everything had to be exactly as she decided—otherwise she got hysterical. Even though I'm a doctor I didn't understand what was happening. I was too close to the whole thing. If I'd made more of an effort, loved her more, been more accommodating, things would have been fine in the end. But it didn't work out that way."

"That's how a lot of things end up in life. It never works out the way you think."

"And now I've met you.... It's a new chance in life, and it scares the shit out of me.... Can you understand?" Anders squeezed her arm gently and looked out of the window at the windblown pines and the sea, glittering beyond the trees.

"I can understand." The car turned into a little track running into the woods. She turned off the engine and faced him. He moved a little closer and kissed her.

"Maybe we should take our chance while the hood's warm?"

"I have a blanket. The moss looks soft there, under that pine."

138

"You tramp. You've been here before, admit it!" he said.

"Yes, I have. It's a favorite place of mine, I usually pick mushrooms here." Erika climbed out of the car and got out the fleece blanket.

Anders's cell phone started ringing.

"Hello, my little love." Erika heard the anxiety in his voice. "I'll come home, right away... I promise.... Right away.... Twenty minutes at the most." He looked resignedly at Erika.

She smiled bravely at him.

Chapter 18

Maria Wern was immersed in a report from the medical examiner when she got a call from reception to say she had a visitor. Quickly she packed up her papers and logged out of the computer. Sara Wentzel, a pretty but very thin woman of about thirty, was standing with her face turned to the window. When she heard her name and turned around it was clear that she had been crying. The rims of her big eyes were red; she was squinting. From time to time she blew her nose in a tissue she took from her pocket. She carried her big brown purse like a shield as she made her way across the floor. Maria came to meet her, shook her hand and greeted her. Sara's handshake was firm but damp.

"Are you the police who was assaulted? Sorry for asking."

"Yes, it was me. It'll be a while before I look normal again." Maria attempted a smile. Her swollen lips stretched. They climbed the stairs in silence. Once they'd installed themselves in the interview room and Maria had noted down the necessaries, she asked what sort of relationship Sara and Linn had. The answer was rather fumbling.

"We were very close." Her gray eyes met Maria's. There was

something pleading in them, which Maria tried to interpret.

"As close as one can get?" Intuitively, Maria felt her question was justified.

"As close as one can get." It seemed to come as a relief to Sara to be able to talk openly.

"Was Linn intending to move in with you?"

"That's what I was hoping and wishing, more than anything." Sara smoothed her long fair hair out of her eyes. She swallowed a few times and searched for the right words. "Linn was having a hard time making that decision. I tried to push her to make a decision. It was making her feel so bad, keeping it all from Claes. The longer we drew it out, the harder it was for her to sleep and do her work. I gave her an ultimatum just to put an end to the suffering, more for her sake than mine. I could see how much it was hurting her being unfaithful. She took pills and drank red wine just to get to sleep. It worried me."

"What was she going to do?" Maria couldn't help but be impressed by Sara's openness. She clearly wanted to cooperate fully.

"The night she was murdered she told me she was moving in with me. She had made up her mind. But there was a hesitation there, I noticed it. She wasn't her usual self. I suppose she felt frightened and under pressure. But the decision was hers. I don't know what she would really have done… if she would have dared go through with it once Claes came home."

"She called you that night?" According to the telephone log Maria had ordered, the call lasted from 10:16 to 10:22.

"Yes, at about ten o'clock. She always called to say good night. I get worried when I don't hear from her… just want to hear that she's got home all right. She'd.… God, it's all so horrible! I can't understand it; can't cope with the thought of how scared she must have been."

"We don't think she woke up. Most likely she was killed in her sleep."

"She must have taken both sedatives and wine. She wasn't sober, I could hear that right off when she called."

Maria didn't say anything to corroborate her statement. Whether she'd taken the sleeping pills herself or was sedated by someone else was still open to conjecture. "What did you do after you spoke to Linn?"

"I couldn't sleep. It just didn't work. My whole future was hanging on her decision. I loved her."

"Did you stay home the rest of that night? Can someone confirm that?"

"I couldn't sleep, so I got dressed and went down to the sea. After the rain there was a full moon. The wind was blowing in hard and the sea was churning; big breakers coming in. I felt exactly the same inside. I stood there looking at the water, frozen to the bone. It was like I knew... we'd never...."

"Did you meet anyone?"

"No, it was the middle of the night. I just stood there crying and then I went home. I may have dropped off now and then, but basically I never slept properly. My neighbor... she works for you, Erika Lund... may have seen my lights on. I don't know. I tried to reach Linn on her cell phone in the morning before she left for work. But she didn't answer. I tried to get her at the hospital, but they said she hadn't come in; she hadn't even called in sick. That's when I figured she must have decided to stay with him. I thought maybe he'd come home earlier than we thought, maybe she'd told him everything. In other words it wouldn't be a good time to call... I mean if he was already there. If they were in the middle of a crisis maybe she couldn't cope with going to work. I decided to keep my head down and wait for her to get in touch."

"So no one can actually confirm you were at home that night?"

"No. Surely you don't think I...."

"I don't think anything. Do you have a car?"

"No, I don't even have a driver's license."

"Who do you think killed her?"

"Claes, of course. He must have found out and flipped out. He's not usually the type—to fight. He shuts up and plays the martyr."

"And if it wasn't Claes... is there anyone else who wanted to harm her? Anyone you know of, or could imagine?" Claes had shown them his ticket, which indicated that his journey had been paid for. Soon they'd also know if he'd checked in and received his cabin number.

"No one. Everyone liked Linn. Well, maybe not everyone. There were probably some colleagues who thought she was a bit of a goody-goody. You know, if you're too willing to work, it makes some people feel useless and lazy. In a workplace with mainly women, everyone has to be as good as each other, no one's allowed to stand out. It's hardly a reason for murdering someone, though, is it?"

"Who knew you were a couple, or soon to be a couple?"

"Linn told me she thought her boss had his suspicions... he was making insinuations. She said she was going to tell him, because it impacted on her work. A nurse is not allowed to have a relationship with a patient. That's why she stopped working at the hospital, even though she liked working in pharmaceuticals. She was moonlighting over the summer so we'd have money to travel in the autumn. As long as I could stay healthy over the summer there wouldn't be a problem. She was going to appeal to his better nature, so he didn't report her. That's what she said."

"You didn't tell anyone else?"

"I told my father. He understood and accepted it. As long

as it makes you happy, he said. As long as it makes you happy... He was worried that we'd run into homophobic people, and that life would become harder for me if we came out." Maria saw a fit of trembling run through her skinny body. "Of course it's hard. Dad will have to tell Mom. I can't tell her myself."

Maria quickly glanced through her notes. "Had Linn started moving any of her things to you? A laptop, for instance?"

Claes was very troubled by the fact that the police had impounded his computer.

"Nothing. When she came to me she only used to bring a little overnight bag. She never brought her laptop. It was a work computer."

"Another question. Did Linn have a favorite flower? Some flower with a symbolic meaning for her? Do you know?"

Sara looked perplexed. "No, she wasn't actually so very interested in plants or nature or anything like that. She wasn't really an outdoors person at all."

"Her body was found on Tempelkullen. In the Pavilion, as you know. Does that say anything to you? Was it a place she liked to go? Did it mean anything to her?"

"Not as far as I know." Sara wrinkled her face. She couldn't control herself any more. The words gushed out of her explosively. "You have to catch the person who did this. It's got to be some perverse, sick pig."

"I think so, too. One last question; think about this one carefully. Has Linn received any threats because of her sexual orientation? Have you presented yourselves in a way that someone else may interpret as you being a couple?"

"We've been discreet about it. I mean, I hoped and dreamed that one day we'd be able to show everyone we were together. You know, I'm not sure Linn would have told me if she had been receiving threats. She found it difficult opening up and talking about things, it took time. You had to ask the right questions and listen for a long time. She didn't want to worry me or make me afraid. Sometimes I was still the patient she was trying to protect. Do you think this is a hate crime?"

"We have to take a broad view so we don't miss anything."

"Does that mean you don't have any clues about who did this?"

"We have a lot of material. It's difficult to know what's important. That's why everything you can tell us is of the utmost importance. If you think of anything, call me direct at this number." Maria handed over her card and a brochure about the hotline for victims. "If you need someone to talk to."

"Thanks, I have friends... and my father."

"I just thought of something else. Do you know what Linn used to keep in her purse?"

Sara shook her head.

"Try, it's an important question," said Maria.

"I suppose more or less the same as anyone else. A wallet with a couple of hundred kronor, her credit card, cell phone, comb and a mirror. She might have had a lipstick. Maybe. A USB memory stick. I was there when she bought it and we figured out how to use it. That's six months ago, but I know she used to keep it in her purse."

"Do you know what kind of information she saved on it?"

"I never asked, but I think it had something to do with her work."

When Maria was taking Sara Wentzel back to the entrance she ran into Hartman.

"I've asked Per Arvidsson to head up the investigation into the assault. He's back on duty, he'll be interviewing someone in connection with it. We're hoping for a fresh lead. In return we're going to be lenient with him and look the other way from time to time."

"Is he up to it?" Maria doubted whether he'd be able to work much more than part-time. There was a risk he wouldn't have time to do what was required, while at the same time being too proud to admit it.

"I couldn't stop him. I felt there was a lot at stake for him. He went to the mainland this morning. Jesper Ek has a son, Joakim, in Svartsjö Prison. The boy's implied to Ek that he knows something, but he wanted to talk face to face. Per wants to have a word with him, it's possible he knows something about a certain person known as Roy."

Hartman smiled warmly at Maria but his eyes were very serious. "I wish I could stay with the investigation into the assault, but now that we have another murder on our books I just *have to* delegate, however much I'd prefer to handle it myself. You do understand, don't you? There are no witnesses who saw the attack, apart from you. We never tracked down the man who walked past, or anyone else brave enough to come forward. All we have is your description and the name 'Roy' . . . but we can't be sure, it may just be a nickname. The assailant could have some scratches on his body. If so we need to nab him before they heal."

"I'd like to question the jerk myself and do a Columbo, you know what I mean? Anything just to get at the truth."

"Listen, you'd do a fantastic job if it was about anyone else. It just won't wash when you're the victim . . . you know that."

"But Arvidsson? Who takes over if he can't cope with it?"

"I already thought about that. Ek will have to back him up. You're right, Arvidsson is experienced, he's the best option we've got but there's a risk he won't stand up to the pressure. Not quite yet."

Maria tried a smile, but it failed to convince. She felt her hands were tied.

Chapter 19

Erika Lund quickly scanned the report from the medical examiner before meeting the others in the conference room. Haraldsson looked as if he'd slept in his uniform, which seemed likely enough. When he closed his eyes, Ek gave him a jab in the ribs, pushing him against Maria who had a mug of coffee in her hand. She managed to slump back into her chair with her legs apart, avoiding getting the hot liquid in her lap. Hartman's gaze was exacting, as if ordering them all to listen to Erika.

"Linn Bogren had a blood alcohol level of 0.2 and a significant amount of sedatives, the equivalent of about four times the prescribed dose. Not deadly in itself but certainly excessive dosage. The incision in her throat was made with a normal kitchen knife, the same knife that was found under the victim's bed, no fingerprints on it except the victim's own. Possibly they were put there after her death. In other respects it's quite baffling how the crime scene seems to lack any fingerprints. It's clinically clean. The head was severed from the body a few centimeters above the actual cut, then moved to the Botanical Gardens and Tempelkullen. I didn't find any signs of struggle or resistance. Everything points to her having been killed in her sleep. The amount of blood left in the body is also curiously small. She was hung like game; drained of her blood. In the ceiling above the bed is a strong hook holding the fan. I lifted it off and found tiny rope fibers . . ."

"Might we be dealing with a hunter here?" Ek felt a vague sense of nausea after Erika's detailed description of the train of events.

"We don't know for sure, it could be someone who works in an slaughterhouse… or a doctor, someone used to handling a knife. The body must have been transported in something: a sack, a box? I found a piece of a black trash bag on Tempelkullen. There were traces of blood on the plastic. Another quite unusual fact is that we found dog hairs from two different dogs. They were most likely tethered to the banister on the front steps, because there's a prevalence of animal footprints there, in the soft ground. The dogs were by the steps during or after the rain."

"I've checked with Claes Bogren and Sara Wentzel, but neither of them are aware of Linn being visited by a dog owner," Maria interjected. "No one she socializes with. But the neighbor Harry Molin has two dogs, an Alsatian and a Labrador. I'm going to question him immediately."

"Very good." Erika was keen to move on. "I found out from Molin's doctor, Anders Ahlström, that Harry bumped into Linn on Sunday evening last week when she was on her way back from work. She seemed worked up, possibly drunk, reeling and unsteady on her legs. Groggy, that's how he put it. You'll have to clarify that with him. Anyway, we know that later that night he pressed his face against her window to see if she was in. This would certainly frighten anyone. She was a nurse; he wanted to ask for some advice."

"Anders? That doctor you met in the bar?" Maria smiled slightly.

"Yes." Erika looked bothered. Work and one's private life

were two separate worlds and should be kept that way. Maria did not allude to it again.

"It doesn't sound quite normal, seeking out a nurse in the middle of the night unless there's an emergency," Hartman ventured. "I'll come with you, Maria. I don't think you should see him by yourself." Hartman's gaze indicated clearly that he was not going to change his mind on this point. "Whoever killed Linn Bogren was strong enough to carry her body more than five hundred yards up and down a hill. Did one or more people do this? What do you conclude from the footprints you've looked at, Erika?"

"It's meaningless even to speculate about Tempelkullen, after all the trampling around there. But there are a couple of finds by the kitchen door to Linn's house in Specksgränd. Prints from a pair of Riekers men's size 8 ½ , a pair of Adidas men's size 10 ½ , and then a vague footprint, size 10 ½ - 11, we don't know the brand yet."

"I took a closer look at Claes Bogren's alibi and it's a little puzzling." Maria took up her notepad and flicked through the last few pages. "The cargo ship he was enlisted on ran into Gothenburg Harbor twenty-four hours before the date he gave us. But the ticket of his Gotland ferry is correct and the ship was slightly behind schedule, just like he said."

"Did he actually check in or just buy the ticket?" Hartman exchanged a quick glance with Maria.

"He checked in, or at least someone did. They don't check your ID at the ticket desk. But there's no reason why one couldn't swap one's ticket with someone else after the trip. A friend. Or if one finds a used ticket in some trash can. It's a bit far-fetched, but a ticket is not really a one hundred percent definite alibi."

"How did he explain his extra day in Gothenburg?" Ek sat with his legs wide apart looking cagey. He already had a clear idea.

"Just that he couldn't remember. They had a serious storm and sometimes one doesn't wake on the day one thinks... or something like that. But can you really sleep through a whole day? I don't think he looks like he lives that way. He seems quite tidy."

"An extra day means an extra lady, in my world," Ek admitted with candor.

Maria smiled involuntarily. No one was surprised; Ek was the way he was. "That was also my thinking and I suggested as much, but Claes denied it. I suppose we have to assume he feels guilty about it. It'll come out in the wash, it's not the last time I'll be interviewing him. Anyway, his shoe size is 44, so those Adidas shoes could be his. I'll tell him to hand in his shoes to the forensic division."

"Were there any results from knocking on doors in the area?" Hartman looked at Haraldsson and Ek. Haraldsson seemed deep in his own thoughts, and Ek responded first.

"Not a lot. Most of them were asleep. We haven't managed to get hold of the closest neighbor, Harry Molin, I mean the one with the dogs. No one opens the door and the telephone's been disconnected. Per Arvidsson lives diagonally across the street and he didn't see anything unusual, either. Linn popped in briefly to see him the evening before she died. I didn't quite understand the reason for it."

Haraldsson stretched his back. He always found it difficult sitting still for a long time. He needed to move, and this meeting looked like it might be a long one. "Yeah, she borrowed his computer. Had to pay for some ticket for an overseas trip."

"That's right. It was almost half past ten. He didn't feel like letting her in. But she was very insistent. I suppose you would be if you had to book a trip."

"Do we know where and with who she was going to travel?" Hartman glared at Haraldsson, who'd sunk into his chair and stretched out his legs across the floor.

"She didn't mention anything about that to Arvidsson. We've asked him to hand in his computer. He'll bring it in when he comes back to Gotland tonight."

"Anything else before we wrap up this meeting?" Hartman had a vague recollection of having seen a woman in reception who'd been asking for Maria Wern. He mentioned this to the others.

"Jill Andersson. She absolutely wanted to talk to you, Maria. I said she'd have to wait until after the meeting. Can you deal with it? She lives in Tranhusgatan above the Botanical Gardens. How the hell could I forget to mention it?" Ek glanced at his watch. "I hope she's still there."

"If we can finish this now I'll get on to it right away." Maria was already half out of her chair as she said it. She didn't wait for an answer.

Chapter 20

Jill Andersson was a woman in her forties with the body of a teenager. She was sportily dressed, with big gold rings in her ears and her dark hair tied up in a vertical, multi-colored pigtail that swayed as she walked with a light, bouncy gait down the corridor.

"You wanted to talk to me," said Maria once they'd sat down on either side of the desk. "I got the idea it was urgent."

At once, Jill looked both startled and serious. She stumbled over her words when she described why she was there. "I wanted to take back what I said before, to the other police. The whole thing was so sudden and I didn't have time to think about it. I really didn't see anything important, nothing at all. It just seems silly now."

"You said you saw a man carrying a sack. On the night of Linn Bogren's murder in her home, not far from where you live. You said it was just past four in the morning."

"Yes, but I want to take that back now. It's just something I blurted out. I don't know where I got it from. Probably I mistook the day. Thought it was the weekend, and anyway I'm not sure it was a sack at all. It could have been anything."

"You're not accused of anything, Jill. In the earlier interview, where you were questioned just for our information, you said there was a man who wore a hood over his face."

"Yeah but that was wrong. I probably got a bit flighty and I kind of added a few things I didn't actually see. You know, you see a lot of that on the TV and before you know it your imagination is running away with you."

Maria watched and waited. Jill rubbed her nose and her gaze darted round the room without meeting Maria's eyes. Her hands were clamped to the handle of her handbag, a cheap Gucci copy.

"If anyone threatened you, Jill… ?"

"No." The answer came rapidly, before Maria had even had time to finish the question.

"We can withhold your identity. You can leave us an anonymous tip. Did you see anything that night?"

"I don't remember, I said. I'm getting the days mixed up." The fear in her light-blue eyes built up, and she blinked emphatically to hold back the tears.

"You know, I think you told the truth the first time." Maria leaned in closer, so that Jill could not avoid looking into her eyes. "I think you saw what you described to us, and that you regretted what you told us because you're scared something terrible is going to happen to you if you do tell us."

"No! Did you hear what I said? I didn't see anything." Her voice sounded like the scream of a bird. Involuntarily Maria pulled back, then regained control of herself. She stayed where she was, leaning back and waiting.

"There could be many reasons for not talking to us," Maria carried on calmly. "Someone could have told you to keep quiet. Someone who's threatened to harm you, or someone you know who you want to protect."

"I don't remember, is that so bloody hard to understand?"

"It could also be because you didn't want to be seen at that hour. Maybe you were sneaking home after meeting a lover.…"

"That's the dumbest thing I ever heard. I don't need to sneak around, I'm single, I can have sex with anyone I want! I just pick up the phone and make a date. There are still quite a few I can choose from."

"Congratulations—how very enviable. What were you doing out at four in the morning, Jill? It must have been something? What's your line of work?"

"I don't work. I'm on sick leave."

"Why are you on sick leave?" The atmosphere in the room was growing more and more loaded. Maria was convinced now. This was where the problem lay. At first, Jill had candidly told them the truth and then once she'd had time to think about it, she'd realized what the consequences would be if it came to the attention of the Department of Social Security.

"My back, but they can't find anything. I get new doctors all the time but no one does anything." She paused briefly. "I couldn't stay in bed, my back was hurting. I had to move, so I went outside."

"This Monday morning at four o'clock?"

"Yes… no, another morning."

"You wouldn't by any chance have a night job you go to, a cleaning job?" Maria saw her facial expression change at once. The woman's cheeks grew very flushed, and her voice was no longer quite as sharp when she said: "How else do you expect me to manage as a single mother? How else can I afford to give my children what other people's children have just like that? New cell phones, computers, flat-screen TV. Trips abroad. How the hell am I supposed to afford all that, do you think? My husband died. We had no insurance policies. Suddenly his income was just gone.

If he'd met someone new and left me and the children, we'd have his child support to live on, at least. But the way it is now, it's just so goddamn terrible. Not a month goes by when we break even. If I have to go to the dentist I can't afford to let the children go on a school trip. Are you going to report me?"

"I'm only interested in what you saw. So in fact it's true, what you said to the police?"

"Yes, I clean at nights and I was on my way home. I'd just passed the Catholic Church. The man with the sack came from behind and passed me. He turned off Vattugränd, down toward the Botanical Gardens."

"Did you see his face?" Maria shivered. If the man with the sack was the murderer… if there were an eyewitness, the investigation would be on a completely different level.

"Not really. He was taller than me. 6'2", perhaps. His face was thin, not round, anyway. He was quite skinny. Smelled of tobacco. I couldn't see the color of his eyes. I sort of didn't dare look at him."

"I'd like you to sit down with an artist and try to produce as clear a picture of him as you can."

"Now? I don't have time. I have to pick up the kids from the youth center and run them down to the soccer field and we have to have time to eat. It's not going to work."

"Can I send an artist over to you later tonight, after they've gone to bed? I can understand it's hard for you to fit everything in, believe me."

"I remember something else." Jill met Maria's gaze with new focus. "He had a funny walk. Clumsy, sort of legs far apart. Hard to explain. He might have been drunk. Or walking in his sleep, sort of thing. My father used to walk in his sleep. It actually looked like that."

Maria went back to the others in the conference room and gave an account of Jill's testimony. During their interval, Haraldsson had also had time to check a few things over the telephone.

"Just because someone passes by with a sack on his back doesn't necessarily mean he's our man. We can only hope. I'd like to get some more leads in." Hartman massaged his gray temples. "Why is everything so quiet?! The streets can hardly have been deserted. Not everyone sleeps at night, people get up and go to the bathroom and look out of the window. Someone else must have seen him."

"Have you checked up on Claes's statement? Do we know for sure when he arrived in Visby?" Most murders are committed by someone who knows the victim well. Claes's booze-up in Gothenburg followed by the memory lapse was, without a doubt, weighing on Hartman, Maria thought.

"Ek was right. There was a lady in Gothenburg. She's made a statement under oath that Claes spent the night with her. He was unfaithful on the night his wife was murdered." Haraldsson sighed deeply. "Poor man. I contacted the captain on his ship. He told me the truth because he thought it was a disgrace. He even knew the lady's name. It's been going on for a while."

"Does he have someone to turn to for support, in case his remorse gets too much for him?" Maria saw his face before her, the way it looked in the morgue. How would he avoid self-loathing after his wife's murder? On the other hand, if he'd been at home he might not have survived either. "What does he have to say about it himself? Have you spoken to him?"

Ek nodded. "He confirmed what the captain said was accurate. When Claes called his wife at night he was in the other lady's bathroom. A rare moment of bad conscience."

"Does he have any theories himself about who might

have killed Linn?" Hartman asked. "He must have thought about it a good deal."

"He says he can't understand who would have wanted to do Linn any harm. She had no enemies. Everyone liked her. Her colleagues may have felt she was slightly too ambitious. Her patients loved her, the manager at the medical clinic only had good things to say about her. She wasn't particularly wealthy, but what she did have will go to Claes. There's a life assurance policy of about a million kronor, so he can keep the house. I don't know what conclusions we should draw." Maria immersed herself in her own thoughts. The ritual aspects of the murder were one of the most curious things she had ever seen. A murderer who was not in a hurry. Someone who wanted to create an exhibition, an almost artistic decoration of the body. Out of love, or hate?

"Was it someone who loved her... too much?" Erika remembered the way the body had lain there in the Pavilion on Tempelkullen. Love and... fury. Could it have been Sara Wentzel? "We don't know if Linn changed her mind at the last moment and decided to stay with Claes, nor are we likely ever to know. The only thing we actually do know is that Sara and Linn spoke on the night she was murdered. But we only have Sara's version of the conversation."

"You think it was her?" Hartman frowned and chewed the end of his pencil. "That doesn't jive very well with a tall man of about 6'2" carrying a heavy sack. The woman is quite frail."

Maria agreed, but nonetheless she wanted to pursue her line of thought to its conclusion. "Sara has no alibi. She was at home by herself. She answered her cell phone and could have been anywhere. At about 23:00 she went for a short walk and then watched television until midnight, but she's had trouble describing what she actually watched. News, weather? It seems to have just slipped her mind. Either she was very upset or tired or her thoughts were elsewhere or she wasn't watching television at all."

"I live next door to her in Lummelunda," said Erika. "But I can't remember if I saw her lights on or not."

"Then we have the neighbor, Harry Molin. We've been trying to reach him today, but he doesn't answer the telephone," said Ek. "I've been there knocking on his door, but no one opens and when I asked the neighbors they don't have a clue about his whereabouts. He usually takes his dogs out several times per day. He's retired, took early retirement because of illness. I heard a dog growling but no one opened the door."

Erika could imagine Harry the way Anders had described him. Friendly but a bit of a nuisance. Hardly some roughneck butcher type.

"Well he hasn't gone away, then. Who keeps an eye on the dogs, who feeds them when he's away?"

"We asked the neighbors about that, and apparently Per Arvidsson usually helps him out. I just had him on the line but the reception was bad. He's at sea so we can't reach him right now; on the ferry to the mainland. Per's on his way to Svartsjö Prison, that's all I can say. He's working full time on the assault and murder case." Ek glanced at Maria to see how she reacted. Maria had insinuated that they should press for more resources. If the police don't solve this case I won't be answerable for what Linus's father will do, she'd said. Ek knew that the investigation was on course, that everything that could be done *was* being done. But Maria, as a plaintiff, had to be kept out of the investigation.

"And if Per doesn't know anything about Harry Molin, what do we do then?" asked Maria as she turned to her boss.

"Then we'll have to get a locksmith to let us into the house, so we can check if he's there."

Maria felt her unease like a cold draft from a fan. It was

too easy letting one's imagination run amok. When a murder's taken place, evil seems to lurk in every alley.

"But he must go back home soon. He has to think about his dogs," said Hartman.

He leaned back and lit a cigarette. The smoke stung his eyes. He squinted at the computer monitor. He had to try and get into the police register and read the interview reports. What had Jill Andersson said about him? She never saw his face, he was sure of that. He'd watched her making her way home after the police interview. He knew who she was and that she lived on her own with three young children. He'd actually toyed with the thought of borrowing the little boy with the close-cropped hair for a few hours, and teach him to sit still. They'd exchanged a few words outside the nursery. The kid was a real little piece of shit. Cheeky and full of himself. It would have been a real pleasure scaring the hell out of him, and hearing him call for help when there was no help to be had. To see that cocky exterior broken down into helpless terror. There was an irresistible feeling of lust in those thoughts. This lust had made him increasingly bloodthirsty with his victims. But for now, pleasure had to wait. He was missing a personal password to crack MajorTwo, the police's computerized case system.

Chapter 21

P er Arvidsson sat in the aft saloon on the Gotland ferry, hiding behind his newspaper. He didn't have the energy to run into some acquaintance. Not now. He had to think and at best have a nap. The school trips were over for the season, but a noisy girls' soccer team with a portable CD player filled the airspace in the saloon with the Smurfs Greatest Hits. Well-known songs, performed in Smurf voices. It was unbearable. The girls shrieked and giggled at trivialities, like teens from an American TV show. Oh-my-God! Their coach was probably so hardened to it all he didn't even notice how much they were disturbing those who were trying to get a bit of shut-eye.

Rebecka had called late last night, crying and asking if he could take the children. She needed a bit of time for herself. Her new love had left her. Things had been difficult between them for a while. She hadn't mentioned it to Per before, she hadn't wanted to bother him with it. It was strange, how little their separation had affected him. She'd been unfaithful with someone else and now, in turn, she'd been deceived herself. If he'd had a bit more energy, he should really have derived some malicious pleasure from it. Instead he simply explained he had a job to get on with, something that couldn't wait. She cried and pleaded but he stuck to his guns, feeling like a big shit. He would have liked to explain that it was all about catching someone who had killed a thirteen-year-old boy and exposed Maria Wern to a possible HIV infection. The question is whether Rebecka would have found the argument convincing, now that her own interest hung in the balance.

After taking a few wrong turns on the way to Ekerö, Per Arvidsson could see Svartsjö Prison up ahead. It was an open facility, where Jesper Ek's son was serving his sentence for assault. Recently there had been a TB scare there, but presumably they had gotten it under control, or they wouldn't have allowed visitors. He'd chosen to introduce himself as a good friend, not a policeman. You could never be sure who might talk, and under no circumstances did Arvidsson want Joakim to feel threatened and thus unwilling to talk.

The white cafeteria building with its integrated solar panels was eye-catching; it looked more like a school than a prison. Joakim had agreed to the meeting on the condition that they meet outside. He didn't want the other prisoners to get a closer look at his face. Arvidsson could understand this perfectly. It had surprised him when his colleague, Ek, had told him that his son might be able to throw some light on the investigation. Joakim had met Maria Wern before and he'd developed a weak spot for her. Per couldn't blame him for that. It was impossible not to be affected by that woman. Joakim was livid when he read in the newspaper that she'd been stabbed with a blood-filled syringe. Now they had to take advantage while his anger was still fresh.

Joakim was waiting for him outside, in the road. Per Arvidsson parked his car and stepped out. They shook hands and started walking in silence. The sun bore down hard on them and the newly-mown hay smelled of timothy grass.

"How are things going for you, have you settled in here?" Per glanced quickly at him. Joakim looked tense. Maybe he was already regretting his offer.

"If you like chopping wood and mucking out pig shit— God the fucking stink!—then it's a pretty decent place. I guess the biggest advantage is you get a fixed income, food, and a roof over your head. I never had that before. For the first time in my life I don't have to worry about a thing. And if some junkie starts playing up, it's not my problem, it's up to someone else to deal with it."

"Your dad said you were studying," Per said, turning to Joakim with an avuncular smile on his face. It was important to establish an understanding before moving on to more important questions. Joakim's facial expression shifted at once. The whole question of studies was probably a sensitive area. The young man mumbled something about re-taking tests in the morning. His eyes filled with timidity. Per felt embarrassed for him, and didn't quite know how to continue. They walked side by side in silence for a while, until Joakim suddenly stopped and changed direction.

"Let's take a different route. There's someone coming." He flicked his dark curls away from his face and poked Arvidsson in the side. "It's a couple of guys I know, they can't see me."

"Your father said you might know something about the person who assaulted Maria Wern and the thirteen-year-old boy. Someone called Roy or something like that. I've brought all the school yearbooks from Visby that I could find.... Do you think you can point him out if he's there?"

"Sorry, I never met him. I've just heard rumors. It was a couple of guys I had a beer with in Visby Harbor. You know, it can take six months before you get to serve your sentence.

It was pretzels and beer, you know. I was pretty drunk so I can't remember everything. They were with the idiot and they were bragging about what he'd done. I don't know who they were. He's a fucking lunatic." Joakim hesitated. "I got the impression he's only there in the summers. Everyone's scared of him. He's a psycho, he'll do anything, he's got no boundaries, you know. He doesn't do stuff 'cause he gets angry, he does it because he enjoys torturing other people. He's like ice, you know. Fucking ice-cold."

"Do you know what his real name is?" Per almost didn't dare interrupt once Joakim had actually started talking.

"No. And I can't ask the right people about it, either. They'll figure out what I'm doing and then I'm dead. Do you get how easy it would be finding me here? What do you think would happen to me if he knew?"

"Is there anything else you can give me? What else did they say?"

Joakim thought about it. He faltered for a second, then said: "They told me he'd scammed money out of people. He used to work from an Internet café. Pretended he was like various women selling nude photos of themselves for 300 kronor. To get paid he asked for the suckers' social security numbers and then got them to punch in some numbers on the little keypad you get from the bank, and then they had to tell him what numbers came up after the encryption. That way he could figure out how the keypads were programmed and empty their accounts. I reckon most people wouldn't even report him. They said he made himself more than two million kronor that way."

"An intelligent young man. And dangerous. Can you think of anything else? Everything you remember is important."

"There was another really sick thing but I don't know if it's true. They said he killed some old bum with a lawn mower blade. Swish, swish, like a Samurai sword." Joakim illustrated with expansive arm movements. "There's rumors about it. But no one knows for sure if it was him. They couldn't ever prove anything. But the guys I met in the harbor told me that this old wino had told Roy he fucked his mom, said she was a junkie hooker who did anything for money."

"Do you know who that man was?" Per felt the cold sweat breaking through. So close now... so close to a name or a connection that could be identified, so they could arrest the bastard.

"No idea. I'm not even sure the police took his name."

"Did you get the impression that Roy's mother was dead?"

"No, one of them had met her. He knew who she was."

"Do you know when that was?" Arvidson halted so that the sound of his steps wouldn't stop him hearing every word.

"Don't know." Joakim twisted uneasily. "I don't even know when he knocked out the wino, or where the old man was murdered.... I was drunk, it was dark. The way the guys were talking they were from the mainland. Sorry... that's all I've got." He stopped. "How things with Dad, then?"

"He's feeling as good as he deserves. All right, I suppose. A bit of time on the sidelines did him good, I reckon. He's pleased to be back on the job."

"That was all my fucking fault, wasn't it? They thought he was gonna squeal to me while the investigation was under way. He came to see me. But shit, it wasn't easy thinking of anything to say...."

"He desperately wants what's best for you, you know that, don't you?"

Joakim turned his face away.

"I haven't got any more time for you now. I have to clean out the pellets boiler. So give my best to dad then."

"You heat the place with wood pellets?"

"Oh shit, yeah. We're environmentally friendly."

"Hold on a second, I want to show you something." Per had brought the artist's impressions of Roy and the others, based on Maria's descriptions. He took them out of the glove compartment. There were various versions. She hadn't been able to remember so clearly, and the fragments she'd managed to hold on to had grown increasingly indistinct as time passed. But she remembered the body types and postures; the facial shapes could be seen even with the hoods, she'd said. It was remarkable the way the brain shut itself down if something seemed too unpleasant.

"Do you recognize them?" Per held out the drawing. It had been published that morning in the newspaper, so far without any results. Joakim quickly glanced at it from the side.

"Not the tall one. Is that Roy? But the other two could be the guys I spoke to."

Per Arvidsson got back into the car and tried to structure what he'd heard. Maria had said the other two men had spoken as if they came from Västerås, with heavily pronounced "l" sounds. As soon as Arvidsson was back on the road he called Hartman and told him what had come out of the conversation with Joakim.

"A lawn mower blade is an unusual murder weapon. We should be able to dig up some information on it, right?"

"We'll work on it," said Hartman. "And we're looking for your neighbor, Harry Molin. Do you know where he is, was he about to go away? I mean, when he does you're the one who waters his plants and collects his mail, right?"

"I have a few times. But not now. Why do you need to get hold of him? Is it something to do with the murder of Linn Bogren?"

"Exactly. He's been on the murder scene with his dogs and we need to know when. We'd like to interview him just for our own information."

"I don't know him so well. He's not the type to make himself conspicuous. Always at home, walking his dogs, a bit needy for company but never gets personal. I guess he has a lonely life. He always talks about his ailments, asks if you know this or that doctor. Because I've also been on sick leave he may feel a sort of fraternal bond with me." Per laughed drily. "He wants to make a sort of blacklist of mistakes being made in the healthcare field, a homepage where healthcare staff would be named and patients could rate them. These reports would be sent regularly to the Department of Health."

"Sounds like a full-time job."

"Probably is, for him. How are things with Maria?" Per regretted the question as soon as he'd spoken the words. He couldn't understand his own reaction: he loved her after all, didn't he? Yet it was too much; he couldn't bear her vulnerability, her fear after what had happened. It worried him that he had become the sort of person who had to turn off other people's misery in order to cope with his own.

"She's steeling herself, fighting it, and trying to think as little as possible about the possibility of being infected. It must be hell for her. It'll be another two months before they can give her preliminary confirmation."

"We'll get him."

"I wish we could put more resources into it. I'm doing everything in my power to get some reinforcements from the mainland. But it hasn't been easy, given that we can't find more witnesses. We haven't had very much to go on. Maybe things will loosen up now if this new lead gives us something."

"You can count on me full time."

"Full time doesn't mean 24 hours a day, Per." Hartman felt relieved and worried at the same time. "As long as you know where the boundaries are. We don't want to lose you again."

"I'll take care of my shit, you take care of yours." His irritation came crashing down like a bolt of lightning. Just because you've been ill doesn't mean people can treat you like a child, or think they have an inalienable right to stick their noses in and tell you how to live your life.

Chapter 22

The dog food had run out. Mirabel stared at Harry Molin with her big brown eyes and whined insistently. Gordon kept quiet, but he stared at him. As quietly as he could and without turning on the ceiling light, Harry sneaked into the cellar to take a piece of frozen meat out of the freezer. This would be his dinner; he'd share it with the dogs. He put a blanket over the microwave oven to stop the light seeping out. The "pling" when the meat had thawed seemed ear-shattering in the silence.

The police had come ringing his doorbell. They suspected him. He'd sat on the floor so he couldn't be seen from the window, and did his best to shut up the dogs. Unsuccessfully, as it turned out. Mirabel had growled. Now they must know he was somewhere in the vicinity, that he'd be back. He couldn't leave his animals just like that. They had to be taken for walks. Mirabel had been pacing anxiously between where he was sitting on the kitchen floor and the front door. Even Gordon was starting to get impatient for a pee. It was almost dark now outside. If he waited another hour. Time inched forward like a snail. Most police worked normal office hours. The risk of them coming late at night was negligible, if one thought about it logically.

Today Harry had missed his appointment at the health center for the first time ever. Doctor Ahlström was probably very happy about it. He was probably getting tired of all the running about, just like all the other doctors. They didn't understand the gravity of the situation. For several nights in a row Harry had been having heart palpitations. His pulse increased gradually as he checked it, until, at one point, he came close to taking a taxi to the emergency room. Instead he moved to the computer, surfing fairly aimlessly through various pages on health and healthcare. He found something that the doctor might be well advised to read. Those pills Anders Ahlström took for his cigarette cravings were liable to make you crazy, according to a report from Japan. One Japanese man had gone sleepwalking and ended up under a train, another had gone out in the nude and sawed down a tree in a park. Harry would inform the doctor of this; he would surely be grateful—very grateful—and understand that Harry was in fact a good person, a considerate human being and not the self-centered egoist the doctor took him for.

Similarly, he had helped Linn find the optimum sleeping pills, with the least possible side effects. And Linus, the boy he'd run into in the waiting room at the health center—the one who was assaulted later with that woman constable… and killed—he'd also given him some good advice. Or rather his mother. If one had constant throat infections one might have to have one's tonsils removed. But of course there were some health products one could try first. He was a nice boy. Doctor Ahlström thought so, too. They even used to do a bit of shadow boxing, and once or twice Ahlström even gave the boy a bear-hug, which almost made them look like father and son. Once when

Linus was walking down the corridor in the health center, his legs wide apart like a cowboy with his hands on his pretend holsters and doctor Ahlström came out of his room with a pile of papers in his arms, Linus cried out: "Draw!" And then the doctor dropped all his papers and drew his pretend guns, quick as a flash and without a trace of hesitation. That kind of presence of mind creates a lot of respect. Afterwards they helped each other pick up the medical documents and prescriptions. Some of the patients probably thought the doctor was behaving irresponsibly, but Harry couldn't stop an inadvertent smile. Now the boy was dead. How unbelievably cruel life could be.

Harry put his dogs on their leashes and went out into the night. For some unknown reason the streetlights weren't working. It had been like that for a few weeks now. There hadn't been any lights since the night he'd found Linn all groggy and drunk outside her house after a night of binging. The odd thing about it was she didn't smell like booze. Now when he thought about it he realized he might have been mistaken. Maybe she had drugged herself with something else? There's so much available these days. Those three men she was with had just left her like that, in a vulnerable state. The age of chivalry was over, today's youth had no notion of how to behave like gentlemen. Of course, he could understand that she had a lot of unwanted attention while her husband was away on a trip. All three men had cleared out as soon as he arrived on the scene. They hadn't even helped her inside.

It said in the newspaper that Linn Bogren's body was found in the Pavilion on Tempelkullen in the Botanical Gardens. Harry usually read the news online first thing in the morning, and then he checked every hour to see if anything else had happened. Claes had already been questioned, then left the police station. The police had not caught any suspect. It was very alarming. The murderer was still on the loose and in a way Harry had protected him (or them) by cleaning away every possible lead in Linn's house. Out of fear. What would happen if the police thought it was him who'd done it? How could one ever exonerate oneself from the guilt and shame? They would take him to the police station. People would see him and recognize him. The newspapers would probably be there and even if he covered his head with his jacket they'd probably have time to get a photo, which would then be slapped across the front page of every newspaper in the country. There will always be those who remember a face and a name, without necessarily getting their facts right. Even if all charges are dropped it doesn't necessarily make things better. One's name and photo will always be associated with the terrible thing that's happened. Linn was dead and he tried to tell himself it wouldn't help even if he did speak to the police.

The dogs couldn't get outside quick enough. They tugged at their leads as if their lives depended on it. They pulled him down toward the Ordnance Tower and out through Fiskarporten. The moon glittered on the black water. The wind was gusting hard, throwing cascades of white foam over the pebbles and concrete edging. The sound of the waves drowned out every other sound. The dogs stayed close at his side now. Gordon growled deep in his throat. Someone was standing at the edge of the wall, watching him. The shadow of the figure melted into the darkness alongside the city wall. Had it not been for the dogs' reactions he'd have thought his imagination was playing a trick on him. And even though he couldn't see the man's face there was something familiar about his posture. He couldn't quite remember where he'd seen him. It was like it happens sometimes when we dream, when the familiar is mixed with symbols we can't quite understand. Maybe the most frightening thing of all is when things that are well known to us change their form and become unpredictable. Harry felt his anxiety crawling under his skin, and he tightened his grip on the dogs' leads. If he'd been alone he'd have spun around and run for his life. He didn't quite know why, but something felt very unpleasant. Possibly it was because he was close to the place where Linn's body had been found. Because he had the dogs, he still had the nerve to go up the hill toward the wall. The shadow had disappeared. Harry looked round, turned and twisted in every conceivable direction. But there was no one on the road. If it had not all been a figment of his imagination—if there actually were someone standing there watching him by the wall—by now he had disappeared into the Botanical Gardens, into the leafy shade under the trees. Harry had no intention of going in there. He chose to go home via Studentallén inside the city wall and then up Fiskargränd. As long as he had the dogs with him, he wasn't so afraid. If someone met him in the narrow lane and attacked him, his dogs would never let him down.

"That's the big difference between dogs and human beings," he said to Gordon. "A dog never lets you down. Women do, though." Harry had long since given up the thought of living with someone he could trust. It was just humiliating to hope and believe and then be disappointed and turn into a figure of general hilarity. Lately he'd sometimes been tempted by the idea of trying some Internet dating. He'd even exchanged a few words with one or two Internet ladies, but the ones online were just as fraudulent as real-life women. Just when you started believing that it was "us"—when you'd attained a sort of togetherness and confidence that seemed to preclude the others, you had a creeping suspicion that she wrote in just the same way to everyone else; that she hadn't stopped dating others, or might even be married. Was this the reason why Linn was murdered? Did she meet someone on the Internet? He'd seen the blue light of the computer through her French blinds at night. She'd been up to something in there. Of course it was up to the police to find out, but he wouldn't be surprised. Someone she'd enticed and toyed with, then deceived. Something to keep her occupied while that husband of hers was at sea. A game she'd thought she could easily step out of. Had she given him her real name, or some hint about where she lived, or had they perhaps met in secret?

Harry stood stationary in front of her house. A curious feeling welled up inside him, turning into tears. It was almost as if he were punishing her, in his thoughts, while at the same time taking the blame himself, the blame for what she had done. He didn't want her disgraced—didn't want them to find something shameful to hold up to public scrutiny. It mustn't happen. She'd been such a good-hearted little thing, warm and generous. Quite honestly he'd been quite taken with her. Her big, cheerful head of hair bouncing as she walked along. Her generous figure, which she wasn't ashamed of, and her red, well-formed mouth. She'd never been stingy about the time she gave other people, either; like so many others are, unless they see some personal benefit in talking to someone. She was always friendly to everyone. While this may have been an attribute of her profession, it was quite an achievement to keep it up even when she wasn't working.

Reluctantly, the dogs allowed themselves to be ushered inside. He unclipped their leashes and in that moment remembered that he'd forgotten to pick up the mail. He hadn't dared leave the house all day. He opened the front door. Gordon growled. When he tried to squeeze past and get outside, Harry grabbed the dog by its collar and lifted him back into the hall. The dog barked. Mirabel pricked up her ears and joined in. Harry felt tired and irritated.

"Shush! Shush, I said. Lie down. Do as I say. Down!"

Gordon glared at him. His black eyes gleamed in the darkness of the hall. Harry closed the door. The dogs carried on barking. They never usually carried on like this. Most likely they were reacting to each other.

Only once Harry was standing by his mailbox and had taken out the pile of letters with one hand while holding the lid open with the other did he notice the man in the garden. He was wearing an ankle-length, hooded cape and standing under the knotted branches of the pear tree. It was so absurd and strange that at first Harry was not frightened, only filled with amazement. He watched as the man slowly made his way forward with an awkward gait. He was expecting an explanation. Most likely he was drunk.

"You've probably taken a wrong turn," said Harry when the stranger still didn't say anything. Maybe this one was getting into the swing of the Medieval Week Masquerade a little early? "This is a private garden," he said, adding: "I live here."

Still the man did not answer. The deep hood kept his face hidden. Only the eyes could be made out in there, in the darkness. Suddenly the situation felt threatening.

"Who are you and what do you want?" said Harry, mentally trying to gauge the distance to the front door. Would he be able to reach it in time and let out the dogs—that is, if the man wanted trouble? It was doubtful. His body suddenly felt stiff and powerless. Probably one had to assume this fellow was here for some trivial reason, in which case Harry would make himself look rather foolish if he suddenly whizzed toward to the door like a startled rat. "Can I do anything for you? Are you looking for someone?" The man fixed him with his eyes and stood as if transfixed. Gordon barked inside the house. A row of white teeth glittered from within the darkness of the hood. Harry had time to see the reflection of moonlight in his dark eyes. There was a solid weapon in his hands, a club or an iron bar. Panic woke Harry out of his paralysis. He measured the distance to the door again and decided to make for the street. His voice seemed to turn into an inhuman croak. The dogs wailed and screamed inside the door. The cobbles of the street flashed under his feet. He stumbled, then felt a heavy hand on his shoulder and wiry fingers enclosing his throat. He fought back with all the strength he had. Tried to twist toward the man so he could hit or kick him, and maybe catch a glimpse of his face. Air. His throat hurt. He must get some air. Harry tugged and pulled at the other's hands, but his kick missed its aim and he collapsed with his face hitting the cobbles squarely. There was a crunching sound, but he didn't hear it, because the roaring sound in his head was louder than anything that was or had ever been, and nothing else would ever come except for that roaring, and when it grew silent there would never be anything else....

Chapter 23

There were more people than usual on the Gotland ferry. The jostling on the stairs was irritating and Arvidsson was among the last to drive off the ship after a choppy crossing. If he hadn't managed to get lost on the way back he would have had time to catch the earlier ferry. Now it was past midnight and his body ached with tiredness. It had never been like this before. Before he was shot he'd been able to stay up into the small hours without needing to sleep in the next day. Now he knew very clearly where the boundaries lay. Reluctantly he was often forced to conserve his energy. It was predictable. Tomorrow he would not be getting out of bed before lunchtime, however much he needed to. He hated not being the master of his own body, no longer being in full control. All he could do was accept the situation and make the most of it.

Rebecka had called again while he was waiting in the line for the ferry. She'd been trying to reach him all evening, but his phone had been turned off. She was desperately sad. He did his best to console her, even though her complaints turned his stomach; tried to calm her down and wind things up, but there was no stopping her.

"Can't you come over tomorrow after work and have supper with me and the children?" She'd sounded so pathetic that he ended up giving way to her, even though he wasn't sure he'd be up to it. Her voice was soft and charming. "I really would love you to come. You don't have to do anything except be with them. They miss you so much."

He promised he would. As he sat there in his loneliness in the line, his memories rose up in him. How he'd met Rebecka for the first time at Örebro Central Station. It felt like a lifetime ago. She'd been a vision as beautiful as the girl on the raisin packages, with long undulating hair and big dark-blue eyes. He'd been absolutely infatuated with her. But the secrecy, at first so enticing, hid a deep crevice which he could never even have guessed at. She'd been married and was living under protected identity, on the run from a man who wanted to harm her. Before he'd realized the scale of the problem she was carrying his child under her heart. From that moment they were linked together forever. One can never undo one's children. They had another child and at that precise moment, when it looked as if they could live like a normal family, he ran into Maria Wern again. Maria, whom he had loved so utterly ever since she first appeared as an intern, working alongside him with energy and enthusiasm. She'd been unhappily married at the time but refused to walk out on it. For the children's sake. He'd understood her. When they met again that summer on Gotland, she had just separated from her husband, in spite of all her earlier good intentions about salvaging the marriage. It was a tremendous reunion. They were drawn to each other with a force that could not be resisted, after so many years of longing. Torn between his love for Maria and his bad conscience, he had nonetheless been willing to finish it all so he could live with Maria. When he spoke to Rebecka about it, it turned out she had also been seeing someone else. It had been going on for six months behind his back. And that was the awful truth of it. They spoke a lot about it at the time. Rebecka explained that she'd never had the nerve to stake everything on one horse; had never been able to love just one man. Her instinct was always to spread the risk so she did not run the risk of falling to pieces if things went wrong. That had been her explanation and he'd been unable to do anything but pity her. And now Rebecka's new lover had made himself scarce and Rebecka, self-assured and proud Rebecka, had turned into a deserted child. A snuffling, snotty-nosed child, he thought to himself, and wanted to push the thought of her away. The only thing he wanted in his life right now was to go home and sleep. His eyes were smarting with tiredness and filling up with tears; he had to rub them even to see the road. He passed Wisby Strand and parked the car by the Ordnance Tower. The waves were slapping hard against the concrete spit. For an instant he thought he could hear a woman's voice beyond the booming sound, screaming. He walked up to the edge and looked out over the black water. It's so easy to imagine things. The myth of the bride that drowned and exacted her revenge on her lover was deeply fixed in human consciousness, and in many ways it was true. Innumerable people through time had been sucked into the undertow and drowned. Their voices are magnified in storms, and in the fury of the waves they seem to be protesting about the unfair brevity of their lives.

Per stood there looking out at the reflected moonlight on the water, constantly breaking up in new mirrors. It was beautiful and dramatic. At the same time it was so desolate. He did not want to go home to the loneliness. Right now he longed for a warm embrace filled with unconditional love. It was almost as if he stood face-to-face with death. And as if Death had asked him: *Are you having any pleasure in your life? Time is running through your fingers and you dither, you stumble along irresolutely without loving, without feeling anything but self-pity. Maybe I should exchange you for one of the unfortunate ones, those who were robbed of their lives while they still had the will to love.* Per shook off the unpleasant thought. At that precise moment Rebecka called again.

"Wilma's got laryngitis again. Her temperature's 103.1 degrees."

"How bad is it—do you need to go to the hospital?"

"I don't know. Maybe. It'll be really tricky waking up Tomas and bringing him, but I can't leave him here by himself. Can you come?" She didn't start crying this time. There was a calm, soft appeal in her voice and he promised. He was already regretting it by the time he was setting off in the car. But a promise is a promise.

Per went directly into the nursery to see how his girl was doing. He leaned forward in the dark, listening to her breathing. Wilma was sleeping calmly and deeply in her own bed. He felt her forehead, which was cool. Then turned with some puzzlement towards Rebecka.

"Things have calmed down. I gave her some ibuprofen. I wanted you to come anyway, so I could get an hour's sleep or so. Things are calmer now but she needs watching." Rebecka had lit candles on the coffee table in the living room and poured him a glass of wine. With a gesture she invited him to make himself comfortable on the sofa. He could surely do with a bit of rest, after all the excitement? Why not allow himself a glass, even though he had to drive home. The wine was peppery and good, she said.

Per Arvidsson felt all the air leaving his body. He'd worked himself up into a pitch of anxiety, and now the danger had passed. It amazed him just how quick everything went.

"I want you to hold me, I feel so alone. Just to hold me, nothing else." She sat close to him and caressed his back without a word. Calm caresses. He put his arm round her and embraced her. The wild anxiety he'd felt came to rest. Everything seemed calm and melancholic now.

"How could life end up like this for us, Rebecka?"

She put her finger over his lips—didn't want to talk. He felt the scent of her perfume, so intimately associated with lust. The body remembered. It had been so long since he last made love to anyone. The anti-depressants had made it impossible for him, and he'd repressed the need for sex so that he could slowly climb out of Hell and start living again. His sense of honor demanded that he had to make a living, pay his way. Now the medicine had been exchanged for a newer drug, and suddenly he felt his desire resurgent again. It made him happy, almost expansive, to feel this physical reaction. Without thinking about the repercussions he drank another glass of wine, which Rebecka poured him. Her hand continually caressed his back while the other hand alighted on his thigh when she happened to lean forward to refill her glass. Her breasts brushed against him. She didn't take her hand away, merely leaned even closer into his arms. Her sweater was cut very low over her bust. The heat spread upwards toward the hot-spot. Her cheek gently touched his and her soft lips searched their way up from his throat to his mouth, while her hand on his thigh started looking for adventure.

There was a half-hearted protest.

When Per woke up the following morning in Rebecka's bed, he wanted to shout out his bad conscience. His icy realization that he had failed Maria made him want to run away, rewind the tape, undo what had happened. How could he have let this happen? So easy, so meaningless. How significant is it within a relationship, every time we make love? We hardly even remember when we make love and when we don't, not in day-to-day life. Often it's just a kind of acquired behavior, something that helps us relax and sleep. So why did his unfaithfulness with Rebecka have to mean so much? Why did it make such a big difference if it happened before or after the break? Per examined his own arguments. No, he couldn't play down the significance of what he had just done. All he wanted now was to get out of there and go home to his own life. Rebecka slept like a dead woman. Her big, wavy hair like a billowing sea over the pillow. Her mouth slightly open, a string of saliva suspended from a corner of her mouth. She mumbled something in her sleep and turned over, exposing her breasts. He pulled on his clothes as quietly as he could, but when he was leaving the room she reached for him.

"Thanks!" He squeezed her hand, and shook his head in response to her unarticulated question, when with her other hand she lifted the comforter and invited him to climb back in again. Her body was beautiful and inviting, but his bad conscience made him abstain. There would be no follow-up. He could see that this upset her, but he didn't have the energy to stay and talk about it. All he wanted was to flee and have everything undone. Rebecka wanted something else. Maybe after all it was better to clearly state what his feelings were.

"What happened last night will never be repeated. It's something between us. I hope you can keep it confidential. "He thought he noticed a sort of flickering of her eyelids which he interpreted as concurrence. Most likely she thought him cowardly and deceitful, but right now he couldn't cope with any further discussion about their relationship.

On the table in the living room stood two empty wine bottles. Presumably Per had himself drunk most of it. The car was parked outside in the street. Dawn was gray and cold and a fine drizzle was settling on the windscreen. He started the engine, turned on the windshield wipers, calculated how much alcohol he'd consumed—dividing this by the numbers of hours that had passed and the rate at which alcohol was broken down—then finally decided to leave the car where it was and walk home. His feelings were conflicted, to put it mildly. How the hell could things have ended up in such shambles? At the same time he couldn't stop himself feeling ecstatic about his restored sexual potency.

The rain intensified, the wet and cold was penetrating to his skin as Per Arvidsson hurried homewards. It was no more than half past six, and there was hardly anyone around. The only people he met were a mailman on a bicycle and an elderly lady with a poodle. Should he tell Maria? Would she ever be able to forgive him? Every time she'd caressingly tried to seduce him he'd rejected her advances, because he knew he wouldn't be able to get it up. She had held him and waited loyally, telling him it didn't matter, she was happy enough just being near him. Damn the whole thing! Of course it makes a difference if one is impotent or not. And now when he'd finally got his potency back, he had ruined everything. Maria would never want to see him again. Maybe they wouldn't even manage to work together any more. How the hell could he have done something so incredibly stupid? He knew Rebecka wanted him back again, yet he'd walked right into her trap.

If he told Maria, everything would be shot. If he didn't, she'd probably never find out. Was it possible living a happy life without telling each other everything? Now when he knew his body was working as it should, he'd be able to give her all the good things they'd both been missing. Now he'd be able to look Death in the eye and say that he deserved his life because he wanted to live and love. He thought about the rope hanging in the hall and the hook he'd put up in his living room ceiling. In spite of his difficult situation, any notion of taking his own life now seemed infinitely remote. He no longer saw death as a way out. Finally he seemed to be returning to full health; in this difficult predicament he found himself in, this made him if not happy then certainly less heavy than he might have been. He decided not to tell Maria. What happened with Rebecka last night was a slip-up. In a way it was even good, because now he knew he was functioning normally. If people belong together and love one another there's no point wasting their lives on separation.

The rain came down even heavier but Per did not take shelter as he walked through the lanes. He wanted to get home. As soon as he walked through the door he was going to call Maria to hear if she loved him and wanted him. He looked in his pocket for the key, but found to his surprise that the front door was unlocked and half-open. He sensed something wrong and walked round the house to the back entrance, where he found the window of the veranda door shattered. Under the outside lamp, shards of glass lay glittering on the ground. He picked up a stick from the ground and poked the front door open to get a better look inside. No doubt about it, someone had broken in. The door wouldn't open completely, there was something in the way. The bookshelf had been moved. The stereo table had been pulled out at an angle in the room. The sofa cushions lay scattered on the floor. The coffee table had been shifted. What the hell! It looked as if there were a sack hanging from the hook in the ceiling where the chandelier had been hanging. Then suddenly it hit him with full impact that there was a person hanging there! Maybe he was still alive? A knife! Per charged into the kitchen. Within a few seconds he'd fetched a knife from the drawer, stepped up on the table, cut the man down, and loosened the rope round his neck. He also loosened his clothes, but there was no pulse and no breathing. For a brief moment he considered giving mouth-to-mouth resuscitation. The tongue of the dead one was blue and swollen, the eyes were bloodshot and pressing out of their sockets. The thought of blowing air into the dead body turned Per's stomach—he was almost unable to control his nausea. He turned away, trembling, and inhaled deeply; then straightened up and looked at the dead body. It was stiff and cold. He must have been dead for hours. Only when Per had calmed himself down somewhat did he realize who he was, even though his features had been so grotesquely transformed by the swelling. It was inexplicable. Utterly absurd. When he called the emergency number he was no longer a police officer reporting a situation. He was a civilian, stuttering awkwardly over his words.

Chapter 24

Ek and Haraldsson were first on the scene. Per Arvidsson met them outside in the courtyard after what seemed like an interminable wait.

"He's dead. There's nothing we can do."

Jesper Ek looked as if he couldn't quite believe it. It seemed so unlikely.

"What, he was just hanging there in your living room? Jesus, that must have been a real shock to you!"

"You bet it was," said Arvidsson in a muffled voice. It was a relief not being alone with the dead man. Everything that could have happened to Harry Molin had already taken place, yet it was still terrible to be in such close proximity to death.

"Do you know who he was?" Haraldsson was on his way into the house when Ek stopped him.

"Erika will skin you alive if you blunder in there and mess up the evidence, you know that don't you?"

"I knew him," said Per. "He was my neighbor, Harry Molin. I don't understand it. I just don't understand why he'd hang himself here. In my place? Was he worried he wouldn't be found if he did it in his own place? He never had any visitors."

"We've been trying to contact him at his own address. Maybe he was thinking of the dogs when he hanged himself here; because he didn't want them to have to see it. I can hear them from here. He was probably worried they'd be left on their own for too long if no one found him." Haraldsson wiped down the green-painted bench at the side of the house and sat down. "Didn't he have any family?"

"A sister in Arboga," Arvidsson recalled. "But I don't know what her name is. I wonder why he did this? Why now in particular? Was he just sick of everything?"

"Maybe he was alone... unhappy." Jesper Ek stood under the roof to avoid the drizzling rain. They waited. "Maria was trying to get hold of Harry Molin all day yesterday. She wanted to question him about the murder of Linn Bogren, for our information. Because he was her neighbor and we had evidence that he'd been at the murder scene. His dogs were left tethered at some point by her front door. We know that Harry and Linn sometimes spoke to each other and now he's dead." Jesper shoved in a pinch of *snus*. "You think it might have been him?"

"What, who killed Linn?" Per let the thought sink in. This was a quiet residential area. Harry had never shown the slightest signs of aggression, quite the opposite. His slow, slightly elaborate behavior may have irritated some, but in fact he was a calm and rather withdrawn man.

"That's one possible reason for killing himself. Maybe he made a few advances and she resisted. What if he found it so humiliating and embarrassing that he couldn't bear it? What if he killed Linn and then took his own life to avoid the punishment?" Haraldsson stood up when he heard the sound of an approaching car. "Erika?"

"Strange that he'd hang himself in someone else's home, though. How did he know that hook in the ceiling would carry his weight?" Per sank down where Haraldsson had been sitting. His tiredness was like a lead weight in his body.

"He knew I was a policeman. Maybe he wanted to turn himself in. Just think if I'd been at home." In the same moment that he spoke these words, he realized their implication. If he'd been at home and not in Rebecka's bed, Harry may have been alive now... or both of them dead.

A car stopped outside the wooden fence. Shortly after, Tomas Hartman, Erika Lund, and a tall gangling man who was the doctor on call appeared at the gate. Erika greeted them tersely and started working without delay.

"We won't cordon off the place until we're done here. The police tape only attracts curious bystanders." Tomas Hartman sat down on the garden bench next to Arvidsson.

"Once we start walking around knocking on doors people will come to have a peek anyway." Ek gave Haraldsson a shove to rouse him out of his introspection. "Because we're not really needed here any more, are we?" They were relieved to be able to leave the place.

"Your observation is quite correct." Hartman opened his briefcase and took out his pen and writing pad. The situation did undoubtedly feel strange. "What's your date of birth, Per?" Hartman took down the necessaries and then asked Arvidsson to take everything from the beginning.

"So you arrived on the ferry last night. What time did it come in? Just after midnight?" Hartman squinted over the top of his glasses to get a better look at Per's face. He wasn't quite accustomed to his new progressive lenses.

"The ferry was a quarter of an hour late, so it was about quarter past twelve."

Hartman was perturbed. "But you only reported it now? That's more than seven hours ago!"

"It's true." Only now did it become clear to Arvidsson

that his overnight stay with Rebecka would not pass detection.

"I was with Rebecka and the children." It sounded a little better than saying that he'd slept in her bed. At best, Hartman might believe that he'd stayed over with his children on the sofa in Rebecka's living room, because she was coming home late and they were staying with her the following day.

Hartman gave him a look that quickly dispensed with that hope. Per felt himself enveloped in a hot flush. His cheeks burned. Hartman shook his head. "Sorry to hear it."

"Yes." There was nothing else to add. It had all gone to hell. And Hartman sat there looking virtuous. Damn him! "Have you never done anything stupid?"

"Yes, but it falls under the statute of limitations. I'm too old now. Not exclusively led by my hormones and a bit more comfortable. Are you going to tell Maria?"

"No." Per felt his fear intensifying into something like vertigo. "No, I don't want to lose her again."

"Okay, that's up to you. I'm not the right man to advise you, but…"

"So don't, then," said Per, feeling invaded and irritated. "Anything else?"

"You came home. And then what?"

Per Arvidsson tried to describe, to the best of his ability, the course of events—from the time he'd noticed the shattered window and then Harry's body hanging from the hook in the ceiling—until the arrival of his colleagues.

"Harry told his doctor something important…."

"Anders Ahlström. He's my G.P. as well. He works at the health center serving this area." Per had heard Harry talking about him on numerous occasions. Mostly, Ahlström was in his good books, but there were days when he was in the doghouse. It depended on the doctor's willingness to consider Harry's various theories.

"Harry told his G.P. that he'd run into Linn in the company of three men late one night about a week earlier. She wasn't sober. The doctor mentioned this to Erika Lund, they know each other...." Hartman's face was like an open book.

"I know. They like to play doctor together," said Per, in an unsuccessful attempt to be amusing. "What are you driving at?"

"Harry also told the doctor that you were visited by Linn Bogren the evening before she was murdered."

Per gave it some thought. In the fog of exhaustion, the days and details all seemed to merge. She'd come to him late one evening. He'd had a good deal more whisky than he should have. "She wanted to borrow the computer."

"Why did she want to borrow your computer?"

"She'd sold hers on eBay or something. I don't know. Surely we can check that. She was talking about some booking she had to make for a trip. I wasn't even in the room while she was using the computer. I don't know what she was doing." Per thought back, tried to search his way back through memory, but all the details were lost.

"What sort of mood was she in? Full of anticipation? Happy? Frightened? Sad?" Hartman clawed at his scalp, making a rustling sound. Per's dullness troubled him. He'd never hold up as a witness when he couldn't remember things with any exactitude or keep a track of days and times.

"Don't remember. I just thought she seemed a bit insistent. I didn't want to let her in, I sort of felt she was disturbing me. I needed to be alone."

"You're aware of the fact that we have to take your computer in, and that you can't live here for a while?"

"Yes, I'll ask Ek if I can crash with him. I mean, he has a whole house, there must be some corner I can rent." The most natural thing, Per thought to himself, would have been if he could stay with Maria. But he wouldn't dare ask her. It was probably written on his forehead, what he'd done. Just think if she found out. What the hell would he do then?

"Do you think Harry murdered Linn?" asked Hartman as the corpse in the black body bag passed them on the way to the waiting vehicle.

"What else could one think?" Per thought about it. "Harry might have been up to something illegal, or maybe he had some shameful secret she was in a position to reveal.... I mean, she was a nurse and they can find out a thing or two.... The murder could have happened on impulse. The actual decoration... the display could have been an afterthought. She was dressed as a bride; was that some way of punishing her for being unfaithful to Claes? Was Harry some sort of guardian of morality or was he in love with her and felt she'd turned her nose up at him?" Per could see them before him. Harry had probably been a bit taken with Linn. "Now that I think about it, he often used to wait for her at the mailbox when the mail arrived. He waited until Linn got there so he could have a little chat with her. She was always friendly and gave up her time for him. She may have been the only person who was actually nice to him, and in his lonely condition he could have misinterpreted this as an invitation, or something like that."

"I agree with you. If Harry came on to her and she turned him away, as Haraldsson was suggesting, might he not have killed her so she wouldn't humiliate him? But what about the decoration of the corpse? The murderer took his time and planned everything carefully. It's not something a normal person would do. I don't believe this is a manslaughter case," said Hartman.

At last he'd achieved a full command of the situation—exactly what he needed, in order once again to experience that sense of divinity pulsating through his veins. A breakthrough.

Now that he could read their thoughts it was so much easier planning his next move. That guy in Svartsjö Prison who squealed would not live long, he'd make sure of that. Right now there was not an opportunity. But later. He'd have to go into the archives to find and delete that story about the old bastard killed with the lawn mower blade. It would also require a short physical journey. Via their computer systems he could monitor the police investigation more closely than they could ever imagine. What a joke to even consider them of the same human breed as himself. An IQ of 100 can be seen more or less as a mental handicap when compared to his own, which was 148. They didn't even deserve the right to vote.

Chapter 25

Maria started her day with a workout at the police station gym. She was on her own in there, and it felt good. She took out her anger, frustration, and anxiety on the treadmill. HIV. She had seen the fear in the nurse's eyes when she was taking the samples of blood. It was given away by the slight shaking of her hand, duplicated in the needle and her anxious eyes, although her voice was calm and confidence-inspiring. Surely sometimes when the patient couldn't sit still and the needle slipped in a different direction, it must puncture the latex glove; followed by three months of hell waiting for the first test result. Healthcare staff live with that risk every time they take a blood test. Police officers also live with it: the risk of serious injury at work. Maria thought of the children, Emil and Linda. What would happen to them if she became seriously ill, or maybe even passed away? Krister would have to take care of them full time. Krister, who could hardly even take care of himself, like some over-ripe, capricious teenager who constantly needed affirmation and the instant satisfaction of whatever neediness he was going through. If he wanted to go out for the night and sleep with some lady friend, he thought the children should be able to manage on their own—even though Emil was only ten and Linda just seven. He never bothered to help them with homework; that was something for the school to deal with, he said. And if the children had to have packed lunches they had to fix their own. He wasn't interested in taking care of them, not even when they were ill or there were snags with parents' evenings or lifts to soccer practice and Emil's games. Every other week had turned into alternate weekends, and now he was trying to negotiate himself out of that as well. Friday evening to Monday morning had turned into Saturday afternoon to Sunday evening.

Maria hoisted herself up on the iron bars into a position of balance, lowered herself again, and did another lift and then another quickly. If she were infected she'd keep fighting and living as long as she could, she'd struggle all the way, maintaining herself carefully and living but perhaps never again having the nerve to make love. There's no fool-proof protection, no guarantee against infecting someone. The thought made her feel so dejected—so how would things work out with her and Per? Would he ever dare touch her again?

But if she did prove to be healthy, what did she desire from life? To live with Per? Would he move in with her in the little yellow house on Klinten? Would he want to? It was her home, after all, furnished and arranged the way she wanted it. Where would his children live when they came to stay every other weekend? They'd have to share a room with Emil and Linda and this would immediately lead to conflict. Either that, or she'd have to sell her beloved house so they could buy something bigger, where they'd all have space to live together. What if she sacrificed her house only to find that they couldn't live together? Every day Maria grew more insecure about whether Per would really wholeheartedly try for a life together. When one thought about it, she and the children were actually doing fine as they were, without anyone else getting involved. Yet things did sometimes get lonely after the children had gone to bed. If Per said he loved her, if he really did love her, no obstacles could stand in their way. They would overcome everything.

Maria tried to do some sit-ups, then finally gave up. She was still in so much pain that her eyes were blacking out. She fetched some dumbbells and continued with her usual routine, while mentally retreating from her private misery and preparing for the day's work that lay ahead. The day before they had been looking for Harry Molin. Maria had reacted to the flowers growing in his garden. Hyacinths, bleeding hearts, and lilies of the valley. Linn did not have those flowers in her garden, yet Erika had found traces of exactly those flowers on the floor by the bedroom door and on the broom. When Linn Bogren was found on Tempelkullen she'd been holding a bunch of lilies of the valley. Most likely they'd been picked in the Botanical gardens. One could only speculate about their symbolic significance to the murderer. Maria got into the shower, turned on the cold water, and tried to deal with the pain. In a way it counteracted the inner turmoil. As she rubbed herself down she thought about Linus's father, Ulf, who'd contacted her once again last night, the telephone conversation shifting between reproachful accusations and despairing tears. You must do something! Something must happen! Maria was seriously concerned. They had to find those who'd done it before he did.

Maria poured herself a cup of black coffee and took the stairs up to her office. As she passed Hartman's door she saw that he'd already arrived and was sitting by his computer. Silently, Maria slid into the chair opposite.

"Did you hear what happened last night?" he said.

"Last night?" Maria gave him a questioning look and Hartman quickly summarized the macabre spectacle in Arvidsson's house.

"So Harry Molin hanged himself at Per Arvidsson's place…. You mean *our* Per Arvidsson? I actually considered opening Harry's door last night but decided it could wait until today. And now he's dead?" Maria was deeply shaken. "And Per, how's he?"

"All right, I think." Hartman dived into a pile of papers.

"What is it? There's something you're not telling me? Come on Tomas, we've known each other for a long time and something's up. Can I see the interview report? This is my investigation as well, you know."

"Okay." Reluctantly, Hartman handed over the transcripts of the interview with Per Arvidsson. It was unavoidable. He couldn't protect either of them. He observed her face with some tension as she read. It would not escape her. He saw her facial expression change from concentration to doubt and consternation once it grew clear to her where Per had spent the night. At Rebecka's.

"Excuse me a moment. I have to make a call." Maria was gone before Hartman had time to react. She dialed Per's number. No answer. So she had to check with Rebecka, then. The truth. Only the truth would do.

"Rebecka Arvidsson." Her voice sounded breezy and happy, as if she'd just had a good laugh about something.

"I'm a police officer. Maria Wern. I want to check an alibi from last night…."

"Per, yes he slept here. Although I don't know if we got very much sleep, really," Rebecka tittered. "I think we've found a way back to each other. It's wonderful for the children."

Maria checked the exact time and automatically, robotically, noted it down on the paper in front of her. This, while the whirring of the ceiling fan seemed to block her ears and press her brain into a hard ball. "Good luck." Maria's voice lost its strength, turned into a dry whisper. She hung up and leaned her head into her hands, fighting the tears. If she was going to call Per now she had to be sure her voice wouldn't crack. Then she felt Hartman's hand on her shoulder, and she released her self-restraint. Her tears ran down her face.

"You knew. How long have you known?" she asked, once she'd collected herself.

"Since this morning. Per is really beating himself up about it, it was a mistake. He loves you, Maria. I know it."

"Bullshit! Leave me alone. I'll come down to the meeting with Erika in fifteen minutes, but right now I want to be on my own!"

Hartman hesitated in the doorway. "Give him another chance, Maria. You love each other, anyone can see that. Listen to what he has to say."

"No! I've had enough. This is quite enough. All the time while he's been ill I've been loyal, I've listened. It's been him and only him all the way. My needs, my hopes haven't figured at all. I've waited, hoping he'd get better. Now when he seems more or less all right, what does he do? It's over, my sympathy is spent and there'll never be anything between me and Per again."

"I hope you'll still manage to work together."

"We'll see. Can you leave me alone!"

Once Hartman had left the room Maria realized how shaky she was feeling. Her fingers trembled as she dialed Per's telephone number. She had to hear him say it himself, that he'd been unfaithful with his wife… with his wife! The thought of it was almost amusing. The divorce wasn't final-ized yet, but in a moral sense he had deceived her.

"Hi Maria, how are you? You've heard what's happened,

haven't you? Harry Molin was hanging in my living room by a rope round his neck. I cut him down, I didn't know if he was alive at that point. It was my rope, I'd even made the knot myself, in case I—"

"When did you find him?" She asked even though she knew the answer. He had to have a chance of explaining himself.

"Now, this morning."

"In the morning? So you came on the night boat?"

"It's in the report. I was at Rebecka's, but it's not like you think. I love you, Maria. Nothing happened." His defensive words flew out of him. He didn't want to lie to Maria; nor did he want to talk about it over the telephone. "Can we meet up... and talk?"

"According to Rebecka something did happen. Don't lie to me, Per. I'm worth more than that. I want the truth."

"I was drunk and I ended up in her bed, but it didn't mean anything. It has nothing to do with us. I love you, Maria."

"It has everything to do with us. She said you were going to try again, that it was a fresh start. I wish you the very best of luck."

"We're not doing that at all. Maria... I'm... sorry. I love you."

"If you say you love me and this is all it's worth, then it's worth nothing. It's over, Per. I don't think I can get over this. The best you can do from now on is stay out of my way."

"Maria... !"

"I mean what I'm saying. Leave me alone." She wasn't flaring up, she was speaking in her calmest possible voice. She felt as if she were not in her own body, as if someone else were speaking through her mouth. Her muscles had stiffened, her shoulders were frozen and hoisted up. She could hardly move her arm to hang up.

Chapter 26

The summer weather was back. The sun came pouring down outside the windows of the police station. Beyond the parking area of Östercentrum was a strip of luminous grass. The swallows emerged from dark cracks in the wall and flitted against the clear blue sky. Erika Lund opened the window to get some air. She'd been working since early dawn. By now she'd received the medical examiner's preliminary report and the results of various analyses she'd ordered. She was late for the meeting. The others had been waiting a while for her; their murmuring voices died away as she entered the room. The air was like a burial chamber in there, so she threw the window wide open.

"Harry Molin died at about 23:00 hours give or take an hour or so, that's the preliminary view of the medical examiner. Per Arvidsson has an alibi for that time, because he was on the ferry until 00:15. Obviously this makes things easier for us, because he can stay on active service. Arvidsson found the murdered man just after seven this morning. Harry Molin was hanging from a hook in Arvidsson's living room. He cut him down and then called emergency services. The rope belonged to Per."

"The murdered man? So Harry didn't commit suicide?" This had been Maria's initial thought when she heard what had happened. It seemed obvious that Harry, for some reason unknown as yet, had taken Linn Bogren's life and then later also killed himself. She had practically considered it as a case solved.

"There are compelling reasons to believe he was hanged."

"But a normal hook for a lamp, is that really strong enough to hang yourself?"

Hartman, looking thoughtful, turned to Erika.

"Arvidsson had changed the hook. I asked him about it, and he changed it while he was thinking of killing himself." Erika looked at her papers so she wouldn't have to look into Maria's eyes. It was about Per's private life. She wanted to protect him but at the same time the truth had to come out. "That's how bad things were."

"But how could the murderer know there was a hook there to hang him from?"

"Any signs of struggle?" asked Ek.

"Take it easy, I'll get there." Erika gave Ek a sharp glance. She needed to talk without being interrupted, needed space to talk without losing her concentration. "Harry Molin was barefooted when he was found. His heels were grazed, as if someone had dragged his body across rough stones... possibly across the courtyard. The lid of his mailbox was open. Possibly he went out without his dogs to pick up his mail, and that's when he ran into the murderer. The medical examiner has confirmed he received a powerful but not deadly blow with a blunt instrument across his left temple. No significant internal bleeding, but a contusion by his temporal bone."

"So he may have been unconscious when he was hanged?" Hartman interjected.

"We don't know that for sure, but it seems likely. There

are no defensive injuries. I don't think he put up any re-sistance. We found a cigarette butt by the mailbox. DNA analysis will take a bit of time, but if we're lucky it'll match something we already have. It had been raining that eve-ning and we have a footprint, probably from when the mur-derer put out his cigarette. A part of this shoeprint is on the actual cigarette. We found a big yellow stain on the victim's shirt, which analysis showed to be urine. If the body had been suspended when he passed urine it would have run downwards and not have ended up at chest height. So we'll have to assume the body was lying down. Possibly the blow to the head made him lose control of his bladder while he was lying down. There are traces of the victim's blood by the mailbox but no blood at all on the floor under the hook where he was hanging."

"I'll be damned," said Ek. "I assumed it was suicide."

"Another find that's confusing is a mark left in the gravel by the mailbox. A 'K'. It could be a coincidence, of course, some child who's just learned the alphabet. I don't want to draw any premature conclusions, only draw a parallel to the bedroom where Linn Bogren died. I found a letter 'K' etched into the blood on the wallpaper; hardly noticeable."

Maria suddenly had a thought. "Do you remember that time at your place when we were brainstorming about Roy and Kilroy? Could it be a 'K' as in Kilroy?"

"It's a bit far-fetched but every idea is worth considering. Did anyone manage to get hold of any next of kin?" Hart-man turned to Haraldsson and Ek. Haraldsson nodded at Jesper.

"I got a hold of his sister. She seems to be the only family he had. They haven't seen each other at all in the last few years, only telephone contact and Christmas cards. Apart from membership in a number of patient associations he doesn't seem to have had any social life at all; just the Internet. There he has a bewildering number of contacts. We took his computer in and I had a quick look through it. All his bookmarks are healthcare-related in some way. It seems to have been his main interest."

"Or his problem." Maria felt irritated at them for making light of Harry. He probably lived his life to the best of his ability, given his available opportunities.

"Nothing's been stolen from Molin's house as far as we can judge. The computer was left, also the flat-screen TV which seems fairly new, must have cost him ten thousand kronor at least. Even his wallet is on the kitchen bench next to the coffeemaker and the car keys," Haraldsson continued. "The door was unlocked."

"The sister told me she found it very strange. Harry would never want to take his own life, she said. Of course, it's a normal reaction from next of kin. But she did say one important thing: he just had a tailored suit made for himself. It cost more than six thousand kronor, we found the receipt among his bills in the desk drawer. You don't have a suit made if you're about to commit suicide, do you? He was planning to wear it on Midsummer's day at his niece's wedding."

"The wallet had more than a thousand kronor in it. In other words, this is not a robbery. The hanging has the same exhibitionist element as the murder of Linn Bogren," said Maria, who'd sat in silence for a while, listening. "The corpse has not been hidden, instead it's exhibited in a provocative way in the home of a police officer. Like when a cat drags a rat in with its head bitten off and leaves it in the hall like a hunting trophy. Who is this show for? Where is the audience? Is it a message that's supposed to scare someone? Or just the work of someone who hates the police and wants to demonstrate his superiority?"

"Someone who gets a kick out of the newspapers report-

ing that there are no clues about the identity of the killer."
Hartman remembered a frightening case many years before.
It was about power. A human piece of scum who'd swung
between feelings of divinity and absolute worthlessness. To
earn respect one had to be dangerous.

"The person we're looking for could be highly intelligent
in one respect and at the same time emotionally stunted, a
victim of his own thinking about the evil of human beings
and the importance of punishing them. Perhaps someone
who has or used to have contact with the psychiatric profession."

"So the victims may be picked at random, you mean?"
Once again Maria's thoughts returned to the assault, in
which she and the thirteen-year-old boy were subjected to
an intense, yet also apparently random, violence.

"Maybe. It's possible. The anger is there. It has to find an
outlet. The perpetrator is only waiting for a victim." Hartman noticed Erika's irritation and stopped himself.

Erika Lund glanced at her papers and then at the clock.
"I've collated the tests I ran at Linn Bogren's with the finds
I secured in Harry Molin's home. As things stand now it
is absolutely conceivable that we are dealing with the same
murderer in both cases. It may be so, but we can't take it
for granted. The materials I found in Bogren's home which
do not directly come from her husband or her girlfriend are
primarily the dog hairs, which can be traced back to the
neighbor's dog."

"Which need not necessarily mean anything more than
that he visited her as a neighbor." Hartman let this information sink in. Later it might come in handy.

"The most interesting thing is some fairly viscous phlegm
coughed into a piece of toilet paper left in the waste paper
basket in Linn's place. Disgusting, but valuable. There
are traces of wood dust in the phlegm, possibly dust from

polishing the wood flooring. The perpetrator is unknown to us, he doesn't figure in any register. But we can probably assume he's either a floor layer or an amateur who recently polished his own wood floor."

"How do we know it was left by the murderer?" asked Ek.

"We don't, but I found something else. A pathetically small dark *snus* stain on one of the strips of torn sheets used to decorate the Tempelkullen. They match. In other words, we have the DNA of someone who was both at the murder scene in Linn's home and on Tempelkullen where the body was found. If we find the same DNA on the cigarette found by Harry's mailbox we've come quite a long way." Erika looked round at them, waiting for their approval.

"I would say it's a breakthrough," Hartman concluded.

"Does it match the DNA that was taken under my fingernails after the assault?" asked Maria.

"Unfortunately not." Erika had been hoping for that.

"I'll ask Claes Bogren to make a list of people among his acquaintances who use *snus*, smoke, and are renovating their homes. We also found a pair of 8 ½ men's size Rieker shoes in Harry's house which matched the footprints at Linn's. The question is, what was he doing there?" Hartman couldn't let go of the thought that maybe Harry was Linn's murderer after all.

"The DNA we found at Linn's isn't a positive match with Harry's," Erika told him.

"Thanks. We should also check stores that rent out floor polishing machines and other DIY equipment." Hartman gave Erika a nod as she stood up to leave the conference room. "I asked a guy from the IT Group to check Per Arvidsson's computer. It felt a bit strange, since it would usually be Per who took care of that job." Hartman distributed copies of the material. "On the evening of June fifteenth at 22:25, Linn Bogren went over to Arvidsson and asked if she could borrow his computer. At 22:30 she sent herself an e-mail, like a sort of back-up on Hotmail. Its contents are a study on plant steroids."

Ek tipped his chair while he tried to interpret the figures. "Maria?"

"I'm not very experienced at reading medical research reports, either. To transfer the material to Arvidsson's computer she must have brought something like a USB memory stick or a CD with her, right?"

"I haven't found any memory sticks in her house and no CDs either." Erika sighed loudly. "I've asked an intern to look through the mail. At least he's university-educated; you have to take what you get."

"Her computer, or rather the clinic's, was not in the house. Her husband assumed she was keeping it in the pharmaceuticals section. She rarely brought it home." Hartman turned to Maria—she was the last person who'd spoken to Claes Bogren.

"She'd been borrowing the laptop for the past year so she could work on the study." Maria outlined the meeting she'd had earlier in the week with the staff at the section where Linn worked. They'd spoken about a range of things, but no one had mentioned anything about a medical study. Linn had been working on it with the clinic manager; no one else had been involved.

"What reason could there be for transferring the material to Arvidsson's computer, other than a fear that someone was going to destroy it? Let's bring in her boss for questioning." Hartman picked up the telephone to inform his colleagues on patrol. "His name is Sam Wettergren."

"I'm going to check his bank accounts and then I'll go and see him there, at work. Surprise him. We've already met, we've established contact. And I won't announce myself at reception." Maria didn't wait for an answer. She was already on her way.

Hartman indicated with a gesture that the run-through was over. Now he needed to get hold of Arvidsson.

Per Arvidsson sat slumped in his chair, his long legs splayed on the floor—he was talking on the telephone. Hartman remained in the doorway waiting for him to finish.

Per waved apologetically at him. He was speaking to a retired colleague who'd been in service at the time of the lawn mower murder.

"I found a newspaper article online. From ten years ago. About a forty-five-year-old man who'd been killed with a lawn mower blade. In your district. I'm waiting to get all the information you have on the case."

The elderly colleague from Stockholm didn't have a lot to say for himself. Per was clearly getting impatient with him for speaking and thinking so slowly.

"Believe me. When you contacted me the first time I tried to find the documents and refresh my memory. I was in charge of the investigation and I remember that summary execution very well. We found the murder weapon but after that we ran straight into a wall. There was nothing to go on, no witnesses. And now all the documents are gone! They're not in the archive, not in paper format or even in our computer records."

"What do you mean? They couldn't just disappear, could they? Have the documents been lent to someone?"

"We're looking into this, but for the moment there are no documents."

"For Christ's sake! What can you remember about it?" Arvidsson chewed his thumbnail frenetically. He had to catch the bastard who beat up Maria, it might even be the only way of getting her back.

"It was never cleared up. No one had heard or seen

anything. The man was found in a ditch torn to pieces. I never saw anything like it, not in all my years as a policeman. Why are you asking?"

"Because there's a rumor among the cons that the guy who did it was someone called Roy. Does that mean anything to you?"

"Roy? No, nothing. I had this case scratched into my retina for three years. There was no Roy in the investigation. In fact, there was no suspect at all. No witnesses. Nothing!"

"Would you be kind enough to write down everything you can remember? What the man's name was, who his friends were, his family. Everything." Per described the lethal assault in Visby and Maria's predicament. "We believe this could be the work of the same man."

"I read about that attack in the newspaper. It touched me. How's Maria Wern doing?"

"The newspaper didn't go into much detail on certain points. The pig stabbed her with a blood-filled syringe; she's just trying to hold it all together now, waiting to hear what her fate is. We've asked the health service for a list of everyone on the island with some form of blood infection, but no one fits. The police have the right to examine this type of information but still we always come up against the same administrative hassle. No one has the guts to grab hold of it."

"Oh shit, it gets worse and worse."

"Get back to me!" Per Arvidsson threw down the phone and swore. Then turned his eyes to Hartman. "Anything new come up?" The others had sat through the meeting without him; he hadn't been allowed any further contact with the investigation until Maria had checked out his alibi.

"Harry Molin was murdered." Hartman took two steps into the room and sat opposite Arvidsson, at his desk.

"What the hell are you saying? I thought he hanged himself at my place because he knew he'd be found there."

Hartman summarized things briefly. "Two murders in your block. People are calling like crazy, the phone lines are jammed. The public demands a beefed-up police presence downtown during nights and evenings. There's a rumor that Linus's father is organizing a vigilante group."

"Nothing odd about that." Per wasn't sure what he would have done if the same thing had happened to his own son. "How's Maria? It's all fucked up, this. She knows I was at Rebecka's place and she won't see me again."

Hartman shook his head ruefully. He felt for them both. "Maria just left to interview Sam Wettergren, Chief Physician at Linn Bogren's workplace. There's no coordination, she's running her own race. She seems more angry than upset, if that's any consolation to you."

"Did she go by herself?"

"Ek tagged along."

Chapter 27

Maria Wern was almost running down the hospital corridor and Ek had to motor along to keep up with her. The smell of fresh-brewed coffee hit them, mixed with other odors from the rinsing room. The door to Sam Wettergren's office was closed. The red lamp was turned on, but Maria walked straight in without knocking. Sam bounced out of his chair, caught red-handed scrutinizing skimpily dressed ladies on a homepage that had apparently been approved by the county council's ratings system. Ek had a hard time keeping a straight face. The physician looked like a bashful boy. It didn't even occur to him to protest about this intrusion. With a click of his keyboard he switched to another site—Stock Market notations.

"Maria Wern, police." She shook his hand, slightly disgusted at the thought of not quite knowing where the physician's hand had been, then pushed away the unpleasant thought and sat down opposite Wettergren. Ek took a seat on the examination table alongside, its disposable paper cover rustling loudly in the silent room. Wettergren's embarrassment soon turned into irritation. He could hardly tell them he was busy without giving rise to hilarity. Under no circumstances did he want them there, but at the same time he didn't dare tell them to go to hell. All these emotions played themselves out on his face over the course of a few seconds, while Maria got out pen and paper.

"What do you want?" he finally said.

"A word with you." Maria leaned forward and turned off the monitor of his computer so that she'd have his undivided attention. They said doctors spent at most twenty-five percent of their time seeing patients. For Sam Wettergren the statistics must have looked even worse. He worked at home at least one day a week according to the clinic nurse, and what he got up to there was impossible for anyone to say. It was probably a hidden perk.

"I've told you everything I know. You've already been here and I have nothing to add." He spoke slowly and clearly, offering a strained smile, though his eyes behind his black spectacle frames were icy gray.

"Let's take it from the beginning. Where were you on the evening of June fifteenth?"

"I've already answered that. I was lecturing on allergies at Congress Hall. I went directly there from work. After the lecture I had a beer with a few colleagues. I went home just before midnight, more or less quarter to twelve, which my wife can confirm as can my friends. I don't understand what the problem is. Why don't you just check my information?"

"We have. Your wife says she was asleep. She can't remember when you came home, and your friends give varying accounts of when you may have left." Maria leaned forward. "Are you in any way involved in the murder of Linn Bogren?"

"What the hell are you saying? No, for God's sake, no! We were colleagues, we worked well together...." Sam Wettergren could no longer sit still. He pushed his chair back, the wheels scraping against the floor. His eyes darting in all directions, he stood up and went to the window where he stood with his back to them.

"At 22:01 you had a telephone call from Linn. Just after midnight she was dead. What did you talk about?" Maria saw Sam Wettergren shielding his body behind his crossed arms.

"None of your business, I have to respect confidentiality, I'm responsible for the staff, you know...."

"We both know it's not like that. We're dealing with murder here. In which case your confidentiality no longer applies. What was your conversation about?"

"She was having a relationship with a patient." Sam stopped.

"Sara Wentzel," Ek filled in.

"So you know. She wanted to come out and be open about it. She wanted me to be the first to know, so I could prepare myself for any problems arising. Very considerate. That's how she was, Linn. A fine human being and an excellent nurse. We always worked very well together."

"You recently completed a study together. What was this about?"

"Linn was always interested in alternative medicine. It may seem a little odd. Those of us who work in orthodox medicine should keep to science, people think, and that is precisely what I do. I want to examine alternative medical treatments in a clinical way, then adopt or reject these attempts to develop new and better ways in which to treat patients. We decided to study whether plant steroids have an effect. If so, they could be used as an aid to existing treatments or even an alternative when patients have unacceptable side effects from cortisone."

"Did you finish the study?"

"I presented it at the annual medical conference this year and it stirred up a lot of interest. In Germany and Holland there's much more openness to unconventional methods, there's a big market for products of this kind. Patients are no longer satisfied that the doctor knows best. They want to decide themselves from a smorgasbord of available treatments, with the doctor as an advisor but not God Almighty."

"What does this success mean for you?" Maria saw how he relaxed and grew less guarded.

"Nothing. I'm doing it to help improve the quality of life of sick people."

"Did you go to Linn's house on the night she died?" Maria dropped her question into their conversation in a relaxed, normal tone of voice.

"I walked past her place on the way back from the bar and was intending to say a few words to her. I thought she might be awake. The gate in the fence was open and the front door wasn't locked. I called her name but she didn't answer."

"For what reason? There must be a reason for going to the home of a woman who's there by herself in the middle of the night. Were you jealous?" Ek leaned back on the examination table and watched Sam's face with a rigid stare.

"I love my wife. I have never had anything but a professional relationship with Linn Bogren. I actually came to pick up the computer which is a work computer, I needed it for my work the following day. My laptop had broken and she had all the material on hers."

Ek gave a whistle. "And did you find it?"

"No, I knocked and when she didn't answer I carried on walking. I thought maybe she'd left the computer at work. Which was correct. It was in her room by reception."

"Which you have access to?" asked Maria.

"There's a master key," said Sam, looking bothered.

"Could you open the study and we'll have a look at it together. I think it sounds very interesting." Maria gave him one of her sunniest smiles and Sam Wettergren melted. He opened the study and patiently explained its bar graphs and diagrams.

"Why did you have to get a hold of Linn's computer in the middle of the night? Couldn't you have picked it up the following day or asked her to bring it to work if she had it at home?" Maria leaned forward and focused on his face. He wasn't going to wriggle out of this one.

Ek stood up and blocked the door when Sam took a quick step in that direction. "Why?"

"Yes, why the heck?" Sam sank back into his chair. "I suppose I was drunk. I'd had an argument with a few colleagues in the pub about the study, in fact, and I wanted to talk to someone. My wife doesn't understand this, but Linn did."

"What was the dispute about?" asked Maria.

"Jealousy, of course, there's no jealousy worse than the academic kind."

"How were they attacking you?" Maria was registering a growing intensity of emotion in the physician. Which was good, maybe he'd be less defensive.

"They were saying the sample was not broad enough for the results to be significant. Several patients had dropped out because of diarrhea. The tiniest bit of resistance and they gave up even though it could have helped them in the long run. Sometimes people don't see what's best for them. In fact the statistical basis of the study was perfectly adequate; they were only questioning the conclusions out of antagonism."

"Did Linn know you were coming?"

"No, it was on impulse. I wasn't sober, I said."

"Before we came we took the liberty of checking your bank accounts."

Maria got out some copies of the pages she'd been given

by Sam Wettergren's bank. "Do you want to comment on a payment of 153,000 kronor from the producer of the material you used in the study?"

"It was for my expenses."

"Expenses of 153,000. What, for pens and paper and a few erasers?" Ek's fingers drummed against the doorframe.

"None of your goddamn business. I've paid my taxes, there wasn't so much left by the time I was done. It's all in my accounts, I've got nothing to hide." Sam Wettergren demonstratively checked his watch. "I have work I need to get on with. Patients who are waiting."

"Okay, we'll leave it for now. Just a couple more questions and then we're done. Do you know a man called Harry Molin? Could be a patient of yours."

"Harry Molin? Doesn't ring a bell, exactly. I couldn't rule out that he's been here, but I don't remember him."

"What did you do with the money? We can see it's not in the account any more. Have you been doing any house repairs at home? Gone overseas perhaps? Or paid off loans?"

"I haven't done any DIY for twenty years. How would anyone have time for that, with my working hours? I divided the money among my children. They're studying and I don't want them to take out student loans. The household budget's leaking like a sieve."

"One last question, and then we're going to ask for a saliva sample." Maria took out a kit of cotton swabs from her briefcase. "What did you think about Linn Bogren's relationship with Sara? How would you have dealt with it if she'd still been alive today?"

"I'm the boss and I have to be fair. Obviously I would have fired her if she refused to go voluntarily. It doesn't matter if the patient is a man or a woman, as a health service employee you're not allowed to enter into a relationship with a patient. I would have reported it to the relevant authority at the Department of Health and Social Security. If Sara Wentzel had reported her it could have led to a civil law case. I have to treat everyone the same, regardless of what I think about them or their sexual orientation. Otherwise my leadership position would be undermined." Sam stared at the cotton swab Maria handed him. "What's that? A DNA test? I didn't fucking do it. Have you asked her husband? Well have you? He if anyone had reason enough to beat the shit out of her. Wouldn't you agree?"

"You think so?"

"Surely you do see it was him?"

"Take this cotton swab and rub it against the inside of your cheek...." He stared at Maria with intense disdain, but did as she asked. "Make sure you're contactable." She rolled the cotton swab inside the circle of the FTA card and covered the sample.

"What do you need the computer for?"

"Just borrowing it for a while," said Ek. "We're aware of the fact that it's County Council property and we'll return it in the same condition as we found it. You should count your lucky stars we're not taking you in as well."

Sam stared at them with the kind of hatred that could have made a concrete bunker self-ignite, but he didn't say anything until they'd closed the door behind them. They heard a long tirade of curses.

"Shouldn't we have brought him in?" said Ek.

"I've put him under surveillance. Let's see what he does once we've left the scene." Ek headed for the driver's side, but Maria was too quick for him. She slipped behind the steering wheel, while Ek had to go around the car to the passenger seat. It was so typical, she reflected, the way Ek always assumed he was driving.

In the virtual world he'd learned to quickly and strategically counter any unexpected events. Any emotional expression at his command was minimal and easily understood. Terror, hatred, the flush of victory—no other emotions were required. There were rules. Everyone had to observe them. The consequences were clear. Unfortunately, in real life things were not always so predictable. Stupidity had an unacceptable amount of room to maneuver. In idiocy there are so many more variables than in intelligence and logic, which have the capacity to boil things down and prioritize. How is it possible to predict situations when people do so many things without any beneficial effects for themselves? They act on the basis of pathetic, irrational concepts such as empathy and love. How could people come up with the idea of doing things for other human beings, when it was actually detrimental to their own interests? The inherent idiocy of it was so provocative, it had to be studied one more time. These delicate and as yet only partially-articulated questions had to be answered: "How much was I worth to you? How much can I cost you now?"

Linn had been a mistake. Yet she was a chip that could be

used in the game he'd set in motion. *The USB stick had been in her purse in the hall.*

She should have taken better care of it. She should have taken better care of herself.

Chapter 28

Erika Lund turned on her private cell phone. Four missed calls and as many text messages. All from Anders. Want to see you again. Miss you. Why don't you answer?

"Because I have a job that's eating me alive," she said to herself as she pressed call-back. "Well I seem to be popular today.... What can I do for you?"

"Can we meet? I want, I want, I want!"

"What do you want?" she laughed.

"Arm wrestling, board games. Anything, as long as it's with you. I'd even play leapfrog around a pole or go for the first swim of the year in ice-cold water, as long as we do it together. That's the whole thing about Midsummer, isn't it?"

"Midsummer. So that's why Maria threw a few herring tails on a plate. I hate marinated herring. The new flavors anyway. Coriander herring. Lime herring. Cranberry herring. Orange herring. Chocolate herring...."

"And sour herring.... When can I see you?"

"I'll just get my things together. We could meet here in an hour."

"A whole hour…. Why does it have to take an hour? I've got withdrawal symptoms, I need you here NOW!"

Erika hurried down to the locker room to take a shower.

She bumped into Maria down there, who was a step ahead of her, blow-drying her hair. Her body lotion smelt of grapefruit.

"I just thought of something."

"No, stop it!" Erika covered her ears. "I have a date!"

"Harry Molin had an article on his desk about sleeping dysfunction and medication for it. Are you listening?"

"Reluctantly!"

"An alarm report has come in from Japan about a pharmaceutical drug called Fumarret, used as an aid to help people stop smoking. But it has side effects. In twelve known cases it has made people sleepwalk. All the people affected in this way were sleepwalkers as children, or were known to sleepwalk at times of stress or if they consumed alcohol. The drug seems to reactivate the tendency. One of them ended up being run down by a car and had life-threatening injuries."

"What are you trying to say?"

"Harry must have been thinking about it. And Jill Andersson, that witness you interviewed, saw a man struggling with a heavy sack that same night Linn Bogren was murdered. She said he walked clumsily with his legs wide apart as if he was drunk or sleepwalking."

"And… ?" Erika waved her hands in the air. "I'd look pretty clumsy if I was carrying my own body weight on my shoulders in a sack. I don't think a lot of people could just casually toss a sack weighing 143 pounds on their shoulders. Why did she think he was sleepwalking?"

"That's how it looked, she said. I've checked the medication mentioned in Harry's article and it's also available in Sweden. It's become a bestseller."

"Fumarret. I recognize the name."

Erika hurried down to reception. It hadn't been her intention to let Anders wait, but she was a good deal later than the time they'd agreed. He sat slumped in an armchair, reading a brochure from the Crime Prevention Council. As she drew close, he pretended to be absorbed in the information leaflet. She winked at him, motioning for him to follow. They would have their cuddle outside; she really didn't want to give her colleagues this icing on the cake.

"So where's Julia, then?" Erika had meant not to mention her, but the question jumped out before she knew it. Hopefully little Miss Insufferable had something more important to do than ruining Daddy's date.

"She's at riding camp in Fröjel all weekend."

"Oh what fun. Does she have friends there?" Erika tried to hide her smile.

"No, but she may make a few new friends. To be honest that's one thing I'm a bit concerned about. She never keeps any of her friends. All girls at that age have a best friend they see intensively for months or years, but not my Julia. They split up into couples and she's been the odd one out. Sometimes she goes home with someone and then there are three of them, so she gets pushed out. Is that some biological law? Do girls get vicious with each other if they have to share a girlfriend?"

"It's like that at a certain age. It usually gets better later on."

"I was supposed to be at the parents' evening last night, but a colleague called in sick so I had to take another shift last night. Julia has taken to a guy who works as a classroom assistant. I was hoping to find out a bit more from him about how she interacts with the other girls in the class. I don't trust Julia's teacher, she doesn't deal with things as they are—just wants to make life easier for herself. But this guy grabs hold of things, even though he's very young and doesn't even have an education. I have to thank him. Sometimes I think about buying her a horse; would it help her get more friends, do you think?"

"I don't think it's such a good idea." Erika felt at a loss. Buying one's friends could never lead to lasting friendship. The fault probably mainly lay with Miss Sulky herself. If one never compromised, always looked in the wrong direction and complained about being unfairly treated while sneering at people and looking for personal advantage, then surely it could never be easy finding friends.

"I read somewhere that girls have best friends as transition objects to break their reliance on their mothers. Don't ask me if it's true, I really don't know. I played mostly with boys, actually."

"Could that be the reason why she doesn't have a best friend? Because her mother died and she doesn't have an emotional reliance to transfer to someone else?" Anders lost himself in his musings while they walked toward the parking area. Erika would have done anything to be able to enter into his thoughts. They were obviously about Isabel. Would he ever get over her death?

"Where are we going?"

"It's a surprise. First back to your place to pick up what you need for tonight and then… I'm not telling you anything else."

"Exciting! What should I bring, you have to tell me what we're doing. A dress or rain boots?"

"If you wear a dress with red rain boots I promise to worship the ground you walk on. Okay, this was my way of thinking: we're invited to Ljugarn for a party. A colleague of mine has invited a group to Pigstugan and then the idea is we go back to their house. I told them we might come, but it's up to you. I rented a cottage over the week-end."

"Fantastic. But I'm a bit curious about your place. I haven't been there yet, you know."

"You can see it when it's ready. I've stripped the old wood floors, polished them up. There's only the kitchen left to do. Then I'll invite you over."

The evening sun lay like a warmer nuance over the sea and the little red cottage with its dove-blue window shutters was absolutely delightful.

There was no wind and the air was warm.

The cherry tree by the corner of the house had already flowered and was full of unripe fruit; the fragrance of the bird cherry trees descended over them like a cloud of fine powder.

"So sweet."

"Just wait till you see what it looks like inside." He opened the door to the main house. "You can bake bread in the wood fireplace. I rented here last winter when I wanted to get out of town for a while. I was going to stay here over Christmas but then Julia came down with cabin fever after two days. So we had to go back. And you know she had her computer with her and the teaching assistant had given her games and other clever things to occupy her. Social life doesn't work the way it did when I was a kid. In those days we played games together, now the children spend time by themselves at the computer."

"They socialize over the Internet and even if they're not in the same room I'm not sure they're so lonely or isolated, really." Erika picked a bouquet of Midsummer blooms—oxeye daisies and columbines with a border of ferns that were growing outside the doorstep—and put this on the table by the window. They got the fire going and opened a bottle of wine while Anders told her about the old bathing resort.

"Ljugarn has been a well-known bathing resort since the end of the 1800s, with five seaside hotels, if you can believe it! Princess Eugènie stayed at Fridhem on the west side of the island. She attracted Stockholm's cultural elite and aristocracy. It became very fashionable to spend your summers on Gotland."

"A sort of Stockholm Week but much earlier, like when the whole of Stureplan moves here in July?"

"Something like that. I was thinking we could bring a picnic tomorrow and go to the Folhammar Rauk Area, with all the stone columns. It's just about right for a decent walk along the beach."

"Sounds nice. Then I'd like to try a restaurant. I read the menu when we drove past Smakrike... lamb chops with wild garlic butter.... It looked really good." Erika gave him a pleading look.

"I'll invite you out another night this summer. Tonight we'll head north along the beach to Lövängens Pension and Pigstugan. The hotel's maids used to live there in the old days but now it's a pub. If you continue up the coast you eventually get Strandridaregården."

"*Strandridare*, Beach Rider, what does that mean?"

"The Beach Riders were customs men working in the harbors where tar, lime, limestone, and wood were exported. And on the other side of the museum is the marina."

Erika sipped her wine.

"What time do we have to be at the party?"

"The others are probably already there, but well-brought-up folk like us always get there a bit late."

Chapter 29

Erika lay in the cool water looking up at the pale stars. Her entire body except for her face was enveloped by water. The sounds of the party faded. Her mouth tasted of salt. Making little movements, she floated weightlessly in the silence. Her loneliness was as great as the universe, it seemed. She'd had more to drink than she should have. That was how it was. She drank more than a woman should, because there were different yardsticks for men and women, everyone knew that. In Anders's group the ladies hardly drank and were coquettish about their weight. She had realized this too late.

The evening had kicked off with a drink. Anders put his arm around her back so that the others would understand they were a couple. Maybe he was already regretting it. The others seemed to know each other well; right from the start they were talking about absent friends. Fond memories were brought up. Insider jokes made everyone roar with laughter. Anders laughed until he was practically yelping, and let go of Erika. He was swallowed up in the bosom of his friends, while she hovered at the edge of the circle with a smile on her lips that grew increasingly strained. He should have introduced her, helped her establish some common ground. She noticed she was being evaluated and judged; more or less like being back at school, standing there in a new classroom every time they moved—which was frequently, because of her father's job in the military. Why does it never end? Why does one never really grow up?

They ate herring and potatoes at a long table on their hosts' veranda, singing drinking songs she'd never heard and even harmonizing with their voices. She tried to move her lips and imitate the others. Probably it looked like a poorly dubbed film, but she wanted so very badly to be one of them. Not to seem like a dull person—Anders mustn't think she was dull. He had been placed right at the other end of the table. He was safe there among his friends and seemed to have no idea that she was feeling abandoned and ill-at-ease. Unfortunately the box of red wine had ended up next to Erika, and she continuously had to top off people's glasses. When it finished, another box was opened. She had more wine than she thought and, though she still felt stiff, her head grew increasingly sluggish.

Then there was the music quiz. They split up into teams. Anders was in top form. One minute he was waving his arms in the air, the next he was grabbing the women in his team, quickly nicknamed Dizzy Tits and Fat Hips by Erika. The girls seemed to know all the songs and they even sang like real pros.

"Who was the drummer in AC/DC on the record *Stiff Upper Lip*?"

"Phil Rudd!" said Anders without even stopping to think, and he got a loud smooch on his cheek from the beautiful blonde woman at his side. She was younger and slimmer than Erika and her halter-top dress was incredibly revealing—Anders couldn't take his eyes off her breasts. Erika hoped she'd spill red wine on it, try to wash off the stain in the sea and then drown.

"What guitarist played on Kent's first CD?" The question was for Erika's team. She didn't have a clue; nor did the others.

"Martin Roos," said Self-Important Jackass who was their quiz master. His name was Petter and he was reading directly from the album liners. To Erika he looked like some overgrown schoolboy on *University Challenge*.

"What, didn't you know that easy one! Come on, Erika!" Anders yelled.

Erika made an obscene gesture at him. Judging by their faces, this was inappropriate. Ladies did not make obscene gestures, not at "Anders parties." Now she knew for sure.

"Okay, I'll give you one more chance. A really easy one. If you can't answer this you're real losers. Big losers!" said Petter.

"What, they're having another question just because they're stupid?" said Dizzy Tits and gave Self-Important Jackass a reproachful stare. She leaned forward to have her glass topped off. When she straightened up she rested her hand on Anders's thigh and kept it there a little bit too long. Then looked too deeply into his eyes. Erika would have liked to claw them out with her sharpened forefinger. He's mine! Do something, Anders! Remove her hand! But Anders just laughed.

"Come on then, let's hear it," said Erika's teammate.

"Who sang a duet with Mauro Scocco in the song: *As Long as We Have Each Other?*"

Erika was quite bewitched by that hand on Anders's thigh. Dizzy Tits leaned forward again and he could not take his eyes off her breasts for more than a few seconds at a time.

"To be frank with you I couldn't give a damn!" she said loudly.

They stared at her. All of them.

"Annifrid Lyngstad," said Fat Hips. "That was actually our question, anyway." She looked at Anders and earned herself an approving smile. That sealed it. Erika stood up and went outside. Tottered through the kitchen, tore off her high-heeled shoes. A hand grabbed her arm. The floor swayed and she dropped into someone's lap. The man's face came much too close to her. His beard-stubble grazed her cheek. In spite of having drunk a lot herself, she could smell his boozy breath. His eyes looked like rolling hand grenades soon to be tossed into a crowd. With a bit of luck they'd all be blown to pieces.

"You know darling, you have to watch out with that fellow. Anders, you know… he knows what makes women tick." He allowed her back on her feet when she started struggling. "When we were students together at Lund… oh damn." He roared with laughter, then his eyes grew shrewd. "At these parties there are no rules about going home with the same person you turned up with. Not at all," he rumbled and slapped her bottom as she freed herself. "A bit of variety is always welcome."

"Erika, where are you going?" Anders's happy mug appeared in the doorway. He didn't seem to have understood a thing.

"Where do you think!?" she hissed and the man twisted up in the chair broke into peals of laughter. Anders joined in. As they laughed their mouths turned into echoing black holes.

"The powder room, I see. Excuse me."

That's when she walked off. Took her shoes in her hand and just wandered off into the dark. Away from the party, away from all those idiots. I hate you! I hate you, you pompous puffed-up shit, and all your stuck-up friends! What the hell had she come here for?

She walked down toward the sea and passed the Beach Café. The outside tables were full of buzzing teenagers in summer clothes. Disco music made the windows rattle like tambourines in the summer night. From Sjöviksgården one could hear the melodies of the older generation. *Take me to the sea… and make me into a king.… A king of the summer and the night.…* What had made her believe in love this time, when it had always gone wrong before? She thought about this while she undressed behind the sauna and left her clothes under a rock.

She walked into the sea until the water came up to her waist. She slid into the black mirror and took a few powerful strokes under the water. Down she went into another world where the shame could no longer reach her. The iciness of the water wrenched her lungs and took the edge off her humiliation, as if she could not concentrate on both things at once. Slowly the water grew more bearable. Indolently the waves calmed her churning inner sea while her thoughts wafted by without her paying any particular mind to them. Here she was alone; no one needed to see her. It makes all the difference in the world to be in one's own loneliness rather than being pitied and stared at by others just because one's alone. She wasn't alone at work. There, she was needed and appreciated and pretty tough. Anders probably thought that was what she was like. That was most likely why he thought she'd be able to take the heat and quickly become one of the gang.

Did I overreact, she asked herself? Like so many times before she regretted not just having gone with the flow, clenching her jaw and joining in with the others, just for a while, anyway; maybe things would have got better. Sometimes things do look up, she thought sleepily to herself as she started swimming toward land. She'd drifted further out than she'd realized. The wind bore away from the shore.

It had been so easy swimming out, but now there was resistance. Her joints were frozen and stiff and the waves washed over her and made her choke. For a moment she was afraid she wouldn't manage it. What an idiot she'd been to swim out like this, drunk and all by herself. She regretted her actions and longed to be back in the warmth. With Anders... if he were still there for her, the way she'd behaved. Maybe he'd already left with someone else. If so, it would definitely be over. She wouldn't have to agonize about it any more. She put all her anger into her swim strokes. One stroke, another, don't give up even though it would be so much easier giving up and going with the current. She saw Anders and his admirers before her and hated them with every stroke. A little further, just a little further. Dizzy Tits putting her hand on Anders's thigh. Fat Hips kissing him on the mouth. In fact, when she thought about it, Fat Hips had not actually kissed him on the lips—but it was only a question of time.

A big wave washed over Erika's head. It came in from the side and she wasn't ready for it. She sank down and pushed down with her feet, feeling for the bottom. Not yet. Was she swimming in the right direction? Yes, in the pale moonlight she could see the white sand, the lights from Sjöviksgården and the outlines of buildings. When after an eternity she came in closer she saw there was someone standing there at the edge of the water, waiting for her. A dark figure. A man. It should be Anders but she wasn't sure. Suddenly it occurred to her that she didn't have any clothes on. They were under the rock. She was alone, naked and defenseless. She wasn't even sure she'd have the strength to scream.

The man was motionless. He should have called out. If it were Anders he would have called out to her as she came wading in, exhausted, through the breaking waves. He would have given her an exuberant wave, he was always exuberant in all his bodily gestures, like a teenager without any real control of his movements. Maybe he was angry. Of course, he must be angry with her for behaving like that and leaving. But something wasn't quite right here. Was it Anders? She rubbed the back of her hand across her eyes to get a better look. His build was like Anders's. He was wearing a beach robe. Probably he was quiet like this because she'd behaved like such an idiot. She couldn't see his face because of the hood. By the time she taken the last few strides, panting and shivering onto the beach and she saw that the man was masked under his hood, it was too late. He'd already come up close and his strong arm had already gripped her upper arm.

"Anders," she said, trying his name even though she already knew this was all wrong. This was a bad dream she'd either wake from with a terrible hangover or not at all.… This was and wasn't Anders at the same time.

The man didn't answer. His eyes glinted from behind the mask in the shadow under the hood of the gown. He turned around to make sure he wasn't being watched, then tightened his grip with ferocious strength.

"Help, help me!" her voice was swallowed by the wind and the waves. "Let me go, what do you want?" She tried to get out of his grip. She was strong and fit and she'd done any number of self-defense courses. But it wasn't doing her any good now; she was drunk and exhausted after her swim. "Let me go! Please! Leave me alone!" If she could only catch her breath she'd recover her strength.

He shook his head. His hand moved up to her mouth. With his other hand, and the weight of his body, he pressed her down toward the water. Slowly. She didn't have the strength. She collapsed, fell backward through the weight of water, scraping her back against a rock. Her head was under the water. Gasping for air she re-emerged, only to be pressed down again. The pressure of his knee over her neck—she was a helpless victim, she couldn't fight him any more. She breathed in water and sand and coughed and inhaled more water until her last reserves of strength drained out of her, and she couldn't resist, couldn't....

Chapter 30

She was awakened by the cold. An icy cold that made her muscles contract and tremble uncontrollably. Someone was breathing very close to her. Something cold and wet slid across her face and the breathing grew heavier. Then came a voice. A woman's voice, screaming. Maybe it was Erika who was screaming?

The scream undulated and pulsated as it grew louder. Erika shivered so hard that her skin smarted.

The voice was there again, now much closer and its words grew intelligible.

"We have to call an ambulance. I didn't bring the cell phone. You're a faster runner than me."

Erika opened her eyes and stared straight into a mouth full of sharp teeth. A pair of round, yellow eyes fixed onto her, watching her every move. A nose pushed into her side. She had a coughing fit, and suddenly felt violently ill, only just having time to turn her head slightly and throw up.

"Shall we move her onto her side?" A man's voice, represented by two legs in denim. Erika didn't even have the strength to lift her head any more.

"I think she's conscious." The woman tugged at the leash, and made her dogs lie down.

"I'll go fetch some help." The man again.

"How are you feeling?" asked the woman as her face drew very close.

Erika was too exhausted to be ashamed of herself. "I'm okay." She tried to gauge whether in fact this were true. She could raise her head off the ground now. And move her arms and legs, although they were trembling and hurting.

"Wait, Jonny! She's waking up." He carried on running. The woman stood up and called out again.

Erika saw him stopping further down and turning round. For an instant it occurred to her that he might be the same man who'd been waiting for her on the beach. The man who'd tried to drown her. He was almost as tall, but nowhere near as skinny. Maybe it had all been a dream, a hallucination.

"What happened?" asked the woman, smoothing away a few strands of hair from Erika's face.

"I don't know. I was swimming." She tried to remember and what she did remember she had no desire to talk about. She'd had too much to drink, far too much, and she'd made an idiot of herself.

"Do you want us to call the police? And an ambulance?" the man asked, out of breath, after coming back to them.

Erika shook her head. This was more than enough without her colleagues finding out what she'd done. The woman had covered Erika with her overcoat. They'd found her lying naked on the beach. She'd been vomiting. *The slut lay there crying out her accusations.* She wished she were dead.

"When you found me, was I alone?" she asked, and her fear of the answer came washing over her like an ice-cold wave. Was the image of the man on the beach created by too much alcohol or had it really happened?

The woman tried to help Erika sit up and sweep the overcoat tighter round her body, while the man turned away politely. "It was the dogs that found you," she said. "They started barking. We couldn't see, the sauna was in the way. We weren't even walking in that direction, but the dogs wouldn't give up."

"We were just taking them for a quick walk before we went to bed ourselves," the man continued. "There are still some people partying at the Beach Café, but we didn't see anyone on the road." He checked his wristwatch and added. "It's quarter past two. It'll hardly get dark tonight, Midsummer's night, before dawn comes again."

"Did something bad happen to you? I mean, did someone assault you?" The woman's eyes were searching and anxious. Protectively she put her arm around Erika and gave her man a demanding look. He should understand the seriousness of the situation and not start rambling about inconsequential things.

"I don't know." Her concern made Erika explore her own feelings. In fact, she wasn't quite sure what had happened. It was so loathsome and horrible that she started crying. How could she even know if someone had taken her body as she lay there naked and unconscious on the beach?

"I do think we should call for help, anyway," said the man.

"No, no, I'll be fine." Erika could see her colleagues before her. Maria would be furious because she hadn't taken better care of herself. Jesper Ek would never stop giving her a hard time about it, and Hartman would be objective and professional without managing to hide what he was really thinking.

"Do you know where your clothes are?" asked the man, who seemed impatient to carry on walking his dogs.

Erika pointed at the place behind the white-washed

sauna where she thought she'd waded into the water. As she stumbled off in that general direction, the man scolded her.

"I'll get them for you." He disappeared and came back with the bundle of clothes under his arm. Still shivering, Erika got dressed with the borrowed overcoat over her shoulders.

"I'm sorry, it's completely wet." She handed back the garment, with thanks.

"Never mind about that. Can we do anything else for you? Shall we go with you somewhere?" The woman looked at her husband, who'd taken control of the dogs, tugging at their leashes. He seemed bothered now. And small wonder. Probably he had a clear idea of what had happened. She'd been vomiting like a proper drunk and wasn't wearing a stitch when they found her. Probably he thought it was all her own fault. She noted where he was looking and felt her hair, sticky and stinking of vomit.

"Me and my friend are renting a cottage nearby. I'll be fine. I'm really grateful to you for following your dogs and finding me."

Once they'd left her and she only saw their backs she felt much better. She went back to the water and rinsed out her hair. Some of the vomit had also ended up on her dress, where the fabric touched her hair. She would change clothes once she got back to the cottage. In the warmth. In Anders's bed, if he wanted her there. How could she have been such an idiot? There was no guarantee he'd want anything to do with her any more.

There again, what about him? Shouldn't he share some of the blame, Erika thought to herself? When she left the party she'd been convinced it was his fault. And nothing else had fundamentally happened to change that. Apart from the fact that she'd vomited and lain on the beach and that some strangers had seen her. But Anders wasn't in a position to know that. And she was certainly not going to tell him either.

Erika hurried past Sörviksgården. The Maypole stood abandoned in the middle of the lawn, decorated with ox-eye daisies, columbines, and other Midsummer flowers tied onto a bed of oak leaves. A little earlier there had been dancing there and accordion music had echoed over the water. The dancing had left its marks in the ground, like a circle in the gravel. There wasn't a single person in sight. It felt unpleasant. She regretted not letting the friendly couple accompany her to the cottage in spite of all. Why is it easier for a man who's had a few too many to accept, than for a woman? Why is the disgrace so much keener and the tolerance level so much lower for a woman who's gone beyond the limit?

Thoughts of what might have happened while she lay there naked and vulnerable in the sand started coming, although she tried to push them away.

What had actually happened? It all felt so real when she looked back at it. A man wearing a cape, like a medieval monk. His hands round her throat. There would be marks, surely? That would prove that it had actually happened. What if Erika had been raped, as the woman feared? The thought disgusted her indescribably.

Erika continued down Storvägen through the village while dawn rose and its gray light filtered down over the road. Smakrike, the Claudelin house, Frej's Magasin, and Restaurant Bruna Dörren—all closed and locked for the night. Directly after Lövängen Pension, a white, single-story building, she turned into Louis Sparres Väg. It wasn't far now to the cottage. Erika slowed down. It felt difficult, having to face Anders again. She saw the kitchen light on from afar, and a bluish light from the computer screen. Was he awake? Waiting for her?

She was just about to press down on the door handle when the door was flung open from the inside.

"Where the hell have you been? Do you understand how worried I've been?" He took her by both shoulders, held her at arm's length and shook her. "What happened?"

Erika couldn't think of anything to say. Her head was empty. All the answers she'd been practicing on the road had vanished. "I went out."

"I noticed!" he said in a hard voice. "We've been looking for you, we've ALL been looking for you! The last few people went home ten minutes ago. I was going to call the police, until I realized it might compromise you in some way. I hope you have a good explanation." He didn't let go, didn't let her into his arms and didn't forgive her, but forced her to look directly into his eyes. "Don't you understand I was worried?"

"Yes." It was as if her own anger had no room when his was so much greater and took up so much room. His voice was much more powerful, his hands so much stronger. His anxiety seemed more justifiable than her feelings of abandonment at the party. They had all looked for her. She had humiliated them both.

"Where were you? Whatever you've done I want to know! Did you go to bed with someone? I want the truth!"

"You're insane!" It hadn't even occurred to her that he'd think she'd been unfaithful. Poor Anders, what would his friends say?

"So where were you?" He calmed himself a little.

"I swam too far out and almost didn't manage to get back."

She saw him grow pale. She realized he was thinking about how he'd lost Isabel. "I wasn't entirely sober."

237

"Goddamn right you weren't!" He let go of her. "Never do that again! Never ever do that again!" To Erika's great surprise he started crying. She put her arms round him and kissed him, rocked him in her arms and he let himself be consoled all the way into the bedroom.

"I left because I felt I wasn't good enough when you were with your friends. And I felt jealous." Now he'd shown his more fragile side and his sadness, it was easier for her to tell the truth.

Afterward, once he was asleep, she lay awake and watched him in the light of morning seeping in through the French blinds. His dark, curly hair, beautiful hands, and his clean profile. What she saw was etched into her memory, and she staked her claim on him. Anders is mine. Get thee hence, Isabel.

Chapter 31

After a couple of hours of shallow slumber Erika woke up and needed the bathroom. Her left arm had gone to sleep and her muscles were dully aching after her exerting swim. Carefully she eeled out of Anders's naked embrace, their clammy skin sticking together in the heat. His arm was heavy. She looked at her pale face in the mirror. Her mascara had caked round her eyes and down her cheek. She washed it off. The water was cold and she had to give it a good rub to get the smear off. Slowly, memories of the preceding night resurfaced in her consciousness. She felt her throat; there were no marks as far as she could see, yet she couldn't get rid of the feeling that the man on the beach had actually been there, had actually gripped her. She should really go to the emergency room and test herself to determine whether she'd been raped. But she'd run into people she knew down there. The thought of this was just as unpleasant as her fears. She could have got herself a rape kit at work; sending off the samples and getting them back herself, involving no one except Hartman.... If she'd been sober and together, that's what she would have done. Erika squeezed her eyes shut and hated herself. If she had been sober and together this would never have happened in the first place.

She got into the shower, letting the ice-cold water rake her skin as it slowly heated up. If I find out you were with someone else I'll never forgive you, Anders had whispered as they pulled close together in the big double bed. He had held her so tightly that she almost lost her breath. And she'd assured him she hadn't. Through ourselves we know others. She had no idea at this point where she'd been, nor did she have the strength to find out. Not now. All she'd wanted when she came back was to be enfolded in warm, forgiving arms. How would he react if she told him the truth—that she actually didn't know what had happened? Maybe she should have told him straight away. If she had thrown herself in his arms, crushed and weeping, as soon as she arrived at the cottage at about two in the morning, or if the friendly couple had accompanied her and helped her explain, then it would have been clearer that she was a victim. But they hadn't seen anyone else on the beach. They had only seen her shame.

"You're so quiet," said Anders, as they sat having breakfast in the sun on the veranda. A fly buzzed round them, insistently landing on the cheese. She tried to wave it away, then looked up at the garden and its newly mowed lawn. She saw the sea beyond the trees. When she didn't respond to his words, he continued.

"What are you thinking about?"

Erika took a sip of her coffee to give herself time to think.

"I was thinking about last night...." She couldn't finish her thought. She wanted to accuse him, but she immediately realized it would be turned back on herself. She wanted to know if he were ashamed of her; wanted to know what his friends meant to him, and particularly what sort of relationship he had with those two women. Had he been seeing one of them? She thought about that hand, resting on his thigh. Those kisses so close to his mouth and kisses on his neck. Fumbling kisses that had ended up almost anywhere—as long as there was an alibi for them, the right answer to the question. Was it true, what his friend had said? Had he been a womanizer in college?

Anders leaned toward her and took her hands, to gain all her attention. "You scared me so much. Sorry. I wouldn't want to lose you for anything in the world." He put his arm around her across the table, and pressed his cheek to hers. "I want it to be you and me."

Maybe she should have been satisfied with his apology and his stated aim to move on with her. Maybe it would have been better if she'd left it at that.

"I felt deserted last night," she said, and those words were not possible to ignore. Now she'd opened herself to his accusations. She moved back, so that his arm no longer reached her.

"Sorry, I wasn't aware of it." He grew silent, thinking it over. "You can't mean you felt jealous of those girls. You don't need to be, they're childhood friends, like sisters more or less. If I'd wanted to be with one of them, I would have had many chances. But it would never work, somehow." He chuckled, as if something had suddenly occurred to him. "Jonna and me had a try while we were at school, but it was nothing very exciting."

"Your friend said you were quite a womanizer while you were studying in Lund." It felt good giving Anders the chance to defend himself, thus evading any shortcomings of her own.

"I was so young then, I wasn't thinking of the consequences, you took it for granted in those days that the girls were taking precautions." Anders reached for the thermos and, with a gesture, offered her a top-off.

Erika nodded. "Did you get anyone pregnant?" Straight away she regretted even asking, wasn't even sure she wanted to know.

Anders jumped at the direct question. "Yes, and I thought it went without saying that she should have an abortion. I didn't want a kid. Not then. I was in the middle of my studies." He put his hands to his head and all of a sudden there was a sharpness in his eyes. "I wasn't even in love with her. It just happened. I panicked, didn't want to see her again. I tried to persuade her to get rid of it, but she wouldn't. I know I was a big shit. We only saw each other once after that."

Erika wanted to follow up with more questions, but Anders stood up and turned his back to her as he walked over and stood by the veranda railing, his cup of coffee in his hand. He clearly did not want to talk about it any more and she left him in peace for now.

They packed a picnic, a portable barbecue, and a blanket in Anders's backpack and headed off to the beach. The sun stood high in the sky, glittering in the water that rippled in the mild shoreward breeze. The light dazzled her eyes, and Erika got out her sunglasses. She felt his arm round her waist. Everything should really have been well with the world.

They stopped at the Beach Café to buy ice cream. There were some new flavors to choose from, and Erika couldn't make up her mind. Once she'd made her decision she realized she hadn't brought her wallet, which was still in her purse. Before she knew it, Anders had opened his wallet to pay and Erika saw a photo inside it—of the woman he kept close to his heart in his jacket pocket. He noticed that she'd seen it. There was no way out of this. An explanation was required.

"Julia wanted a mom like anyone else. She wanted me to get the photo out when we were reading her bedtime story so her mom could be there, too, and ever since the photo has been left in my wallet."

"She was very beautiful, Isabel."

He confirmed this almost inaudibly. Then took her by the hand.

"You're quite similar, in many ways." They walked up the beach in a northerly direction. "As you understand, I haven't had much luck with women. If you think I'm a bit rigid and careful there are some pretty specific reasons for it. Maybe it's time to change Isabel's photo now. Do you have some nice photo I could have?"

"Should I take that as a promotion?"

Vitvärs fishing huts were low and gray, with small windows. There were no nets hanging in the net enclosures. Beyond them lay some remains of lime ovens last used in the 1600s. Erika looked out over the green-blue sea and thought with a shudder about the events of last night. Anders put his arm round her and probably thought she was cold.

"The Donner trading house was in business here until a merchant called Claudelin took over the company at the end of the 1800s. His farm is still standing, along with the warehouse, in the village." Anders kissed her neck.

Only now did she dare ask what the others had said when she was left the party in a mood, and they couldn't find her. She steeled herself against his answer.

"After you left we played games for a while, but when you weren't in the bathroom and no one had seen you for an hour or so I got worried. To be honest, I was afraid you'd gone home with Stefan. He left more or less at the same time as you."

"I don't even know who Stefan was."

"You were sitting in his lap when I came into the kitchen." He gave her a look that spoke volumes about his opinion of that. "I suppose it wasn't completely true what I said about *everyone* looking for you. I went straight to his house and asked if you were there."

"What did he say? It must have made him wonder?"

"He laughed right in my face and said I should keep you close, or he'd consider you a single woman. I asked to have a look inside his cottage and he let me have a quick look round. I mean, you could have been hiding anywhere, so I tried to have a peek through the windows, but the lights were turned off in the house, I couldn't see anything."

"What? You were jealous!"

"Then I sat behind a spruce fir so I'd see you if you came sneaking out of the gate. I must have fallen asleep. Not for very long, but an hour or so, and then when I got back to the cottage and you weren't there I didn't know what to do. I was frightened and angry and upset. Sorry. I'm not usually jealous."

They took a shortcut through the woods. Folhammar Rauk Area was full of limestone formations polished by the sea into pillars, prehistoric animals, and dragons. It all looked so playful that Erika had to smile. An old man with a giant nose in limestone. A little door in a huge boulder that a six-year-old would have wanted to crawl through. Ugly trolls with overgrown heads. In the middle of nature's haphazard playground someone had put out tables and arranged a neat and tidy barbecue spot.

Anders unpacked the trout he'd stuffed with lemon butter and fresh herbs then wrapped in aluminium foil. They lit the disposable barbecue and put out the couscous salad, bread, and wine. Anders was in a good mood again and telling anecdotes from the hospital and his military service.

"Military service is one of the most dangerous things you can do at that age. Every year more and more young men are wounded or killed, and that's in peace-time. I was lucky enough to be sent home."

Erika was just about to ask why, when he put his head inside her sweater and kissed her stomach, nibbling her belly playfully.

"Stop, it tickles!" She couldn't stop herself from laughing. It had been a while since she last laughed as she did that day. Once they started they couldn't stop.

"If you're going to cope with jobs like ours, I'd say laughter is almost a matter of mental hygiene. I mean, sometimes you feel like vomiting in the trash. When you hear about the abuses patients have been exposed to, while still managing to carry on, I'm filled with admiration. And I could only guess the things you see in your work."

"Shall we have a swim?" she interrupted. Work was the last thing she wanted to think about.

"It's shallow. You'd have to walk almost all the way to Russia to have a dip. What did you do to your back?"

"What?" She tried to turn round, but she couldn't see.

"It's a scratch. Looks like a letter, actually."

It was difficult for her to push the thought away, but at the same time she was worried that Anders would ask if she grew too remote. When they got back to the cottage she went straight into the bathroom and locked the door to have a look at her back in the mirror. After she pulled her sweater over her head she stifled a little cry with some difficulty. There was a letter. A large if not entirely clear letter: "K." Just like the blood in the bedroom where Linn was murdered and in the gravel outside Harry's place. It could not be a coincidence. The letter may not have been very symmetrical, but it was there, engraved in her own flesh.

Never before had people in a civilization left so many traces of themselves, he thought. Every bill, every receipt, every time one logged onto a computer, there was an exact time and purpose. Every human life could be mapped out in detail. Books taken out in the library were only a password away from the observer. Interests, political alignments, and leisure activities could all be extrapolated. Secret e-mail messages exchanged between lovers might as well be sent as postcards—that's how easy it was gaining access to them if you knew how. The real problem was how to filter the information. Faces gliding past surveillance cameras in a pedestrian underpass could be scrutinized hundreds of miles away. There was no longer such a thing as private lives—nothing personal. That was the price we had to pay for our security and comfort and our access to information. That was why one should not upload everything on the Internet. He had collected his secrets in an old-style scrapbook. Here, he nostalgically kept his most cherished moments from a summer on Gotland more than ten years ago. It had been his birthday. They were having a party. He wanted streamers in the trees. But Isabel had forgotten to buy streamers. So she tore up an old sheet into thin strips. It had been really beautiful, and for a moment he almost did not hate her at all.

Chapter 32

And then came Midsummer's Day, with its sun and clear blue sky. Lightly-dressed people jostled in Visby's streets, but for Maria Wern it might as well have been any old weekday. Operation Door-Knocking in the neighborhood of the Botanical Gardens had yielded some results. On the night when Harry Molin was murdered four witnesses had seen a man wearing a dark cape. It was something that had not yet been publicized in the media, and thus more valuable. One of the witnesses, Louise Mutas, even lived on the same street as Harry Molin.

Maria Wern was shown into a pleasantly furnished living room in Specksgränd. Admittedly she could not actually see Harry's house or the mailbox—because these were on the same side of the street as Louise's house—but she had a very good view of the lane itself.

"It was from this window that I saw him," said Louise. She was a bony woman of about eighty with a wonderful curly head of white hair like a halo around her friendly face. "It was about half past eleven. I sleep so fitfully. By nine o'clock I'm exhausted and have to lie down even if there's something good on television. I sleep like a log. But then it's completely impossible; I wake up after just a few hours and can't go back to sleep. This was precisely what happened."

"Did you hear some noise, or what made you wake up?" Maria went up to the window and stood in the exact position from which Louise saw the man in the cape wandering down the road.

"Harry Molin's dogs were barking like there was no tomorrow. He usually keeps them under control, and it surprised me they kept barking for so long." Louise kept moving nervously around the room. "Would you like a cup of coffee?"

Before Maria had time to answer, Louise had disappeared into the kitchen and started bustling with cups and saucers. Maria remained by the window. The old lady hadn't turned on the lamp; she stood there in the dark. The man had come from Rostockergränd. Louise had perceived him as inebriated. Because the streetlights were broken, she hadn't managed to form an opinion of his face or any other features, other than his unsteady and rather stiff gait. He seemed to be carrying a piece of firewood or some other weapon in his hand, but she couldn't say for sure. It may have been something else he was carrying, but since hearing about Harry she thought it probably was a weapon.

"So, coffee then. Let's not be formal about it, shall we sit in the kitchen?" Louise gave her a friendly smile, wiped her chapped red hands on the striped tea-towel and hung it up in the cleaning cupboard. They sat down at the kitchen table, where she had placed two rose-patterned cups in delicate porcelain. Most likely her best porcelain, Maria reflected and held the cup carefully with both hands. Louise offered her the platter on which she'd piled all the best the house had to offer: fritters, crullers, Tosca cakes, saffron buns, cardamom turns, and little biscuits with marzipan and red icing. Maria understood what was expected of her.

Cakes were the pride and joy of this lady, and they had to be tasted. Each one of them would take at least twenty minutes on the rowing machine to burn off. She really hoped they were homemade, so at least they'd be worth the bother.

"I'm staying with my sister in Endre. I daren't sleep here at nights after what's happened on this street. First Linn, our sweet nurse Linn… and then Harry Molin. I haven't seen Linn's husband, either, since… she was found in the Botanical Gardens. It's so terrifying it doesn't bear thinking about. I feel so sorry for Claes, poor little man. What will he do with himself now? I don't think he has anyone to talk to." By the time Maria stepped back into the street she was off-duty. The Midsummer sun was lavishing itself on everyone, the weather quite sparkling. Her children were with their grandparents in Uppsala. Erika had made off to Ljugarn with Anders Ahlström; this time it seemed to be for real. Maria hoped it would last, for Erika's sake, so that she wouldn't have to be disappointed again. She'd grown very aggressive toward men, and it didn't suit her at all. Tomas Hartman was at a family reunion in Martebo. When Maria called Jesper Ek to ask if he wanted to do something, she learned that he was off fishing with Per Arvidsson. She was invited to tag along, of course.

"I'd rather stick needles in my eyes," she'd replied, and Ek said he'd been expecting something along those lines from her, but if she changed her mind there was space in the boat.

"But I expect you'd freeze the water with your looks. Can't you try to forgive him, Maria? He's regretting himself to death. It's terrible seeing him now. He'd do anything to have it undone. Do you know how hard it is ripping him away from work for a few hours? He promised to come fishing but only if we used the time to talk about the investigation. He's obsessed with finding the people who assaulted you. He's doing his utmost, Maria."

"That's lovely. Best of luck with the fishing."

"Maria...." His voice was pleading.

"No, I've had enough! I'm not even going to discuss it."

She had difficulties concentrating after the call. Her feelings for Per had already grown murky while he systematically failed to give her anything back—countering her hopes and dreams with irritation and constantly changing plans. What was it Jonatan Eriksson had said? Sometimes one makes do with the crumbs from the table because that's all one seems to be worth. This was not the same as bitterness, she decided; this was about self-respect pure and simple—saying "no" before she got so humiliated or sick of the situation that she grew hard and nasty. But what about the rest of her life? Who would she think about now, who would she miss? It all felt so scarily empty.

Maria went back to the police station and clocked out. She'd taken on the extra shifts partly because she didn't want to feel lonely, and partly because she couldn't stand the idea of the murder investigation slowing down over the public holiday. As time elapsed, witnesses progressively forgot what they had really seen. Once they'd had time to confer with each other or read the newspapers, this also affected their stories. The brain looks for order and credibility and subconsciously probes for meaning and context. Maria repeatedly went through all the material collected from the murders of Linn Bogren and Harry Molin, only pausing occasionally to replenish her mug of coffee whenever it grew cold. She called Claes and checked up on a few details. The shoes he'd handed in had matched the shoeprints, as expected. She asked a few other questions, to clear up some details concerning the suit Harry had ordered at a tailor's in town.

She checked up again on Claes—how he was feeling. Once he understood that she was actually concerned for him, his sadness and anger and guilt came pouring out of him in a torrent of words that seemed never-ending.

"Do you have anyone else you can talk to?" Maria didn't feel she could leave him hanging on the other end of the line in his current state. "Someone who could stay with you?"

"If you mean that woman I met in Gothenburg, it's over. Definitely over. I never want to see her again. I can't even explain how it happened. I ended up at her place one time after we'd gone to the bar after we came ashore. I stayed the night. I didn't love her but she kept getting in touch and wanting to see me, and I couldn't resist her expectations. Do you understand? Once it had happened I thought seeing her again wouldn't make things any worse. It was ruined anyway between me and Linn, I'd already broken what we promised each other. I didn't think it could get any worse, but I was wrong. If I'd only come home right away. I don't have anyone to talk to because I don't want anyone to know about this. No one."

"You're staying with your brother right now?"

"Yeah, but we've never really been able to talk. He's much older than me and he knows the way everything's got to be. It's been a relief, though, having somewhere to go. I'll never be able to live in our house again. It's not a safe place any more."

"One last question. Did Linn used to call Tarot hotlines?"

"She did sometimes when we first met. I asked her why and she said it was good sometimes looking for support when you were facing a crossroads in your life."

Several hours later when Maria left the police station, the sun was low but the air was still warm. She took a deep breath and stretched her limbs. Her back was stiff. Probably she'd sat all twisted up in front of the computer, like a staple. A boy of about ten or eleven was standing outside the main entrance, looking around confusedly. Maria went to him and asked what he was doing there.

"I want to talk to that police who tried to save Linus."

"That would be me." Maria gave the boy a searching look. He shuffled his feet nervously and looked down at the ground.

"Are you Maria Wern?" Round-eyed, he looked at her. His freckled cheeks grew flushed, then with a toss of his head he flicked his raven-black bangs out of his eyes so he could get a better look at her. "Straight up?"

"Yes, it's me, it's really me." He was so sweet in his embarrassment that Maria started laughing. "What's your name?"

"Oliver." He twisted uneasily. "There was one thing I didn't tell that other police who came to our place. Something I forgot. I never got a phone number so I didn't know how to get hold of him again and anyway I didn't want to talk to him any more. I wanted to find you." The little boy's gestures grew expansive and his voice sounded eager.

"If you like we can go to my office and have a chat. I'm not in a hurry."

"No, I don't want to go in there...."

"So let's have an ice cream at Max and you can tell me there instead. The officer you spoke to is probably not working today, it's a holiday. I'll write down what you tell me and then I'll give him your telephone number, so you can talk some more if he's got any other questions. An ice cream would be nice, wouldn't it?" They sat outside in the sun. Maria dug out pen and paper. "What was his name, the policeman you spoke to?"

"He didn't say. He didn't even have a uniform. It felt a

bit creepy." Oliver gave Maria a glance, then dived into his ice cream again.

"What did he look like?" Maria wondered if it could have been Hartman himself or maybe Jesper Ek or Arvidsson who'd spoken to the boy. But his description of a tall, very thin man with a black pulled-down hat, leather jacket, and sunglasses didn't fit. Arvidsson's red moustache would have been the first thing the boy commented on. Hartman was definitively not thin and Ek could hardly be described as tall. Haraldsson would never wear a hat in the summer. Maria couldn't think who the boy was describing, but let it go for the moment so he could unburden himself.

"The police, I mean the one who came to see us, asked if Linus knew a doctor whose name was Anders, Anders Ahlström? He wanted to know if Linus thought he was a nice guy, like a sort of dad type. And I said he did think that. He was his favorite doctor."

Maria could well imagine. But the question puzzled her nonetheless. "Did he show you his ID?"

"No. He just said he was a policeman."

"There was something you'd been thinking about," she prompted.

Oliver's cone had started dripping and he bit off the end and plugged it with his index finger.

"It was something Linus said. I promised I wouldn't say anything about it, not to anyone, 'cos he reckoned it was bit embarrassing." Oliver stopped and waited to be disencumbered of his vow of silence.

"If it helps us catch the people who hurt Linus, he'd probably like you to tell us, don't you think?"

"Yeah." Oliver looked relieved. "It was like this. Linus couldn't get to sleep because he was scared. But he didn't dare tell his dad 'cos he'd get angry and tell Linus to stop imagining things and be quiet and get to sleep. And that's exactly what he couldn't do. Linus said he'd seen a nasty man outside his window in the street. Like a nazgûl, if you know what that is?"

"An evil black knight, like in the Lord of the Rings, a creature in a black cape?" Maria felt herself breaking out in goose bumps. Had the information about a man in a cape leaked into the press after all?

"He didn't have a face, it was really creepy. He was just a black sort of thing, and his eyes." Oliver grimaced. "Linus saw him loads of times, once in the garden. But he never dared tell one of the adults. Maybe not even his favorite doctor and definitely not his mom, 'cos she'd get really hysterical and want to drag him off to some children's shrink if he said it was for real."

"Has anyone else spoken to you about nazgûl or men in capes? Have you read about it anywhere?"

"I've seen 'The Lord of the Rings,' if that's what you mean. Do I... do I have to talk to the other police? I prefer talking to you. I didn't like talking to him. He smiled all the time but his eyes were angry. I don't want to talk to him any more."

"I'm the one who got attacked, you see, so I'm not allowed to investigate this. But I'll talk to my chief. His name is Tomas, he's a sensible man and he's smart, too. I think you could talk to him, he'd be very interested in what you just told me. Can you remember anything else about the policeman you spoke to? You said he wore dark glasses and a black hat. Did he ever take off his sunglasses? You said his eyes were angry."

Oliver hesitated. "You could see his eyes through the lenses even though they were tinted black. His eyes were evil."

Chapter 33

Maria Wern walked home with Oliver, taking Smittens Backe toward Stora Torget. They zigzagged between the market stalls, all offering exactly the same as in other street markets—printed T-shirts, bronze and silver jewelry, sweets, and braided hair extensions—whether in Crete or Paris. Only the odd stall here and there offered local items such as blueberry jam, Gotland mix tea, Gotland mustard, and mint jelly. She tried repeatedly to get Hartman on the cell phone, but most likely he couldn't hear the phone over the noise of the party. It was just as impossible getting hold of Arvidsson and Ek.

"Are either of your parents at home? I'd like to talk to them." Oliver thought they would be. His mother had told him they were having guests for dinner in the evening and that he had to be home early. They crossed the square diagonally and Oliver walked ahead through the lanes until they stood in front of a white-washed house with climbing roses on both sides of a low, green-painted door. There was movement behind the lace curtain: someone was at home. The front door was opened by a barefooted woman in summery clothes and lavishly curly hair. She stepped into her sneakers as Maria was introducing herself.

"Can I come in a moment?" Maria showed her ID.

"We've got guests coming in a minute." The woman looked troubled.

"I really don't want to barge in and this won't take a minute." Maria knew exactly how those last minutes felt before the arrival of guests.

They sat down in the glass conservatory, where climbing vines across the ceiling providing some shade against the sunlight. Oliver disappeared into his room.

"Linus was like a son in our home. We're desperately sad and torn up that this could happen. It could just as well have been Oliver who was attacked on the way home from Linus's house. The first few days Oliver wouldn't speak to anyone else at all. He just sat in the dark in his room and when we tried to talk to him he'd shout at us and tell us to stop lying about Linus being dead."

"It must be so difficult for him to comprehend...." Maria felt tears pressing just behind her eyes and she cleared her throat when she felt her voice thickening, "that someone he was just playing with is suddenly dead."

"In a horrendous way!" Oliver's mother moved her hand to her throat and then tossed her hair out of her eyes. "I was afraid Oliver would be damaged psychologically, so I insisted that the police had to bring a child psychologist if they wanted to question him. By the time they managed to get hold of someone with the right expertise, Oliver wouldn't speak to her."

"When Oliver came looking for me he told me he'd been visited by a male police officer. Are you aware of that?"

"No, if that's what happened it must have been yesterday when we weren't at home. We went up to our summer house yesterday and Oliver wouldn't come. He never mentioned this to me. If a policeman did come here I'll be furious, that's not what we agreed with the police."

"I promise I'll double-check that with my chief and get back to you."

"What do you mean?" Oliver's mother looked worried.

Maria hesitated briefly and then chose her words so they wouldn't be more frightening than necessary. "Don't leave him unsupervised until I've checked this."

As soon as the door had closed behind Maria's back she tried again to reach Hartman. This time she was successful. The party mood in his voice instantly disappeared when she revealed her fears to him.

"I'll come in straight away. If someone questioned that boy without a psychologist it was done expressly against my orders." Maria repeated Oliver's description of the policeman. "In which case who was he? He didn't show his ID."

"To be honest, Maria, I don't know. And it's scaring me."

The anxiety would not let go, nor the feeling of powerlessness. Their lack of insight into the assault case was frustrating. Maria was caught between extremes. Had she needlessly scared Oliver's already anxious mother when she said the boy should not be left alone? Or should she have taken the boy to the station to protect him from someone who wanted to harm him The thought crashed down like a bolt of lightning. If the evil was already here, in uniform, then he wouldn't be safe here, either. No, she mustn't think like that. It wasn't realistic. She'd probably been working too hard, and now she was seeing evil everywhere. Anyway, the investigation lay with Arvidsson. She hadn't managed to get hold of him and now the ball was in Hartman's court. She couldn't do anything else.

Linus had seen a man in a dark cape, just like Jill Andersson and Louise Mutas. Each of them, entirely based on their own subjective experience, had described him as a sleepwalker, a masked monk, a drunk, or a black and faceless knight. Either the perpetrator was inept because people saw him at the crime scenes, or there was actually an intention for him to be seen. A third alternative might be that he was unaware of his actions—was it really possible that these crimes had been committed by a sleepwalker? Suddenly Maria remembered Jonatan Eriksson. She'd promised the infection specialist that they'd have a coffee and a chat. Maybe he could fill her in about sleeping disorders? Maria called the hospital. Jonatan was not on call. She reached him at home. Half an hour later they met outside Skafferiet, a charming café on Adelsgatan where one could choose between pies, salads, and other light meals. The atmosphere was very pleasant. Maria had not been there since Christmas, when there had been a cozy fire crackling in the hearth. Now the doors to the outside tables were wide open. He came toward her with open arms and she couldn't quite stop herself from chuckling. People were looking and assuming they were a couple. She gave him a quick hug.

"Good to see you."

"At last," he said a little sulkily, then smiled. "I was hoping you'd get in touch."

They ordered a prawn salad each, with homemade bread, and sat down indoors with a view through the window of Adelsgatan. After a sun-drenched day on the beach, many tourists were seeking their way into Visby in the evening to have something nice to eat. They were lucky to have found a table, Maria realized, as she noted the line building up behind them at the register.

He looked at her with happy eyes and smiled, but said nothing. So much was unexpressed. Maria chose to bring up her formal errand first.

"What do you know about sleepwalkers?"

The question was completely unexpected. Maria looked so deadly serious that Jonatan burst out laughing.

"What was that?"

"I'm serious. Is it possible to kill another human being in your sleep? Are there checks and boundaries in the subconscious that prevent people from doing things they don't want to do, like in hypnosis?"

"Are we talking shop now?" he asked.

"Yes. But I can't tell you anything else about it."

"There is one case involving a sleepwalker. A man drove to his stepparents' house and stabbed them with a knife. Both of them died from their injuries. He woke up in his own bed. There was an exhaustive investigation into his sleeping disorder... to evaluate whether he could be put on trial for the crime."

"So there's no way of faking it?"

"No. If you're really sleepwalking it's verifiable by something called an EEG test. In fact, it doesn't happen while you're dreaming, which is what a lot of people think, but in deep sleep, right at the cusp between dream sleep and deep sleep. The longer this transition the greater the risk of sleepwalking. The motor-dynamics aren't deactivated, as they are in dream sleep, otherwise we'd do everything in real life that we do in our dreams, and the consequences of that would be quite awful, wouldn't they? A sleepwalker moves robotically, the body motor is not fully activated but it is in motion. Sleepwalkers can even talk, but the voice sounds mechanical. Afterwards, the sleepwalker can't remember anything."

"I walked in my sleep when I was a child and had a high temperature," Maria remembered. "Once I woke up in the greenhouse and I'd wet myself."

"It's quite common for children to walk in their sleep,

but it usually goes away. Among adults suffering from it, sleepwalking can be triggered by alcohol, a lack of sleep, or stress. It can be very debilitating and awkward for the person afflicted by it. Anything sleepwalkers may damage has to be removed, and it's best if they sleep on the ground floor with locked windows and closed doors."

"It must be terribly stressful not to be in full control of what you're doing."

"There have been cases of people stripping themselves naked and doing the most extraordinary things. If you're not in command of what you're doing you can't be put on trial for it, either. Or what do you think, as a police officer? It's an illness."

"There's a new prescription drug to help people stop smoking. Fumarret. Have you heard of it? I read an article about how in certain cases it led to confusion and sleepwalking."

"That's off my radar. I'm an infection specialist. If you want to know more I can contact a colleague, Sam Wettergren, one of the country's leading specialists on sleep, who works here at the hospital."

"Sam Wettergren!"

"So you've heard of him? He's been working on smoking prevention and sleep dysfunction but he's basically a lung specialist. Recently he presented a study on plant steroids. I haven't had time to read it yet, but I know it caused a stir at the medical convention in Gothenburg last autumn. I think he also published an article on it in 'The Lancet'."

"Sounds very eminent." Maria was having difficulties containing her excitement, and Jonatan read her like an open book. The flame of the candle flickered in the draft as more guests walked in.

"You saw him, didn't you? Questioned him about Linn,

who was murdered. I mean, she worked with him." Suddenly Jonatan realized where the questions were leading.

"Did you know her?"

"I ran into her sometimes when I was on duty at the hospital. We all miss her." Jonatan was lost in his own thoughts for a while. "Surely he's not a suspect?"

"I can't tell you. You if anyone should understand that. As a doctor you have to respect your patient's right to confidentiality."

"Can we meet again?" asked Jonatan when Maria made a move to stand up.

She hesitated. Wanted to. But couldn't promise anything.

"You're someone I'm very fond of, Jonatan, of course we have to meet up."

Chapter 34

Per Arvidsson sat at the prow of the old rowing boat, looking down into the sparkling green water. The churning
of the outboard drowned out the rushing sound of the water
against the hull and the screeching of gulls. Ahead in the
haze he saw the high, rocky coast of Lilla Karlsö and, further in the distance, could just make out the flatter profile
of Stora Karlsö. Jesper Ek cut the motor and took up the
oars.

"What a fantastic day. Can you see how lovely it is?"
He couldn't stop himself from saying it, though Arvidsson
looked just about as miserable as the semi-dehydrated earth-
worms in the old coffee tin.

Arvidsson squinted at the horizon and pretended not to
hear him. They prepared their rods and cast. They should at
least get a little perch or two. In his first summer on Gotland, Arvidsson had gone with Hartman to catch cod. The
zinc barrel had been overflowing in just over an hour, and
the boat lay so low in the water that they didn't dare fish
any more. Now the cod had disappeared and before that
the salmon, and the last few summers the sea had been full
of algae.

"It's like the Baltic is vomiting," he mumbled sadly. "If you want to catch something now you have to put out nets. And even then you only get a couple of plaice. Possibly."

Ek laughed without a care in the world. "You're incredible. Come on. You're not the only person in the world who's blown the love of your life. Been there, done that, bought the T-shirt. Happens to me all the time. You think you're going to die, that life will never be worth living again. Then someone buys you a cold beer and you realize it might just be worth hanging in there a little bit longer."

Arvidsson shook his head. What Ek had just blurted out was as dumb as it was true. His affairs were superficial, short-lived flames, in no way comparable to what he felt for Maria.

"Hartman said you were in Märsta the day before yesterday. Anything come out of it?"

"Yes, I have to go back again on Monday. When I tried to find the file we're looking for, the one about the man who was killed with a lawn mower blade, it wasn't there. I didn't believe my colleague, so I actually went there to help him find it. They can't explain where it's gone. The place in the archive where it should be is empty, and there's no way of checking if it's been lent to someone."

"Damned careless!" Ek spat on his worm and threw out the line again.

"Or theft. With the help of this colleague who was in charge of the investigation, I sketched out the main events as well as I could. If we're talking about the same man responsible for the lethal assault, we might get some more clues here to help us track him down." Suddenly, Arvidsson's float was pulled under.

"You've got a bite." Ek helped him haul in the line.

"Only seaweed," said Arvidsson, disappointed, as he untangled the green mess from his hook.

"But something came out of it? It must have or you wouldn't be going back."

"There's a woman I want to talk to. Malin Karlsson. An ex-heroin addict. One of the lucky ones who got herself out of the shit and managed to find a job at the register in a DIY superstore. She's in Greece and coming back on Monday. I've already spoken to the others who figured in the investigation. It's a long shot but we might get lucky...."

"What's her relationship to the dead man?"

"She accused him of repeatedly raping her, according to a girlfriend of hers. It was never possible to prove anything. She never reported it. I suppose she was afraid she wouldn't be believed. And then he was butchered with the blade of a lawn mower and thrown in a ditch. She had an alibi. She was in a rehab clinic at the time of the murder."

"Damn. Someone must have been pretty angry." Ek put on his sunglasses. The light breaking against the still surface of the water was blinding.

"Precisely. Here you can really talk about excessive violence. Every bone in his body was broken. The head was severed from the body. He was unrecognizable. They had to identify him using dental records."

"But Malin Karlsson had an alibi?" Ek repeated.

"She'd taken an overdose but miraculously survived it. For a couple of days she hovered between life and death on a life-support machine; then she was sent to Bredgården."

"And the girlfriend who talked to the police?"

"She was also in rehab at the time." Arvidsson tossed out his bait again, wedged his rod between his knees, and reached for the cooler. "A beer, you said. It won't help a lot, just dilutes the misery, you know."

"And if that trail doesn't lead anywhere, what then? Time is not on our side here." Ek took the sandwich and beer being handed to him.

"You're telling me. I've been working night and day on this. We have the murderer's DNA because Maria had the presence of mind to scratch him where his skin was exposed. If we find him we've got him. But the only tip we have right now is what I got from your kid at Svartsjö Prison. There are no witnesses. Weird, isn't it? Two people are assaulted in the street and no one sees anything of any value. Local residents hear some shouting and then three men leaving the scene, but none of them are capable of giving a description. What are people doing with their spare time? Getting drunk and watching TV?"

"Maria described a man in an overcoat and cap who walked past while the assault was in progress."

Arvidsson remembered. But the witness had never come forward.

Ek continued: "We had a tip. A woman living in Ryska Gränd saw the witness walking up toward the Cathedral. She's almost sure she recognized him. He used to work for the Tax Department but he's retired; the woman used to be an accountant, and often met him through her work. She wasn't sure of his name and didn't have a record of it in her papers, but she says she could identify him. I'm seeing her on Monday at eight o'clock."

"It's pretty weak. It's unlikely he'll be able to say much more than Maria did. Someone must know who these guys are. If they were boasting about what they'd done, someone must have overheard them. And this assault can't be the only crime they've committed." Arvidsson thought about Ek's son, Joakim. He could get hold of more information, Per was sure of that. But the lad would probably have to pay for it with his life. They couldn't take that risk.

"The DNA we took under Maria's fingernails didn't match what we found at Linn Bogren's. Even so, there are parallels. Linn was also harassed by a gang of young men.

Harry Molin told his doctor. It would be nice if there was a connection here. To make something understandable out of all this."

"Maria only got a skin scrape from one of them, the one she thought was their leader. What if it was one of the others who murdered Linn and left signs of his presence there?" Per had tested that thought before, yet he continued to focus on the leader.

"In which case one has to ask why would one of them go back for Linn, and then Harry?"

They ate their picnic in silence. Arvidsson didn't enjoy what he was eating, it was as if the food expanded in his mouth. For Maria's sake, for the murdered boy's sake, they had to catch the perpetrators. Every day the trail grew colder. Witnesses started forgetting. The criminals had the chance to destroy evidence. And yet the disappearance of the files on the lawn mower murder was good news, somehow. One had to assume it was a case of theft. This had not been risk-free, far from it. But someone had weighed up the risks and benefits and deemed it necessary to go in. It gave one hope that this was something important.

Ek pulled the outboard's starter cord and they headed back toward Djupvik. The sun was boiling over the shore meadows and the fishing harbor. The land was parched and there were radio warnings about possible forest fires. Arvidsson fumbled in his pocket for his cell phone and realized he must have left it at Ek's place, where he was sleeping on the sofa nowadays. He'd already started looking around for a new apartment—moving back to the house where Harry Molin had been hanged seemed impossible. Ek hadn't brought his cell phone, either.

They spent the rest of the day at Tofta Beach, playing miniature golf and eating pizza while Ek kept his eyes peeled for red-headed sirens. Some of his pickup techniques made Arvidsson gag. He kept in the background as much as he could, so he wouldn't be associated with his colleague. Even as a temporary roommate, Ek was a goddamn trial sometimes.

Only in the evening did Per see that Maria had called. He went out on the balcony to get away from Ek's curious eyes. His heart raced, and the pulse thundered against his eardrums. Had she changed her mind, did she want to see him after all? He hoped it could be so, more than he had ever hoped for anything. His hands grew sweaty as he pressed the call-back button and waited.

"Maria Wern!" She sounded tense. Not a god sign.

"You called." It sounded silly, as if he had to make an excuse the first thing he did.

"It's about work."

"Right," he said, dragging out his answer. She didn't want to give him cause for optimism, that much was clear. Probably he should be glad she wanted to talk to him at all.

"Linus Johansson's friend, a little lad called Oliver, sought me out today. He had a visit from a policeman who never showed his ID. I suspect he was bogus."

"None of us have spoken to him, I can promise you that. We waited for a child psychologist, but when we questioned him he didn't want to say anything. According to his mother he's refusing to see the psychologist again. We were hoping she'd be able to get him talking about what he knew." Arvidsson stopped, waiting for Maria to continue. "So Oliver got in touch with you?" he prompted, when she didn't say anything.

"He told me Linus was afraid because he'd seen a man in a dark cape waiting outside his bedroom window, both when he was staying with his father and his mother. They had him every other week."

"Sounds very serious, someone impersonating a police officer. Where's Hartman?"

"At a party in Martebo. But on his way in. You have to decide how to move on this. If Oliver wants me involved, you know where I am."

"That's good."

She was just about to hang up, but something in his voice stopped her.

"Maria...." Everything he wanted to say got caught in an echoing vacuum.

"Listen, you really do have to respect the fact that I don't want anything to do with you any more, not outside of work. It's over." As soon as she'd spoken the words she regretted them. She wanted to add something to make them less harsh, but by then he'd already hung up.

Chapter 35

It was Monday morning. A sharp sun was shining in, accentuating the dust particles dancing in the air over the officiously brown sofa from the seventies and the stained, grayish armchairs. The fabric was indestructible, timeless and nondescript. The table in front of the sofa was scratched and rickety, and the picture on the wall belonged to the County Council's art collection which neither caused offense nor made anyone happy. The Midsummer weekend was over and the waiting room was full of patients.

Anders Ahlström got to thinking about Harry Molin. After a long weekend he would usually be there, checking appointments with Agneta in the reception and loyally pacing back and forth in the waiting room. He remembered how Linn Bogren had sat curled up behind a newspaper, over by the window, to shield herself from curious glances. It hadn't been so easy suddenly being a patient in a clinic where she had only just started working. The same sun had illuminated her brown curls, making them seem almost purple. In that moment she'd been almost preternaturally beautiful. Could he have helped her more? If he had listened more carefully could he have helped avert the danger? The very thing she feared most had actually taken place. If only he'd been aware of her terror of an unknown male intruder at night. What at first sounded like a fantasy had later had a natural explanation, when he heard Harry's story. But by the time Harry Molin admitted that he'd pressed his face against Linn's window to see if she were in, the problem no longer seemed very pressing. Anders hadn't seen any reason to contact the police.

And Linus Johansson, that little toughie with asthma, he was no longer in this world either. His infectious laugh would never again be heard in the corridor, when he drew his imaginary pistols and won the duel. His mother Katarina, her anxious face lighting up in a wonderful smile, had not been seen again.

He would never see them again. Three of his patients had died terrible deaths in the course of a month, all in the same part of the city. It really was terrifying. These were Anders Ahlström's thoughts as he fetched in his next patient. A small, straight-backed lady in her eighties whose name, according to the journal, was Agnes Isomäki.

"What can I do for you?" he said, offering her a seat. He hadn't had time to read her file yet, and it seemed impolite to do so before the very eyes of this old lady, who seemed perfectly lucid. Better to listen to what she had to say for herself.

"My granddaughter's getting married and I don't want to go to the party wearing slippers."

Anders leaned across the desk to see what she meant. Sure enough. The lady wore slippers in a checkered brown pattern, with a frontal zip.

"Can I see your feet? Are they swollen?"

Agnes made a face as she took them off.

"Just look at the state of them! I don't know what I did. I don't think I've been bitten by an insect, not in both feet, and I haven't twisted my ankles, either."

Anders squatted beside her and squeezed her ankles and feet. His finger left an indentation in the swelling.

"I'd like to listen to your heart and then we'll do an ECG and run a couple of tests. Have you had any pain round your heart or felt out of breath?"

"That's not the problem. It's the slippers," she corrected patiently, as if talking to a child. "I have a pair of lovely shoes with a heel, I'd wear them if my legs weren't so swollen."

"Typical girl, you only think about the way you look," he joked, adding in a more serious tone. "I think the swelling may be because of your heart. Once it starts playing up, you start retaining water in your legs."

"I've always been a bit proud of my legs. When you get older and your decent legs are the only thing left of whatever looks you once had, you end up feeling even more particular about them. I want to look my best at my granddaughter's wedding. We've only had misery in the family. This wedding is the first good thing that's happened for a long time." She looked at him, expecting him to ask what had gone wrong in the family.

"My husband...."

Anders Ahlström glanced at his watch. One couldn't just dismiss people when they started talking about their disappointments.

"... my husband's gone senile and I can't manage him at home any more. It's so terrible. He leaves the house and gets lost. We've lived together for fifty years through good and bad times. I love him, but I can't cope with having him wandering round the house at night, and turning on the oven. He gets so unaccountably angry when I tell him he's doing something wrong...." Agnes Isomäki burst into tears and all Anders could think of doing was to take her in his arms. Over her shoulder he could see, through the window, a tall, thin man standing there, with a hat pulled over his face even though they were in the middle of summer. Only for a split second—then he was gone. Something about the appearance of the young man stirred memories and a strong feeling of unease—he'd looked like a younger version of himself, twenty-five years ago. Anders forced himself back into the here and now.

"Is there anyone helping you or do you want me to contact the social welfare officer? I can understand the problem's too much for you."

Agnes Isomäki let go of him and looked embarrassed. Her face was red and her nose running. "Sorry doctor, it just came over me. I'm alone. My daughter lives on the mainland. The wedding will be in Gnisvärd Church. I don't know if I can bring Gösta.... What if he becomes agitated and ruins everything? At the same time it's awful excluding him, and who'd keep an eye on him if he's left at home?" Agnes started crying again, and Anders carefully patted her arm. It would probably take a week at least to get an appointment with the social welfare officer, then an unknown quantity of days and weeks before a short-term bed could be arranged at a care home. It would be quicker if the husband were admitted to a hospital for some other reason, and the wife then found herself unable to take him back into the home.

"I'll have a word with the social welfare officer, we'll try to sort this out in the best possible way," he said vaguely. Many times while working at the hospital he'd been amazed at the immense labors these women managed at home. Out of love they tended and took care of their men, night and day. Fed them, washed them, helped them go to the bathroom many times every night—an unsteady dance on four legs. Why? Well, because it had to work and there was no other way. At the hospital one relied on a mobile lift or the muscle power of two comparatively strong young people. How much money had she not already saved society by putting in all this voluntary labor? Then, when her reserves of strength started waning, society did not have the resources to help her.

Anders glanced again at the window. In some strange way he felt observed by the people passing by outside.

When Agnes Isomäki had left, clutching her prescription for a diuretic and medicine to reduce blood pressure, Anders stopped the clinic nurse in the corridor and asked her to set up an appointment with the social welfare officer. He explained the importance of it. The nurse sighed audibly. All of Anders Ahlström's patients were very important. But there were another four doctors to attend to.

Anders had arranged to meet Erika Lund for lunch at the Restaurant Trädgården at twelve-thirty. He'd sensed it would be difficult getting away, nonetheless he'd given in to her enthusiasm. Now he'd have to disappoint her. Judging by his earlier attempts at relationships, he wondered how long she'd be able to put up with it. Just then, his telephone started ringing.

"Darling Anders, I can't get away. Things have piled up. Can we do it another day?"

"It's fine." He hoped his voice wouldn't reveal his relief. Maybe she'd be more understanding of the nature of his work when she also had to put a hundred percent into hers.

Anders drank a big glass of water to dampen the worst of his hunger pangs and decided to close his eyes for five minutes before asking in his next patient. He went into the staff room, where he found a couple of stale cookies and a biscuit which he brought back to his room. Whenever he allowed himself to feel, he realized he was dead beat. It was as if he could never quite get enough rest. Even when he got his eight hours' worth he sometimes felt exhausted when he was getting up. Just as he'd put his legs up on a box of files and closed his eyes, he remembered he'd forgotten to take his smoke aversion pill. He reached for his briefcase and found the box straight away. He swallowed the pill down with a mouthful of water. If one holds a pen in one's hand and goes into a slumber—then by the time one drops the pen and wakes up—it equates to a whole hour of sleep, according to current thinking. His colleague Sam Wettergren had said so in his talk on "The Importance of Sleep on Human Health." Wettergren recommended a power nap at work.

He was awakened by ill-tempered banging on the door. Although he felt he had only just closed his eyes, when he glanced at his watch he realized that over an hour had passed. So much for that falling pen waking him up. He surveyed the room morosely, where files and papers had scattered in an almighty mess, and the bookshelf had moved almost three feet so that it partially blocked the door.

"Yes, come in," he croaked in a hoarse voice, unable to take his eyes off the bookshelf. What had happened?

The nurse's face appeared in the chink of the door.

"What are you doing? The waiting room is filled with patients!" She looked pale and annoyed. Everyone was working at full steam here. Anders rearranged the furniture.

"Help me with the bookshelf," he pleaded lamely, grabbing one corner to push it back into position.

"You're goddamn out of your mind," said the nurse, but there was a hint of amusement in her eyes. "What the heck were you doing?"

"I don't know," he replied. "I really don't know." And at that moment he noticed his big window was wide open.

Chapter 36

Agnes Isomäki rushed out of the health center so she could get to the pharmacy in Östercentrum before Gösta woke up. He usually messed about in the night, then slept like a dead man in the mornings. There was a line at the pharmacy and Agnes ended up next to a talkative woman named Mrs. Levide, who'd recently moved to Jungmansgatan and was lamenting the geographical locations of the health centers.

"It's just ridiculous. There'll be three health centers lumped into one if Gråbo Health Center is moved. We already have both Visby North and Visby Southern in Korpenområdet, and if Gråbo moves there as well there'll only be one big health center in Visby to choose between. Unless you opt for private healthcare, of course. For those of us who live in Gråbo, Korpen seems very remote. I wonder who came up with the idea?"

Agnes hummed her concurrence, but her thoughts were elsewhere.

"It ends up more expensive if people can't walk to the health center but have to take a taxi," the Levide lady continued, checking her number tag for at least the fourth time

275

since Agnes got there. "Our whole society is going to the dogs. Where are we heading?"

Agnes didn't have so much to add to this, either. She had enough on her plate already with her personal miseries and felt no pressing need to add to these by dwelling on the problems of Gråbo.

"At any moment you can be set upon or robbed or stabbed. It's just too awful what happened this last month. The woman found murdered in the Botanical Gardens and the old man who was hanged. They don't even think twice about attacking children or police. What lies in store for us now?"

Agnes agreed. Nowadays she locked the front door with both locks. Both so that Gösta wouldn't be able to slip out, and because she was afraid of the murderer. How many waking nights had she not spent, lately, standing behind the curtain and keeping a watch over the dark garden.

"I've bought a color spray," said the Levide woman, scrabbling about in her worn-out brown purse. "If someone attacks you, you just spray him right in the face. The paint doesn't come off for a week. It can save lives, you know."

"Can I see? How does it work?" Agnes found herself curious.

"You put your finger here… and then you press here. You can have one. I bought two."

Agnes thanked her and said she wanted to pay for it, but this was ruled out.

"Be careful though so you don't spray some ugly-looking man just because he asks you for directions or what the time is. Once you start thinking about being attacked, your trigger finger gets a bit shaky. You hear the slightest sound behind your back and.… "

The Levide woman's turn was next and, soon after, Agnes's number came up. She hardly had time to say thanks and goodbye.

On her way home, her thoughts returned to Gösta and her granddaughter's approaching wedding. Agnes would probably have to bring him along, there was no other possible solution. As long as he didn't get chaotic in church. That was the moment you remembered your whole life. It had to be solemn and beautiful. Maybe she could sit outside on the bench with Gösta, at least she'd get to see the bride, and ClaraMaj might not notice they didn't go inside. Then there would be the supper. The worst possible scenario would be if Gösta got it into his head to give a speech. In the old days he'd been a brilliant speaker at parties. Back then, people had listened to his subtler witticisms and applauded him. But in recent times he no longer held it all together, everything seemed to turn into these long, disjointed harangues, sometimes even with expletives and excruciating remarks. There was also the risk of him soiling himself, which had been happening more and more of late. When Agnes thought of it the tears rose up in her eyes and her nose started running. It was so humiliating for him, and for them both when she had to help him. He wanted to take care of himself, but when he tried the damage was even worse. It would probably be best for everyone if they stayed at home, thought Agnes. The thought of it made her weep heedlessly, because she wanted so badly to be there for the festivities.

When she unlocked the front door he came to meet her with his pants on backward, his fly open across his bottom, and his overcoat draped over his bare, skinny shoulders. A damaged milk cartoon lay on the floor bleeding to death and the tap was gushing. She hurried inside and turned off the water. Living with Gösta was worse than having toddlers in the house all over again, because he was so much bigger and stronger. The worry of him hurting himself or burning the house down or something else she hadn't thought of yet and hence could not take preventive measures against, was constantly a torture to her. There was a sense of being captive, never being able to go out and visit a friend or have guests over. Sometimes it felt like being locked up in a tomb, waiting for death. You have to think about yourself, ClaraMaj used to say with a hint of reproach in her voice. You should go to the Canaries with a friend or start a dancing course. She was so naïve, her little girl. But maybe it was Agnes's own fault that no one got involved, because she protected family and friends from seeing just how bad things had gotten with Gösta.

It had felt good talking to the doctor but at the same time it had been frightening. Gösta would be in despair if he were moved out of his home. In the day-to-day routine things were not always so terrible, and at certain times he even managed to pull himself together. But he could also grow unaccountably angry at times. There had been moments when Agnes feared he'd kill her, but she hadn't mentioned it to anyone. In fact, he had lost all self-restraint on a few occasions, and lashed out at her.

Agnes turned the last few herring fillets in the frying pan and served them up on the dish.

"Come on, Gösta, the food is ready."

"Delicious." He sat down and smiled at her; his smile was warm and self-aware. "Delicious!" He helped himself to a decent spoonful of mashed potato and looked out of the window. "Looks like rain."

Agnes leaned forward so she could see the sky. Sure enough, the clouds were building up and there was rain hanging in the air. At times like this, things were calm and quiet. Agnes got a bad conscience about arranging to see the social welfare officer behind Gösta's back. He turned on the radio just in time to catch the news, like he usually did, and she cleared the table and put the coffee on.

"This last month a number of violent incidents have taken place. The police are interested in hearing from anyone who noticed something of interest on the nights of June twelfth and fifteenth, when a man in a dark cape was seen near the crime scenes. The man is about six feet, two inches tall and thinly built."

Gösta twisted nervously in the kitchen sofa. The graven voice and Agnes's nervous facial expression worried him.

"Where are you going?" she wondered, when he hurriedly shoved the table over to get past. He slapped her hand away, the hand reaching out to caress his back and still his fears. He stared at her; his gaze was wild and inconsolable.

"I didn't do it!" He threw the radio at the floor, so its plastic casing cracked.

Agnes tried to appear calm, although she was trembling inside.

"Come and sit down, let's have some more coffee," she said in her softest voice. But inside, her thoughts were whirling round, making her quite dizzy. "Come on, I'll tell you what ClaraMaj has written about her preparations for the wedding." Gösta loved his granddaughter and liked to hear what she'd been posting about it online. Agnes had never had any problems adapting to the new technology that had replaced the old letters written on paper. "Come and sit down, my dear heart."

"You shouldn't fight with the police. She was a woman, and he was a child!" His eyes narrows and he put up his hands as if to defend himself.

"What kind of nonsense are you saying?"

"You mustn't kick. I got scared. There were so many of them." He stared, as if he could still see them as they had been in that moment. "I didn't dare." He burst into tears and was inconsolable.

"You've been dreaming, my love. Come and sit down here with me. There's nothing dangerous. Everything is fine. Peaceful and nice."

"I hid in a car. In the trunk. I was afraid. Didn't know where I was. I saw the tall one. And the others. In a house. Where we got to."

"The way you talk. Shall I read what ClaraMaj has written now?"

"I got the trunk open. Air. It wasn't locked. I had to pee. It was by Norrgatt. They were nice at the café, they gave me hot coffee. They called you."

"That's right. You must never run off like that again."

In the evening he fell asleep as usual in his armchair by the television. They'd seen an old movie starring Humphrey Bogart. Gösta couldn't keep up with the storyline at all, nonetheless he enjoyed the familiar faces.

She'd long since given up trying to get him to come to the bedroom at nights and get his clothes off. Better to let him sleep where he was, or he only got angry. In a few hours he'd wake up again and create a mess. Agnes went to check the front door. It was locked with both locks. She stared out into the garden, where she saw the rain dripping from the trees in the light cast by the garden lantern. Everything was peaceful. She put a chair in the kitchen doorway, so she'd hear the scraping sound and wake up if he tried to get out. The stove was in there, and the knives that he could hurt himself with, and the freezer where Agnes had amassed food for those days when he was extra difficult and she didn't even dare leave the house for a quarter of an hour to do a bit of shopping. Not so long ago he left the freezer door open and they had to throw out hundreds of kronor's worth of food.

Agnes stretched out on the sofa and tucked her purse under the pillow so he wouldn't be able to get his hands on the keys. At best she'd get a couple of hours of sleep. She needed all the rest she could get now that she'd been forced into a morning appointment at the doctor's. Other days she tried to adapt her sleep patterns to his. As she lay there listening to his regular, calm breathing, she wondered if he would have done the same thing for her? Would he have taken care of her in the same way? She wasn't sure at all about that.

In her dream she stepped right through a windowpane. It was the front window of a needlework shop. She was embarrassed, trying to explain to the people gathering round how it had happened, how she hadn't seen the door and therefore walked straight through the window, although obviously she hadn't intended to steal anything. That's when she realized she was naked. She tried to cover herself up with her purse and arms. The windowpane carried on breaking up in big white shards like strips of bed sheets. That's when she woke up. In the faint light of the garden lantern she saw Gösta, still slumbering in his chair. Yet there was a sound of steps in the bedroom facing onto the veranda. No, she was not imagining it. She was wide awake now. Agnes sat very still in the sofa, clutching the can of spray paint in her hand. Slowly the door opened, with a screeching sound. Gösta also woke up. His most lucid moments were just after he'd been sleeping. Before Agnes had time to react, Gösta leaned forward with a bread knife in his hand. She should have locked the knives away.

Seeing people embrace each other always created anxiety. The feeling of touching and being touched was so strongly associated with unease. When he'd seen them through the window holding one another, he'd wanted to kill them both. The action was more about ownership than anything else. Is death really a punishment if one isn't aware of dying? Obviously not. To be punished one has to feel fear and realize the horror of no longer having a choice. The degradation is only complete if someone can see it.

Just like his mother he suffered from the curse of a photographic memory. To never be able to forget. She had chosen to dull herself with drugs. He drugged himself on the feeling of power. But if he killed the one he wanted to punish most of all he would find out the answer to the question he still had not dared ask. The question about the world's frightening lack of logic and tactics, the incomprehensible fact that someone would voluntarily—without any personal gain—sacrifice himself for the sake of another.

By now it must be obvious to him who was behind all this. First, it would come as a whimsical thought and then, once it had acquired some weight, the rest would fall into place and hell would be a fact from there on.

Chapter 37

When Agnes Isomäki finished her account, Maria Wern fetched her chief so he could also hear what she had to say.

Tomas Hartman sat immersed in a memorandum from their superiors.

New guidelines, new rules about improved transparency to the general public.

"Can you come to my office for a bit?" Maria's face was excited.

Hartman immediately realized this was important. He stood up and followed her.

"What's going on?"

"We have that witness here from the lethal assault. I recognized him at once, the man in the overcoat and cap. It was him! But that's not why they came."

"So I'll get Arvidsson to question him right away. Is he here yet?"

Maria stopped, shrugged, and looked at him. "I don't know if he's come in yet. But we have to do it now. Can't you do it? It's not very straight-forward. The old man is senile, I only more or less pieced the whole thing together with the help of his wife. An outline, but it wouldn't hold water in a court of law. If I understood it right, he actually hid in the trunk of the murderer's car. Don't ask me how he got there, he doesn't even know himself. The best he can do is remember where the murderer parked. It was somewhere close to the Norrgatt's Bakery by the roundabout close to the hospital. He may be able to remember what sort of car it was."

"Well I'll be...."

"There's more. Someone broke into their home last night. The wife contacted the police but by the time they got there the intruder had fled. A man in loose-fitting ankle-length clothes. Together they managed to drive him away. Agnes Isomäki had a color-spray, she thinks she may have hit him with it on the leg of his pants as he was exiting through the veranda door. The man, Gösta, lunged at him with a bread knife but missed."

Hartman shook hands with the Isomäkis. The old man was more incoherent than he'd expected, but his testimony was still a step forward in the investigation.

Agnes recounted the events of the burglary again and tried to describe the intruder as best as she could. She was clearer this time, she felt less overwhelmed by the authority vested in those in front of her. She described a tall, thin man in a dark cape. His gait was stiff and he was mumbling something.

"It was like a macabre joke. I got scared when he wouldn't say anything, just hid himself in his masquerade outfit. First I thought it was someone we knew. One of ClaraMaj's friends, maybe." Agnes looked at her husband. "Gösta moved toward him with the knife. It was very brave and very foolish of him. It was a normal serrated bread knife, quite blunt, too. I was so afraid I could hardly breathe. I thought one of them would be hurt, even if it was only a thief I didn't want that."

"A thief!" Gösta was impatient and wanted to leave. "A thief," he repeated. The conversation was worrying. "Thieves deserve a good beating!" Agnes held his hand in a firm grip.

"He gives me the slip sometimes," she said. "The whole night between the sixth and the seventh he was gone. I looked for him and didn't know what to think. I even contacted the police, the report must be somewhere, even if I did call back later and cancel it. If he did see something there's no guarantee he'll remember it. Sometimes things just come out wrong."

Tenderly she caressed his cheek, and the tenderness in her eyes was very moving. "I didn't know where he was until they called from Norgatt in the morning. Isn't that right, Gösta? You must never do that again."

"I want to go home." He tried to tear himself out of her grip, with repeated mighty yawns.

"He usually has a sleep this time of day," Agnes explained. "He's very, very tired now. He's not at his best in the mornings."

"I used to be picky, now I'm pesky." Gösta looked so full of mischief that, for a moment, Maria wondered if he were messing with them. She offered him an armchair and squatted down in front of him to make eye contact. "We're so grateful to you for coming in. Do you think you can remember what the car looked like?"

Gösta shook his head, then closed his eyes.

"Things usually get better if he can rest for a moment," said Agnes. "He has his better moments."

Hartman offered to run them home and continue the conversation there. At that moment Per Arvidsson appeared in the doorway. He did not say a word to Maria but his expression said it all. Although his words were for Hartman, he couldn't take his eyes off her.

"I'll come along. We can take my car."

Maria sat down at her computer, digging into the report she had started writing when reception had first called up to say Agnes Isomäki was there. She was angry at herself for allowing Per's presence to affect her so strongly, when she'd rather just blot him out of her life. All morning she'd been dreading his showing up, trying to prepare herself for it and looking for some inner calm. But she'd not been prepared for his pleading eyes. If it carried on being this difficult they wouldn't be able to work together any more. In time he would surely come to understand there was no way back.

She had to stay true to her own convictions and not doubt herself, had to concentrate and do a good job. Just as she was starting to find the right formulations in her report and building up a head of steam, Erika's brown locks popped through the door.

"Hartman? You know where he is?"

Maria explained the situation while Erika listened impatiently.

"He went back with the Isomäkis. Anything I can pass on to him when he comes back?" she asked, gesturing at the empty chair in front of her.

"Not exactly." Erika looked as if she wanted to say something. "Some archaeologist wants to see him. Maybe you can deal with it instead? I wouldn't mind sitting in on the conversation. It's about a find they've made on Galgberget. I've been keeping up with the excavations and I'd like to hear what he has to say."

A man in a white shirt with rolled-up shirt sleeves, jeans, a leather vest, and half a week of beard stubble sat down at the conference table and accepted their offer of coffee.

"Kent Wiklund, archaeologist." He stood up and shook hands when Erika walked in.

"You wanted to tell us about a find on Galgberget," said Maria, slightly puzzled once she'd noted down the obligatory information. "I read a few weeks ago that the area was going to be excavated."

"The area is rich in finds. We've found scores of bones belonging to the unfortunates who were executed there. Some thirty bodies, at least. Shattered bones without any order to them, just chopped up and buried like that directly after the executions. But in the middle under the stone pillars we found two coffins with three complete skeletons."

"How incredibly exciting," said Erika, leaning forward and hanging on his every word, as if afraid to miss something.

"Two of them were affluent men from the medieval era. We were able to date the find using carbon-14 dating. They were buried in coffins because they were slightly wealthier, more upper class. We're trying to establish who they actually were. But one of the skeletons is from another time. A woman. We believe she's been in the ground for no more than ten years. That's why I got in touch with you."

"A murder victim," Erika filled in.

"We have to assume so." The archaeologist got out a drawing to show the position of the bodies when they were found. A man in one coffin, and a man and a woman in the other.

"Can we say anything else about the woman? How old she was? What was the cause of death?" Maria felt the same excitement as Erika.

"She was about thirty, had recently given birth. Her pelvis was distended, there were signs of what must have been pelvic girdle pains. She was buried in a piece of white material. Possibly a bride. Her hair was long, dark, and curly. The cause of death is something I'll leave to you. We can't judge whether or not she was murdered, just that someone chose to bury her in this strange place."

"Where on the other hand no one would have come

looking, if you hadn't started these excavations," said Maria. "And as time passes it gets more difficult to see how long someone has been in the ground, to the naked eye at least."

The archaeologist rubbed his chin and his eyes filled with something tentative. Maybe he had not wanted to describe his own work so contemptuously. "Maybe the person in question did not stop to think that we employ a good deal of care when we date our finds."

Maria saw the murder victim before her, on Tempelkullen. Linn Bogren had been dressed as a bride, clutching those lilies of the valley in her thin, yellow-white hand. Erika had the same thought.

"The story repeats itself. A bride. Disappeared ten years ago. She must have been reported as missing. Is the body still there at the scene or where can we pick her up?"

"She's been put back in the grave. We'd be grateful if you could arrange for the transport. We don't have the resources to guard the body, either. I stayed in my tent on Galgberget last night, guarding the find. It was quite eerie, I'll have you know."

"Why didn't you contact the police at once last night when the dating results came back?"

"You work office hours, don't you? It didn't seem very urgent, given that she'd already been there for ten years."

"True. I need to see her on the scene before she's moved." Erika disappeared out of the door and was gone for a short while.

"She must be entered into our register if she was reported as a missing person in Gotland." Maria turned to the archaeologist. "Did you talk to anyone about this?"

"You mean did I say anything to the media? Not yet. I thought you'd want this information first. I mean, there could still be relatives alive," said Kent Wiklund. He stood up when Erika came back; his joints seemed stiff. It had probably not been very comfortable in that tent.

Maria logged into her computer. Between 1998–2003 twenty-two women on Gotland had been reported missing. She drew up a list and started ticking them off. Of the nineteen who were found, seventeen were still alive, and two dead. The remaining three missing persons cases had never been cleared up. One was a case of a suicide-prone blonde woman who had disappeared from a psychiatric ward while on release, the other a young woman of about seventeen of Asiatic origin.

Both could be excluded on the basis of their age and the color of their hair. But the third one remained. She had been lost in a drowning incident below the Hotel Fridhem a few miles south of Visby. Her clothes were on the beach. The woman had most likely been sucked into the undertow and the body never subsequently found. She had drowned on her wedding night, while taking a swim after the party. Under the effects of alcohol. Alone. The continuation of the story was even more puzzling. Who had dressed the woman in white and buried her on Galgberget, and why? The body may have been taken by the current and swept out to sea, that was the assumption made in the earlier investigation. Using dental records they should now be able to establish who she was, and then notify her next of kin. There was a husband and a young daughter who must be eleven years old by now. Like the archaeologist, Maria hoped this could be done in a calm and orderly manner before the details emerged in the media.

It would be a terrible shock to them so long after the actual events.

Chapter 38

Erika Lund read through the medical examiner's system-atic examination of the murder victim from Galgberget. Her wavy brown hair framed a cranium with high cheek-bones and regular teeth. Erika thought about Linn Bogren who'd been exhibited under the rippling strands of fabric on Tempelkullen. Seeing both of these women was like seeing one's own death and progressive putrefaction.

"Can you say anything about the cause of death? The archaeologist Kent Wiklund was speaking of pelvic girdle pain. Could she have died in labor?"

The medical examiner straightened up and shook his head. "She's given birth to children, but the damage evident here... " he pointed with his gloved hand, "... has started improving. I don't think she had any major problems with it any more. I'd guess the child would have been somewhere between six months and one when she died. I mean, if the child survived; we don't know what happened. Maybe she chose to take the child with her when she died, a sort of collective suicide. These things happen."

"What do you think she died of?"

"I don't think, I know." His hands parted the woman's

long hair over one of her temples. "Here is the lethal blow. A blunt weapon. As if someone struck a hand-sized stone into her head, with the sharp side towards her."

"A rubble stone. There are plenty of those all down the coast, the ones you use for stone skimming."

"Precisely. It could well be something like that. The hole is little less than half an inch wide and three inches long, and the impact has penetrated to a depth of almost an inch, which would unfailingly have led to unconsciousness and bleeding. Are there any dental records? Have they managed to identify her?" he asked.

"Maria Wern will be in touch as soon as they have them."

They had finished their day's work. Erika passed by the parking area and took her bag out of the car. Her tension had been there all day. Now it was time. Every time she had a free moment, she'd felt that sucking feeling in the pit of her stomach about the evening ahead. It would either bring them closer or end in all-out catastrophe. Anders had invited her back to his place for the first time. She was expected to stay the night. Julia would also be there. I have to show her we're serious about this, he'd said. She kept an eye out for him as she walked down Östercentrum, nervous and insecure like a teenager. Anders had also been sounding nervous the last few times they'd spoken. There was a new restlessness and anxiety in his movements; but also a remoteness, when he seemed to disappear into his own ruminations without listening to anyone else. Something very important was occupying his thoughts. When she asked, he made a joke of it. Maybe he was afraid of change, just like she was.

When she saw his tall, elongated figure on the other side of the parking area, she felt joy whirling round in her breast.

She stumbled forward without looking where she was going. Her steps grew ungainly and she didn't want him to look at her as she approached; almost like a phobia. She was aware of it but unable to do anything about the feeling.

He took her in his arms and kissed her on the mouth for a long time. People standing round could not stop themselves from smiling at their happiness.

"So you had the guts, then!" He laughed.

"Of course I have the guts to meet your daughter. Do you have the guts?" She looked at him with great seriousness.

"Yes," he said in a light-hearted tone. He didn't seem so sure of himself.

"So what did Julia say when you said I was coming over to stay the night?"

"She said 'oh right.' It wasn't much weirder than that." His forced joviality didn't quite ring true. It would be easier, much easier, if he'd share his anxieties with her. "Whatever will be will be from now on. I'm all Julia's got, of course she feels her position's under threat."

At last Erika would get to see Anders's home. The white villa was embedded in greenery, great clumps of poppies and viper's bugloss edged the drive and, by a corner of the house, a jasmine bush spread a wonderful fragrance.

The kitchen window was lit up. A green-checkered curtain framed the terracotta pots of herbs. There was a smell of coffee as they stood in the big, airy hall and on the kitchen table was a plate of chocolate balls rolled in dried coconut. The entire kitchen counter was smeared, the table stained, and the floor in front of the pantry was sprinkled with coconut. Anders walked up to Julia and took her in his arms.

"It's looking lovely in here!" He swung her round a

turn, then released her. "Why have you put four cups on the table?"

"Because we've got a visitor. He said he was a friend of yours from your military service so I let him in. He's in the living room."

"What!" Anders could hardly believe his ears. Erika watched a series of emotions passing across his face as he searched his memory. "Who?" he whispered to Julia.

"His name is Guran. Can you really be called Guran?" she whispered back. "He called because you have a reunion coming up, that's when I invited him over for coffee. You have to be polite sometimes." Julia looked triumphant. They couldn't just turn up here and plan their evening any old way they wanted, while telling her what to do.

Erika followed Anders into the living room and cast her eyes around with interest. The furnishings were rather minimalist. Wide, open spaces made the newly polished floor look its best. A beautiful, wrought-iron chandelier hung over the dining table, which was made of light oak. The bookshelves were made of the same wood, but they weren't filled with books but DVDs—a plentiful supply of films, certainly enough to outdo all the repeats offered by the terrestrial stations. In the midnight-blue sofa sat a swarthy, heavy-built man with lots of curly hair and a full-length beard. With extreme reluctance he tore his eyes away from the television, where Barcelona had just taken a 3-2 lead against Seville. He gave them a broad smile, showing his big, even teeth.

"Paul Gustavsson, it's been a while!" said Anders, once he'd managed to control his initial surprise. Erika watched him switch into an entirely different mode of behavior, helping himself to a decent dip of *snus* from the can he was offered, stuffing it under his upper lip until it bulged.

"I thought you'd stopped." The words slipped out of her.

"Heck no, you have to have *snus*." Anders laughed as he looked at Guran. "So how are things?"

"I've started my own company, traveling salesman, sell motorcycle spares online and travel around making deliveries, no fixed address." He sniggered at Erika. "Damn taxman's after me." He spluttered and rubbed his big hand against his beard. "I was thinking maybe you'd like to invest, become a partner or something?"

Erika felt she'd seen the man before in less auspicious circumstances. Drunken driving? Fraud? Disturbance of the peace, maybe. But she wasn't sure.

Anders ushered Julia toward the kitchen and pleaded with Julia. "Maybe you can check if the coffee's ready?" He was not entirely comfortable with the situation. Julia walked in front, largely satisfied with the way things were going. Erika wiped the worst gunk off the kitchen table and considered whether it was normal for eleven-year-olds to make such an infernal mess or if that were also a provocation.

"It's nice of you to bake! Is that your own recipe?" she tried.

"No, Mom's. Mom was very good at cooking and very beautiful." Julia studied Erika's face to see how she took it.

"Yes, she was," said Erika. "And I'm sure you will be, too, you're already so pretty now."

"So you did your national service together?" Erika said, once Anders and Guran had parked themselves at the kitchen table. Anders's army pal slurped his coffee, The chocolate balls smeared round his mouth and he talked endlessly so that no one else could get a word in. Julia rolled her eyes and looked at Anders, but his attention was elsewhere. She focused on Erika and for the first time there was a hint of understanding between them.

"Yeah, we did our service together. But not for long, you can't have guys like Anders in the military, it's too dangerous."

"What do you mean, too dangerous?" Julia said eagerly. Erika was also curious.

"Oh it's all water under the bridge now. It was a hundred years ago." Anders picked up the coffee thermos to refill Guran's cup.

"You wouldn't have a bit of the strong stuff would you?"

"Spirit?" Anders wasn't surprised. Guran must have already checked the contents of his liquor cabinet.

"Yeah, please. First you put a sugar lump in the cup…" he demonstrated to Julia, "… then you add the coffee until you can't see it and then schnapps until you can. That's how you do it."

"Why was my father dangerous?" Julia asked again.

"With a guy like your father in the army there's no need to worry about the bad old enemy ambushing you. Oh heck, he scared the hell out of me."

Julia's eyes grew big and round. Anders tried to get Guran to control himself and not worry his daughter.

"We were in Norrland, camping, it was freezing, mid-winter, by some lake or other, can't remember what it was called. The tent was so goddamn cold you had to keep the fire going. Either your hair caught on fire and your feet froze or the other way round if you turned your sleeping bag round toward the wood-burner. I was on fire duty and I must have dropped off. What the fuck, you know, you were wiped out from carrying all the gear. Sometimes we hitched a lift on our skis or bicycles behind a tractor, that was goddamn lethal, too. More injuries than soccer. Your feet were full of blisters because of the boots and you were so tired you'd sleep standing up."

"You were on fire duty…." said Erika, helping him back

on track after his digression. Guran peered at the bottle of schnapps. First he needed another shot, like putting some more money in the jukebox slot.

"I fell asleep on duty. I admit it. When I woke up it was cold as hell but the stove was still full of glowing embers, and in front of it stood a dark figure with an AK4 in one hand and a heap of ammunition in the other. He walked like a zombie toward the wood-burner and was just about to chuck the whole lot on the fire. That would have meant a one-way ticket to eternity for the whole lot of us if I hadn't lunged at his feet and knocked him down. Your dad, I mean. He was walking in his sleep. After that he was discharged, lucky bastard."

Chapter 39

"I don't want to go up and sleep on my own." Julia's voice was puny and anxious. She looked at Anders, who was concentrating on his cards behind the colorful stacks of chips.

"I'll raise," said Guran.

"Dad!" said Julia insistently.

"Big girl like you don't need to make a fuss, do you," said Guran with a chuckle.

Anders had already half-risen out of his chair; now he sat down again. After all, Guran had come all the way from Norrland to visit him.

If he'd only called first, a babysitter could have been arranged.

"I'll go with you." Erika had just staked everything on a bluff and lost to Anders. He was as bad at winning as she was at losing. She couldn't avoid feeling slightly disgruntled at his crowing, his smug announcement that everyone was a loser and airhead except for the winner. Julia, after playing for a while alongside her father, had grown tired of the game earlier and turned on the television instead; also the stereo and the computer, progressively turning up the volume until it crossed the pain barrier. Anders was hardened to it, he seemed not to hear it. Guran didn't notice or pretended he didn't. But Erika developed a formidable headache. This was not what she'd been expecting of the evening.

Julia scrutinized Erika from head to toe, evaluating the advantages of her company against the desire to push her away and maintain distance. "All right, then." She gave her father a goodnight kiss on the cheek, then followed Erika up the stairs.

Erika looked around with a searching gaze. The security gate was still there, from the time Julia was a toddler, although now held up with a piece of string. Julia followed Erika's eyes.

"It's like Guran says. Dad sometimes walks about in his sleep. Sometimes he closes the gate before he goes to bed." Julia clucked with laughter and unexpectedly took Erika by the arm. "I'll show you my room."

"Yes, I'd like to see it." Something about her touch made Erika's eyes fill with tears. It just came over her. Her loss. Her own girl would have taken her by the arm like that, if only life had treated them better. She was grateful about Julia unexpectedly confiding in her, which made her feel emotional and warm. Maybe her loss of contact with her own children had made it difficult to handle Julia's truculence in the beginning. It had confirmed what she already knew, that she was no good with children.

"Ta-da!!" Julia opened her bedroom door with a theatrical gesture.

"You like horses, don't you?"

Julia's face was overwhelmed by a big smile. She nodded. The whole room was *horsified*. There were three large posters of thoroughbreds, foals in the green grass, a muzzle touching a girl's face. The bedspread was decorated with an image of two horses lovingly grazing beside each other. The border of the wallpaper consisted of a long row of ponies. In the bookshelf were magazine holders with various issues of "My Horse." There was a riding helmet on the desk, also some very fine charcoal drawings of wild horses. "Who did those drawings?"

"My friend Ronny. He's a classroom assistant, really cool and totally brilliant at everything."

Erika also used to ride when she was growing up. She'd even competed for a couple of years in dressage. But when the children arrived and she took time off work because of her breastfeeding psychosis, the hobby became too expensive. Julia's eager questions brought back old memories. Riding camp. Adventures. Injured horses and her great sorrow when her favorite horse had to be put down.

"My mom was world class at dressage. Well, maybe not world class but almost," Julia added.

Erika didn't know what to say, so she just nodded to indicate she was listening.

"Do you want to see how beautiful she was?"

Erika wasn't sure that she did. She felt her smile draining from her face and her body stiffening. The presence of Isabel was so pervasive, even ten years after her death and even though Julia could not possibly have any memory of her. She was a fairytale, a legend constructed gradually by recourse to excellent character traits, fantasies, and all the perfections that normal mortals couldn't aspire to. An impossible rival. Julia took Erika by the hand and led her through the corridor to a room on the other side.

"This was Mom's study." Julia turned on a lamp. The light fell on a large portrait over the magnificent oak desk. A bridal photograph. Erika stared. It was like seeing her own face. The woman in the photograph was younger, of course. But her facial features... her cheekbones, eyes, and hair, even her smile, were strikingly similar. There was also something of Linn Bogren about her. The soft outlines of the round face, the nose and chin. The voluminous curly brown hair, the dark brown effervescent eyes—all three of them had these in common. When her eyes fell on the bridal bouquet, the air went out of her lungs and she felt a heavy weight pressing down on her chest. Was it pure coincidence that the wedding bouquet consisted of lilies of the valley?

"You look funny." Julia gripped Erika's arm.

"She looks like someone."

"She looks like you, can't you see? The ones he brings home are dark and curly haired. But you're the best one." She squeezed Erika's arm again.

Erika smiled mechanically. The thought gave her vertigo. That woman who'd been found on Galgberget.... Her mouth dried up. She tried to control herself for Julia's sake, while her suspicions dug a deepening hole in her trust. Could it really be like this? Anders was a sleepwalker. Was he also a murderer? Was there any risk of him hurting his own child? He loved Julia more than anything in the world. Erika's immediate impulse was to take the girl in her arms and flee to a safe place where she'd be safe. Should she contact the child's grandmother and ask her to take care of the girl, and then contact the police? No, she had to calm down. There was no evidence. Anders, her beloved Anders, was sitting down there playing poker. She could hear their talking and laughter downstairs. She might be wrong. Maybe her suspicions were just a product of her overworked mind.

Erika went back with Julia to her room. Managed to have a few jokes with her while they were brushing their teeth together and using the same mirror, so that one body seemed to have two heads on it, like a totem pole. Erika's dark hair looked strange with Julia's fair eyebrows and lashes.

"I like you, Erika." Julia gave her a goodnight hug and

then crawled into her bed and turned out the light. The words lingered in the dark like a warm breath. I like you.

That was why she had to stay and protect Julia until she knew how things were. For her sake and for Anders's, only with them was there a meaning in life. It was madness staying, but she couldn't leave them. Erika fiddled with the cell phone in her pocket. She didn't dare call, in case someone in the house overheard her, and more than anything she wanted to avoid worrying Julia. She went back into the bathroom and opened the medicine cabinet. She must find evidence. Julia and Anders had their own sections in there. On the left were girlish perfumes and a pink comb, hair grips, and a little nail brush with a horse's head on it. On the right, his shaving things, his aftershave which he liked so much, some lesser-known brands of deodorant. A small, sharp pair of nail scissors which she pocketed. A dark blue comb, unfortunately without any hairs. For a single strand of hair to be usable in DNA analysis, it still had to have its root. She dropped a foot file, which had not been so well cleaned, into her toiletry bag. She undressed, shivering with cold. She had to behave normally, had to pretend to be asleep when he came up. The house was completely silent now. The army pal must have left. Suddenly she heard the sounds of scraping chair legs and footsteps across the wooden floorboards. How could she have been so blind? She thought about what they had found in Linn Bogren's bathroom. Some coughed-up phlegm containing polishing dust. Most likely from Anders's newly polished wood floor. Everything had been served up right before her eyes, yet she had failed to see.

Erika crawled into the bed, lay completely still and tried to breathe deeply, as if she were asleep. She heard him brushing his teeth, getting undressed. Then felt the large mattress shifting its center of gravity.

"Are you awake?" He kissed her neck, caressed her back. "Erika? I want you to stay here with me." He took hold of her shoulder to turn her toward him. She made her body as heavy and limp as she could. "There's something I'd like to tell you." She came so close to opening her eyes. So close to hearing the truth. But instead she sighed deeply and stayed on her left side. She could feel his member throbbing against her behind when he embraced her and caressed her breasts. Her heart was beating fast. Maybe he could feel this through her skin? Hard, rapid heartbeats that demanded oxygen and whipped up her rate of breathing.

"I love you so much." His breath smelt of booze.

She'd have liked to scream and run away or simply give up all resistance. The way things were now, she was in a vacuum where everything was a lie. He pulled her silk nightie over her hips, rolled down her panties and tried to force himself inside, without success. His thrusts were hard and painful. She tensed herself. It was dry and smarting down there; her fear made the pain even worse. After what felt like an eternity, he gave up. There was a swaying motion in the mattress. She heard his steps on the stairs. She lay there for a long time, listening. The dishwasher started up with a scraping sound. A door shut somewhere. Or was she imagining it? What if he were no longer in the house? They could flee. No not yet! She had to steel herself, had to stay and get her hands on more evidence. Before she abandoned him she had to be one hundred percent sure that he was the guilty party.

Carefully Erika lifted the comforter and placed her feet on the floor. Step by step she moved toward the stairs, then stopped on the ledge in the middle. A blue light was shining from his study. She could see him in the hall mirror, through his doorway. He was sitting by the computer and she could observe his facial expression. Concentrated and grim. His eyes stared at the screen. He inserted a USB memory stick. She saw his fingers moving over the keyboard. Suddenly he stood up and Erika rushed back to bed. She heard him make some slamming noises in the kitchen. The tap was running, the fridge door opened and closed, but the other sounds were drowned out by the churning dishwasher.

He returned to the bedroom again, collapsing into his side of the bed without taking any notice of her, even though she was facing him. His breathing grew deeper and slower. She squinted at him; he seemed to be asleep. Was it a wise idea to get up and give Hartman a call—ask for advice? The cell phone was on the bedside table next to the scissors. She reached for them, touched the cold case of the telephone, snatched up the scissors. He moved. Quickly she drew back her arm under the comforter and lay on her back so she'd have a better view of what he was doing. Suddenly he sat bolt upright in the bed. She opened her eyelids just enough to see without showing him she was awake. He stood up stiffly and went to the wardrobe. His bathrobe was hanging on a hook, and he put it on. With ungainly steps he started moving toward the stairs, opening the gate as he did so and disappearing out of her field of vision.

Erika followed him, glided along barefooted like a shadow across the floor. Ready to flee, fight, scream for help. Her stomach muscles were tense and cramped, her breathing controlled. She had to find out the truth. Was he really sleepwalking? Or was this just an extenuating factor, an excuse for the repulsive deeds she'd been forced to see? Maria had once jokingly suggested that Anders might be a psychopath or married or weird in some other way—after all, normal men were rarely ever available. In fact he *was* too good to be true, wasn't he? How could she ever have thought anything else? But she loved him. What a relief it would be just to give up; to embrace him, love him as if it were their last moment on earth, give herself over to unbounded passion and then accept the lethal blow when it came. No, she had to find evidence. For her own sake she had to know if he were guilty or innocent, conscious or unconscious of the terrible things that had been done. Only then would she be able to give up or stay. Nothing was worse than the uncertainty.

He went out on the veranda. The hood of his bathrobe covered his face completely. He lit a cigarette. The red glow followed his hand to his mouth, then hung limply at his side.

He traced a few circles in the air with his wrist, let go of the butt, and stepped on it. He stood immobile for a long while, then slowly and apparently aimlessly started wandering round the garden under the apple trees. Erika hurried back. She'd seen what she needed to see.

The challenges he faced on the computer screen were so much easier to deal with than reality. Logged into the surgeon's program on the simulator, he could perform advanced stomach surgery, brain surgery, or an autopsy on his intended victims. He liked the thought of how vulnerable they were, anaesthetized and immobile, just waiting for his knife. When their lives were in his hands in this way, he was raised above all human laws and morals. A god creates his own rules.

He'd decided to spare Erika Lund for a little while longer. The knowledge that she was a policewoman turned him on. She had been chosen as the observer of the degradation, thus earning a full punishment. Later, once she'd fulfilled her purpose, it would be a real pleasure to see her agony.

Chapter 40

"I'm not well, I've got a migraine. I'm taking the day off."
Erika leaned back against the pillows. When the alarm clock went off, she'd sat bolt upright. How amazing that she'd managed to sleep at all.

"I didn't know you suffered from migraines." Anders's clinical doctor's eye scanned her.

She almost spoke of a temperature and sore throat, then stopped herself just in time. He would have felt her forehead and dismissed it all as nonsense.

"It doesn't happen very often, it already started last night. That's why I went to bed so early." She held up her hand, shielding her eyes against the light.

"Yes, things didn't work out last night the way I'd planned them. Sorry. Can I get you something, what do you usually take?" He had such a charming way of giving his whole attention to the one he was talking to. She almost melted, then pulled herself together.

"Nothing. I never take pills." Did he suspect something? Would he drug her and... and then, what would happen after that?

"Can I bring you a bit of breakfast?" He crawled onto the

bed and put his cheek against hers, kissing her forehead. "I love you, you know that? Whatever happens I love you."

"I love you," she mumbled back, her face pressed into his shoulder. Whatever happens... why had he put it like that? It added fuel to her fears, her sense of balancing on the edge of the void.

"You want coffee and a piece of toast? An egg?"

"I feel sick. I'll try to eat something later. As long as it's dark and quiet it usually goes away."

She heard them bustling down in the kitchen. The washing machine started up. The tumble dryer. Julia's voice, and his deep rumbling voice. A car started. Was it his? It was difficult to tell whether they'd left the house. Erika sneaked out of bed and up to the window to look down at the garage and driveway. His car was still parked there. If he would only leave soon, make himself scarce so she could search the house. Could she bring a pair of his shoes? Those loafers he was wearing today had not been on any of the crime scenes. But there had been other shoeprints. Maybe she could blacken his soles and make an imprint of them on paper?

Erika jumped when she felt an arm on her shoulder. She gasped for air, wanted to scream but stopped herself.

"Did I scare you that much?" He took her face in his hands and looked into her eyes, utterly serious. There was no way out. He kept a firm grip on her. "How are you?"

"I don't know. I feel sick." She removed his hands, ran for the bathroom, then locked herself in. Coughed and spluttered, splashed with the toilet brush in the water so it would sound as if she were being sick.

He knocked on the door. "You want some help?"

"No, I want to be left alone. I'll be fine. Just go to work. I need to rest, that's all." Why hadn't she waited a little longer before getting out of bed? If she'd waited a few more moments he would have given her a kiss and left.

She heard the front door shut, then the car starting. Sitting on the closed toilet lid, she waited a few more moments before daring to move. There was a risk he'd realize he'd forgotten something and unexpectedly come back. She started looking over the bathroom more carefully. The contents of the laundry basket. There wasn't much there, just a towel and a pair of Julia's jeans. The washing machine was churning away downstairs. She'd already gone through the medicine cabinet. She felt along the top of the shelf over the mirror. There was an expired, unopened pack of condoms up there. Expectations that had not come to fruition? She opened the drawers of the chest by the window, lifted out the towels and put them back in the same order. She sank down on the floor, leaning her head against the wall and closing her eyes. Then, as she was about to get up and leave, she saw some material under the bathtub. Carefully she pinched a corner of it and pulled out a pair of pants. She held them up in the light, turning them this way and that. There was some red paint on one of the pant legs. From Agnes Isomäki's self-defense paint? She could hardly breathe, or move. No, no, it couldn't be! Please God let there be another explanation!

Quickly she got dressed and scrabbled her belongings together. At the bottom of her bag she put Anders's robe and a pair of boots that might conceivably match those shoeprints. Her tears were running, her vision grew misty and her heart raced hard and fast. She could hardly swallow, her mouth was so dry. Only when she got back to the police station and closed her door did she dare relax a little and think things through. First she had to make some prints of the shoe soles, remove fibers from the robe, take samples of the stains and paint on the pants for analysis, then take the things back during her lunch hour. She worked intensely, disconnected from her feelings.

"You were a bit late today, has anything happened?" Maria gave Erika a searching look when she appeared at the reception desk.

"I overslept."

She should at least have told Maria, but something inside stopped her. Maria would only tell her to leave him immediately, forcing her into something she wasn't ready for. Afterward she would understand that she'd been emotionally blocked and unable to make correct decisions. She should have been taken off the case. But right then, at that moment, the only sensible thing seemed to be to wait for the DNA analysis. Well-founded suspicions were not enough. Her love for Anders required evidence of his guilt before she could leave him—if, indeed, she'd even be able to leave him then....

"Want to go out with me for lunch or did you bring something with you?" Maria asked.

"I'm going to swing past Anders's place." Her stomach turned as soon as she thought about food.

Maria said nothing, which was almost worse. "There's a meeting at one o'clock, you know that, don't you? In the conference room."

Erika checked her watch. She might just manage it. Anyway, she'd been late for meetings before.

"Do you know how Arvidsson and Ek are doing with the assault investigation?" Maria hadn't been able to ask Per herself, but every day she had to wait was one day too much.

"He's back on the mainland, I haven't seen very much of him. I mean one does wonder how much fun it can be for him, lodging with Ek. They don't have much in common."

Erika tried to take everything in as they walked briskly toward the parking area. She was in a hurry. "The worst thing, apparently, is they have a different taste in music. Arvidsson says Ek's favorite songs are not much better than German porn film music."

"How would he know?" Maria smiled slightly, then grew serious. She looked as if she were going to say something. Erika was worried that she'd say something about Arvidsson, which would take time. She had to take preventive action. Once Maria had started a conversation on the subject, it wouldn't be possible to cut things short.

"So, see you at one then?" Erika speeded up and was almost jogging to the car. Maria only saw her back, bearing away.

Chapter 41

Sam Wettergren sat in the wing chair in his homely study, furnished in the English style. He was skimming through a doctoral thesis on acupuncture as a treatment for specific sleep disorders, when suddenly the doorbell rang—first a single pulse, then a couple more in a very insistent manner. His wife had just gone to bed and he rushed to the door so she wouldn't be disturbed. Who could this be, so late at night?

"Anders, this is very unexpected! What can I do for you, my friend?"

"Can I come in?" Anders Ahlström stepped into the hall and hung up his coat. "Can we talk privately somewhere?"

"It sounds serious, has anything happened?" Sam thoughts raced through any possible problems. "I'm not on call," he added.

"Neither am I. This is not anything work-related." Anders looked round for Sam's wife, but she was nowhere in sight. Good.

"Coffee and cognac?" asked Sam. "No, no, it's no problem, it's in the coffeemaker, I was going to have a drop while watching the late news. It's a little ritual of mine. Take a seat in the study and I'll be back in a minute."

Anders remained on his feet in the room, watching his colleague through the open kitchen door: a tall, well-trained man in excellent physical shape, still exceptionally ambitious in spite of just having turned sixty. There were many rumors about Sam at the hospital, but nothing that rang true about any amorous adventures. Sam loved his wife and his family was sacred to him. The rumors were of an altogether different kind; they concerned his eruptive anger and almost sick intolerance of free-thinkers. His word was law at the clinic and whenever there were any changes, he would inform his staff of them as a *fait accompli*. On Sam's instigation, one of his assistant physicians who had earlier questioned a diagnosis of his was later cautioned by the disciplinary committee for a minor offense. A nurse who demanded more interaction and dialogue had been transferred by him to the emergency room, which he knew she didn't have the stomach for. And on one occasion he'd sent home a patient whose treatment had not yet been concluded, because the latter had been rude to a nurse. There was no pardon or discussion. Either one was loyal and enjoyed Sam Wettergren's full support or one became his enemy.

Sam served his colleague, then sat down in the armchair with his cup of coffee. Slowly he took a sip, then looked up at Anders.

"So what's on your mind?"

Anders hesitated for a moment, not wanting to seem too eager. What he wanted to say now was something he'd been preparing and running through mentally every spare moment since the visit of his old pal from military service. "I was wondering whether you'd be able to get hold of a clinical report on me. For personal reasons I don't want to do it myself. But with your contacts I'm sure you'd manage it.…"

Sam put down his cup and drummed his fingertips against the table. Then, leaning back and looking as inscrutable and immutable as granite, said: "You'll have to give me a bit more than that. A report on whom?"

"Me. It's from 1979 when I did my military service at Kronoberg Regiment. An investigation was held and I was discharged."

"What would be my reason for requesting it, would you say? I have to be able to answer that if someone asks me."

"I'm sure you'd find a convincing reason. I can't think of anyone who would challenge you about it." Anders made an artificial pause, watching Sam, who according to popular rumor was susceptible to a bit of flattery. If you laid it on thick you could maneuver him more or less any way you wanted, as long as you took things at his own pace, calmly and in a dignified manner. "They investigated my sleeping habits."

"I see. So you got sent home because of sleepwalking? Of course they couldn't have a zombie among all those weapons. Any movement that's automated can be replicated by the sleepwalker and activated without conscious thought. I suppose that's precisely what you were trained to do: assembling, loading, and shooting a weapon. There won't be a problem getting hold of it for you." Sam smiled in an avuncular manner, handing Anders one of the cognac glasses and sipping his own. "Of course, you make me rather curious. Why is this document so important to you?"

Anders didn't answer that one. But he could follow Sam's entire thought process in his face, from the newspaper reports on a murderer who behaved like a sleepwalker to the fearful conclusion.

Anders took a gulp at his cognac without taking his gaze away from Sam's eyes. He waited for him.

"You really think you might have done all this?" Sam whispered.

"I don't know. How could I know?"

"Are there any other indications that it might have been you?" Sam's eyes opened wide at the implications of it. "They were all your patients, and the murders were in your part of town." His immediate curiosity was stilled. Now he was on guard instead.

"Is it possible for a person to do things in his sleep that he'd never do while awake? Can you be convicted of murders you committed in your sleep?"

Sam slid to the edge of his seat, then stood up and started pacing across the floor, still holding his glass of cognac.

"Yes, it's possible to commit crimes one would never have committed if awake and in full control of oneself. I'd say 'no' to your second question. You wouldn't be given a prison sentence, you'd be placed in psychiatric care but only after a rigorous investigation. And that would be something for the police and the medical examiner, not me."

"I'm asking you as a friend and colleague, I must know where that document is. If I knew myself I would hand myself in to the police and explain the situation to them. Sometimes I've awakened in the morning and my room's been rearranged, my shoes covered in mud by the bed, my robe's got blood on it. But I can't remember anything!"

Sam stood by the window, looking out at the street where the raindrops were dancing in the wind under the street-light. A car drove past. He opened the window. Anders wondered if he were opening up an escape route or giving himself a chance to call for help.

"You have to help me. We're colleagues. If you don't, who else could I turn to? You can do this for me if you want to!" Anders was growing increasingly desperate.

"It's out of the question. Precisely because we are colleagues I'd never even want to be consulted about this. It would only complicate things for you if you got me involved."

"All I need is a miserable piece of paper from the military and a certificate that I've come to you for help with my sleep disorder."

"I won't do it, you must leave now. I don't want to get involved."

"But I prefer to stay." Anders stood up and went to the computer. "Before I leave your house there's something I'd like you to see, concerning your study." He turned on the computer and told Sam to log on.

"What do you want?" Sam's voice, otherwise so strong and deep, sounded dry and frail. "What the hell do you want?"

"Scratch my back and I'll scratch yours." Anders plugged in a USB memory stick, tapping his way to the study on which Linn Bogren and Sam had worked. The figures were Linn Bogren's.

"Where did you get that from?" Sam looked very old all of a sudden.

"It arrived in the mail. I don't know who sent it. Maybe Linn."

"There was so little missing," Sam admitted. "Yes, I faked a couple of answers. Linn wouldn't agree to it at first, but I persuaded her. For the good of the cause, because I knew this would benefit our patients even if was beyond their own understanding."

Anders took back the USB memory stick, hid it in his hand. "I'll give this to you if you give me my certificate."

Sam logged out and turned off the computer. "What are you going to do?"

"If I go down, you go down. I want you to make sure I get the material I need if there's a trial. Do we have an understanding?"

"I'll follow you out."

"I want a certificate now and I want the excerpt from the

clinical report I need within four days. Otherwise I'll be very disappointed. Your children would probably also...."

Sam's eyes were oozing bile, but he was forced to capitulate. "I'll arrange it."

Chapter 42

The days passed in a cold sweat, waiting for the DNA analysis of the samples Erika had taken at Anders's house and sent off without notifying her chief. She'd be given hell about this later, she knew that. From time to time she popped into the laboratory to ask about the results, whether they'd come in yet and if they could hurry things along a bit. On one of these occasions she got the result for Sam Wettergren's DNA. It didn't match any of the samples taken at the murder scenes, nor the material taken from the lethal assault. He was innocent. Erika had devoted a couple of hour's work to reading everything that could be found on Fumarret. It was Sam Wettergren who had introduced it into Sweden. The money on his account, which initially seemed to have something to do with the study of plant steroids, might equally be a bribe pure and simple for maneuvering the drug into the Swedish market. Both involved the same pharmaceutical company. Whether or not anything criminal had taken place would have to be determined by the Board of Health and Welfare.

Erika had more or less moved in with Anders and Julia. She slept in Anders's bed, ate at his kitchen table and chatted with Julia as if they were quite safe. At night she kept vigil over Julia and nervously guarded Anders. She often thought about leaving, but outside there was nothing but meaninglessness waiting. In the nights Erika kept him under observation. He did not sleepwalk again. She noticed that he was tense. Maybe her anxiety was infectious, because he grew increasingly restless. Erika slept with her service weapon, loaded, in her purse. Whereas it should actually have been kept locked away at work. She hoped no one would notice. What she'd do if there was a serious situation, she did not know. Would she be able to shoot him to save herself and Julia? She should have brought up the situation with Hartman straight away. This decision was not hers alone. She only wanted to keep him with her a little longer, and love him for another few moments. They'd find him soon enough.

Erika would never forget Anders's expression when the police came to take him away. When he looked at her and knew that she'd known all along. But Erika refused to shoulder the guilt. She had to turn him in once the evidence came back. She was a policewoman. His DNA matched what was found at Linn Bogren's home and on the cigarette butt by Harry's mailbox and the white cotton strips on Tempelkullen. She could still see him, deep in shock.

Each of Anders's movements took time, as he walked clumsily across the drive and was shoved unceremoniously into the patrol car. Before disappearing he called out to her through the open car door.

"I love you, Erika!"

She looked at him, feeling as if a knife had been twisted in a wound at the top of her ribs. To think that words could hurt so much! Julia screamed when the police took away her father. Her grandmother was there to soothe and console her, but her eyes were full of despair.

"My darling, everything will be all right. They don't want to harm him. They're only going to talk to him at the police station."

"Why can't they talk to him here? When is he coming back?" Julia started crying when she saw her grandmother's grave expression.

"I don't know, darling. I don't know."

"I'll give you two a lift home." Erika caressed Julia's hair, prepared at any moment to be pushed away by the child as the traitor she was. But Julia only stood there frozen to the spot and clutching her grandmother. How does one explain to a child that her father is a murderer? Eye to eye with Hartman, Erika let go of the whole charade. He had fetched coffee and stuck the mug in her hand. She drank mechanically, with shaking hands.

"I didn't want it to be him," she said and wiped her nose with the paper towel he handed her. "I didn't want to understand even though it was so obvious. I love him."

"Maria Wern picked up on it at an early stage—the idea that Anders might be the guilty one. All the victims were his patients. Their worst fears came true—exactly what they confided to their doctor. We've been able to confirm this by looking at his patient notes. Linn Bogren's fear of a male intruder. Harry Molin's fear of dying. Arvidsson's thoughts of suicide. Did it never occur to you? Maria has been very worried about you. We kept you out of the discussion, but we had you both under surveillance."

"Why didn't you say something?" Erika stared at Hartman, hardly able to believe it.

"Until we had some actual evidence we felt you were safer if you behaved normally. Just like you, we wanted to have some consideration for Julia. But we were there: on the balcony outside the bedroom, in the lilac bush outside the kitchen window, on the veranda behind the plank. They contacted me from the laboratory and told me you had handed in some samples for DNA testing. They found it strange that the results had to be sent directly to you, in person."

"What's going to happen to me now?"

"For the moment you'll have to go home. I'll be in touch." Hartman's conflicting emotions played themselves out in his face. He decided not to raise his voice at her, given her fragile state of mind.

"But I have to know what's happening! Please, you mustn't shut me out!"

"Right now you're of no use to us as a police officer, but you could be a support to Julia."

"I'm having a hard time believing that a man who's so loving and warm could turn into a monster when he's asleep. I just don't understand it."

"All the evidence points to him. We even found the USB memory stick that went missing at Linn Bogren's place. It was in his house. Arvidsson saw her put it in the inside pocket of her purse and zip it up. The USB was never found in Linn's home, but we found it next to Anders' computer. He had even copied the material to his hard drive."

Suddenly it struck her. There was too much evidence, it was almost prescriptive. "This is too much. Think about it, it's never this clear. If he was guilty he'd try and get rid of the evidence. He would have hidden the USB, for instance. It must be someone else."

"Erika, you have to see there is no one else. What do you know about his late wife?" Hartman's voice was muted.

"She drowned. Do you really believe he killed her as well? He loved her, loved her beyond all measure.... I don't want to hear anything more, I can't take it."

Maria Wern stood to one side in silence. Now she came forward and put her arm round Erika. "You have to try and tell us everything you know. Not to let him down. You hear me, Erika? To help him. The Anders you love is the doctor who wants to do good, who wants to save lives. That's how he wants to be. I also believe that, but it's more complicated. We're after Mr. Hyde, and he's the one who'll go on trial. We've consulted a doctor who's an expert on sleeping dysfunction. If Anders is a sleepwalker he can't be convicted for murder. He'll need help to stop it, do you understand? He'll go through a major neuro-psychiatric examination. We've also asked for the services of a psychiatrist who's an expert on split personality."

After giving Erika a lift home, Maria felt terribly inadequate. Erika should not be left alone in the emotional chaos she was in. She wouldn't have a quiet moment until the investigation had been concluded and the trial was over. Until then Maria would have far more to do than she had time for. There was a great deal to think about. If Anders Ahlström was found guilty the girl would be taken into care. A grandmother of almost eighty could not be the sole guardian of a child. Social welfare would have to be involved as soon as the trial was over. It might even be advisable to inform them now, so they could prepare for it. A good home for a lost little girl. Maria thought about her own children—one always wanted all the good in the world for them. Anders had never hurt Julia, although she had been in his immediate vicinity throughout. Whenever she thought of the murderer she'd always seen him as an outcast, a loner and social misfit who'd started offending from an early age, who'd been punished for crimes of increasing severity with longer and longer prison terms.

She'd never conceived of him as a socially competent father and popular doctor.

In the car on the way home Erika said: "Remember that time at your place, when we were brainstorming about Kilroy? Did you know Anders was known as Kilroy when he was doing his military service? He popped up in all sorts of impossible places, he really had no sense of direction at all." Maria hadn't given any real thought to Erika's remark until now. She slowed down, pulled over by the side of the road and stopped to think. KillRoy. Roy. Could it be the same person? Could the man who killed Linus and stabbed her with the blood-filled syringe really be Anders?

At eight in the morning Anders Ahlström was taken to a special section of the department of neurology. He'd been kept awake all night so that he would be exhausted and thus fall asleep easily. Maria Wern watched him conversing politely with the nurse as she fitted a cap on his head, consisting of a number of rubber bands with electrodes fixed to them, for the EEG registration. Then a belt round his stomach to take a reading of his breathing frequency and a mask under his nose to measure levels of carbon dioxide. By the time he had the EEG connected by cables to his wrists and ankles and a pulse oximeter on his finger, he was practically tied to his bed. The lights were turned down. The nurse came in to Maria in the control room. She could see the wavy curves on the computer but they didn't tell her anything, although later in the day the neurologist would be able to deduce a lot more. While the monitoring process was under way, Maria asked the nurse what she made of it.

"We'll see his electrical waves once he's asleep. His pulse has already started slowing. I have to go now and hook up another patient, but I'll be back in a minute."

It felt unpleasant to be left alone there, but Maria didn't have time to stop the nurse. Anders tried to roll over onto his side but the equipment impeded him and he remained on his back. Everything grew silent. All that could be heard was the whirring of the computer fan. The dim lights also made Maria feel sleepy. She hadn't gotten to bed until the small hours the night before, and this morning she'd been up at dawn. She waited, but nothing happened. Could not one other police have stayed on duty in the control room? The nurse had sent them all to the waiting room. They found it difficult keeping quiet, which disrupted the monitoring process.

"Do you see the change?" The nurse, who'd just walked back in, pointed to the computer screen. Maria took her eyes off Anders and watched the curves change. They grew calm and flattened out. "He's sleeping peacefully." Suddenly the curves grew chaotic and confused. The nurse sucked in air and when Maria looked up from the monitor, Anders had got out of bed. He tore himself free of the electrodes and reached for a yellow staff coat hanging on a hook beside the bed. He put it on with awkward movements and started moving clumsily through the room toward them. His eyes were vacant and his mouth chewed the air robotically. Stiffly he kicked a chair out of the way, then took another step and pressed down on the door handle.

"He's sleepwalking. We can't wake him up now." The nurse looked at her patient with evident fascination. Maria looked round for something to use as a weapon—in case she had to defend herself.

Chapter 43

"Just because Anders Ahlström is a sleepwalker doesn't mean he killed Linn Bogren and Harry Molin. Our strongest evidence is DNA." Maria Wern, who'd spent three days questioning Anders, was having an increasingly difficult time associating this thoroughly charming man with his supposed, terrible crimes. "I have a gut feeling about this."

"Gut feelings don't stand up in court," Hartman pointed out to her.

"Anyone can plant DNA," she disagreed. "Think about it. I'm inclined to agree with Erika. There are so many bits of evidence against Anders and they're all so clear, served up so perfectly. Okay, that is *my* spontaneous reaction. So what I did today was to check Anders's alibis on the murder nights."

"I'm listening." Hartman sank into his chair without taking his eyes off her.

"Anders wasn't even in Visby on the night when Linn Bogren was killed. His mother got ill suddenly, she had a fainting fit while at a sewing circle meeting at her house in Öja. He stayed there overnight. One of his mother's friends can also back this up because she stayed, too."

"Could he not have taken the car and gone back?" Ek interjected.

"No, he slept in a walk-through passage with his mother on one side and her friend on the other. They would have woken up. Anyway, Julia was also sleeping in the same room with her father."

"What about the murder of Harry Molin? Does he have an alibi for that night as well?" Hartman looked skeptical.

"On that night Anders had thirty minutes notice to take the shift of a friend at the emergency room. They were really busy all night, any number of witnesses will back that up."

"Does this mean we have to release him, or do we have anything else on him?" Hartman seemed to deflate where he sat at the table. It would not be an easy matter, going out to the media with the announcement that they were releasing their only suspect.

"We have the fact that his wife Isabel died." Maria didn't need to look for her notes, she knew them by heart. "It was assumed that she drowned below Sjöstugan on Fridhem during the wedding night. Her clothes were found on the stony beach and the body never recovered."

"Anders has an alibi for that night as well until three o'clock. According to his friends he was in a total stupor. They helped him into bed. It's unlikely he would even have managed to get down the stairs without falling. Isabel's best friend had the room next door. She's a light sleeper and he was snoring non-stop until he got up at about five o'clock. That's when he went down to the beach, found the clothes, and raised the alarm. The earlier investigation concluded that it was an accident, or possibly that Isabel had swum into the undertow on purpose."

"And then the body was found now during the excavations on Galgberget. The injuries to the head point to murder. The medical examiner said that she could not have fallen and injured herself in that way." Ek felt as disconsolate as Hartman.

"Isabel's bridal dress was still there in the room. What we saw as a wedding dress in the grave was in fact a lace curtain wrapped round the body. It was an early summer wedding. One could pick lilies of the valley, Anders' mother arranged the wedding bouquet herself. Another remarkable thing Anders pointed out himself is that the murder of Linn Bogren took place on the same date, but ten years later. On June eleventh."

"Only because you would have found this out anyway. He can't be innocent, there are too many links to him. How else could all this have happened?" Ek twisted uneasily. To leave the guilty man to commit new crimes was a very unpleasant thought.

"Assume he's innocent," said Hartman, turning to Maria. "How would you say it happened then?"

Maria rubbed her eyes and tried to collect her thoughts. "Someone could have planted the DNA, we've seen that before. If I was planning a murder and wanted to pin it on someone else, I'd choose times when this person did not have an alibi. Which Anders wouldn't have had, if lucky or unlucky circumstances had not played into his hands. His daughter was staying with his grandmother on both occasions. He would have been at home by himself, without anyone being able to confirm his whereabouts. If someone has tried to put the blame on Anders it's certainly someone who knows him well."

"What about the red paint, then? Agnes Isomäki, who by the way is also Anders's patient, sprayed the intruder and we found the exact same paint on Ander's pants." Ek had thought the case was solved, but now nothing made sense to him any longer.

"Yes, that's right. But there was no red paint on his skin.

Either he's guilty, in which case I really can't see how he did it, or someone really wants to do him harm."

"Linus was also his patient." Hartman tried to push away the images that came back to him from the lethal assault. "But the DNA that ended up under your nails did not match Anders Ahlström's DNA. So it's not the same assailant there."

"I'd hoped there would be a match, so I'd know for sure." Maria fell abruptly silent. It was a big disappointment.

"If we follow Maria's reasoning and say Anders is innocent, and that his DNA was planted, then in theory it could be the same man who committed all these crimes." Arvidsson had come in during the conversation and was sitting in the background as far away from Maria as he could. "I have a lead in Märsta and I'm flying there tomorrow morning. It concerns the murder of a man eleven years ago, a man who was killed with the blade of a lawn mower. I think the same assailant killed Linus."

"You're free to go, Anders." Maria sat down next to him on the bunk in the holding cell. Instead of the great happiness and relief she'd expected, his face registered fear.

"Why? What's happened?"

"We don't have enough evidence to hold you. I just have one question. Is there anyone who would like to do you harm? Anyone who'd like to blame you for these murders? In theory you could have been picked at random, but I have a feeling this is about something else."

All the color drained from Anders's face. He shook his head.

"You're thinking about someone, I can see it." Maria wanted to shake him. "Who wants to make your life a living hell, and why?"

He tried to laugh it away, and his laughter was more horrible than if he'd wept. A hollow, hoarse croak. "My life is already a living hell. As soon as the media gets wind of the fact that I was arrested, the printing presses will be working overtime. There's no worse punishment than trial by media. It's the pillory of our time, anyone can throw stones at you. We both know that. I will always be associated with the murders. 'Oh that Doctor Ahlström, no thanks, I don't want to be treated by him… didn't he have something to do with those murders in Visby?'"

"I am sincerely sorry but we had to take you in when your DNA matched what we found on the crime scenes. Do you know who might have put it there? It has to be someone who could get close to you, someone who could get into your house and leave the stained pants under your bathtub."

"Or else I went somewhere in my sleep and somehow made contact with the murderer in the night."

"Do you really believe that yourself?" Maria stared insistently at him. "Tell me who you're protecting? Who knows you're a sleepwalker?"

Anders Ahlström paced back and forth in his living room. He had already called his mother to tell her he'd been released. She was both relieved and angry at the same time. Julia had cried into the phone and wasn't even able to speak. Right now he was too upset to bring her home. He had tried to make himself call the school a number of times to talk to her teacher. Rumors would soon be rife and it was important that the school knew how to handle them in the best possible way, so that Julia was not bullied again. After four attempts he gave up and looked in Julia's address book for the telephone number of the classroom assistant. He explained his errand to Ronny, who promised to take care of it. He was friendly and approachable. Such a pity they had not managed to see each other at the previous parents' evening. Anders would have liked to thank him in person for everything he'd done for Julia.

Anders sank into the sofa and closed his eyes. Maria Wern had come very close to the truth, and it was only a question of time until she took the thought to its logical conclusion. What would have happened if he'd confessed? Would they have believed him then?

His thoughts searched their way back to that dawn when he woke up, hung-over and ravaged, to find that Isabel was not lying at his side. He'd asked his mother to stay with Julia, then hurried down through the beautiful park to the sea. His anxiety was very much present, although ameliorated somewhat by the beautiful surroundings. The morning was crisp and sunny. The clear blue sky filtered down through the laburnum trees with their rough, twisting boughs. The path wound down the hill alongside a stream, whose water flowed over soft, round stones. The fragrance, the droning of bumblebees—all seemed to breathe of calm, as if there were no such thing as evil in the world. He leapt down the wooden stairs to the beach. Then, on the final landing, he turned round. On the bridge over the enchanted waterfall, just by the sea, stood a figure partially hidden in the dark green gloom under the trees. Not even then had he understood what had happened. Only when he saw her lifeless body in the water did he understand. Her blood, coloring the water a rusty red. The rooms in Anders Ahlström's house were suffused with the glow of dusk. He did not turn on the lights. His head ached with all the thoughts he'd tried to turn off for so long. Is there anyone who has a reason to hate you? He would have liked so much to call Erika, just to feel her embrace without any words. But most likely she was as upset as he was right now, and he wouldn't have the energy to answer her questions. Suddenly he heard a strange churning sound outside the window. Then a stone came flying in through the window. Anders stood with his back to the wall by the window and peered into the street. A large crowd had assembled outside his house. Another stone came flying in, skimming his shoulder. In spite of the failing light he could make out their grim expressions by the glow of the streetlights. He fumbled for the cell phone in his pocket and called the emergency number. The churning sounds picked up. A man freed himself from the crowd and rang his doorbell. Briefly Anders debated with himself if he should answer and try to speak to them. But all his energy had run out. What could he say? "It wasn't me." The sharp sound of the bell cut through the silence. Then came the sound of a tool, progressively inching the door off its hinges. Only then did he get through to the police. Burglary in progress. The address. That's all he had time for. Next, a stone hit him in the head and catapulted him backwards.

Once more odious coincidence had been victorious against intelligence and strategy. He who should be punished had been released. Twice, fate had saved him. But even though Fortuna stood at his side, he was not immortal. Now he must die. An anonymous telephone call would be enough. Why dirty one's own hands when people were so willing to make themselves into instruments in the service of hatred? Linus's father would certainly feel a quickening lust in torturing the doctor to death, if he were released. Don't we all have these tendencies? Malicious pleasure when a rival fails, satisfaction and reassurance when rule-breakers are punished. Such feelings are only the lesser siblings of the pleasure of actually torturing the victim directly. The feeling of power, of having the upper hand and seeing someone else's fear and humiliation. Like both those men he'd had to punish for their gossip, punish them because no one else would, when they showed a lack of respect and obedience. They were dead now. But before then, they had both been under his knife. Dosing them with Curare had paralyzed them without taking away their pain, while he slowly flayed them alive. His pleasure had greatly exceeded his expectations.

Chapter 44

Per Arvidsson got off at Märsta Station and walked down Västra Bangatan toward Nymärsta Kulle 6 to meet with Oskar Wallman at the local police station. It was a fresh sunny morning. He entered the red brick building and went up the stairs. His colleague was waiting in reception. He was older and looked far worse-for-wear than Per Arvidsson had thought. His crutch under one arm and contorted lip pointed to a stroke. He regretted his irritated tone when earlier he'd pressed the policeman with his questions about the lawn mower murder. Oskar Wallman had probably done his best.

"You wanted to question Malin Karlsson? She refuses to come in," he said, his speech slightly slurred. "She doesn't want to speak to us at all. But I managed to get her to agree to see you if you're out of uniform. She's also a health freak who does sixteen classes a week at Fitness First and only drinks green tea produced on uninhabited islands. She felt she could squeeze in a meeting between the body pump and aerobics."

"So… a fitness addict."

"It's probably hard to stay off kicks when you've been on

332

drugs for so many years. The ones who manage to go clean either end up working with addicts twenty-four hours a day, or turn into workaholics, or go all out for some religion. This is her address. It's a stone's throw from here if you're good at throwing."

"Is it appropriate for a policeman to go to her on his own, if she's been subjected to rape and lived off prostitution? I know it's more than eleven years since she started her new life, but wouldn't it be better to meet her on neutral ground."

"She doesn't think of the police station as neutral ground," he replied drily. "If you want her to talk to you it's going to have to be one-on-one, even though I do understand your reservations about it." In her exterior, at any rate,

Malin Karlsson seemed to have left her past far behind. Her sports bag was packed and ready in the hall. She wore a pin-stripe suit and a white turtleneck sweater. Her hair was cut in a short, severe style, she wore a long pearl necklace, and her makeup was discreet and well harmonized with her sun-tan. Her shoes were low-heeled and elegant. Possibly her un-revealing clothes hid a tattoo or two. She showed him into the kitchen and put away a crossword magazine and a book of advanced Sudoku. Per Arvidsson had bought it himself a month ago and given up. Malin was on the last page.

"They don't last me long but it's a nice way to make the time go by," she said. "Can I offer you something? Tea, cof-fee? There's decaffeinated coffee and I have a selection of green teas."

"Tea, if it's not too much bother. I've been having a few stomach problems."

"Gastritis? You're not having love problems, are you?" She seemed to be able to read him like an open book. Per had thought of Maria all night, agonizing and regretting. When morning came, his coffee had made his stomach cramp up.

"It's possible," he said, noticing to his own vexation that he was blushing. On the other hand, maybe it wasn't completely wrong to open up a bit and create an understanding.

"Love and guilt, right?" There was nothing teasing about her question, just a plain statement of fact. If the situation had been different it would have been good to confide in someone who might be able to understand.

"Something like that," he said.

"There's probably nothing that creates so much guilt as love. Love and a debt of gratitude, love and deception, love and everything one is prepared to do so the other party does not leave."

"It's true." Per felt more and more empathy. This was a woman of experience and worldly wisdom. But something held him back, thank goodness. One could be personal, but not private. Right now they were heading toward the most private thing in his world—his love for Maria.

"I won't press you," she said with a little smile. "I just wanted to see if there was some common ground where we could meet and both agree that life's not always as simple and uncomplicated as in a police report. We all have our private infernos. You've probably read about what I've been through and I can guess what your life looks like. Is she worth all the agony?"

"Yes, she is. And the guilt is all mine."

Malin smiled inwardly and poured the tea. "You've come to dig in the past. And I'm doing everything I can to forget it. You've come from Gotland and I've read about the murders in Visby. What do you want from me?"

Per watched her for a moment and made an assessment of the situation. Malin Karlsson seemed to be an intelligent and psychologically stable woman. It wasn't how he'd imagined this woman who'd been a drug abuser for fifteen years, he was perfectly willing to admit that. How could things have gone so wrong in her life?"

"There's a rumor in the criminal fraternity that the same man who assaulted and killed a boy, Linus Johansson, earlier butchered a man with the blade of a lawn mower. You featured in that investigation, but you were discounted from the list of suspects because you were in a rehab clinic."

"You're wasting your time. I've already told you everything I know." She leaned back and crossed her arms over her chest.

Their understanding was broken. He had to recreate it.

"You seem to have beaten your drug dependency in an amazing way. How did you end up there? What happened?" He shifted focus from the essential question without dropping the subject. The conversation was right on the edge of what she was willing to discuss. There was a risk that she'd ask him to leave.

Malin Karlsson closed her eyes. Her face was expressionless.

"I was studying law in Lund. My studies were a piece of cake, I have a photographic memory, never needed to try very hard. There were parties and I always wanted to be the center of attention. I was good-looking in those days.... Sex appeal can be a curse, it can put you in trouble. Suddenly I was pregnant. I really loved him, but he wanted nothing to do with me and not the child, either. I didn't want the child by that time, either, but I was too far gone. I met another man who took care of me and the child, and consoled me with drugs. I didn't have the energy for the kid, who made demands on me night and day. Always had colic. My studies went to hell. Life went to hell. The child was taken into care. I was allowed to have him sometimes, when I said I was feeling better, but I failed again and again. They should have realized at the social services that it's no good for a child to be his mother's therapist and get ferried back and forth. He never had a chance to develop an emotional bond with anyone. Already by the time he was five he grew uncontrollable, he was moved from home to home. He was devilishly manipulative, played his foster parents against the social services and the social services against me. I never coped with him. It's my greatest sorrow."

"But he had a father as well."

"I had a tiny bit of self-respect left in spite of all. We managed without any help from him. Without maintenance. I didn't want anything to do with that bastard." Malin's face changed, her eyes became hard. She straightened up in her chair and leaned forward. "I hated him so much...."

"Did the boy never ask about his father? At some point in one's teens, one usually wants to know where one comes from. Didn't he demand to know who his father was?" Per drank a last sip of his bitter tea, which had grown cold.

"When he was thirteen he managed to find out for himself by threatening my mother. He found information about him on the Internet, found out everything there was to know. Found newspaper articles. He made a scrapbook and interrogated me. He wanted to know everything, and he found it especially interesting that Anders, his father, used to sleepwalk. Just after his fourteenth birthday Roy went to see his father. He found out that he had a little six-month-old sister. Anders had met the love of his life, Isabel, and he was getting married. I think Roy felt mostly in the way. He came back fairly quickly and never wanted to see his father again."

Roy! Anders Ahlström and Isabel! Per Arvidsson did his best to hide the fact that the insight made his skin crawl. Had Roy used a lawn mower blade to kill the man who raped his mother? Presumably she stayed silent to protect her son.

"When did you decide to start a drug-free life?"

"Eleven years ago. I was in rehab and then I came home. Suddenly I had to make a choice." Malin stood up and started slamming around with some cups and saucers. Clearly, the turn the conversation had taken was upsetting her.

"Directly after the murder?"

"Yes," she said, her face averted.

"It was Roy who did it, wasn't it? He was taking his revenge on you, and the shock made you stop." He waited for an answer. But she was silent and her face was inscrutable. "When you read about the murders in Visby you must have known it could be him, because the anger in him would never run out. Are you afraid of him, Malin?"

She nodded mutely, and her eyes grew big and shiny.

"The best thing you can do for Roy now is help me catch him before he kills more innocent people. He needs professional care. Do you know where he is now?"

Malin sank down on the chair. Her face, so tanned a moment ago, now looked gray and pale. She swallowed repeatedly, but she didn't answer now, either. Per assumed there was a battle going on inside her; a battle between her wanting to talk and at the same time not—or did she not dare give her son away?

"Do you have a photograph of him?"

Malin showed no sign of wanting to get up to fetch what he was asking for. Her whole body seemed to express a deep anguish. It pained him to see it, but he had to get hold of Roy.

"Is it all right if I look around?"

Malin still didn't react.

Per found what he was looking for in the living room. A photograph of a boy in his early teens, with a soccer ball pressed to his chest.

"Was it Roy who killed that man with a lawn mower blade?" He held out the photograph in front of Malin's eyes.

"You're not letting him down, you're helping him if you answer the question. Was that what happened?"

Malin shook her head.

"I'm going to tell you about the people who've been killed in Visby. I want you to listen carefully. All three people were patients of Anders Ahlström. Curious coincidence, isn't it? The first was a young boy of thirteen, he was kicked to death. His head was crushed, but he was alive until he arrived at the emergency room. At the same time a woman police officer was stabbed in the leg with a blood-filled syringe. He welcomed her to hell, he said. And then there are two more unsolved murders, which he could easily have committed. A woman was dressed up as a bride and then had her head cut off. The bridal bouquet consisted of lilies of the valley, just like in Isabel's bouquet. A sick elderly man was very pointedly strung up in the home of a police officer soon after being beaten unconscious. He used to visit Anders daily. I suspect it's Roy who's behind all this."

"Stop, I can't hear any more.... I want you to stop him. I am so devastated, so very devastated. Yes, it was him who murdered that man. I kept quiet because I thought we'd be able to live with it and move on. But when he came back from Gotland and at the same time I read about that woman who disappeared on her wedding night and I understood it was Anders's wife, I realized it was him who'd killed Isabel, to defend his family. The thing he wanted was me and Anders to be there for him. I'm not sure he knew at all what a family was. I suppose it was what he had dreamed up in his scrapbook."

"Do you know where he is now?"

"No, but he knows where you are. He's a computer genius. There's no information he can't find and get his hands on. Roy is abnormally gifted. I don't know if it's an asset or a handicap. He only went to school sporadically. His classmates were scared of him, the teachers, too. He took his high school examination when he was seventeen, highest possible grades. And since then he's devoted himself to correspondence courses. How he makes money I don't know, but I think he makes a living playing online poker."

"Think again. Is there anywhere on Gotland where he can hide out, has he said anything about his whereabouts?"

"He lives above a car repair shop. Some company that fixes trucks. It's a ten-minute walk from an ICA store. I don't have an address but I have a cell phone number."

"One last question. Is there any risk that he's a carrier of a blood infection of some kind?"

Chapter 45

Erika Lund knew nothing about Per Arvidsson's trip to Märsta when she picked up Anders Ahlström late on the Friday night. He was in a bad way after his lynching and might not have survived, even, had there not been a police patrol car in the vicinity. Erika had tried to make him go with the ambulance to the emergency room for a head X-ray, but he refused. Like a wounded animal he curled up and wanted nothing else to do with the clamoring interest of the media and the general public. The police had logged his report and told him to stay within reach on the cell phone. Linus's father and the other more active members of the vigilance committee had been brought in for questioning. Anders only wanted to go far, far away, to a quiet place where he could be left in peace to think. Erika had called Fridhem Pension and booked Sjöstugan. All of Sjöstugan, so no other guests would be able to disturb them. During her time off she had done a great deal of thinking. If they were ever to have a chance of living together he had to tell her about Isabel and then let go of the past. In her state of despair, it seemed if they were back in the same place where Isabel disappeared, it might help him remember and talk about it.

Outside Visby it suddenly felt as if life were taking on a different, slower rhythm. They drove past Fridhem's coffee shop at a crawl and then up the slope, passing an old stable with a Celtic cross in the stable yard and a flowering acacia with a honeysuckle clambering along the bole, a twinned bloom. On the other side of the gravel track was a garden pavilion so enmeshed with branches that it was impossible to say where it began or finished. Beside it lay a fallen tree that was still growing, although it had snapped against the ground. Erika took it all in with a resigned feeling of life always being wasted. She wanted to stop time and experience everything. They parked outside the large yellow main building of the pension and listened to a blackbird mimicking the telephone at the reception desk, accompanied by two wood pigeons. They caught the aroma of a nearby bakery. On long lines behind the laundry, white sheets flapped in the evening breeze. The friendly lady at reception gave them their keys. She showed them the dining room and the drawing room, where the furnishings still breathed the atmosphere of Oscar II's social life from the turn of the century.

"How are you doing?" Erika gripped Anders's hand as they walked out onto the upper floor veranda.

"Why are we here?" He looked at her with resignation.

"I think you know why we're here." They gazed in silence over the park and the sea. The smell of jasmine reached them even up here, the cherry trees were already ripe with fruit and in a month or so the roses would bloom overwhelmingly. He took her hand and asked to her to turn round. Behind them was a large glass window divided into a multitude of leaded panes. The room was screened off by a thin white curtain.

"You want to know the truth and you're going to have what you want. I only hope you know what you are asking for." He turned to the main building and pointed at the window. "That's the wedding suite. The party was over. Isabel took off her bridal gown, we made an inept attempt to make love. Suddenly Isabel wanted to have a swim, and I didn't have the energy to go with her. A couple of the guys were having drinks in the reception hall. I joined them. When I woke up at five o'clock Isabel was still gone. I went down the stairs just as we're doing now and hurried down to the beach."

They continued out of the door facing the park, while he continued his narrative. The painful memories made his eyes fill up with tears. He'd tried to call the police but the reception was very poor. The best places were either at the flag-pole or down by the sea.

"When I saw her dead body on the beach I tried to call the police again. But the sea was coming in hard and we couldn't hear each other." Erika didn't interrupt him. Two calls had come in to the police on that night, Maria had told her. The second call twenty-five minutes after the first. He had told the police that Isabel had disappeared and probably drowned. He'd only found the pile of clothes. Now he was going to tell her the truth: that he'd seen her dead on the morning after the wedding.

They went down the wooden steps to the beach. The sun was sinking into the sea, and the silhouette of Stora Karlsö och Lilla Karlsö grew increasingly dark while the sea was colored red and golden.

"There she lay and when I looked up at the bridge over the waterfall I saw my son standing there. "What have you done!" I shouted at him. I was out of my mind, in despair, burning with anger and shock. I realized he had killed Isabel. He was fourteen years old. My son had destroyed his own life and mine. Isabel was dead. I couldn't get her back." Anders picked up a stone from the place where she lay. Absentmindedly he stroked it. "Without any time to think about it, I had to make the decision whether to report my own son or cover up what had happened. At that moment I was even willing to take the blame myself. Because I owed him such a huge unpaid debt. His determination was so strong, I had no will of my own, I followed his commands. He'd already planned how we should get rid of the body. We carried her back and hid her in the cellar under Sjöstugan for a couple of days. There was a trap door in the floor. Then one night we fetched her and buried her on Galgberget where no one would ever think of looking for her among all the bodies. She would still be lying there, had it not been for that archaeologist." Anders looked at her, frightened. "I just obeyed him. I can't explain it. He had a way of making decisions, an absolute sense of authority. He stayed with us for a month before the wedding. He made Isabel's life a living hell. Played us against each other. Time and time again I had to work things out, take the blame myself. He wanted to live with us. Isabel said no. She said I had to make a choice. And I did. I thought I did." They sat down on the beach. When Anders put his arm around Erika she felt he was shaking.

"I love you," she said. "Whatever happens I love you and want to be with you, but you must never lie to me again."

"I'll never lie to you again." He squeezed her shoulders tightly. "But I'm scared. God, I've been so scared without being able to tell you about it, because I was afraid I'd lose you if I did. For a few terrible days I even believed I was the one responsible for those terrible murders while I was sleepwalking. And then when I realized I had alibis I understood who was behind them. Another sort of fear took over. He's capable of absolutely anything."

"I think this is a safe place right now." Erika hadn't told anyone where they were going, and when she booked, the woman at the Fridhem reception desk had promised to be discreet if anyone asked about them. Erika leaned her head against his shoulder. "You see the foundations of Sjöstugan? It looks like it might just glide into the sea the next time there's a storm. You can't get closer to the water than that. We'll be able to hear the waves when we're going to sleep."

"If we can sleep." Anders doubted it. "I'm worried about Julia. Just think if he harms her to get at me?"

"Would you like them to come here?" Erika could understand his anxiety.

"Let's call them and ask them to come here. Now, right away. It would feel safer."

Chapter 46

Maria Wern was sitting in Hartman's office when the call came in from Per Arvidsson.

She understood the seriousness of the situation at once, when Hartman summarized Per's conclusions.

"Erika is in grave danger. Anders has a son, Roy Karlsson. Per believes he murders anyone Anders shows any affection or love—such as Isabel or his patients. We have to get hold of them right away! Erika isn't at home and she's not answering her cell phone. Anders isn't, either."

"Ek has been looking for Anders all morning and went there to ask him a few supplementary questions. No one seems to be home there, either. He called Anders' mother. She said her son wasn't there, but she might be lying for her son's sake."

"In that case our top priority right now is finding the apartment where Roy Karlsson might be staying. You have to keep out of this, Maria. It's damn terrible, because I could do with you. What do you want to do instead?"

"I'll talk to Anders Ahlström's mother and bring her and the girl in. They may need protection."

"Wise move. There's the duty officer on the phone."

Hartman's face lit up. "They know where the apartment is. We may have him. I'll go with them to Havdhem."

The area round the workshop was surrounded by a high fence, but the gate was open and in the courtyard were a number of small trucks in various states of disrepair. In the office sat a man in blue overalls, a can of beer in his hand. He was talking on the telephone while panting in the heat. When Hartman walked in he waved his hand dismissively. "We don't have time for more jobs, not before we close up for the summer." Only when Hartman showed his police badge did he hang up.

"Do you have a tenant upstairs?"

"What the hell, he's borrowing the place. Who said I was renting it?"

"Is he up there now?" Hartman wasn't interested in small-time tax dodging. "This is about murder."

The garage mechanic gave Hartman a dubious look, then pulled down his cap over his face and scratched his neck. "His car's here. Sometimes he takes the bus and sometimes a taxi. He lives in goddamned luxury, could afford a bit more rent."

As they talked, the police had moved into position. Hartman took the megaphone and called out. They waited. Nothing happened. Hartman repeated his call, and then they decided to go in. The garage owner had a spare key. At the top of the stairs they were met by an expansive hall, into which daylight only entered via a ceiling window.

"This is the police! Roy Karlsson! Open up, come out with your hands over your head." They unlocked the door and went in. Not a sound could be heard. But an invasive, sweet and nauseating stink hit them, like forgotten prawn shells. They searched the apartment.

"He's not here," said Jesper Ek at the same time as he heard Hartman calling out from the living room. He hurried into the bright room. The white walls encompassed the oblong steel tables on wheels. Hartman walked up to the nearest bier and saw the dissected corpse. He could hardly believe what his eyes were seeing.

"He's flayed them. The monster. He's flayed them alive, otherwise the blood wouldn't have run like this."

Jesper Ek couldn't stop staring, although he would have preferred not to look at the repellent sight. All the skin had been peeled off except on the face. The victims looked as if they were wearing white masks. "Who are they?"

Hartman closed his eyes briefly and breathed through his mouth to avoid having to smell the stink. "Perhaps Roy's accomplices from the assault? Maybe Joakim can identify them."

"Anyone who'd do this to his friends… I hardly dare think what he'd…" Ek couldn't finish the sentence. He was thinking about Erika.

"If you let a fox into the henhouse it kills all the hens, not out of hunger but lust." Hartman gestured for them to go outside. The fewer the footprints in there, the better for the technicians who'd be taking over the crime scene. Before he left the apartment he took a look at Roy's workroom, consisting of a bank of computers on a semi-circular table. A little further off was a bed. On the wall, a large number of charcoal drawings were pinned up. Isabel, Linn, and Erika were a three-headed goddess. Julia was a creature from the underworld, with dead eyes and her flesh partially torn off her skeleton. Anders Ahlström was the Grim Reaper, arrayed in a dark cape. Harry Molin hung with a swelling tongue. The battered body of Linus. Sick, twisted but very expertly done drawings. There were also several drawings of prostitutes in violent situations. Death was everywhere.

What you are we have been, what we are you will be. Hartman read the well-known text under a drawing of the dead rising from their graves. Vaguely he remembered the words from the crypt of the Capuchin monks in Rome.

On the floor beside the bed lay a pair of jeans of the Kilroy brand, and shoved under the bed a pair of boots like those described by Maria from the gang's assault. He went up to the wide, unmade bed and looked under the pillow and mattress. He was seeing something, an explanation perhaps, or a contradiction. Pure evil must be gainsaid in some way. At some point Roy had been a child. Afterwards, life and circumstances had created a monster. He found what he was looking for under the mattress: a well-thumbed scrapbook with Pinocchio on the cover. A fairytale of truth and lies. On his way into town he flipped through it. Ek drove. It was a diary with cuttings from newspapers and quotes from the Internet. Sometimes there were cartoons, interspersed frame by frame with a child's drawings, thoughts and longing for family. A birthday party with long, flapping serpentines in the trees and a strawberry cake.

Chapter 47

Maria had been sitting a long while at the kitchen table with Anders Ahlström's mother. Julia stuck like glue to her grandmother and Maria had no decent opportunity to speak to the woman about the overhanging threat to the child. When they did not want to go back with her to the police station, Maria had shown them what an alarm unit looked like. Anders's mother wasn't interested. It was technical and complicated and she had no energy for learning anything new, not any more.

"I just can't understand where Anders went. It makes you worried. I have to stay here in case he needs me. Am I also being accused of something? Otherwise I'd rather you just left."

"Think about the girl," Maria tried. There was a risk that Roy would want to hurt her, just as he'd hurt all the others to whom Anders had shown any kind of feeling.

"There's no one who wants to harm her. Can't you stop tormenting us now? It's enough what you did to Anders, even though he's innocent. I don't want anything to do with the police! Just go!"

"Please, I'm begging you. Come with me. For the sake of the child!"

Anders's mother opened the front door. "Out!"

Maria couldn't force them, though she was sick with anxiety. Instead she went to Lummelunda again to try and get hold of Erika. She wasn't at home now, either, and she still wasn't answering her cell phone. Anders had taken quite a beating, but he'd refused to go to the hospital. The media had followed on the tail of the vigilantes group. Presumably he was keeping out of the way somewhere with Erika, but where? Maria made an attempt to find them in the cottage they'd rented in Ljugarn, but found out that there was another guest staying there. The more Per Arvidsson's words sank in, the more certain she grew that Roy was after Anders and Erika. Maybe he also wanted to harm Julia. Did he see her as his sister or only as a rival? What places did Erika know about where one could get some peace and quiet?

Hartman came back. They reviewed the situation. There was frantic activity. Police officers on vacation were called in. Joakim was able to identify the men he'd met in Visby, who had been with Roy during the assault, by reviewing the grotesque photographs faxed over by the technicians. Maria wasn't as sure—they had been masked. But their body types and length fitted. They were soon found on a list of missing persons. Hartman took on the duty of contacting dependants to ask them to identify the victims. It was a task no one envied him. Roy was still on the loose, and Anders and Erika had apparently gone underground. Not a good combination. At midnight, Hartman decided to go home and catch a few hours' sleep. Police on duty were free to contact him whenever they wanted; he promised to keep his cell phone switched on.

"You need to rest as well, Maria. You'll think more clearly if you do. There's nothing more we can do right now. Roy Karlsson is wanted, his photograph will be on the front page of every newspaper tomorrow."

Maria reluctantly followed his advice, went home and stood in the shower. Then she ate a couple of sandwiches in front of the television and drank a few strong cups of coffee. She called Erika again but the number was temporarily unavailable. Could they really be so sure that Erika would think primarily of the need Anders had for peace and quiet? When Erika was taken off duty the most urgent question in her mind had been whether Anders was guilty or innocent. A new thought popped up in Maria's head—admittedly one that was fairly wild and farfetched. What if Erika intended to carry out some of her own police work, taking him to the crime scene where Isabel had been murdered? The more Maria thought about it, the more likely it seemed. Erika needed the truth if she was going to be able to live with Anders. Maria didn't even give herself time to finish her coffee. On her way outside to the car she called central command and told them she was on her way to Fridhem Pension.

Chapter 48

When Anders called with fear in his voice, his mother immediately picked up on it. Maria Wern had been right, they were in danger. Anders' mother had shared her son's terrible secret over all the years, loyally keeping silent. She had not visited Fridhem, the place where his wedding had been held, since the murder. Now he wanted her to go there and she obeyed him without hesitation. She woke up Julia, who'd fallen asleep in the sofa, and swept a blanket around her shoulders on the way outside to the car.

"What's happening, grandma?"

"Dad wanted us to come."

Instead of going to the coffee shop to buy waffles, as Julia had wanted, they contacted the hotel kitchen. Dinner was served at five but they were willing to make an exception and send down food to Sjöstugan. Erika was grateful that they could eat on their own. They sat at the garden table outside the house by the edge of the sea. The dusk spread out, mild and blue, and the laburnum hung in great clumps. The river sighed. Everything was calm and still. Anders could hardly eat at all, which his mother commented on. Erika glossed over his comments. What Anders had to say to his daughter wasn't easy.

He pushed his plate away. "Julia, I'd rather you didn't have to hear what I'm going to tell you now. The first thing is, you have an older brother. You can't remember him because you were so small when you met. He was there when me and your mother were married."

"Great, what was his name?"

"It's not as great as you think. His name is Roy. He's twenty-five years old." As mercifully as possible Anders told his daughter the events of her parents' wedding night.

"You told me my mother drowned. You've lied to me!" Julia stood up to run from the table. Anders caught her in his arms. "There's something else I have to tell you. And you have to listen, because we're in danger!"

Erika admired his way of talking to the child about the horror, making it understandable and not scaring her more than he absolutely had to. Maybe all his experience of passing on unwelcome diagnoses to patients helped him find the right tone. He listened to her questions, waited on her reactions, and helped her take in the truth bit by bit.

"There's a risk Roy wants to hurt us. So no one must know we're here. You understand that, don't you?" said Erika.

Julia stared at Erika. "He wants to kill you because you're with dad?"

"I hope it's not like that, but we don't know." The thought had never struck Erika before. It might actually be like that. The sleepwalker murders had started when she met Anders. Maybe Roy could not put up with his father having any kind of fond feelings for anyone else? Anders had joked with Linus, listened to and cared about Harry, and given Agnes Isomäki a hug. Linn had also been his patient. Was it Anders's care and commitment that had sentenced them all to death? In which case, what kind of punishment would he not like to inflict on Erika? Or Julia? Had he saved them till last, slowly ramping up Anders's suffering beyond all understanding, so that he could ultimately blame his father for the things that had happened? A demonic plan.

For a long time Julia lay in bed next to her grandmother, listening to the waves breaking against the shore. All other sounds disappeared in the sound of the waves. It felt as if her body was in the waves, rolled up and straightened out by the all-encompassing sound. Grandmother's light snoring. Dad's feet on the floor on his way to the toilet. Whispering in the adults' room. She felt alone. After she'd been asleep for about an hour there was a "ping" of a text on her cell phone. She put the blanket over her head and checked who'd written to her. It was Ronny.

"Are you in Sjöstugan?" he wrote. Daddy had said she mustn't tell anyone where they were hiding. But Ronny already knew, because he could check by GPS where Julia's phone was. He was so smart and fun to be with. Almost like a magician.

"Yes," she replied. "And do you know I have a brother? A real one."

"Cool," he texted back.

"He killed my mother." Julia's eyes filled with tears and she tried to hold back her crying as much as she could, so her grandmother wouldn't hear.

"We have to talk about it. I'll come right away. Can you sneak out of the house and down the wooden steps and I'll wait for you on the beach?"

"Yes."

"I've hung up some strips of white sheets in the trees so you can find your way in the dark."

"Almost like Hansel and Gretel. Good. I'm coming," she wrote. Ronny understood everything. She could tell him everything, she could be small and sad with him. When dad told her all the horrible things she couldn't say whatever she wanted, not without making him even sadder. But with Ronny it was something else. He always knew completely what had to be done. He was never upset. Never angry. He was just Ronny. What would she have done all those lonely afternoons when Daddy was at work if Ronny had not been there with her?

Julia crept out of bed as quietly as she could. Grandmother lay on her side facing into the room. The tiniest sound would make her open her eyes, and then everything would be ruined. Julia pulled a sweater over her nightie and looked for her shoes, but couldn't find them. Barefoot, she tiptoed across the floor then opened the door, which creaked slightly.

"Julia. Where are you off to?"

"Just to pee," she whispered and disappeared down the passage and into the night. The strips of cloth were hanging in the trees. It looked fun. All the way to the stairs they were flapping in the wind. As she took the last step onto the sand she looked up and saw him. He was standing at the edge of the water, and came toward her with his arm waving.

"Give me five!" The palm of his hand slapped against hers. He smiled broadly. "Come on, let's go for a swim!"

"But it's the middle of the night," she laughed.

"Yeah but you're probably quite dirty. You're dirty right here." He picked her up in his arms and held up one of her feet. "And here on the other foot you're dirty as well, you little piggy. So you have to take a swim. I'll carry you out so you don't have to step on the stones." He held her in his arms and dialed Anders's number on his cell phone. Anders answered at once, as if he'd been lying there with the cell phone in his hand. As if he knew something would happen—but not how.

"Say hello to Dad, Julia."

"Hi, Dad. We're having a swim."

Anders's voice came out as a strangled cry.

"Come on your own if you want to see her alive," Roy hissed.

A splashing sound. Julia's scream was the last thing Anders heard before the call was cut off. He jumped out of bed and shot out the door. Erika woke up but Anders didn't have time to explain anything to her. White cotton strips bordered the path to the sea. He ran toward the stairs. Far out he could see them, heading out toward the undertow. He made his way down the stairs without breathing and charged into the cold water.

"Come and get her if you can." The waves amplified Roy's voice without the loss of a single syllable. He held the girl's head under the water, then let her come up.

"Help, Daddy! I don't want it. Help!"

Anders swam toward them. If he'd had time to think he would have brought a weapon, a club of some sort. But in his huge fear he had just run off to save his daughter.

"Don't hurt her. She's your sister, she trusts you." Anders coughed water between his words, swallowing a good deal, too. If he exerted himself too much he wouldn't have the energy he needed once he got there. He forced himself to slow his swim strokes, to save his energy in order to give himself a chance of measuring his strength with his son's. The moonlight fell on the surface of the water, glittering against the knife Roy was holding in his clenched fist just under the surface.

"Come and get her. Your life for hers."

Chapter 49

The yellow hotel building lay in darkness. Only the lights by the parking area gave her some point of reference. Maria heard Erika's screams, faint and distant, as soon as she stepped out of the car. Maria ran down the hill through the park, taking the path that led to the beach. From the edge of the cliff by Sjöstugan she could already see them, like dark shadows in the water. Roy, Anders, and Julia's long hair. Erika was also in the water. Maria clattered down the stairs, stumbled, fell, and hit her knee against the stones on the beach. It took a few seconds before the pain hit her. Maria didn't feel the cold. She surged through the water. When it got too deep she started swimming. Erika was still screaming, her eyes were closed. She only stopped when Maria touched her.

"What's happening?"

"He has a knife. He stabbed me really deep in my leg." Erika could hardly keep her head above water. Maria hauled and dragged her onto land. The blood was coloring her pants red.

"Can you move your leg?"

"No, not my right leg, it hurts too much. You have to help the girl first. Be careful!"

Julia screamed at the top of her voice. Had the lunatic stabbed her, too? Maria swam out to them at full crawl, then dived under the water. She only surfaced when she needed air. She stopped a few feet away, rubbing her eyes so she could see. Anders was holding Roy's hand, with the knife in it, and trying to make him come to his senses.

"She's your sister. She trusts you."

Julia clambered onto her father's other arm. He tried to keep her away, while at the same time holding the knife at bay. He didn't have many more seconds. Roy looked as if he were only toying with them. Only now did he notice Maria.

"Come here, fucking cop cunt, and I'll slice your stomach open."

While he was distracted for a moment Maria managed to snatch the child out of his hands. Anders got a free hand. At the same time Roy lashed out with the knife, grazing Anders's lower arm.

"Can you swim, Julia?" Maria felt the current growing strong. She could hardly keep herself from being swept out. With Julia under her arm she swam toward calmer water.

"I have to help your father. Can you swim?"

"Yes." Julia looked terrified, but if she had a task to get on with she might manage it better.

"When you get back to the beach, help Erika. Tell her the police are on their way, and the ambulance." Julia nodded. Maria watched her—she seemed to be doing all right— then dived and swam back toward the other two. Took a mouthful of air and then dived again, so that Roy wouldn't know where she was. Maybe Anders could also gain some advantage from Roy's divided attention. Fifty yards away, Anders no longer had the strength to resist. He received a powerful stab in his upper arm and one in his shoulder. The next lunge carried the knife straight through his hand.

"Nothing's going to get better by killing me!"

Roy smiled derisively by way of an answer.

Only now did Maria meet Roy's gaze. They were the same eyes that she'd seen in her nightmares these last months. Scornfully he aimed the knife again at Anders. Maria threw herself between them, catching the knife mid-air and being thrown backward as she did so. At the same time as she cut herself, she also managed to twist the weapon out of his hand. The knife sank toward the seabed. Roy also glided back toward the sea, then sank into the water and disappeared. He could reappear at any moment. Maria stared down into the water round her. If he decided to pull her down under the water she wouldn't stand a chance. Anders was hurt; he wouldn't have the strength to help her. A slightly lighter nuance in the water and a stream of bubbles showed where Roy was. Maria fought the current. Roy glided away.

"He's drowning!" Anders swam after him. Maria couldn't stop him. "I can't let him die."

"Stop, you won't manage it. You'll both drown!"

Maria felt the force of the water pulling her toward the abyss. She couldn't do anything right now but fight for her life. The pain in her chest made her eyes blacken. She could no longer see any of them. Then, for an instant, she managed to get her head above water again. In the far distance she heard the sirens of the police cars. And, in the moonlight, a glimpse of Julia and Erika on land. She looked round for Anders and Roy, but they were gone. The next wave pulled her under the water. She swallowed water, and felt her strength waning. She must have air. Her lungs were almost exploding in their hunger for air. By sheer force of will she managed to get up to the surface again. Concentrating on each stroke, her chest paralyzed with pain, she slowly inched away from the edge of the coastal shelf, and was pulled down again, taking in more salt water. Her ears were singing. An angry, shrill note cut her head to pieces.

The pressure against her eardrums was unbearable. She was pulled even further down. Maria no longer even knew which direction to swim toward the surface. She must go up. Must have air. Air.

When she woke she was lying on the beach, in recovery position. She saw the rubber dinghy. And the body carried ashore by the policemen. Erika's crying was mixed with Julia's screaming. Maria saw a glimpse of the face.

It was Anders. His face was pale blue, his lips white.

"Is he dead?" Julia waded toward the men in the boat. "Is my father dead?"

Per Arvidsson squatted down and took her in his arms. "Yes, Julia. He is." Julia let go and ran over to Erika, sitting against the wooden construction of the stairs. She curled up there. Erika grimaced in pain and put her arm round her. "Is he really dead? He can't be!"

Erika couldn't answer. She pressed the child closer to her. Julia's grandmother stood at the top of the wooden steps. Her aching legs made it difficult for her to make her way down.

"Did you find Roy?" Maria tried to push herself up on her good arm. At that moment she saw him sitting on the beach, a short distance away, between two policemen, awaiting transportation to the hospital. Maria managed to get up somehow. She had a fit of coughing but she made her way to him. She had to know, she had to see him face to face and hear him say it.

"Why did you do it? Why did you kill them?"

Slowly he turned his head, smiling derisively at her pathetic presence and inserting his finger into his mouth like a child. "Because they took my father." His voice was like a child's. "That was my dad. Only my dad. But he didn't give a goddamn."

"He saved your life." Maria saw the lonely little boy in him, and for a moment all the fear and hatred was gone.

"Yeah, he did." A big smile spread over Roy's face. "I don't get it. Why did he do that?"

Maria went over to Erika and Julia with a blanket she took from the boat. She swept it round all three of them, and wept.

Four days later Maria ran into Jonatan Eriksson in the Café Siesta. He had something to tell her, which couldn't wait until they'd ordered their coffees.

"You can stop worrying. Roy doesn't have HIV and there's nothing in your tests to indicate you've been infected."

"Thanks." Maria felt a lump in her throat which she could not quite swallow.

"How is Julia doing?"

"She wants to stay with Erika if her grandmother doesn't get custody of her. No decision has been made yet. I have hopes that things can be resolved for the best."

"And you? How are things for you?"

"They're okay. But I can't stop thinking about Roy. Do you think there's any chance that he can ever be released into society again… and function as a normal human being without hurting others? Can someone who gets a kick out of harming others ever be reprogrammed? And what happens if he reaches some insight into the terrible things he's done? Will he ever be able to forgive himself?"

"I don't know, Maria. I really don't know." Jonatan put his arm round her and felt her trembling.

"Just for an instant I saw the child in him." Maria's eyes grew moist. "He's a monster, but in that moment I actually felt sorry for him.…"

Translations of streets and places

Adelsgatan - Noble Street
Bredgården - The Broad Farmhouse
Bruna Dörren, Restaurant - The Brown Door Restaurant
Donnersplats - Donner's Place
Fiskarplan - Fishermen's Square
Fiskarporten - Fishermen's Gate
Galgberget - Gallows Hill
Hästbacken - Horse Slope
Hästgatan - Horse Street
Jungmansgatan - Deckhand's Street
Klinten - The Mount
Klinttorget - The Mount Square
Korpenområdet - Raven Field
Kärleksporten - Lover's Gate
Lilla Karlsö - Little Karl's Island
Louis Sparres Väg - Louis Sparre's Way
Norra Murgatan - Northern Wall Street
Paviljongplan—The Pavilion Square
Pigstugan - The Maid's Cabin
Rostockergränd - Rostock Alley
Ryska Gränd - Russian Alley
Sjöstugan - Cabin by the Lake
Skafferiet - The Larder
Smittens Backe - Smitten's Slope
Specksgränd - Speck's Alley
Stora Karlsö - Big Karl's Island
Stora Torget - Town Square
Storvägen - High Street
Studentallén - Scholar's Parkway

Södra Kyrkogatan - Southern Church Street
Sörviksgården - South Bay Farmhouse
Tempelkullen - Temple Mount
Tranhusgatan - The Whale-Oil House Street
Trädgården, Restaurant - The Garden Restaurant
Vattugränd - Water Alley
Wallers Plats - Waller's Place
Östercentrum - Eastern Center
Österport - Eastern Gate
Östra Tullgränd - Eastern Tollgate Alley

www.stockholmtext.com

KILLER'S ISLAND